THE FAE CHRONICLES

Fighting Destiny

AMELIA HUTCHINS

ISBN-13: 978-0991190911

ISBN-10: 0991190912

Amelia Hutchins

P.O. Box 11212

Spokane Valley, WA 99211

Amelia-Hutchins.com

Ordering Information: https:www.createspace.com

Quantity sales. Special discounts are available on quantity purchases by corporations, associations, and others. For details, contact the publisher at the address above.

Orders by U.S. trade bookstores and wholesalers. Please contact Amelia utchins ameliahutchins@ amelia-hutchins.com

Printed in the United States of America.

Dedication

To my husband who is my best friend and my biggest fan. Who has stood beside me from the very beginning of this journey.

~~*~*~*~*~*~*~*~*

To my kids for being patient while mommy sat glued to her computer writing.

~~*~*~*~*~*~*~*~*

To my grandmother and mother who never limited my imagination and for the endless stories that made my own imagination soar to endless boundaries.

~~*~*~*~*~*~*~*~*

The beta group who read the story many times over until it was perfected, there are too many to name, but ladies you know who you are.

~~*~*~*~*~*~*~*~*

And to Gina, for her endless hours of dedication, editing, tossing ideas and dealing with me while I spoke Atlantean. Without you, this book could not be what it is. And to Gina's husband for allowing her to work with me through endless nights of editing and the kids for being art gurus.

~~*~*~*~*~*~*~*~*

WARNING

This book contains sexually explicit scenes and adult language, and may be considered offensive to some readers. It is intended for sale to adults ONLY, as defined by the laws of the country in which you made your purchase. Please store your files wisely, where they cannot be accessed by under-aged readers.

~~*~*~*~*~*~*~*~*

This book is not intended for anyone under the age of 18, or anyone who doesn't like lip biting, throw your ass on the bed, tear your clothes off and leave you panting dominant alpha male characters. It's dark, dangerous, intense, gritty and raw book. Scenes are dark, disturbing and scorching HOT. This read is soul crushing, tear jerking, leave you hanging on the edge of your seat, fast paced read.   Side Effects may include, but are not limited to: Drooling, lip biting, wet panties, crying and screaming at the author. If any of these things happen, do not seek medical attention— get the next book in the series and enjoy the ride!

Chapter ONE

"Comm. Check. Adam, come in?" I said over the traffic noise I was hearing through the small device hidden in my ear.

"Roger that," Adam said from his safe distance behind the old shipping warehouse a few blocks away.

I pulled the leather coat up tighter around my neck as a woman and child passed me on the street beneath the Dark Fortress. I'd been given an unusual assignment from Alden, the leader of the Guild, where I worked.

Break in and steal the Dark Prince of the Fae's crown. Normally, given my history, I'd have walked away or given this particular assignment over to another from the Guild. But Alden, the Guild leader, had demanded it be me who took it. It was an overly risky and stupid assignment as far as I was concerned, but I had no say in the matter.

Adam and I typically worked as enforcers and assassins for an organization of Witches that kept Otherworld creatures on the right track and out of the local newspapers. Thirty- some years ago, those of the Otherworld crept out of the shadows and made it known to the Human race that they were no longer alone here on earth.

Of course, Witches had always been among them, but we'd been content just to watch from the shadows. Until the Fae who, taking matters into their own hands, came out and let the Humans know they were no longer the top of the food chain. It had changed everything. Governments were now run with the help of the Otherworlders.

It had been a huge adjustment for the Humans, but, eventually, most had come to terms with it, and those that were considered royalty of the Otherworld creatures had been given safe passage, as well as diplomatic immunity. Even now, I was walking on sovereign land that had been legally declared a section of Faery.

Normally, my job was supposed to be easy— enforce the laws and protect Humankind from becoming food for the Otherworld creatures. Today, it wasn't that simple. I was stepping out of my comfort zone and into the realm of the Fae, where no Human rules could be applied. If I failed, they could kill me, and no one would ever know.

It was a small price to pay for what I had been given. When I was young, my parents had been brutally murdered by the Fae. I'd gone to live inside the safety of the Guild soon after and, while it hadn't been ideal, it had become my home.

I had more than what most orphaned children had, and I'd been trained to take my place among the Guild. We were taught that life wasn't about being selfish, it was about giving back to those who needed it or those who couldn't protect themselves from the deadly creatures who wanted to feed off of them. That's where I come in. I keep them safe, even if they never realize it. I'm not looking for payback or gratitude; I'm in it to keep this world safe.

I turned, watching the wide glass doors open as an entourage of Otherworld beings that guarded the Dark Prince emerged from the embassy. Ryder was reported to be a notorious playboy—right up until last week when he announced his engagement to the Heir of the Light Fae who had seemingly appeared out of thin air.

The Fae normally kept their lives out of the spotlight, but this story had hit every major newspaper around the world in a matter of hours. It wasn't every day that the Fae announced weddings, or anything for that matter, and this one was going up on a grand scale. Two royal houses combining together was big Fae business. The papers loved it.

"I've got movement; seven guards and a male in a dark leather trench. They're heading for the black limo, over," I said, pulling my magic around me and making myself look like one of the everyday Humans on the street just milling about for a paper or a look at the royal Prince.

One of the challenges for the Guild was how little we knew about the Fae. They were incredibly secretive, and what we did know came from rumors. The Dark and Light Fae were friendlier with the Humans. However, there was grapevine chatter that there were other castes of the Fae that we had less information on. There was even one caste called the Horde that was supposed to be the stuff of nightmares, and there were whispers that the Horde King had gone walkabout a little over twenty years ago.

Without a guiding hand on that group, who knows what kind of trouble could happen? As it was, there were hints coming back to the Guild of skirmishes within the Fae castes, and this was probably why we were experiencing such an increase in the Fae population in our world.

The secrecy just contributed to the problems. Some Humans were infatuated with the Fae; others were simply terrified. It was a mess and some just wanted the Otherworld creatures to pack up and leave our world, or be shipped to camps where they could be monitored. Bad idea. They're powerful, immortal, and, even with the sheer number of Witches being trained, it would be an all-out bloody war if we tried it.

The comm device in my ear hit static before Adam's voice came out clear. "Confirmed. It's the Prince. You are clear to engage, Syn. Chandra's in play now, as well. Good luck."

I let out a shaky exhale. No one had ever tried this before, nor should they. It was basically suicide. There was a reason this embassy was called the Dark Fortress.

Five hundred highly-trained Fae reportedly guarded this Fortress. Our sources told us the crown was inside a vault that had one of the most deadly security systems known to every Otherworld creature.

I placed my finger to my ear. "Are we sure it was the DP?"

"Confirmed, Syn—be careful. There's no contingency plan," Adam replied quietly.

"Wouldn't have it any other way," I said with more bravado than I was currently feeling.

If I got caught, we cut ties. I would be stuck at the mercy of the Fae who were notorious for not having any. I waited until the door opened once more, slipping in as a tall blonde walked out with a radiant smile on her face.

The Fae were beautiful, ethereal creatures. Many had taken jobs as movie stars or models. They were the ideal creatures to be on the posters representing the Otherworld beings as they never aged. Timeless beauty frozen right around the age of thirty.

I scanned the room and found two sets of elevators against the far wall. There were guards stationed in front of the one I needed to get on. I scanned the faces of the Fae guards who were armed to the teeth and dripping with testosterone. I checked the rest of the lobby before heading to the front desk. I had on a long, flowing skirt that made me look similar to the only woman working in the lobby of the Dark Fortress.

"Hi! My name is Angelica. I should be on the list for the walk-through for the Embassy tour. I know I'm a little late, but the press outside today was crazy." My voice came out more calmly than I thought it would.

The busty blonde looked up and glared at me with annoyance. She probably wasn't a fan of the Fae groupies. "First elevator; here is the badge. Attach it somewhere security can see it, or you will be removed from the building." She handed me an identity badge that held the false name.

"Thank you so much!" I said with a bright, fake smile on my face, turning to make nice with the Fae guards—who didn't play nice back.

"Identification," the taller of the two said, holding his hand out without even looking directly at me.

"Oh, of course, sorry," I smiled and handed him the picture ID. "Here you go."

"Angelica Jolie?" he mocked.

Adam was toast.

"My mother loved the actress," I said, over-emphatically shrugging my shoulders.

The guard didn't crack a smile. "Spread your arms and legs," he said with little interest in his voice. I spread my arms and my legs obediently.

His hands came up and patted me down, checking under both breasts as if I might have had a gun parked between them. When he was satisfied that I held no weapons on my person, he turned and hit the button for level 2 before moving back to his post.

The elevator doors opened with a small ringing noise and I silently slipped inside after one male had exited it. Inside, I scanned for cameras and found one in the corner. Two more were beneath the glass two-way mirrors they had embedded on the elevator's walls.

When the doors reopened again, I stepped out and surveyed the empty hall before heading in the opposite direction of the tour that would be rounding the corridor any moment now, if they stuck to schedule. The door to the next elevator opened, and a tall male Fae stepped out smoothly with a radiant smile.

"Are you with the tour?" He inquired.

"Yes, I was a few minutes late though. The press outside is crazy thick today," I gave him my best dumb-blonde smile and looked up and down the halls as if looking for the group.

"You're a pretty little thing. You sure you want the boring tour—and not something a little more personal?" His voice lowered seductively.

I fluttered my eyes and bit my lip. "You could do

that?" I asked with awe in my tone.

"And much more, if you'd like." His smirk was all teeth.

If I hadn't planned on him falling for my act I'd be tempted to kick him into next week. I pretended to consider it for a moment, my teeth pulling at the fleshy part of my lip. "Are you sure we won't get in trouble? I would hate to get kicked out," I fussed, twirling a stray lock of my hair around my *You Only Live Once* OPI painted fingernails.

He smiled, his gorgeous chocolate-brown eyes lighting up at my uneasy performance. He was tall and well-muscled. His black pinstriped suit made him look older than most of the Fae normally did. His thick auburn hair sat in silky spikes along his forehead, framing his beautiful face. "Mmm, I promise you won't get in trouble. I'll take good care of you."

Oh, I just bet you would, lover boy!

I smiled wider and agreed. He took me silently down a hall, through another corridor and into what looked like a lounge of some sort.

The room held a long cream-colored couch and rich chocolate-brown walls. The carpet was plush, extravagant, and a matching brown.

"This room is where the Prince holds more *intimate* meetings," he said.

"Seriously?" I asked, letting the pleasure of the room show on my face. It really was a beautiful room with its rich, natural colors.

"My name is Dristan. Yours is?" he asked, his eyes roving up my covered body. I removed my coat, letting his eyes travel over the tight black tank top I'd worn today.

"Angelica," I whispered nervously, playing it up.

He moved closer, his hand reaching for the jacket I still held in my hands. He gave me a reassuring smile as if I had no clue on his intentions. "You're beautiful. One would almost confuse your beauty for that of a Fae."

"Really?" I beamed.

"May I touch you?" He asked. His words sent alarm bells off inside my head, but I needed him close to me.

"I—I don't know—"

"I don't bite. I promise," he said, moving over and touching my arm.

He ran his long fingers over my forearm, moving up slowly. I gave a small, shaky laugh as my hand sank into the pocket of my jacket, finding the small flat piece of magic vellum. "Your eyes are beautiful, Dristan," I said, blinking slowly as he allowed his eyes to change. The chocolate-brown turned into a mass of lime green, outlined by a deep emerald.

All Fae had double colored eyes and the ability to shield them when the need arose. He smiled as my eyes grew wide from the true beauty of his. "I want you to see me. All of me," he replied, roughly cueing me that it was time to move before I ended up as his dinner.

Fae were of the few creatures to feed from emotions. They had come to the Human world since Humans had emotions in abundance, unlike the other Otherworld creatures. The Fae's preferred method to generate the highest emotion in Humans was sex.

Seems there was some truth to those old stories about Succubi and Incubi, and the Fae not only consumed emotions—they could also take all or part of the soul while feeding.

"You're beautiful," I inched closer as if I was being drawn in by his Otherworld attributes as some women were. I raised my hand, touching his cheek, and almost smiled as he tried for a seductive smile, but failed. The other hand holding the vellum came up and softly planted it on his neck before I allowed him to kiss me.

His lips were soft, his kiss gentle. He pushed me gently toward the couch, fully thinking he had me where he wanted me. His hands pulled against my skirt and I let him, since I was ditching it soon anyway.

His mouth started going slack, and his voice murmured like he had been over-indulging in spirits. "*Somnus*," I whispered, sealing the spell on the vellum against his neck with the Latin word for sleep.

I held his hand and it dropped like a rock. I stood scanning for cameras, knowing there wouldn't be any placed where the Dark Prince held his personal meetings. Someone should tell the Fae that being secretive wasn't always a good thing.

I moved, pushing the sleeping Fae from my body, and removed the skirt, revealing black spandex shorts. It matched the skin-tight tank top I'd allowed him to see. I quickly pulled my hair up and then removed the extra garments, tossing them into a wastebasket, along with the purse, and whispered the word for burn. "*Exussum*."

"Syn, you still with us?" Adam's voice was loud inside my ear, but it pushed away the small ripple of fear that was creeping into my stomach at the job I had ahead of me.

"Copy that, Adam. It's raining men," I whispered with a smirk on my ruby red lips.

"Next floor. Twenty minutes on the clock," Adam replied.

"On my way," I whispered, looking at the sleeping Fae. I walked back over and pulled the small, special camera phone from my pocket before opening his eye and flashing the device silently. "Thanks, Dristan. Sorry," I whispered, before moving to the elevator and slapping another vellum onto the door.

"Open, *patefacio*," I said, adding the Latin to intensify the spell. When I was inside, I quickly kicked from the side of the glass wall and jumped to the top. Luckily, the glass double-pane elevator window didn't cave from my weight. I pushed the top open from where I stood, with two feet pushing against the glass, and removed it before making the small leap and grasping the opening with my hands to pull myself up.

When I was on the top of the elevator, I paused, checking for more cameras. I held my hand up to my ear and relayed to Adam. "Clear; heading up to the vault," I whispered.

"All is quiet outside, Syn. Good luck."

"Who needs luck?" I gave a soft, nervous laugh after the comm had gone silent. I looked around, still kneeling, since the elevator had yet to stop. There was an overhanging ledge from the top floor, which would mark *his* rooms.

When the elevator had finally gone up close enough that I could jump, I did, sailing through the air with no margin for error. My fingers touched upon the thick metal and held. I inhaled slowly, letting it out even slower. After a brief second, I pulled myself up and used the small picture of Dristan's eye at the sensor to gain entrance into the chamber.

I held my breath and, after a second that seemed to last for an eternity, it finally beeped. The doors slid open, revealing the Dark Prince's personal rooms. These were not warm and neutral as the other room had been. They were masculine shades and vibrant. The walls were a bright shade of red with artistic Celtic designs that seemed to encircle the entire top of the walls where they met the ceiling. Expensive white couches had been strategically placed throughout the room, the longest of which was placed in front of a wall bearing a large, ornate mirror that was actually embedded in it. By the look of it, I had pretty good idea that it wasn't just for decoration. The elaborate frame held expensive double-pane glass so you could watch those who sat in the entryway without them knowing they were being observed. *Shit.*

I ripped another piece of vellum from my pocket. This one was designed specifically to look for hidden passageways, and slapped it on the wall bearing the mirror. Quickly whispering the same words, I watched as a small portion of the wall opened up. I quickly stepped back and took a fighting stance.

I didn't hear anyone approaching. I relaxed once I saw it revealed nothing more than a single walkway into the next room. I approached it cautiously, slipping around the large couch, my eyes searching for anything out of place. When I was satisfied that it was only a passage and not an actual portal into their realm, I stepped through. Thick, spelled walls moved, pulsing with a life of their own.

We had suspected that the Fae had brought parts of Faery into our world to bind the two and keep their entrance open, but this was more than we could have imagined. It also indicated that the Dark Prince probably had a Witch working with him.

The spelled walls were a dark blue, with a vibrant green that seemed to be pulsing, moving, and twisting as I walked beside it. It begged to be touched; calling out with a siren's song. I knew better, but even knowing it would probably lock me in place wasn't helping much. When I finally spotted another entrance, I took it.

This one opened up to his bedroom—not exactly where I would have chosen to go. The bed was huge; red silk sheets covered the entire frame snugly. Black pillows that matched the color of the walls were propped at the top of the bed and silver chains had been sewn into a few of them—so the Prince had a dark side. *Go figure.*

Pathetic. I scanned the room, noting there was only a single camera inside this room and it was aimed at the bed—yup, guy had issues. I left the room without a sound, scanning the few doors that were open to other rooms down the long hallway. I grinned when I finally saw the one I needed.

It was a thick type of wood and would take a few strips of vellum to open it. After I applied it and spoke the words very carefully, the door popped open with a small thump. I entered the room and cussed violently. It was not lost on me, the irony of it all. It had been relatively simple getting to this point.

Before me stood what appeared to be a torture chamber. And if that wasn't bad enough, a medieval obstacle course ran the length of the room up to the vault doors. It wasn't the torture chamber that had my knees shaking, nor was it the wicked looking tools either; it was the course. Whatever Fae had designed it had either spent way too many hours watching bad B-rated movies or had a perverse sense of humor thinking this would deter Humans.

Wicked looking curved blades swung from the wall in a synchronized pattern, while thick twelve-inch axe blades swung from another part and fire blared to life right after those nasty little bits. Of course, it had been crazy easy to get inside. No one in their right mind would try the damn course.

"Syn? How are we looking in there?" Adam's voice vibrated in my ear.

"Peachy," I growled, trying to figure out the pattern of the blades. I wanted to turn tail, go home and eat some chocolate just from looking at the damn thing. I'd live longer. My ass might not like me come morning, but I would be *alive* for it not to like me.

"Peachy as in smooth or, peachy as in you found something you didn't like?" Adam persisted.

"Hey, tell Larissa she can have my OPI collection if I don't make it out of here," I said, moving up to the course.

"Syn—"

"Enough, Adam. If you don't hear from me in twenty minutes, you need to head in and report to the Guild."

"That doesn't sound good," he said in a small voice.

"I need silence—no noise on the comm, Adam," I growled, trying to make myself grow enough balls to take the first step into the course.

I turned, eyeing the glass walls. What was it with

these guys and glass? I noticed my platinum blonde hair looked darker inside the room. My azure eyes looked a little too big with the thick eyeliner covering them. I looked like a mess. My shorts were just that; very short. The tight tank top hugged my size Ds seductively, drawing my eyes to them instead of the star brands on my shoulders.

My mouth was actually quivering, and I was never afraid of anything—except the Fae. I turned away from the mirror, since it wasn't helping me. I needed to do this now, before the Prince returned. I re-pulled my hair back into the tight ponytail and stepped up to the gauntlet.

I inhaled, watching as the blades moved. I bit into my bottom lip and shook my head. There was no way to get past the knives. I was pretty sure the moment you tossed something in to their space, more bad things would pop up. I let out a shaky breath and took off from a dead stop that would lock me into the deadly course.

The wicked looking blades shot out the moment I entered their path. One sliced through the small of my back, but it only drew a thin line of blood. Sure enough, as soon as I turned around, wicked looking poles shot up to keep me locked into the course.

"No going back now," I said to myself. I turned and ducked, rolling on my stomach as the blades whizzed past me. I was flat on my back as they swung mere inches from my face. I took a quick breath before I turned my head slowly, watching as the axe blade gouged two inches from the ground next to me.

I was skinny, but not that skinny. I counted and then rolled quickly to the next thing before standing effortlessly and twirling my body through yet more sharp blades and axes. When I had successfully made it past them, I barely avoided the flames that shot from the walls.

"Fire in front of me, water beneath me. Meet." I brought my hands together to give the spell more force without needing the ancient language.

Nothing happened. I hated *his* Witch, whoever it was—someone had used a lot of blood to ensure those flames were magic proof. *"Aqua within,* come to me," I whispered, allowing the magic to pulse through me. My body used the water inside to cover my skin, turning it slick and wet enough to quickly step through the flames and up to the vault door. "Take that, Witchy Witch," I growled, already tossing a few pieces of vellum onto the thick metal door. *"Patefacio,"* I said, even as the thought crossed my mind that the course had been a little too easy.

I gave a wicked little grin at my success and stepped through the door—to guns pointing at my face. I swallowed and looked around, calculating my chances of escape. I met a pair of eyes so golden that it startled me. The face they belonged to was harsh and beautifully masculine. Shit.

"Abort; that's a direct order," I said, with more calm than I was currently feeling.

"Syn?" Adam shouted.

"Run."

* ~ * ~ * ~* ~* ~ * ~* ~*

Chapter
TWO

I reached up carefully, so as not to get shot in the head, and removed my comm. I tossed it to the floor, knowing if I did more I might end up dead before I could figure out how to get out of this situation alive. The Dark Prince stood before me; his hair so black it almost appeared blue in the lights. Golden eyes stared at me, no emotion in their endless depths. He was the most beautiful thing I had ever seen. *Would* ever see, since my life was about to be cut short prematurely.

"Search her," he ordered. His voice had a slight brogue to it.

My knees were kicked out from behind me, making me hit the floor ungracefully. I bit into my bottom lip to keep from crying out or making any sound. Rough hands searched me from behind for weapons and came up empty.

"She's clean," the Fae who was still behind me said after he was sure I held no threat. As he continued to search me, he found the thin paper in the tight pocket of the spandex shorts I wore. They had been tipped off. It was the only way they would have been waiting for me. I glared as cuffs were secured around my wrists from behind.

"You came for the crown?" The Prince asked as his eyes slid down my body slowly, his men bringing me back up to my feet.

I remained silent. Nothing I said now could save me. I would never tell them why I was here or who I was with, and nothing on my person would give that away either. It was why I'd left all weapons at home. They could be traced back to the Guild through serial numbers, and, while I knew how to use them, I wasn't a big fan of guns.

"Your silence will do you no good. Help yourself out and I'll make your death quick. Remain silent, and I'll enjoy killing you *slowly*," he purred, closer to me than he had been seconds before; my eyes hadn't even caught the subtle movement.

"I'm with housekeeping," I ground out, breathlessly since he was now inches from me.

"Take her to the chamber," he said to his men. To me, he whispered in my ear in a strange language I'd never heard before. An ancient language, that much I was sure of.

Everything inside of me screamed against the pressure that was building as everything started shutting down like clockwork. My mind pushed together as if something was fighting to gain control of it. Darkness swallowed my vision, my limbs grew heavy as if replaced by lead, and everything inside of my mind went dark.

~~*~*~*~*~*~*~*~*

I awoke to ice water being tossed over my head. I was strung up like a spring chicken on market day. My arms were hung high above my head. I had to fight against the darkness to get my bearings back.

Thick metal bands held me locked into place; chains hooked to my feet kept me from doing more than standing upright.

My mouth was dry and felt as if I had eaten an entire bag of cotton. My shorts and tank top had been removed, leaving me in nothing more than my small black thong and lacy bra. My hair had been taken out of the ponytail and left to hang in my face.

I could feel no new injuries to my body—no abuse while I had been knocked out. Whatever spell the Dark Prince had used on me packed a wallop that left me feeling weak and drained.

"Ready to talk?" *His* voice came from a speaker in the middle of the room.

"I—I told you—I'm housekeeping," I whispered since it was the best I could do, which sucked. I sounded weak.

Silence reigned until a door popped open, and the Dark Prince strolled in wearing a white shirt and old jeans, which he probably used for torturing unwanted guests. "Tell me who sent you and I will go easy on you."

I laughed coldly.

"Something funny?" He inquired, moving closer to me.

"Bring it, Fairy," I growled throatily.

His head tilted, showing off his sharp, exquisite bone structure. He was simply breathtaking. His hair clung to his face, hanging low over his ears. Those golden eyes had changed, showing his Fae features. Golden pupils surrounded by obsidian black circles, marking him royal in his breed. He had a day's worth of stubble, which only drew the eyes to his sharp jawline. He was taller than the Fae who had surrounded me earlier, standing well over six feet in height.

"You will tell me what I want to know. In the end, everyone does," he whispered huskily with a wicked twist lighting up his face, his eyes still watching me intensely.

"Is that so?"

"It is. Tell me, do you prefer torture? Or, I can easily feed to get the information I want out of you," he asked as if we were discussing the weather, instead of my immediate future.

"Torture—" Shit! I realized my error as soon as I said it.

"Feed it is," his hands reached out, smoothing down the lines of my body leisurely, seductively soft as he touched my flesh. His eyes never left mine. I inhaled slowly, waiting for the anger to take hold of me. With anger, would come power—only, it never came.

My body burned from his touch, awakening something inside of me I had thought would never come alive again. Lust. Oh fucking hell, wrong place and wrong guy. I watched a smirk take hold of his full lips.

His fingers traced elaborate patterns over my skin until they stopped at the lace of my panties. "I think I might actually enjoy this," he growled, ripping one of the small thin sides from them, exposing the soft lines of my pelvis.

"Bet you would," I scoffed, finally finding my voice.

"I could take your emotions and make you think I am your God. If I turned you FIZ, you'd give me *anything* I wanted."

I blanched. I hated that they called the poor saps they fucked to the brink of death FIZs. *Fae Induced Zombie.* "Go. To. Hell. Fairy. Boy."

One side of his sensual mouth tugged up as if he were fighting the urge to laugh. "I will show you how much of a man I am," he purred, placing his head too close to my face.

"Oh, baby, don't hold back on me now," I said mockingly.

"I never do," he whispered, letting his fingers move over my soft folds, making my body shudder violently in their wake.

I struck without warning, slamming my face into his and crying out at the same time he did. I fought against the chains, knowing that pain was up next. I'd smashed his too-sexy face. No way was he going to allow me to live now.

Surprisingly, he seemed unaffected after a moment. I, on the other hand, had blood oozing down from my smashed nose. He stepped back, reaching slowly down to the bottom of the shirt he wore before pulling it up and over his head slowly.

I flinched. He was ripped and looked like he had stepped from the cover of a male fitness catalogue. A solid six-pack flowed down his abs, disappearing under the rough jeans he wore. A thin trail of dark hair started below his navel, flowing in a seducing trail into the waistline of his jeans that clung loosely to his tapered hips. He was covered in Celtic brands that looked similar to tattoos, but moved.

The door opened as another Fae walked in. As he got closer, I saw he wasn't Fae exactly—he was a Demon. His skin was covered with brands similar to mine and Adam's, which were usually invisible to the eye, and if I invoked my own, they would glow and match his Celtic patterns. The Dark Prince didn't have a Witch. No, he had a fucking Demon.

The Demon was taller than the Prince. His silver eyes swirled with black patterns that were common for his kind. His hair was long and straight and looked as soft as silk and was the color of freshly poured ink. His forearms were covered in thick brands that I could tell flowed up and covered his neck stopping just below his face.

"Who do you work for?" The Prince continued to question me, his sharp eyes watching, searching for a weakness.

"Your mother. She wants you to clean your bedroom," I quipped sarcastically. A silent shiver raced down my spine as I remembered his bedroom. I flinched as he held his hand up until it touched my face. An earthly scent whirled through the room as cool waves touched my face. The bleeding stopped as he lowered his hand from my face.

He ignored my taunts and nodded to the tall, exotic Demon of his. A few minutes of awkward silence descended on the large sterile room. I watched him from beneath my lashes—his glyphs were beautiful. Thick black Celtic markings covered a single shoulder, flowing gently onto his chest and down his side, further onto his back, out of sight.

"I found something that might make you talk," he said, interrupting my thoughts.

I was still trying to figure out what his brands

meant when a familiar cry ripped from the hallway. My heart accelerated, my mouth going dry again, but this time with fear. Chandra and Adam were led inside the room, both bloodied from fighting for their lives.

I felt angry tears push against my eyes as I met Adam's vibrant emerald stare. They were told to leave, to run, so why hadn't they? I pulled all emotion back from my features, sucking in air until I wanted to choke on it. Chandra's lip was swollen and bloodied as if she'd been assaulted.

They were pushed in together, and Adam was shoved to his knees in front of me. His shoulder-length black hair clung to his bronze face, his eyes begging me to forgive him. I wanted to scream at him. He should have been clear. If he'd done as I'd said he would've been. I'd tried to buy them time with myself as a hostage. If I'd known he hadn't listened, I would have fought them.

I lifted my gaze from Adam to Ryder who was watching me closely and judging my reaction. He materialized a Rugger 9mm from thin air and cocked it before holding it to Adam's temple.

"Talk, or he dies."

A gun—seriously, even I knew these guys didn't need guns to kill, so he had to be doing this so I could see the threat. I couldn't talk. It was part of my training. If Adam spoke of the Guild or gave anything away—I myself would be killing him. It was part of the blood oath they made us take when we graduated. Our eyes met and held, his saying that it was okay, mine showing everything I felt. Frustration at not being able to help. Anger for what was happening and pain for what I was losing—my closest friend.

"Use the girl," his Demon said, when I refused to

answer.

Relief washed over me as Adam was spared from death and chained beside me in the other set of hanging manacles. Chandra was pushed in front of me, and shoved to her knees the same way Adam had been. She was fairly new to the Guild, and I didn't know her as well as I did Adam.

I met and held Chandra's eyes, telling her I was sorry, but her eyes didn't hold remorse, or regret— deep malice sat smoldering in her hazel eyes. I almost choked on my tongue—I knew that look. Shit—she *would* talk.

"My name is Chandra—" She smiled coldly at me.

"Shut up Chandra," I growled in warning, making my voice sharp.

"Fuck you. I'm not dying here!" she cried.

The Prince was watching us closely. His eyes moving from my red face to hers, which showed not an ounce of remorse. I wasn't as attached to Chandra like I was the others in my small coven. If she spoke, I'd take her out, and, while I hated doing it, she knew the rules. She'd taken the same oath I had; the one to protect our coven by every means.

"Who does she work for?" Ryder gently asked Chandra, who looked only too willing to give up who I was, and why I had come.

"She's the—"

I closed my eyes, feeling a slight twinge of regret as I did the only thing I could to prevent her from pointing blame at the Guild.

She coughed violently as I sent my dark magic

inside her with a whisper, seeking her lungs with thousands of needles that would stop air from entering them. It wouldn't be completely painless, but I was trying to make it a clean death so she wouldn't suffer more than she had to. She cried out as blood exploded from her lungs, flowing freely from her lips, seconds before she suffocated and collapsed to the floor with a soft thud.

The Dark Prince watched with mock amusement on his hard beautiful face, his golden eyes rising from her crumpled form to my face. I couldn't look away from Chandra. She had panicked and given me no other choice but to take her life. She was dying slowly, drowning on blood that filled her lungs—because of me.

"You killed her?" he asked, surprised, but I ignored him.

For what seemed like minutes after Chandra had slumped onto the floor, cold and lifeless, I continued to push dark magic inside of her until Adam spoke low and leveled calling me by code to keep our names secret. "Mags, stop; she's dead."

Her dark brown hair was now taking on an angry red tint from the blood that still flowed from her lips to create a pool around her face. I'd done what I was taught. I'd had no choice. I kept telling myself this over and over inside my head as my heart rate increased at what I had just done—I'd *killed* her.

Guilt crept up my spine. I hated killing, even if I was good at it. To talk of the Guild, or to tell a mark who sent us, was treason. If you got caught, you went silently to your death as I would surely do now at the hands of this deadly Fae.

"Mags, look at me," Adam said, gently but firmly.

I raised my eyes, meeting his gentle green eyes. His hair was covered in perspiration and clung wildly to his face. His face showed no fear, no anger for the kill; only acceptance. "Blood oath, Mags. You had no choice."

"It was a good kill—painless." I choked on bile with each word. "Hecate, keep her safe." I felt hot angry tears push against my eyes again. "*Exussum, Chandra,*" I said the word, focusing as I pushed enough power into the words, drawing from the limited reserve I now had after pulling from dark magic.

Smoke billowed from the body inches from my feet. Flames erupted from her body, and the ferociously awful smell of putrid flesh misted the air. I raised my eyes from Adam's comforting face to the Dark Prince's, and found him still watching me.

Intense eyes met and held mine. A look of respect and awe entered them fleetingly before he turned to look at Adam. He waved the gun away with a magician's flourish, placed his large hands on his hips and shook his head as if he was trying to piece together why I'd killed her.

I coughed and choked on the smoke billowing up from her body. Flesh burning is something you never get used to, no matter how many times you've smelled it before. The smoke burned my eyes, causing water to rush from them.

"That was—interesting," Ryder said, stepping up to face Adam who also hadn't taken his eyes from me.

"Mags—" he whispered, placing all his love into his voice.

"Who is it you work for?" Ryder asked Adam.

"Go to hell, Fairy," he growled, still watching me.

Ryder brought his fingers up to pinch the bridge of his nose in frustration. Shaking his head, he turned and looked directly at me. His eyes taking in everything about me, so slowly I couldn't miss his intentions. "Bring her down, Ristan; place her on the bed."

I fought down the surge of panic that threatened to seize control of my brain with his words. He was Fae. He could seduce and feed on me until I told him *everything*. He could take away my mind and will with his skillful fingers, leaving a shell of who I had once been.

The Demon moved closer, his oily magic slithering over my skin, leaving me helpless against its deadly touch. The chains they had used must have been spelled with magic to keep me from escaping.

Instead of undoing the chains, he released them from the hook, leaving me locked inside their manacles, and kept from using blood magic. I exhaled, accepting the fate that was to come with a surprising calmness I shouldn't have felt.

The bed looked more like an exam table—the same kind you'd see inside a doctor's office—with a simple white cloth draped over it. Like the room, the bed looked cold and sterile. Shivers raced to the fore, memories of another rape pushing against my temples, wanting to allow the fear I had locked up since I had been a child out to run rampant through my veins.

As I was moved slowly, methodically, to the table, I was looking around for anything I could use to get away from the Fae, but they'd taken precautions and placed everything inside the room out of reach of the table. Adam cried out, not from pain but from what was about to happen to me. I prayed he had the sense to look away and not watch what was about to happen.

Being turned into a brainless, sex-induced corpse was not my preferred way to die—but it would be painless. When we reached the table, rough hands grabbed me from behind and swung me over it effortlessly as if I weighed no more than ten pounds.

A deep timbre shivered against my supple flesh as he whispered against my ear, "Last chance, *Mags*." His fingers still bit into my soft flesh, refusing to leave my skin. They sent heat soaking into my bones, pooling in my core like molten lava. Fucking Fae.

"Screw you," I said, trying to hide the fear I was feeling.

I sat with my back to him. My legs clumsily draped half over the other side of the small table. My back was flush against the hard rippling planes of his chest, his heat entering my skin as surely as if I was siphoning it from his pores.

"I intend to screw *you,* and by the time I am done, you'll not only beg me for more, you'll tell me anything I want to know."

A shiver licked my flesh, sending small rivulets of sweat pooling at the base of my neck. I wasn't sure how long the spell laced in my hairline would hold, or if it would work against a Dark Prince at all for that matter, but I needed it to.

I'd had Titus, our local tattoo artist who spelled his ink, place them there when I was only thirteen. He reinforced the spell every year like clockwork. Most Witches, when they hit adulthood, were covered in ink, spelled for protection or against memories.

I'd kept my memories and my internal scars. They were reminders of what I had lived through and how close I'd come to death over the years. The one on my neck was to make sure I had a fighting chance against the Fae, unlike my mother years ago.

"Lock her in," Ryder said, stepping away from me.

His Demon stepped forward, pushing me down gently, which was surprising since I was about to die. Fucked to death by a Fae—life just kept kicking my ass. I held my breath as my arms were held above my head once more, this time flat, and then the metal chain was attached to a hook at the top of the bed. My feet were slipped into similar chains and locked in place.

I turned my face to Adam when I was secured for the bastard Fae Prince. Tears ran down his cheeks. I felt for him, because if I started blabbing or gave a hint of who we were I'd meet Chandra's fate at his hands.

"You fucking bastard! Use me!" Adam roared, fighting against the chains that held him in place. Anger rolled from him in violent waves, mixed with despair. "Mags—fight him dammit!"

I smiled sadly. He knew I had no chance against the Dark Prince. To the best of our knowledge, he was among the most powerful of the Fae. I didn't speak. I couldn't. Tears made my throat grow closed, pain poured through my heart as I imagined seeing myself from Adam's vantage. I swallowed past the tears and spoke clearly, proudly. "Close your eyes," I told Adam, and watched as he shook his head with tears threatening to fall at my words.

Adam strained against the chains—normally so composed and confident, he was now reaching a breaking point with anger at what he knew was happening. His sharp features, normally smooth and young, now strained with it.

"How cute," Ryder growled.

We ignored him. We both knew what was coming, and I didn't want the closest thing I had to family watching this happen to me as I had once watched it happen to my own mother. I felt Ryder pull the magic around him, thick and devastating.

"Chance, please, don't watch this." My words cut off as lust tore through me so violently I almost exploded in pleasure. My body jerked tautly, my eyes seeking the one responsible for these seductive feelings; the one that had created the fire inside of me.

All of Ryder's fingers were touching my skin, sending a battering ram of need through my mind as his Fae magic pushed against my will. I wanted to beg him to stop, but if I did—he'd know how afraid I was, and I couldn't allow that. He placed his face closer to mine, making sure I could see him.

My lips quivered as his eyes turned to molten lava, golden as a mint-pressed bar in the National Reserve. His tongue snaked out to lick his lips before he lowered his head to mine. "Last chance to tell me."

I shook my head, my eyes lingering on his lips for a second too long before moving to look into his golden haze. He smelled divine; sandalwood mixed with Otherworld spices, illegal to Humans for their aphrodisiac proprieties; he must have been pushing the scent from his pores in succulent waves. Lips of the finest silk touched against my cheek, moving slowly over flesh until they lingered briefly over my own.

He took my breath away and fed it back to me slowly, just from his close proximity. His fingers moved, releasing the magical hold for mere seconds as he moved them down to inside of my thighs. My breathing grew labored as his fingers met my delicate flesh, stroking and exploring. His eyes searched my face, watching every minuscule expression, every hiss I made from his touch.

His breath hinted of rum, and, against my better judgment, I wondered if he would taste of it. I didn't have long to wait to figure it out as his mouth crushed against mine in a hard, demanding kiss. His fingers released my leg where they had been making small swirling patterns and slid up to hold my head back; one hand was buried deep in my hair, the other along my jawbone demanding I open to his kiss.

The kiss lasted only a few minutes, but in that time heat had flooded to my core, drenching my panties. My body shook from the need to release, just from his kiss. I moaned against his mouth; wanting, demanding more before my mind could grasp what I had done. A throaty purr vibrated through his chest as he pulled back, releasing my mouth but not his touch.

"You're wet for me already," he growled huskily.

His eyes were alight with his own need, filled with a million stars; as if the solar system lived inside their fiery depths. My own eyes felt glazed; my body was a mass of need. My lips quivered for his, my chest lifted for his fingers, needing him to grace them with his heated touch. I bit my lip to keep from begging as I struggled from his powers.

I could feel the burning on my neck from the brand, the tattoo trying to work, but failing. It wasn't working. I would be killing Titus when, or if, I got out of this alive. It should have been working against his seductive powers.

I played out why I was here and who was depending on me. Adam would have to kill me if I gave in, and he'd never recover from it. He'd end up as damaged as I was. I bit my lip harder, drawing blood to the surface. "More," I growled huskily, much to his delight and my utter horror.

"Unchain my saucy little sex pet, Ristan, please." Ryder's own voice was filled with lust. His eyes watching me feverishly, intensely. I watched him from beneath my lashes.

He was well-built. Muscles covered his torso, as well as tattoos. Smooth and bronzed, unscarred perfection. The tattoos, or brands as we called them, pulsated—proof he was pushing his magic into my mind, consuming my will to become his own. It was working. My body wanted him more than I had ever wanted any man before.

I felt a tug, first on my hands, and then the clinking of chains falling haphazardly to the floor met my ears. Adam's shouts now sounded as if they were coming from far away, but still there. I only needed Ryder. I needed him to fill me and take away the throbbing need between my thighs.

The chains on my feet were also removed, giving me free reign to sit up, but my body felt useless as if my bones were gone, and the muscles had been replaced with Jell-O. My mind fought to keep a hold on why I was there, but with Ryder so close, it was becoming impossible to remember even my own name.

Ryder released my face and moved to the end of the exam table, deftly lifting himself up and moving my legs around his hips as he did so. I groaned as he lifted my body, slowly, effortlessly, his hands placing my own over his shoulders as his slid gently down my back. I ground myself against him and enjoyed the deep rumble that ripped from his chest. I was on fire, and he was the cure.

The contact was too much, too fast. My mind went completely numb once more as his mouth found mine and devoured it hungrily. Sparks ignited inside me, a storm built to dangerous levels in my core. I was so close to reaching the precipice he had me standing on. I wanted to go over—*needed* to.

I melted into his kiss ardently, needing more of him inside of me. I was on fire, burning from the inside out. My panties clung, soaked, to my pussy. His hand on my back was pissing me off—I needed his fingers buried deep inside of me to stop the pain eating away at my mind. I growled with need, but instead of giving me what I wanted, he pulled back panting.

The look of surprise in his molten depths fed my inner vixen—he wanted *me*. I smiled with victory until something echoed inside of me; a warning I wanted to ignore, but couldn't. Someone needed me, someone other than my master; it was important that I not give in to this sexual beast—but why?

"I ache," I whined, bringing my hands around from where they had been holding him against my own flesh. They strayed with a mind of their own down my smooth belly, reaching lower to stop the pain, but his hands grabbed them, pulling them away and bringing them back up to hold against his chest.

"Tell me what I want to know and I'll make it better for you." His voice was rough and guttural, as if he was in as much pain as I was. I wanted to stop his pain, but he wouldn't stop talking. "Who do you work for?"

I blinked, my mind going blank—I was supposed

to remember something and, yet, I wanted his cock more than anything else in the entire world. I opened my mouth and closed it a few times, like a fish gasping for breath outside of its tank.

"What's your name?" he asked when I didn't reply.

"Who the fuck cares? I hurt." I pulled my hand away from his, only to grab it back and push it toward my wetness. "Down here."

He growled hungrily, but yanked his hand away. His eyes narrowed as if he was trying to figure something out. That nagging feeling inside my mind came back with a vengeance, itching against my scalp and then going deeper.

My lip quivered from the pain inside my head, at the force of the pull to listen to the white noise blaring inside my mind. I tilted my head as I focused my gaze on his full mouth. I leaned closer, needing to taste them again, and he let me.

He groaned as I caressed his lips with my tongue, nipping at his lip between my teeth teasingly before pushing my tongue inside his mouth seductively. His hands lifted from where he had allowed them to drop and grabbed the back of my head, bending my neck back to allow him more access. I moaned against him, allowing him to open my jaw until it was as far as it would go for his hungry mouth. His tongue stroking mine, relentlessly.

And then it hit me—coming back with the force of a truck hitting a wall at sixty miles an hour. Enemy. Fae. Adam. Torture.

~~*~*~*~*~*~*~*

Chapter
THREE

I came alive like a lightning bolt. I pushed away from him, falling to the floor with a bone-jarring thud that woke me up better than the cold bucket of water I'd tossed in my face earlier. I was on my feet and backing away from the two deadly creatures who stood shocked that I'd been able to move at all.

I was pretty sure that it was the shock that kept them from attacking. I pulled the anger that had been hiding inside me, along with Adam's, into my mind and pushed it out of my body in a solid wave, clearing the room of the Demon's oily magic until mine was the only magic inside the room.

I allowed the magic to run through me riotously and seductively. My mouth opened and whispered a binding spell. Hate and fear made for hasty decisions. I needed something that could get me and Adam out of this alive. The Dark Prince wouldn't know what hit him.

In the seconds that it took for them to understand what I was doing, the door behind them was thrown open, and Alden was suddenly there in front of the Dark Prince. I was beyond hearing. Everything inside the room was silent inside my head. I'd evaporated it with the blood from my lips where I had bitten into them for the blood needed for the spell.

I said the words, sealing us together—I and the Dark Prince. If he killed me, he'd follow my fate. Everything was moving in slow motion. The horrified look on the Warlock's face as he stood in front of the Prince, as if to guard him from what was coming, gave me pause.

I could hear my own heartbeat. It was the only sound inside my head. I inhaled, readying the words to take us both out, but something grabbed me from behind and took me to the floor before I could say them.

Adam was shouting against my ear, but he sounded far away, distorted. He'd been in chains only moments ago—how the hell had he gotten loose, and why had he stopped me? He had taken me to the floor, and before I could understand it was him, sound came back with a deafening roar of violent voices, all cursing. Alden was screaming at me to cease, Adam was cursing, now as confused as I was, but he'd connected something I hadn't.

Or he better have, since he'd knocked me flat on my ass—and into the pile of ash that had once been Chandra. I watched as Alden said something to the Fae and then the Demon only for all three to turn as one and look at me. I fought to get my breathing under control. The feel of his searing kiss was still lingering upon my lips.

I turned and narrowed my eyes back at the three men, wondering what the fuck was going on. Alden was from the Guild—*my* Guild. He was the leader of the Eastern Section of Washington State. He'd basically been a father figure to the orphans that came to us—.which had included me up until a few years ago when Adam, Larissa, and I had moved out of the Guild complex into apartments of our own in the same building.

Alden stood with his gentle blue eyes narrowed on me. His thick brown hair was streaked with gray and instead of it making him look older as it should have, it just made him look distinguished. He wore the Guild leader's crimson robe over black slacks. He didn't look a day over thirty-five, but I knew different.

I still didn't trust my voice not to quiver from the effect the Fae had upon me. My insides still quivered with need for him and *only* him. It burned me; my anger rose by the second, even though I'd sent it away. It was one of the few ways an immortal could be killed outright. Bind his soul to a weak Human and drag him to hell with you.

Souls were tricky that way. You couldn't live without one—you wouldn't want to anyway.

"Synthia, listen to me closely," Alden said sternly, as if talking to a wayward child. "You need to release him this instant. He's the fucking Dark Prince for fuck's sake girl. What the hell is wrong with you?"

I digested his words—what was wrong with *me*? "Alden—" I growled, knowing what he was going to say next without needing the words.

He said them anyway. "This was an interview— he wouldn't have hurt you."

I laughed, but it was cold—more pissed than happy. "A fucking interview?"

"They asked for the best, but they wanted to see you in action and to see your skills without you knowing it was an interview."

Bile rose to the back of my throat as I stood, pushing myself off the ground still only garbed in my unmentionables. "A fucking interview! Chandra's fucking *dead*. I killed her, Alden! He tried to turn me. He fucking *kissed* me!"

"No harm was done, Synthia."

I blinked at Alden—hadn't he heard me? "Chandra. Is. Dead," I replied slowly, enunciating every word. Making sure he couldn't miss the anger I was feeling or what I was telling him.

"Yes, she is. Shame, but she was being tested, as well. Synthia, she was new to our Guild. You know that better than anyone; the Guild rules must be kept. You were under the Dark Prince's powers, yet you refused to give up the information—she sang like a bird at the first chance she got to save her own skin. You did as you were taught, child—you did well."

I wanted to scream. I wanted to cry. I knew what I had to do, and it was neither of those things. I had to bury my dead. Chandra deserved to be given the Rites. She deserved to go into the Fade; to be reborn.

I turned and erected an invisible wall with what strength I had left, much to the horror of those around me who had no idea what I intended to do with the life of the Dark Prince still attached to my own soul.

It wasn't until I turned and smiled sadly at Adam that they knew what I was going to do and started to freak out. Alden rushed to the invisible barrier, while Ryder and his Demon stood still as if afraid to move. I knew better, I was willing to bet there wasn't much Ryder was afraid of—not even dying.

"You can't send her to the Fade. She turned on us!" Alden screamed, outraged that I would try to send her, even though she had betrayed us.

Try was the key word. I would take her death unto me. If I could manage to keep my mind from thinking it was happening in reality. I'd done it only once before. Not many had the balls to even attempt it, since the mind was a dangerous thing to play around in.

I silently looked around the room, finding my target. A radio sat in the corner, turned off. I sent my magic flowing through the room to it, finding Creed's *My Own Prison* within its database, and turned it up. I bent down, kneeling upon the cement floor in front of the ashes.

Adam tried to turn it off, but as the words flowed he stopped. I could feel the weight of the stares in the room burning into my flesh, heavy and unrelenting. I pulled a knife from the Demon's boot without having to leave the sanctuary of the circle; magic, swift and silent, pulling it inside and sealing the hole before anyone knew what had happened.

I brought up the cold, wicked looking blade and cut my palms, slicing an X across both hands. The sting burned as flesh opened up in thin red lines to release the blood needed to complete her Rites. I painted the sign of life and death on my torso, the sign of fear and courage on my cheeks—and then whispered the chant to bring life to the ashes.

A small wind flowed through the room as I pulled myself up to meet Chandra's soul as she came alive, briefly. Her soul would need a host—I would become that host until I could release her soul. The soul gets lost without a host. It's why we take them in and release them with magic.

Her hazel eyes opened as she stepped from the

ashes. She had no voice, but it didn't keep her from trying to use it. Telling the dead they're actually dead is not always a bright idea. They tend to think they can be reanimated. Only Necromancers can do it, and it doesn't always end well for the soul.

She glared, and it might have been comical except I'm the one who killed her, so technically, I'd hate me too. She smiled—it was cold; her brown curls rustled soundlessly as she laughed and it too was silent. She noted Adam and Alden outside the sanctuary I cast to protect us from being disturbed. She tilted her head before accepting my offer to carry her. Pain erupted as she entered through the small cuts. Her soul was pulsing as it entered my own. I felt her inside of me; her animated soul gone as she entered my body. And then it came.

I felt my lungs start to fill with fluid—blood. I was taking her death echo into my soul. My brain makes me experience it for myself. As if it was really happening to me. This is where it would get tricky, if my brain, at any time, thought it *was* actually happening—I would die.

Adam pounded against the invisible barrier—he's yelling at me to remember. To remember it wasn't happening. And it wasn't, not really. God, did it hurt. It wasn't supposed to hurt. It was supposed to be painless. She suffered because I'd lost focus.

I felt her rage as she made the connections and then the bitterness of denial as she figured out it was me who had killed her. I could barely feel my own body at this point. I could feel the tears flowing down my face from the pain as my soul made room for her inside of it.

My hands flew to my throat as oxygen was ripped and starved from my esophagus and then I felt my lungs giving out. Chaos broke loose outside of the shield as the Dark Prince coughed and grabbed at his own throat.

Our eyes met and held. If I died—he would die with me. He could feel my distress, because I'd linked him to my lifeline—my soul. I would undo it when I was done gathering her soul and consuming my sin. He became enraged as he understood that, at that moment, he was as mortal as I was—and if I lost this battle, he would join me in death.

I coughed and hit the floor at the same moment he did. Our eyes still locked on one another; his in anger, and mine in awe. Even choking, this asshole was hot—seriously, someone needs to break his nose and make him a little less pretty.

My mind cried out in warning. Adam and Alden were both chanting—trying to take down the barrier. The Demon was using his dark powers—did they think I hadn't considered all this before I erected it? It was foolproof. I was that good. Seriously, sometimes I scared myself with just how badass I was.

Ryder spat blood the same moment I did, and then it stopped. He stood up as I did. I smiled coldly— he'd felt her pain. He'd felt mine. He had touched my fucking *soul*. He knows now that I am darker inside; that I have secrets. I hated it.

I wiped my mouth off with the back of my hand and moved my other hand, flicking my wrist to remove the barrier. "Come, Fairy, let's get this over with." I wanted him out of me; his soul was slithering seductively against my own.

~~*~*~*~*~*~*~*

Chapter
FOUR

Clothed in my shorts and tank top once more, I grabbed his hands and met him face-to-face. His hands, surprisingly warm, gave me a sliver of remembrance of how his seductive touch felt on my skin. I placed them palm up, with my much smaller hands resting lightly on top, and enjoyed the anger flowing through him, until he spoke.

"If you ever connect us again—I will kill you, Witch." His voice was low, raspy.

I raised my eyes to meet his head on. "You ever try to Fae-fuck me again—I'll kill you, Fairy."

"I'll show you a fucking Fairy—if I remember right, you wanted it."

I raised a blonde brow, which was probably red at the moment, since I was still covered in blood. "You used the haze, which is basically rape."

"Did I?" His voice purred, leaving it a statement more than a question.

I growled, which only made his lips turn up in the corners, reminding me of the kisses we'd shared. I tried to push his essence out of me, but it was like it was locked inside a box inside my mind. I rolled my eyes and tried again as sweat beaded on my forehead.

"It's not working?"

"Pretty *and* smart. Better alert the press," I replied sarcastically as I put everything inside of me into pushing his essence out of my body.

"You think I'm pretty?" he asked incredulously as if I'd just handed him the biggest insult of his life.

I narrowed my eyes on him and bit my lower lip. I tried, yet again, to get his essence from mine as my legs shook. His hands landed on my waist before I fell. "Pretty much. Maybe you should wear less makeup and add some scars. Toughen up that pretty boy image you got going on." I smirked, watching his jaw tick with anger. My eyes slid to his full mouth, remembering it and how it felt pressed against mine.

"Syn, need a boost?" Adam asked me from where he stood a few feet away, trying to dispel the tension building inside the confines of the room.

My body trembled violently—it was still adapting to the new soul inside of it. I winced as aches and pains made themselves known, now that the adrenaline rush had passed. "I just need a few minutes," I lied, not knowing if I would be able to give him back what I had stolen from him.

No sooner had I said it, when my legs gave in against my weight. I was caught by Ryder before I landed on my ass on the floor at his feet, and carried to a couch. We'd left the torture room and entered what appeared to be an unused office. It was drab and barren of any personal items.

Whitewash walls and matching white carpets—

the only object inside the room being a single black couch that wrapped around and covered two walls. "Sit down and do not touch anything," Ryder ordered as he dropped me none too-gently on the couch.

"What the hell would I touch?" I grouched back, feeling bitchy about needing to be carried at all— much less by him, of all people!

He looked down his nose at me, and then at his hands as if I had stained them—I laughed.

His eyes narrowed. "You were not laughing a little while ago—shall I remind you of where you wanted me?" He looked down at my black, skintight shorts, as if he could tell by scent that I was still having him dance around in my inappropriate thoughts.

"You fucked with my mind, and I *resisted* you," I said, allowing my lips to turn up in one corner, before gently biting my lip and wincing.

Oh yeah—I'd bitten it hard. *Ouch.*

"Keep lipping off, and I'll find a use for that tongue."

"Keep dreaming, man-whore."

He made a disgruntled sound of irritation, but I was too tired to care. My body felt drained. My mind kept replaying his damn lips pressed against mine and Chandra, poor Chandra, had died for this guy's stupid interview.

"I don't need to dream about fucking. If I wanted you, Witch, you'd be mine," he growled heatedly, his voice rough.

I glared back. I was tired of everything that was going on in this place. However, I knew I wasn't walking out those doors until I could fix this. The noise coming from the hallway drew me from my irate inner thoughts and back to Adam, who was now coming through the door with steaming hot coffee.

I accepted it carefully, noting how my hands shook as I reached for it. After a few minutes of intense silence, Alden walked in, his eyes sharp as a predator's as he took us all in.

"Any luck yet?" His voice's sharp, angry tone made me want to slap him.

It was one of the first things we learned in training. Never argue with an elder, or any Witch for that matter, in front of someone from outside the Guild. I shook my head and indulged in a long drink of the rich, hot nectar.

The room once again grew silent, until I set the cup aside on the floor, since there wasn't a table or anything to place it on. "Let's give it another shot," I whispered, noting Alden was watching the two of us very closely.

I stood up slowly and stepped closer to the dark and seductive Fae Prince, my hands coming out from my sides to hold his. It would have been a hell of a lot easier if I didn't have to touch him to complete the transfer.

His hands were warm and soft, as if he'd never seen or endured a hard day's work ever in his life. His fingers curled around my own, sending heat raging through every part of my sex-starved tissue. I raised my eyes, meeting him head-on, even though I had to look up to do so. I watched his lips curve wickedly. Those eyes of his were glowing bronze fire, as if he felt the same intensity I did. The spell shouldn't have been cast. If I had known I wasn't going to be killed,

I wouldn't have used it. I exhaled slowly, feeling his strength combine with my own as he pulled his soul essence from my body.

It caressed me from the inside; touching, testing, as it flowed through me and reattached to him. His eyes smiled mischievously, as if he was commanding it to do so. Heat flowed through me, and his hands offered more support as my legs trembled once more with the need to come. He watched my face hungrily, intensely, as I felt even more moisture pooling at my junction and saturating my panties. His soul was fucking me from the *inside,* and it was intensely seductive and powerful.

The minute I felt the last of his essence leaving my body, I pulled away, as if his touch was scorching my flesh. I wiped his touch off on the tank top I wore and turned to Alden on shaky legs, ignoring the husky laugh from the dark seduction behind me. "It's done."

Alden wasn't looking to me, though. He was looking over my shoulder to the Prince. *Whatever!* I just wanted to go home and curl up in my bed and sleep for a week. Maybe indulge in a few buckets of Ben and Jerry's ice cream.

"Sit, Synthia. We have business to discuss," Alden growled, as if he was upset with me—nothing new there.

I sat. Not because he had told me to, but because my legs wouldn't stop shaking with need and lust. Much to my utter horror, Ryder sat beside me—way too close for my state of mind. "Talk."

"The Prince has a job for you," Alden said without any emotion on his face.

"No."

"No?" Three voices said as one—Alden, Ryder, and the damn Demon who had just walked back in.

"Need a dictionary to figure the word out, boys?" I offered lamely.

Alden pinched the bridge of his nose in annoyance. "This isn't a *would you*; it's a *you're going to*, Synthia."

I smiled coldly. "Well then, why didn't you just say so to begin with, Alden? And what if I flat-out refuse? Besides, with my past history being what it is—you sure you want me working with *them*?"

"Then you will receive a mark, and it won't bode well for your coven for refusing a direct order. Past history aside, Synthia, this is something you *will* do."

I growled.

Adam, who was swallowing a sip of his own coffee, spit it out and cussed.

"Syn," Adam warned with stark fear in his eyes.

I swallowed past the swelling in my throat. "What's the job?"

"Impersonating the Light Heir at the Engagement Ball," the Demon said smoothly, as if I hadn't just been threatened, yet again, today.

"I think I'd prefer death. Besides, Alden, that's a waste of my talents and you know it," I snapped. Impersonator? I was not a freaking impersonator. I was one of the best enforcers in the entire state of Washington—don't even get me started on the jobs requiring my skills as an assassin!

"Enough! Do you know why no one else has asked to join your coven, Synthia? Because they're afraid you'll get them killed, like everyone else you grow attached to! If anyone gets too close to you, they die. Adam stays beside you, because he knows if he doesn't, you'll probably get marked and become an easy target. Damn it, girl, you know what happens when you've been marked."

Ouch, that was going to leave a bruise on my ego. My eyes swung to Adam, who wouldn't meet them. "Adam?"

"Syn—" he said carefully as if he didn't want to go there in front of our present company.

"Fine, I'll impersonate her."

"It's not just impersonating. That is only part of what we want you for. You will be told the rest later on," Ryder said, "I was informed you could cloak your appearance and take that of another so well that it would be completely undetectable?"

I officially wanted to scalp Alden, Indian style. I just needed a really cool doeskin skirt, and a very sharp knife to do so. I nodded. It was the only confirmation he would be getting out of me.

They all looked at me expectantly. I looked back at them, bored already.

Alden spoke first, after a few moments of silence. "Change."

"Can't. I've never seen her before," I snapped with exhaustion showing in my tone.

"Ristan?" Ryder raised an eyebrow.

I chewed my lips while Ryder dusted off an invisible piece of lint from his jeans. The Demon materialized a tabloid with a picture of a blonde beauty on the cover. The two would have cute kids together. I studied every detail I could see, and memorized it. I straightened up and pulled the glamour around me from head to toe.

A small sliver of magical current shimmered over my skin, rippling in the air around me. I looked down, taking in the tight jeans and designer top she had been wearing in the photograph, which were now on me.

"That is incredible," Ristan said with wonder in his voice.

"She didn't change," Ryder said, narrowing his eyes on me with close inspection that I felt all the way to my OPI *Paint Your Toron-Toes Rose*.

"She looks just like her," Alden replied, stepping closer, unaware of the death wish I had for him at the moment.

I felt a moment of panic. No one had ever seen through the glamour spell before—not even my friends. "What do you see then?" I asked, narrowing my own eyes to mirror his.

"You," he spat angrily, and it had never sounded more like an insult.

"Sorry to disappoint you. I guess I'm not up for the task at hand."

"If they see you as Arianna, then it doesn't matter what I see. The assassins will mistake you for her as well," Ryder sneered.

I almost choked on my own tongue. "Assassins?" *Now they tell me this?*

Everyone in the room ignored me, and the three men started discussing me as if I wasn't even there.

It felt as if something bigger was going on here; something that wasn't being said to me or Adam. More Fae bullshit; games within games.

"She looks exactly like her," Ristan said excitedly.

"But will it hold up against Fae, or is it only me who can see her true form?"

He didn't have long to wait for an answer as the door was opened, and the tall dark and kiss-me-lips I'd been about to make out with in order to get inside, walked in. "Next time, Brother, a little heads up would be nice."

He stopped, turning to look directly at me and bowed low at his waist. "Arianna, I wasn't aware you would be joining us today."

I rolled my eyes and looked back at Ryder who was grinning mischievously now. I bit my bottom lip under his penetrating gaze.

"Dristan, do you see anything off about Arianna today?" he asked carefully.

Dristan stopped and narrowed his eyes, his head tilting to the side slightly. "Am I supposed to see something different?"

"Good. Now, about letting that little wraith of a Witch seduce you—*don't* do it again. Is the ball still on schedule as planned?" Ryder asked.

I let the glamour fade, since it took energy I didn't have to keep up. The moment I did, Dristan cussed and threw a left hook. I ducked, barely avoiding it, dropped like a sack of potatoes, and came up behind him.

"You bitch!" he snarled, angry with my appearance.

"So I've been told. Do try *not* to attack me again," I said coldly.

"You fucking drugged me!"

I ducked his second punch and landed a solid kick in his side before Ryder pushed me away, none-too-gently, causing me to hit the wall hard. The wind left my lungs violently as I landed on my ass at his feet.

"Enough, Dristan—Syn will be working with us."

"Put this stupid bitch in her place, Ryder. Her kind need to be reminded of where they belong," Dristan snarled.

I said nothing. I wasn't afraid he would do it; I was just tired of hearing dire predictions about my immediate future today. I lowered my head and remained silent as the room grew tense once more. I hurt everywhere—my ego was bruised that I had been caught, I'd killed one of the only Witches who had wanted to join my coven, and I'd played kissy-face with a freaking Fairy.

"What, no snappy comment?" Ryder said.

"Are we done here?" I asked after a short pause.

"For today, yes we are. You will be here at seven tomorrow morning. Wear something appropriate to train in. We only have a short time to teach you what a Fae Princess should act like and, from the looks of it, it's going to take a lot more time than we have."

Chapter
FIVE

Adam and I left the Dark Fortress as fast as our feet would take us, both refusing to speak of what had happened inside. I'd had enough shit for one day. I'd known why the two had stayed with me, but hearing it out loud was a reality check.

I was going to be covered in bruises from head to toe come morning when I had to face his *Highn-ass* again, and I wasn't looking forward to it at all. I'd rather face an angry mob of Witch haters than face him again.

"Syn—"

"Not now, Adam. It's fine," I snapped, hurt over the entire mishap. I'd killed today, and, while everyone else thought it was okay, I had to live with it forever. They could pretend it didn't happen. Me, on the other hand—I had her soul *inside* of me now. I'd basically been dry-humping the Dark Prince, and it was *not* something I wanted to talk about.

We walked into our apartment building in deafening silence. I couldn't bring myself to say more than, "I'm fine." I'd grown up with Adam and Larissa. They were the closest thing to family I had.

It hurt to hear that they only stayed beside me because of it, but what hurt the most was Adam had stayed in the coven, instead of moving on to study war-craft as he had wanted to. That knowledge sat heavily on my heart.

He'd wanted to be more than just a tech guy for me, but he'd stayed because I was reckless and a loose cannon. Okay, that was a little harsh. I wasn't a loose cannon—I just didn't take shit from anyone.

"Syn, we need to talk about this," Adam said as we entered the ancient elevator to our floor. It creaked loudly, and, just as I was afraid I would be stuck dealing with the problem of the truth, the alarm went off.

"Sorry, I just can't deal with this and the Prince in one day, Adam. I need to go in and check on Larissa anyway. See you tomorrow?" I mumbled, already heading out of the elevator, back into the stark white dreary lobby.

"Don't you have to meet up with pretty boy tomorrow?"

I groaned loudly. "Yeah, thanks for reminding me."

~~*~*~*~*~*~*~*

I opened the door to the apartment and checked the safeguard spell before tossing my keys onto the coffee table and heading into the kitchen. "Honey, I'm home," I mumbled, inhaling deeply of something divine.

Larissa could cook like nobody's business, and did, often. My stomach chose that moment to make its needs known. The smell of freshly baked bread lingered inside the room; Larissa must have been baking while we endured the Fae.

Larissa lifted her sparkling green eyes and smiled. "You're alive."

I exhaled and threw my limp form into the small wooden chair next to the little nook table we'd bought secondhand. "Barely. You almost inherited my entire OPI collection today."

"Seriously? How bad was it?" she asked, limping to the sink to wash the jar out, before tossing it into the recycle bin. She tossed her chestnut-brown hair over her shoulder and turned to me with a curious look on her beautiful face.

"I killed Chandra today," I blurted. Shit, I really needed to get a filter for my mouth. I watched as Larissa's eyes grew wide in horror. I chewed my lip nervously as she digested the news.

"Was it within sanction?" Her question caught me by surprise. How easily we could kill one another without remorse; but not me. I took it in and beat the crap out of myself over it. Sanctioned or not.

"It was. We got caught, they had Adam, and I was chained to a wall. The Fae Prince never left the building—instead, he was inside the vault when I opened it. We were drilled for information; she was going to spill the beans—it was a set-up. Alden set the entire thing up!"

Larissa exhaled and shook her head, her eyes flooding with guilt.

"But then you knew that, didn't you?"

My stomach clenched from the knowledge. How could she have known and not told me? The desire to eat was suddenly gone. I closed my eyes before pushing off the small table and standing up.

I entered my room in a daze. Had Adam known? No, no—he'd been just as distraught as I'd been. I wanted to cry, to scream at those who could have stopped what I had done—I'd taken a fucking life! I walked to the small cherry wood dresser I'd brought from the Guild and tried to find something clean to wear to bed, but gave up with a sigh when I found the drawer empty. I missed the Guild's laundress. It beat doing my own laundry any day.

I could still smell sulfur and ash on my skin. And Fae. The bathroom was an ugly olive green from the seventies, but at least the water worked. Who cared what it looked like? Rent was cheap, and, unlike the other places that we could afford, this one was close to the Guild.

I turned the water on, watching the steam curl around to lick my skin gently, beads of condensation forming over my hand. I closed my eyes, but the instant I closed them, all I could see was a devastatingly primal pair of golden eyes.

It was like he was watching me. As if the Fae Prince was sitting inside *my* bathroom! I instantly opened my eyes and started to strip down to nothing. It didn't take much. He'd trashed most of my clothes and, in my haste to redress I had only ripped them more. The entire walk home had been one of shame.

I sank into the water, letting a blissful sigh steal from my kiss-swollen lips. Freaking Fae had made them puffy, and I'd be damned if I hadn't enjoyed it. Sparks had flown from his touch. The fire he'd created inside of me, and the feelings I'd felt, were dangerous and exciting. It was why they were considered the most deadly of the Otherworld. They could make you like it as they fucked you to death.

I let my nose sink beneath the water, holding my breath as the heat from the bath blistered across my lips, hoping it would erase his taste and touch—only it didn't. The moment I popped back up, I could still feel it. His kiss, his mouth, *his* fucking taste. My traitorous body wanted more, but my mind wanted him dead.

I quickly washed, ignoring the darkness of the dimly lit bathroom and ugly green walls. After I was done scrubbing my skin raw to get his touch from my skin—still unsuccessfully—I growled and got out. I looked in the mirror and noticed I was bruised below one eye, more than likely from fighting against him. Thankfully, I heal quickly—it was some sort of running joke within the Guild that Adam and I should have been brother and sister in truth, as we healed much faster than the others. My azure blue eyes were too bright from using magic. My normally platinum blonde hair was a few shades darker when wet, making my skin look pasty white.

It wasn't as if I had a lot of spare time for tanning, though. My spare time was used for reading so I could escape from reality for however much time I could. This was never enough, in my opinion. I turned while wrapping the towel around my body and picking up my clothes to discard them in the trash.

I groaned, frustrated with how today had turned out. I'd killed a fellow Guild member. Sure, I'd passed their sick little fucked-up test, but I didn't want the job. I hated the Fae, and everything about them stunk in my book. I wanted nothing to do with them. I left the bathroom, ignoring Adam as he entered the small apartment, leaving Larissa to deal with him, since all I wanted to do was sleep and forget. Tomorrow I had a job to lose.

~~*~*~*~*~*~*~*

Chapter
SIX

I awoke to a disturbance. Something was inside my room. I pulled the eye cover I used to sleep off of my face and screamed. Golden eyes looked over at me from the other side of the bed. "Get the fuck out of my bed!" I hissed, sitting up before remembering I'd fallen asleep naked.

"You're late. I do not accept tardiness, Synthia."

"Fire me, *please*," I grumbled, trying to pull the covers from beneath him to wrap myself up for modesty's sake. It was like tugging a blanket from beneath a solid boulder. "You mind?" I asked after a moment, noticing there was no way to get up without him seeing me in the buff.

He sat up, resting his long frame on the duvet. His eyes flickered over the top of my breasts where I had been unable to move the blanket to cover them, lingering a brief second before he stood and moved to look out the single window inside my room.

"Stunning view," he said, after a quick inspection of the building across from our own. Yeah, it was crappy, but again, rent was cheap. It was something he had probably never seen—rich boys had way better views.

He kept his back to me and I studied it briefly. His suit was black and hugged his form well enough that I could just make out every muscle in his ass—

He turned, those damn disturbing eyes smiling, as if he had followed where my mind had gone. I glared as I finally managed to bring the covers up far enough to cover myself. I wanted to pull it over my head completely and die from suffocation, which would be better than working for him.

"My car is waiting downstairs. You have exactly ten minutes to be ready and inside it, or I will be back up to dress you myself. I do not like to be kept waiting; nor will I stand for you to be late again."

I raised my brow line and allowed my lips to curve into a small smirk. "You think you could, Fairy boy—"

I was off the bed and on the floor, covered in six feet of Fae, before I finished talking. My head hit the floor with a jarring thud that made my eyes explode with tears. His hands held mine above my head. My body was pressed against the rough carpet by his much larger frame. Lust, thick and dangerous, erupted inside of my core.

"Never challenge me. I promise that you will lose. Every. Fucking. Time."

"Get off me!" I shouted angrily. I was trapped and exposed. His knee was pressed against my naked heat, as if to show me just how exposed I was to him.

"Think you can make me?" he challenged, with his mouth entirely too close to my own; images of last night came rushing back with a vengeance.

"Now!" I yelled, tired of whatever game he was playing. I wasn't stupid. I got that he was higher in the immortal food chain than I was.

"All bark and no bite?" he asked, raising his eyes from where they'd been on my mouth, to meet my own.

I struck, sending my hips bucking against him, using the element of surprise against him, but it was futile. Ryder just ground his knee further in, making pain and pleasure pulse through my junction as he effortlessly held my arms in place.

"By all means, fight me," he purred as fire lit up his amber eyes until I could see them pulsing, thousands of stars locked in their fiery depths. His nostrils flared, and his tongue jutted out to lick his lips, as if he was considering kissing me.

I was pissed. Anger was pulsing, rushing through my veins as surely as a fire through a dry forest. Not to mention, I had zero possibility of getting up without him seeing me naked. I think he realized it at the exact moment I did, if his cocky grin was anything to go off of. He started to sit back up, but I pulled him back down the moment he released his vise-grip hold on my arms.

"Don't even freaking think of it, Fairy boy," I warned.

"You want me, don't you?" he asked as his eyes latched onto my lips, encouraged by my seemingly sudden change of mind.

I pushed him up, making damn sure I went with him. "Dream on," I growled.

"I don't fuck Witches, so if you—"

I pushed him up to his feet, pushing off of the floor with my bare feet, never allowing my eyes to leave his. My breasts were pressed against the softness of his suit jacket, my legs inches from his. I walked him backward, and he allowed it. I inched him further back as he kept eye contact, up until the point where I reached behind him slowly, surely, allowing my hands to caress him softly but firmly, as I reached for the door knob behind him. I quickly pulled it open and enjoyed his look of shock as I pushed him out of my room, managing in the process to keep him from seeing my nether region at all.

I smiled frostily at the door and the cussing Fae behind it. "I don't fuck Fairies. So at least we agree on that subject, pretty boy."

I thought I heard a soft laugh, but I couldn't be sure.

"Ten minutes, Synthia, or I come back in and drag you out," he growled through the door, making it quiver as much as I was—and it was solid oak.

I listened to his shoes as they thudded down the hallway, and my beating heart didn't calm until I heard the door close behind him on his way out. How the hell had he gotten through the protection spell enveloping my room?

I looked up at the incantation spell and narrowed my eyes, glaring at it for turning traitor. It was written on my ceiling in white ink, so it was invisible to the naked eye and intruders. It was supposed to keep creatures like him out and away from me while I slept. It had failed; just as I had done for the second time where that freaking Fairy was concerned.

I replayed his shocked image in my mind a few times, before putting on a silk robe and grabbing a few items of clothing to take with me to the shower. I was smiling as I opened my bedroom door and ran right into the solid chest of the Dark Prince. Hard.

I flew backward and landed flat on my ass at his feet. I looked up and glared angrily at him.

"Pay back is a bitch. I don't fuck around little, girl. Remember that."

"Cocky much?" I barked, already standing back up, so he didn't have as much of an advantage as he did with me being flat on my ass.

"Self-assured; I always win," he replied with lips too full and too fucking kissable for his own good.

I pushed past his body and headed toward the bathroom, dismissing him completely from my mind. Okay—so I tried to, anyway. He was the most beautiful, exquisite creature I had ever laid eyes on— also the most deadly, which I was humming inside my head to keep the hormones at bay. Not that it was helping me any.

"Ten minutes. If you're not out by then, I will dress you myself," he growled deep in his chest to drive his point home. It sent shivers racing down my spine.

I shut the bathroom door in his face and leaned against it, catching my breath. The man was incorrigible. What the hell was he doing *inside* my house? Larissa was going to hear it from me if she had allowed him inside. Didn't she sense how deadly he was? I was pretty sure she wouldn't have allowed him inside my bedroom, unless he'd fucked her funny— no, he wouldn't have done that…would he?

I shook my head. He needed my help. Touching my friends wouldn't achieve that. She was probably off his radar for now. I dropped my clothes and rushed beneath the water, quickly washing my hair, before jumping back out to toss my hair in a quick ponytail, apply some lipstick and a touch of blush.

"Two minutes," he said from behind the door.

Seriously? Was he sitting with his damn ear against the wood? I slipped into a black satin thong and matching bra, and quickly pulled up the low-rise jeans I'd chosen, before slipping on the tight black, sleeveless shirt in a hurry. I took a quick peek in the mirror and opened the door.

His eyes raked down my body with a hint of disgust in their golden depths, but he remained silent. I followed him down the hallway and to the front door, stopping only to look at a note from Larissa— she'd gone shopping. Figured. I was paying the rent and Miss-Shopaholic was out shopping, which meant she better be bringing home coffee.

"Problem?" Ryder asked when I didn't move fast enough for his Highn-ass.

"How the hell *did* you get inside my house?" I asked as I closed the door and we headed to the elevator. His only reply was a cocky grin, which left me with my question still burning inside my head.

The elevator was waiting on my floor with the doors open, so we didn't have to waste time waiting for it. I stepped in and felt the pressure as it shut me inside firmly with the Dark Prince. I'm not normally one to fidget when nervous or uncomfortable, but standing next to six plus feet of pure, masculine, grade-A alpha male? I was *so* freaking fidgeting! My hands fisted and relaxed, only to fist right back up again. I chewed nervously on my bottom lip, with my eyes plastered to the floor.

The silence was deafening; bad enough that I was suddenly wishing we had some corny elevator music. I could feel the sizzle of his power more so now that I was shut in a tight space, alone with him. When the doors opened to let us out, I gave a loud sigh of relief. If he noticed, he said nothing.

His car was a Lamborghini Aventador LP 700-4, orange in color. I whistled and just stood gaping at it for a moment, before a subtle cough pulled me back from making love to the car with my eyeballs. His eyes went from mine, back to the car, and back again.

"Try not to drool on the upholstery," he said.

I was going to have to touch everything inside of it just to piss him off, now. I watched the door rise with a soft smile on my lips. I'd never been in a car that cost as much as this one did. Hell, I hadn't even actually seen one in person until now!

"How fast does this thing go?" I asked, unable to stop myself. The leather seats were black, and actually real leather, I noticed as I slid inside.

"Fast enough."

I met his golden eyes and narrowed my own, "Bet you've never taken it past the speed limits."

He said nothing. He wasn't rattled or moved by my goading—damn. I wanted him to let loose and floor it. Instead, he slowly pulled out into the light traffic of downtown Spokane. You would think that he, being Fae, would let loose and break pretty much every law that the Human race had.

I reached over, making sure my hand stayed far enough away from his leg as I turned on his stereo. Godsmack's *I Stand Alone* blared, rattling the windows of the expensive car. I don't know what I had been expecting him to have in, but it wasn't that.

He turned his head slowly, inHumanly. His eyes glowed iridescent amber as he growled. I swallowed, to keep myself from gasping audibly. "Do. Not. Touch. Anything."

Okay then! I jerked my hands back and then folded them on my jeans, wishing I'd brought a jacket or something since he'd turned the air-conditioning on when we'd gotten in.

I was watching traffic, right up until the point that I could feel his eyes bearing down on me. I looked over at him, his eyes still doing that glow thing, lowered down at something below my face. I looked down and blushed from head to toe. My nipples were straining against the thin shirt and completely visible, due to the air-conditioning. I crossed my arms and held my tongue. Not having caffeine running through my veins was sorely testing my temper.

His lips quirked up, and then he was once again watching the road. We drove with the music now off. I didn't want a repeat of the earlier performance. I thought the elevator was bad, but this was ten times worse. I could actually feel his strength and power pulsing against my skin. It was like standing next to a transformer with the power on full capacity.

"Where are we going?" I asked, after the silence had gotten to be too much.

"This way," he replied, without turning his head.

"Do you speak more than four words? Or, do you lack the brains to?" I asked after another few moments of the blistering silence.

He ignored me.

"Seriously—"

We hit the highway, and he floored it. The motor hummed, and I smiled. I was pressed back against the cool leather seat, my hands instantly going to it for balance, as if it would help. I sat like that, listening to the motor until I looked back over at him. The smile left my face instantly.

"Stop looking at my boobs!" I said more sharply than I wanted to.

"I don't play with my food," he said calmly.

"I am *not* your food," I said through clenched teeth.

"If I wanted you, that fucking spell on your neck would do little to stop it from happening. I assure you of that."

My hand flew up to the back of my neck, and my fingers trailed over the white ink that was invisible to the naked eye. "How did you know it was there?" I asked, uncertain I wanted the answer.

"I watched you sleep," he replied, unamused or affected by my surprise at his words that showed all over my face. He turned his head, and he stared directly at me as his foot pressed down further on the gas pedal, pushing the speed even faster on the deserted highway.

Disturbing. He had actually watched me sleep, and I hadn't even noticed he was inside my bedroom. The ward inside the bedroom should have stopped anyone not marked as one of our group. The one for the apartment was only to ward or restrain anyone intent on harming us. Still, it set my nerves to *fried* just thinking about how long he'd been inside my room—and I'd been naked, since I'd gone to bed too tired to care.

The car decelerated and started pulling off the highway, which caused my attention to jump back to where I was and who I was with. There was nothing but pine trees on both sides of the highway. As far as I could see, the road was still deserted, but he pulled off anyway onto the soft shoulder.

"If you brought me all this way just to drop me off in the middle of bum-fuck-nowhere, think again," I warned, irritated that we'd stopped.

"Get out of the car. We need to discuss some things before we hit Darklands."

Darklands? No freaking way! The Sidhe Darklands was an exclusive invitation-only club, owned by Mister Highn-ass himself. It wasn't somewhere I'd ever wanted to go either. I fumbled at the door, but he was out and around the car with those Fae freaky movements of super-speed before I could continue to fumble for more than a second. The door was lifted, and I glared up into his beautifully-etched face.

I stood, smoothing out invisible lines from my jeans, and waited, for what I had no clue. When he stepped closer to me, I stepped back, only to fall on my ass inside the car at an awkward angle. He grinned, amused.

"They told me you were one of their best. I'm beginning to think they lied," he growled, now unamused with my reaction.

"They told me you were taller…guess they lied to me too." I instantly regretted saying it, because it was a lame thing to say.

I stood up again, my hands fisted at my sides, frustrated with my own nervous reaction to him.

"I need to put my scent on you, Synthia." His evil little smirk came back.

"Excuse me? Is that some lame-ass Fae joke?" I cringed.

"My club is invitation-only," he said, as if I didn't already know that; everyone knew that.

"And?"

"And, you are either owned or food, so if you want to take your chances and come in as a free agent, be my guest. But those who come in unclaimed are unprotected."

"Which means?" I asked, already twirling the implications of that inside my over active mind.

"Which means, if another Fae claimed you, he could make you his *bitch*," his voice lowered on the last word.

"And if I allow you to claim me, then I'm *your* bitch?" I wasn't doing this. I hated the Fae. They used Humans as food, and, while a lot of other creatures did as well, his kind could leave a shell behind of whomever they fucked.

"You work for me, Synthia. You are already my *bitch*," he replied coldly, deadly. Chills ran over my skin and my heart sunk to meet my toes in the dirt that I stood upon.

"I. Am. *Not. Your*. Any-fucking-thing!"

"You will be," he said, with an air of confidence that only pissed me off more.

"You wish. I won't sleep with you. Period! If I wanted dick, I'd take it. And yours is so not on the list of dicks I'd take, buddy."

"If I wanted you, Witch, you'd crawl to me. Begging for release—" he stopped talking, his eyes doing that Fae-fuck glow thing again. And then I was. Crawling, in the freaking dirt no less!

"Stop it!" I shouted, even as I pushed my ass out and up for him. My skin was afire with need. My sex grew moist and ready for him. I wanted to crawl into the fetal position and cry. I wanted to get up off the cold ground and smash his pretty fucking face.

"Beg me," he purred, his arms folded over his massive chest as he watched me continue to crawl to where he stood leaning against the car. "Are you wet for me? I could make you show me just how wet you are. I could make you do a lot of things right now, if I wanted to. I won't, but know that I can do this at any time. So can those inside the club we're going into. So make a decision—go as my property, or take your chances with those who would take you. I won't babysit you. I just figured you might care who fucks you."

I growled angrily, my hands biting into the sharp rocks on the ground while my ass was in the air, hips spread wide with fuck-me-hard vibes coming out in heated waves. I could feel the moisture pooling between my thighs, and my nipples were hard and in need of his mouth. I wasn't feeling this. It was his Fae-fuck mind game, I knew that, but the heat was too much.

"I ache," it came out husky and filled with the need he had created.

He said nothing.

Did nothing.

Watching me silently as my hips gyrated with a mind of their own.

"Please," I cried. Not from fear, but from a need so hot and fucking raw that at this moment in time, under his influence, under his power, I'd let him drive himself into my body just to make it stop.

"Touch yourself for me, Syn," he said roughly, sending my pulse soaring.

I ground my teeth together, a strangled noise tearing from my throat as I rose up on my knees, unable to stop myself from doing what he had said. I knew the Fae could use compulsion, and even worse, they could do this. Make you crawl in the dirt, like some fucking dog, with no more than a single heated look. He was able to override the tattoo and control me.

I glared up at him—or tried. My eyes had slanted, filling with lust for him. His were no longer on my face, but on my hand that was now cupping, stroking my junction through the rough jean fabric. I wanted to die as I moaned, the storm building inside of me demanding to be released. Demanding he remove my hand and replace it with his own, more skillful touch.

"So, have you made a choice? Or shall I make it for you? I could always use a snack," he replied seductively low, his tongue coming out to lick his full lips, his eyes searching and locking with mine.

"Fine, just make it stop!" I winced as my voice, which was weak, filled with heat and a roughness that bruised my pride.

"Stand up," he ordered, and my traitorous legs obeyed him instantly, as if they belonged to him.

"I have to touch you," his head tilted as his nostrils

flared, "to mark you as my own."

As my own—

I hated it! I was being reduced to nothing. My bones felt like heated putty. My blood was flowing in a heated rush to parts that I had left neglected since Adrian. I hadn't been laid in so long that I couldn't even remember how long it had actually been.

I watched him slide forward, his eyes intense and still piercing me with his glow. I wanted to step back—needed to—but all I could manage to do was arc my flipping hips! My body strained for his touch, anticipated it. *Begged* for it.

"Are you wet?" He whispered softly, his lips touching against my ear as he pulled my body flush against his.

I wanted to scream at him, but the most I could manage was an explosive "yes" to his question. His hands reached out, removing my own that had continued to stroke where the wetness was now visible through the jeans I wore. He held my hand in his much bigger one as it continued to move.

I thought he would drop it, but, instead, he brought it up and held it to his nose, inhaling deeply for a few seconds as a deep blush stole up my body to flood my cheeks. Drawing my scent in, before his lips moved down to my flesh and softly touched my palm, his heated breath made me growl my need from deep inside my chest.

"You smell good, Witch."

I moved closer to him, even though it wasn't the direction I wanted to go.

"Tell me to fuck you. Tell me to fuck you until you

come."

My lips quivered, but as much as I despised myself for weakness, I said it. "Fuck me, please—I ache. Make it stop. Oh God, just make it stop, please." Another violent moan exploded as soon as the words were out.

He moved closer, finally dropping my hand, as his body closed the distance and pressed against mine— hard. "You hate this, but you need to know your place and what can happen. There is a reason no one fucks with me. Next time you want to push my fucking buttons, remember this," he pressed a magnificent erection against my navel. "Because next time, I *will* fuck you. I don't play games. Nor do I take shit from anyone. I take what I want. I don't fuck around. If you mind-fuck me—well, I will *fuck* you. Next time, you won't get a warning."

I said nothing. It felt as if by speaking I would violate him—crazy, I know, but whatever spell I was under, be it compulsion or something worse, was making it impossible to say anything besides what he wanted to hear from me—which sucked, because I had so many comments to throw in his face.

His free hand came up, grasping my chin between his fingers as he tipped it up until I was looking into those dangerously endless fiery pits. He leaned in closer to mine at the exact same moment his other hand applied pressure against the fire he had started in my core. I felt sparks ignite from his touch as his mouth claimed mine gently but firmly. Tasting me, softly.

His mouth went from soft to forceful as his teeth grazed against my lips, demanding more. Demanding I open for his pleasure. I was lost. I opened for him, giving him back what he wanted, what he demanded.

The combination was overwhelming. His slight pressure, combined with his kiss, made the storm intensify until my legs quivered and refused to hold my weight any longer.

I didn't fall as far as I thought I would. Instead, his leg was there to catch me, his hands pushing back against the cold metal frame of the car while he stroked me with his hand and his fingers magnificently. My heart raced as liquid heat poured from my core. I was about to explode, and he knew it.

"Good girl," he whispered as he pulled away to watch my reaction.

"Ahhhhh—stop—please," I stuttered over my tongue, which was refusing to work around him.

"If I stop, you agree to be mine while inside the club. You need to be wearing my mark as well."

He pulled his hand away and damn it, my body cried in response. It was as if he'd ripped my heart out and my mind felt battered, as if he'd been in control of it instead of me. "—Fine."

"I think I like you better obedient," he replied hoarsely.

I struggled to get my mind back, to make the raging storm inside of me calm. I was still being held by him. He'd released my chin and nether region, but if he released me completely I'd fall, so he held my waist, his thumbs caressing where my shirt left the skin exposed.

I wanted to fall. I deserved it for being weak. The spell on my neck was useless with him, useless against him. He removed his knee slowly, letting me feel it as it was withdrawn from where it held me up. "Can you stand?" he asked after another moment. I nodded, but started to fall, only to have him once again save me from falling.

"Lie to me again and I will punish you for it… *severely*."

"Suck—*it*." I had to force my teeth not to clatter together audibly while getting the words out.

He was up against me instantly, his hard muscles pushing me once again into the unforgiving frame of the car. "Make no mistake, Witch, if I wanted you it would be simple to part your legs and fuck you right here, right now. I am in full control of you at this moment, and unless you want to be fucked on the hood of this car, you will cut the fucking comments!" He was growling from low in his chest.

I bit my lip. No way in hell would I give him an excuse to do as he had threatened. I flicked my eyes up to meet his probing stare, my lips trembling with need for him to follow through with the threat. Hell, I think my entire body wanted him—even my little toe!

"That's better, now let's try this again. Can you stand?"

"No."

I was picked up deftly, and with little effort I was deposited on the car's sleek hood. He took measures to ensure my head didn't fall back too fast as he placed me on my back on the warm hood of his exquisite sports car.

"Stay."

Like I could go anywhere if I tried? I was a hapless mess of liquid heat. This was embarrassing. I'd never been more so in my entire life. I didn't hear or see any cars go by, thankfully. My body was still shuddering from the loss of his touch, and I resented it to no end.

The crunch of his shoes over the gravel made me hiss. I hated him. I'd hated what he was for this very reason. He'd just reinforced my hate. He'd just made me feel weak, and worse—he'd made me his, even if it had only been for a short time.

"Pouting? Sit up."

I rolled my eyes and tried.

Nothing happened.

Fuck buckets! Why me? There were a thousand other Witches in Washington State… Why the hell did they have to pick me?

"Ask for help. Pride will do you more harm than good here."

My eyes flew to his—which now had the royal Fae lines inside of their endless depths, swirling hypnotically, searching—only to discover I saw passion and desire inside of them as white-hot as my own. That's something I never wanted from a Fae, *ever*.

"I need your—"

"I know what you need," he tilted his dark head, probing my eyes, searching them. "Tell me how much you want it."

"I need your help," I whispered it. It wasn't something I asked for often, if ever. I was self-sufficient. I was the person they called when shit went awry. When someone couldn't get to their mark, they called me.

"I bet that killed you to say," he growled as he

moved his massive frame closer to the hood, which I was laying on uselessly.

I exhaled a deep, shaky breath and averted my eyes away from him to the trees behind him, or tried to. His hands grasped my legs and pulled me closer to where he stood between them now. Then he grabbed my shoulders and pulled me up, draping my useless arms over his shoulders while he produced something from his pocket.

He pulled a thin silver chain out and reached up with one hand, moving my hair from my neck gently, his finger rubbing over the naked flesh seductively, enticingly sending my heart into another fit of beats. A Celtic knot was etched on the chain, along with a tribal dragon—the same one he had tattooed on his upper chest. His voice was low, but steady when he spoke. "By accepting this, Synthia, you become my property until I say otherwise. I can either be the one who protects you—or the one who hunts you. Decide."

My anger rose again, even higher than it had been before. "I am not yours," I argued.

He laughed. Coldly. Harshly. He lowered those damn lips of his and pressed them against my ear, his breathing steady, his breath hot and erotic against my over-sensitive flesh. "I can smell you, Witch. I made your pussy wet—*for me*. I can make you feel things no other man can, or ever will. If you're not mine, then you are open to be hunted by me and the other Fae. If you say no, little Witch, you better fucking run and run fast—" His word's trailed off, his mouth pressed more forcefully against my ear as a soft, throaty growl resonated from deep in his chest. "I like to hunt, but I like to fuck more. Can you guess what will happen when I catch you, Synthia?" He pulled away, which caused my body to sink without his added weight against it.

"And this ownership, what does it entitle you to?" I asked, knowing that somewhere there would be a catch. We were taught that there was always a catch when dealing with the Fae, because they were incapable of lying, but that made them masters of manipulating their words. His kind loved to play games. Loved to mind-fuck you and turn you inside out. All the Fae did.

His lips rose into a twisted smile which unnerved me to my bones. His hand came up to cup my face beneath my chin. "For now, it means no other of my kind can touch you without my consent."

That wasn't so bad. I didn't want to be touched by any of them—including him. I still couldn't bring myself to say the words, but neither did I say anything as he released my chin and moved his hand to place the ends of the chain together.

I *felt* it.

A violent bolt of white hot pleasure ripped through me, my body jackknifed against him and would have fallen to the cold ground had he not reacted just as fast, catching and holding me against his chest. This was stronger and more violent, this lust he'd just made me feel. "Shhh, it will only last for a moment."

I inhaled and let it out slowly, carefully tasting the intense pleasure as my face pressed against his enticing scent. He smelled different than most Fae. Instead of smelling like otherworldliness, he smelled of ambrosia—crisp, and clean, and foreign.

He stood there, allowing me time to come back to my senses. "Can you make it stop aching?" I asked.

"I can put you in the car, Witch. The effects should

wear off shortly," he replied, already lifting me, even though I had yet to agree. He pressed my core against his navel, bringing my face up entirely too close to his. "Stop your fuck-me vibes, Witch, or you will cause a fucking riot inside my club." He growled sharply.

"That is not my fault, Ryder. I never asked to be Fae-fucked on the side of a highway," I retorted, seething that he would choose to belittle me for something he had done in the first place.

~~*~*~*  *~*~*~*~*

She's so fucking green. Untried. Un-sampled by *my* kind. I should have bent her over the hood and taken what I needed, what I wanted. Could have stolen the memory, erased it from her mind. She's a puzzle that I want to tear apart, and watch as she struggles to put herself back together.

Her scent is driving me bugfucked crazy. I want to push apart her sweet pink flesh and sink my cock in until she knows nothing else, wants for nothing else. I want to fill her, feel her as her warm, sleek muscles clench my hard length lovingly.

Feel her from the inside. Abuse her insides until she screams for me. I get what I want, and right now, it's her. She should run, but I'd catch her. I always catch my prey. I take because I can, because no one else can stop me. I am what she fears. I can smell it coming off her in succulent waves and it drives my inner beast insane.

She is trying to hide it. Useless, futile fucking attempt—I can smell it as I can smell her fucking sex begging me to tear off those tight fucking jeans and savage it. She's a hot blooded woman, and she needs to be fucked. Hard. Soon. By. *Me*.

She denies it in her mind, inside her blood. She's young, untrained in the bedroom. Her only lover was a damn child as green as she is. Her supple curves, her sweet smell when she's ready—un-fucking-believably addictive.

Inside me, *he's* fighting for control; fighting to get out and take what I deny him. I tell him it takes time, to be patient, and he growls. Impatient asshole. She isn't like the others I feed from; her hate could feed me for years alone, and her lust will be a fucking feast. If she fucks like she fights—she will be worth chaining in the white room and keeping around as I wanted to do from the first moment I saw her.

Ahh, the white room. She'd like the toys—I'd become her ultimate fantasy from hell with them. She thinks this is bad—that I Fae-fucked her, but she hasn't tasted of my cock. She will. The chain that now binds her to me will wear her walls down, giving me the fullest access to what I want. She believes it is for protection. Stupid. No one would ever dare to approach a female who walks in beside me.

They fear me. They know what I am; know my plans. Know I am the biggest, meanest fucking thing on this planet right now. She's smart, though. I can see it in her eyes, endless depths of knowledge. If she sees through this charade we play, she will become my slave. I'm going to make her scream my name; make her tremble and explode on my cock. I *will* have her.

Maybe I will keep her as a pet. She'd look good in chains. She'd look better with my cock between her sultry lips, fucking it with her full mouth. I smile. She flinches. I show her teeth, and when she does the same I narrow my eyes, flashing her with my hungry glow and watching as her eyes register the hunger deep inside of me for what it is. She turns and my beast screams. He wants to play with her—it's *not* a good thing.

I lean over her, making sure my body presses hard against her lithe frame while I fasten her seatbelt. I enjoy the breath she expels as I make contact. I smile inwardly, but it is all teeth. I just found a challenge in her hate, in her scent; her bloody fucking scent. My cock is straining, pressing against the fucking suit I despise, but it's needed to pull off this fucking charade; this part of my brilliant bloody fucking plan.

She moves her head away, refusing to make eye contact with me. She's mocking me. I can smell her need. Inside her room, I could smell her wet folds begging me to take them. She has refused all men who have tried since *he* died.

I've been watching her for a very long time now, planning and determining why Marie wanted me to find her. She smells of magic, wild and untamable. Wild magic is dangerous. She's different than normal Witches. Marie discovered this, sent me a letter to protect her, but died before she could explain more. She's a puzzle, and the challenge in her eyes excites me.

She's challenging me. Even now, her eyes narrow on me, watching me as I watch her back hungrily. *Challenge fucking accepted.*

Chapter
SEVEN

We finally pulled off the highway a little over thirty minutes later. The road wasn't well traveled, but it was paved. More trees separated us from the world. Good. I needed them right now. My oxygen level hadn't gone back to normal since his mouth was on mine. My legs still trembled with need. I hated it. Hated him. Hated this day.

Wished it was over.

I could tell it was far from it.

"Why am I here *again*?" I asked, testing my weight on my legs and smiling when they proved to work once more.

"To sign a contract," he replied, with disinterest, mocking me. "If you embarrass me inside, you will regret it. Try to act like a lady."

My jaw dropped. I *was* a lady! "I can act like a lady."

His eyes mocked me, as if he was saying *prove it*. He stopped me briefly, and, with a flick of his hand, righted my appearance to the way it was before our little roadside stand-off.

I had no sooner grasped what he had done before he was moving again without a single word. I hurried to catch up with him, but by the time I reached him, the doors to the club were opened by two giant Fae, both dressed in dark shirts and low hung jeans. Both were brunettes with the same shoulder length hair and dark green eyes. *Twins?*

"Ryder, good to see you, Brother," the one on the left said, followed by a nod from the one on the right.

"Savlian, Sevrin, are they here yet?" Ryder asked, already walking away without waiting for an answer from the twins.

I tried to follow him, but was body checked by both men. Today was not my day. I was going to need a donut pillow by the time I got home for my behind! I came back up onto my feet like a firecracker. "I'm with him!" I growled fiercely.

"New pet, Ryder?" The one called Sevrin asked over his shoulder to where Ryder had turned to watch us. The guy's green eye were looking me over which was making me sweat from the intensity inside them.

I looked to where Ryder stood, his eyes raking over me as well with his cocky grin locked into place. "She is. Let her through."

"Anything else?" The tall Fae asked, his eyes telling me he enjoyed this job entirely too much.

"Assemble the team. We'll be in the third room; the warded one," Ryder said, sweeping his hand in the direction of a staircase.

The club was huge inside, and unlike the non-descript wood on the outside, the inside was lavishly decorated. Beams stood out prominently from the ceiling every few feet, going from one side of the room to the other. The high ceilings had chandeliers that hung from each beam, made with spiky coral. The tables had similar ones, only much smaller, that hung from chains from the same beams, lighting up the tables and also dimly illuminating a more private setting in the back.

Celtic designs were highlighted on the walls, light shining through them from behind the frosted glass paneling. Brighter blue lights lit up the bar area through more frosted glass. The stage was set up for a performance, guitars and other instruments laid out as if the band had just stepped out for a smoke.

The stairway he was walking to lit up before his foot could even touch the first step, as if it was aware he was on it before he actually was. I watched as each step he climbed changed to a different color, before I attempted to step on it myself. My eyes bulged as I stepped on it and a siren went off across the room.

My eyes went up to meet Ryder's golden stare. He turned and kept walking as if nothing had happened. So I continued to follow him, watching each step he took, change from the beautiful rainbow colors to crimson red as I stepped onto them. It was an alarm system, as if the stairs could tell the difference between my steps and Ryder's.

When we reached the top, a long winding hallway stretched out before us. Ryder's long strides were difficult to keep up with, but I managed—just barely. While I wasn't short by normal standards, I was, compared to his long legs. I had to jog to catch up, just to fall behind as soon as I did.

"Why are we *really* here?" I asked, looking behind me as I felt something slither over my skin. I shook my head and brought my eyes forward just in time to collide against Ryder's chest. I jumped back as if he was on fire.

"Consider it another part of your interview."

I rolled my eyes and rubbed my arm where I had felt something touch my skin. There was nothing there, but the feeling had yet to leave my skin. I stood, shifting from foot to foot, wondering what he would make me do now. I didn't have long to wait before ten well-built Fae dressed in dark colored clothing walked up behind us, blocking my exit.

I stepped back away from them. The odds of fighting them all were slim if they decided they wanted a fight. Hot breath touched the side of my neck, and I instantly realized I'd stepped toward Ryder for protection. He'd probably help them beat the shit out of me.

"Behave, or I will make you," Ryder growled low and huskily into my ear, quiet enough that those striding toward us wouldn't be able to hear him.

I watched the men get closer, their features hidden in the shadows by the hallways dim lighting. As they all got closer to where I stood, motionless on high alert, my hands itched for weapons I'd left at home. I hated that I was defenseless, except for my spells.

They nodded dark heads in Ryder's direction before he opened the door beside us and walked through, the others waiting for me to follow his lead. I did, but the moment I passed over the threshold I felt it again, the slithering. And then a violent pain rocked me and nausea fought to get out from my throat.

"What the fuck!?" I shouted, even as I tried to keep the bile at bay.

"It is magic proof," someone behind me said, pushing past me into the room. "Well, at least from *your* kind of magic," he snorted.

I held my hand out in front of me. The scars normally hidden by the faint glamour I usually generated to hide them now showed vividly. Whatever they had inside this room stripped all magic from me, all glamour. I was officially one hundred percent fucked. They watched me, seeing me.

A Witch was normally covered in spells. Most ran out of room and would be forced to use their faces or necks to complete their spells. Most were ruined of flesh by the time they had hit my age. I had one spell to bar Fae from using me for sex, and that had been done at the hairline of my neck. Two stars sat on my shoulders, marking the two deaths that had touched my soul, and another on my hip, to always remember what had happened. The rest were not visible, unless I chose them to be, or unless I stepped under a black light.

"Fuck me, she isn't all fuglied out," the Fae whom Ryder had referred to as Savlian said, as he came around with his eyes narrowed slightly. He took in my features more carefully.

I glared at him and then closed my eyes briefly as I felt nausea rolling deep inside of me; removing power that quickly was dangerous, and it was taking everything I had to stay upright on my feet. Ryder was watching me intently. It took a very powerful Witch not to succumb to the loss of their powers. Most would be flopping on the floor at his feet like a fish out of water.

I flicked my gaze to the walls—white walls to the naked eye. Sanction spells were written upon them, rendering anyone not of the Fae defenseless inside the room. "Cool trick," I growled, righting myself and squaring my shoulders firmly.

"You have no visible ink. Explain," Ryder said in disdain.

I smiled coldly, unwilling to share my secrets with him.

"Want another example of why you don't want to fuck with me?"

"I don't need ink," I whispered, narrowing my eyes at Ryder.

"Explain."

"I can't explain it, not here."

"Try," he barked angrily.

"I can't! Not without having a fucking target on me. So, unless you want to give me one—" I let the question trail off, leaving it for him to figure out. I was bluffing, of course. If I stepped out of the room, I could call up the power to light up my spells, but he wasn't on my need-to-know list as far as I was concerned.

"Sinjinn, bring me the contract. Zahruk, get to it."

I wanted to leave, like, this instant. The slithering feeling had yet to go away, as if something was literally crawling over my skin. I hated being unarmed—I felt weak—and the worst part was, they knew I was. I knew how to fight better than most, but the odds were seriously not in my favor.

"On your knees," the one called Zahruk growled with a thick accent I tried to place.

"On my knees?" I exhaled slowly. I was in severe

need of a stiff drink.

"Zahruk, give her some options first," Ryder said, moving to lean his shoulder against a barren wall. There was nothing else I could immediately see inside this room, other than white walls and marble flooring, also white. It looked sterile, and that just made me want to run away.

"Choices are overrated. She won't tell us anyway," Zahruk said. He was dressed in a white *Assassins Creed* looking robe. His face was hidden before he turned and looked directly at me. "Tell us why you hate the Fae. Marie couldn't explain it, since it was not her story to tell us." I watched him push his hood back, revealing yet another Fae, beautiful, yet deadly. His eyes lit up in an electric blue color, which only made him more stunning, with his dark, shoulder length, wavy blonde hair and perfect bronze skin.

"Fuck. You." I snarled, tearing my eyes from him and leveling Ryder with a murderous glare. They had no fucking right! "You want me to work for you? Fine, but that doesn't give you the right to ask stupid questions!"

"Told you. She's got stubborn written on her forehead, Ryder," Zahruk laughed harshly.

My knees were kicked out from behind me violently. It was the same as had been done the day before, inside his vault. I kept my eyes leveled on the Dark Prince. "I came with your fucking mark on me, because you said it would protect me!"

I flinched as a knife blade was brought to my throat and my hair was grabbed hard from behind. "You will address him with respect, bitch." The words were cold, calculated and filled with promise of death dripping from each syllable.

"I said no other Fae could touch you without my permission, Synthia. Do it Zahruk, no more fucking around. If she won't tell us—we will take it." Ryder's voice trailed off, sending shivers racing down my spine. The knife was removed from my throat, and the slithering on my skin intensified.

The room's air grew thick and tainted, dark magic running through my skin and searching inside my mind. My lips quivered, and my hands shook where they were still balled up at my sides. "Ryder, don't— please." It took every ounce of pride inside of me to say it. I could feel something searching my memories.

Too little.

Too late.

I was no longer in the room with the Fae.

I was in a worse place than the Fae club now. One I hadn't been to since that ill-fated day. Tears swam in my eyes, but I refused to allow them to fall. I knew what was coming, knew it like the back of my hand. Voices I'd thought to never hear again laughed in front of me echoing around the walls.

"Darling, she's too young. She needs time," my mother's gentle voice sang with laughter as her ocean blue eyes lit up with her smile.

"Nonsense, she's old enough to dance with me, Syrina," my father's deep baritone came seconds before his features smoothed out enough that I could see him motioning for the child who looked on with uncertainty. My father's dark brown hair framed his face perfectly, as his eyes smiled with their perfect navy blue depths.

"Daddy, play our song!" The soft voice sent chills down my spine. That child was weak, pathetic.

I hated her.

I wanted to bury her.

 And I had.

Long ago.

Journey's Faithfully *came on, his hand never touching the stereo. Magic. He'd been the Head Master for the Spokane Coven. He'd been my hero and my teacher. I turned my head to the left and watch as the child decides if she should go, unsure of her place.*

"Come darling," he said, with so much love in his voice that a single tear dropped from mine and the child's eyes in sync.

My mother laughed and slowly walked over to the five year old I had been, her hand coming up to catch the tear and wipe it away with a smile. I was such a crybaby as a child, unsure of my place in the world, unsure of so many things that I shouldn't have been.

The child moved closer, a small smile on her face. My father smiled warmly, welcoming her into his arms before allowing her to step upon his feet and dance with him. I watched them from where I sat on the thick blue carpet of my family home's floor, my stomach flipping over with horror, regret, and fear of what was to come.

I hated Ryder more for this; more than I did for his Fae-fucking me on the highway.

My mother laughed as she sat on the wooden chair she had always despised, even though my father loved it. Her radiant smile was like a knife through my heart. I wanted to scream, to warn them, but I knew nothing I do now would change what is coming.

I'd relived this nightmare until I knew every detail intimately.

The song ended, and the child stayed. She was mesmerized by him—my father. He was her everything. Always kissing scrapes, and scaring the fears away. He'd always been there. Always. Until they took him from me.

I looked toward the door. I knew what is coming. It always did.

The door shook from the impact of a heavy fist pounding on it. They both went stiff. The wards in the house pulsed and flared with angry red lettering, warning them of evil intent. They knew. Every time I saw this, it was obvious they knew what was coming, what was happening. And, every time, they were still helpless to what was in store for them. I wanted to scream. I needed to, but I didn't. I settled for shaking my head; it too is useless.

"Synthia, come with Mommy. I need you to be big for me. Can you do that?" Her voice was low, and trembled.

Every. Fucking. Time.

I want it to end. I search wildly with my eyes for a way out. I hate this part. I don't want to see it. "Stop this!" I cry, to no avail.

"I can, Mommy, I promise."

I want to slap the child, make her blind. Make her not see it and then maybe, just maybe, I'd have lived a normal life. One not haunted by this dream.

My mother opened the hidden door behind the fire grate. She stopped long enough to kiss the child on her cheek. She wanted to say something, but the door was splintering and crashing into the house as it was kicked in. "Go," she whispered, pushing the child through and closing it.

Five men swarmed the room, death in their eyes. Their strides. Fucking Fae. All of them, Dark and Light. Working together. Fucking Fae. One swung what looked like an oversized bat to my five year old mind, threatening my father. Now I knew it was called a cudgel, or a club.

"Where is the Gift?" The tallest one screamed, his voice shrill as it came out in layers.

"Gone," my father said, standing up tall, undeterred by that wooden club or the deadly creatures he was facing. Pride swelled inside of me, inside of the child me. He was so brave.

"I can smell the Gift. Show us, or the pretty blonde gets to entertain us until you do," the dark haired one growled, his voice multilayered. His eyes were black and gray, marking him Fae. Even at five, I could tell they were evil.

I turn, looking at where my child-self had been hidden—she should've turned away. She should have done something; fight, scream, give them something to use besides her parents. But she just stood there behind the grate, watching with horrified terror. I glared at her, as if it would make her do something. This happened so long ago. Nothing changes, ever.

My mother screamed as they descended upon her. One held the ropes and attacked my father. I was their weakness, they knew it. They couldn't fight, to use magic would have disrupted the house, and, to keep me safe they'd had it balanced far enough away from the leyline they needed to use for casting. In the end, it had cost them their lives.

More screaming followed as my father was tied to the wooden chair and left helpless to do anything but watch as they tore into my mother. He tried fighting them to get to my mother. This was when it turned ugly. The sound of wood breaking bone was hard to forget; sickening, the crunch audible and unforgettable.

Blood was everywhere.

The sound he made when he tried to call for my mother took my breath away. I wanted this memory to stop. I didn't want to watch this. I sank the rest of the way to the floor. It was too much.

Chapter
EIGHT

The child didn't know what was going on; only that the bad creatures were hurting her parents. Now that four of the Fae were raping her mother, stealing her mind, and killing her soul. She couldn't know that the grunts and grinding were torture to make her father talk. That her mother's cries were from pain and pleasure alike.

Her father's outrage covered some of the screams, but not all. Shock kept her eyes locked on the horror that was befalling them. The club smashing into her father over and over again, her mother screaming and moaning until it was nothing more than moans leaving her lips.

When the last one climbed off my mother, I could finally see her beautiful face. She was beyond pain, her mind fractured. She begged for more, wanted more of what they had done to her. Bile rises in my throat. The child was just now figuring out what has happened.

My mother caressed herself and lifted her white skirt for more. She begged them to finish her, to continue the assault. She was weak. My father yelled at her, trying to reach inside her mind; he was horrified by what she was doing. And yet he told her he did not blame her and that he would always love her; he understood.

Another sick thud sounded from the club. This one smashed against his face while I stood behind the grate and covered my mouth with my hands. Stupid child. Weak child. One fucking word from her and this could have been averted. One whisper from her lips and they could have died, just one—

Another sickening blow and, with it, the only sound left inside of the room was the Fae snickering, and my mother's barely audible gibberish as she begged them for their touch. I turned from where I am sitting on my knees, watching as the child I had been tilted her small blonde head and wiped away the useless tears that streaked down her face.

If I'd been stronger.

If I'd not been so weak.

I'd still have my parents.

I noticed a new Fae had arrived. I wasn't sure what kind he was, and he appeared to be arguing with the other ones who had savaged my family. The taller Dark Fae that seemed like the group's leader smiled, unaffected by the newcomer's outrage.

"This wasn't supposed to happen here. We were only supposed to question them and retrieve the Gift! What have you done?" The new Fae argued angrily.

"Consider them questioned. The weak fool should have never agreed to retrieve the Gift. He brought this upon all of us by changing his mind! Maybe now everything will right its course and we will go to war as should have happened long ago." He slid closer to my mother, "The next person who comes through the

door…you will shoot them, my sweet little whore." He smiled with his cold, lifeless smile, and whispered his heartless words against my mother's ear.

"I will," my mother whispered softly. Her eyes flickered on the bloody lump that had been my father. He wasn't dead, but my child-self didn't know that; she was waiting.

I'm not sure how long I had waited in that hiding place, or how much time had passed before I climbed out. It felt like an eternity to me back then.

I watched as the Fae tore the house apart. They were looking for something, searching. Time passed. I kept still, not daring to move, or uncover my mouth where my hand was holding the scream at bay. I listened; the door closed, and still I didn't come out.

My mother was holding the gun; the one they gave her. The silver caught in the sun's rays as it streamed through the windows. When I finally did climb out, she just watched me. I wasn't sure if it was because I didn't walk through the door that she hadn't shot me right away.

She was alive, and, yet, her mind had been cleared of everything. She was a blank slate. No memories of us remained inside her mind. No recognition showed inside her eyes. Nothing. "Momma," I whispered.

She turned and held out the gun and took aim at me. I didn't back down, didn't falter. "Momma, please!" My voice shook. Stupid child couldn't see that she was gone; couldn't tell that her mother had been turned FIZ.

"Syn—" my father's voice was shallow. The blood he was choking on floods from his lips.

"Daddy?" I moved toward him, but the gun

followed me.

I stopped, glaring down the business end of the gun. My eyes were swimming with tears. I could feel the life draining from my father. His breathing grew shallow with each attempt he made to get more words out.

"Never—forget, Syn—secret—our secret—never forget." His eyes rolled back in his head. The child struggled to understand his words; struggled to understand why he was staring at the ceiling. He'd died right in front of me that day. She didn't understand death, but she will.

What secret? I never understood this part, or what he'd told me.

She turned to go back to her mother, the gun still aimed at her. She was going to pull that trigger soon. Her finger was locked on the trigger, her void eyes seeing nothing. "Mommy, please, I'll be good!" the child wailed.

The gun went off.

I watched as the child's hand flicked the air and deflected the bullet.

It went back the way it had come from.

Blood splattered and covered my face. I stood there and watched her, without making a sound. The only sound inside the room was the sound of my heart beating with magic. I killed my mother. Instead of sending the gun out of her hands, I killed her.

I look at the child I'd been. Her shoulders dropped as she fell to the floor, trying to figure out how to fix her mother. In my mind, I'd thought I could. I'd been five. I found new words that day. Death, destruction, despair, and, most of all, I learned what it felt like to hate.

I watched as she struggled to pick everything up, slipping and sliding on the blood around the corpse. She hears a noise; the door. She throws up the protective shield—the one she should have thrown up to save them, had she been stronger, faster. Smarter.

Marie screamed. Her voice was shrill as she took in the horrors of the room. I winced as my child-self turned, covered in my mother's blood. I didn't let her into the protection of the spell, and she wasn't stronger than the child I had been.

Alden came in behind her. His gasp grated on my nerves.

"Synthia, are you hurt?" Marie asked her voice low and clear.

"My mother is broken. Father is sleeping," the *five year old said, as if it was true, but she knew better. She knew by then that they were dead. She could feel the loss of them inside of herself. Where once there had been love, was now an empty void of death in its place.*

"Did she do this?" Alden's *whisper made my skin crawl. This was the work of evil; even the child knew that much. In the end, she would blame herself because Father had been a warrior, and he'd died to protect her.*

"They were looking for something. Was it me?" The child asked with eyes too old for a five year old.

"Alden, enough. She's in shock," Marie whispered, as if the child wouldn't hear.

I pulled back, shoving the memories of what

happened next away—my hands ripped into my memories as if I could shred them. I won't relive the next part—taking their souls. At five, I was stronger than any other Witch. History would record the next details of what transpired. I'd be a lab rat for Alden for years after the deaths of my parents because of it.

"Enough. We risk damaging her mind if you continue," Ryder said softly, his voice penetrating the illusion.

The room turned white again, my body shaking with violent spasms. I ground my teeth together, wanting to kill them for seeing what happened.

"Interesting. They were looking for something," the Fae behind me said.

Dristan cleared his throat. "I don't recognize any of them. They look—"

"Enough," Ryder interrupted sharply and glared at him.

I blinked, bringing the room back into focus as I fought for air and stood before I found my balance. My chest heaved from the pain of reliving the worst day in my life. My eyes flickered to Ryder's golden gaze. He looked almost puzzled and disturbed by what he had seen. I turned to push past his men, but I was boxed in, as if they knew I would leave. I hated what I found in their eyes. Pity.

"Move," I snarled, wanting to get the fuck out of there. To go home and curl into a ball until the feeling of hate and hopelessness passed. It normally takes days.

"She was a victim," Zahruk said softly.

"I am. Not. A. Victim!" I growled low and clearly

pronounced each word.

"No? Then what are you?" he asked, angered by my words.

"I'm a survivor."

Zahruk bowed his dark blonde head. I'd never allowed myself to be a victim from that day forth. I'd fought hard and was best in the class I graduated with from the Guild academy. Marie had been there every step, helping me, cheering me on. Alden had blamed me, but with good reason.

I'd pulled their souls and refused to allow them to leave me. Fear was a bitch. It could make you do things you never thought yourself capable of. I'd pulled their souls before I had known what I was doing. It had been grief which made me act hastily, mixed with young age and too much power. I'd ended up branded with two stars upon my shoulders as a reminder of my first failure in life.

"She's damaged," another inside the room said, as if I wasn't standing right there.

You have no idea. Damaged makes me look normal.

"She is; can she do the job we need her to?" Dristan asked.

I hated that they had ripped these memories from my mind. And yet, this time when they replayed it, my father's words had not been so silent. When it was happening, my mind wouldn't grasp what he'd said.

"Fuck you, and fuck your job, Ryder. I'm out of here," I growled and turned with every intention of walking out.

"Call the Guild; get Alden on the phone," Ryder said smoothly.

I exhaled and closed my eyes slowly, fighting for composure. "I'm damaged, and others can use glamour," I offered him a solution to his problem.

"I don't want others. I need the best, and you came highly recommended by Marie."

I blinked and turned, looking at him over my shoulder. "Marie is dead," I snapped angrily.

"She is, but she was a friend of my father's," Ryder supplied.

"Find someone else," I barked, wanting out of the room. I felt as if the walls were closing in around me.

"Call the Guild," he snapped at the Fae closest to the desk that sat against the back barren wall of the room.

"You just fucked with my head! What do you expect me to do? Kiss your fucking boots, Fairy? Wrong. Fucking. Girl!"

"Quite the opposite…I think you are the right girl for the job," he interjected.

I wanted to tell him where to stick it, but he knew from Alden that if I didn't take this job it would be my last one. I could run, live by myself, but I'd probably be signing Adam and Larissa's death warrants too. That was something I wouldn't do. And he knew it, which made him dangerous.

"I have a contract written up. You *will* sign it."

I glared at him, without confirming, or denying I would be signing anything.

"You sign it. I will *not* yield to you, Ryder," I snapped.

His lips tightened. "Oh, but I think you will yield. You will do more than just yield to me," he snapped his fingers and the door to the room opened. "You will lie down and yield, even it if includes you begging me to allow it."

"Syn," Adam's voice pushed me over the edge, my anger boiling over the rim. Startled, I looked at him sharply. How long had he been here, and how much had he seen?

"You asshole," I snarled at Ryder, uncaring who heard, or who pulled a knife. I was ready to attack.

"Syn, be careful. Alden is signing his own contract right now. It's why I was sent over here," Adam advised at my side.

"I bet he is." Alden could count his fucking days. They were numbered by forcing me into this damn corner. It seemed like he had been abusing his power since Marie had been killed. It was widely rumored that he'd been taking jobs from the highest bidder, and that was against the laws of the Guild. It had been created to protect the Human race, not line our pockets.

"Fine," I snarled, holding my hand out for the contract.

He smiled coldly as if he'd won. I rolled my eyes as he grabbed my hand, instead of handing me the contract. His fingers curled around my own, reminding me of what had happened on that abandoned stretch of highway. I tried to pull it away, but he was stronger and his pull brought my body flush against his.

"Let me go—now!" I cried, the memories of my

mother came to the fore with a vengeance.

He released his hold as if the memories had also flooded his own mind. His eyes narrowed as he took in my ashen color. Maybe, if I was crazy enough, I could get out of this before signing his stupid contract.

His lips turned up wickedly at the corners. I narrowed my own eyes, wondering if he was reading my mind. I knew some Fae had the ability to do so, but I was unsure what powers he had, and until I could figure it out, I'd be damn careful what I allowed to enter my mind. I discarded the thought and walked to the desk.

The vellum which the contract had been written on, was gray and it sent chills up my spine just looking at it. Legend had it that the Fae made contracts on the skin of those who committed treason against their race. They skinned them alive and kept them in a suspended state until they grew more—only to take the next skin the traitor grew. Put a whole new spin on recycling.

I wasn't going to touch it—didn't matter what it said and if I didn't sign it. I would be signing death warrants—for those of my friends. I looked around for a pen, but the only thing on the small wooden desk beside the parchment was a bone handled knife.

A sinking feeling took residence inside my stomach. I turned and glared at Ryder. His smile was still all teeth.

"Read it," he growled huskily.

I raised a single brow. "Does it really matter if I read it? I either sign this, or I go to war with the Guild and that's not something I want to do." I had friends inside the Guild, more than just those of my coven.

He picked up the knife, and, as I watched him, sliced the palm of his hand wide open. Thick blood turned crimson as it hit the air. My eyes were riveted to his hand, my own balled into a fist and I stepped back. His voice was rich and husky as he asked for mine.

"Uh—"

"Give me your hand," he interrupted my moment of panic.

It took all of my willpower to raise my hand for him while he held that knife in his other hand. My inner-self was screaming. Something more was going on here than just signing his damn contract, and my mind knew it. I winced as he cut shallowly into my hand. A hiss left my lips as an audible caress. I had scanned over the contract, but it wasn't as if it was a choice. Larissa and Adam's lives were on the line if I didn't.

"I ask of you to honor this contract by blood. Do you agree to honor it, Synthia Raine McKenna?" His voice was low, hypnotic, like a caress inside my mind.

My eyes flickered up to Adam's and back to Ryder's. "Yes," I said quietly. The moment I said it, he placed my hand in his, palms together, and violent waves of pain and pleasure mixed together, shocking my senses until I was holding onto him to stay upright. I cried out, feeling something tear through me. He must have been feeling the same thing. His eyes turned hard as a tick started in his jaw.

When the violent reaction had slowed and our pulses were once again at a semi-normal rate, he slammed both our hands on the graying parchment. The walls lit up with a glowing fluorescent blue color, and then it was gone just as fast as it had started.

"What the hell did you just make me do?" I shouted.

His eyes narrowed considerably as they snaked from my head, down my body slowly, his tone low and dangerous as his words filtered out, penetrating me sharper than the knife had ever come close to doing. "I took your blood. Now there is nowhere you can hide that I won't be able find you, Pet. You took from me; I took from you. Tit for tat, so to speak. I suggest, next time, you read the fine lines inside a contract before blindly signing it. *I own you.*"

Chapter
NINE

I was freaking out, yet I managed to keep it hidden—just barely. I hadn't been able to see a way out of signing it, and now the deed was done. Now, reading it in a booth across from Ryder, I was considering a long jump off a tall bridge.

"I am not feeding you! Ever," I snarled, reading the page again.

He snorted and slammed his own copy down onto the table. "It says only in the event that it is an emergency situation, for which my needs take higher demand than your prudish pride."

"I'm *not* a prude." I wasn't. *Was* I? Some at the Guild said I was, but, then, I wasn't a virgin either, so I didn't consider myself to be one.

"I bet you have never been naked with a man; not completely. I'm not speaking about clothes either."

Uh—wasn't that what being naked meant? I groaned, rubbing my fingers over my temples. Adam sat one booth away from where I'd sunk into a booth in the back of the club to lick my wounds alone. Ryder had followed me, like a proud peacock that was ruffling his feathers with his damn contract.

"That is so none of your business," I sneered, not knowing what the hell he meant; only that I didn't want to go down that road of discussion right now. I needed coffee, or tea. Anything with an insane amount of caffeine would be welcomed right about now.

I scanned through another section, finding yet another thing I wasn't about to let happen. "You want to pick my clothes? What the hell is wrong with my clothes?"

His eyes took in my sleeveless top and sank lower, as if he was sneering with disdain at my jeans. They were jeans for monkey butt's sake! "I have a certain reputation, Synthia. I won't have it smeared with being shadowed by a child who wears the clothes of an immature teenager."

"I'm wearing jeans. Half the country wears them!" I cried, pissed that he was nitpicking everything about me.

"Don't worry. You can pick out your own panties—for now."

I grumbled and continued to read, regretting being so hot-headed and not reading before he'd taken my soul—*if* that is what he had done. I could still feel the heat boiling in my veins, but I had yet to determine if that was him or my anger.

"Why can't I date while in your employment?" I squeaked. What the hell was up with his sudden interest in my personal life, anyway? Did it matter who I dated, or what I wore?

"It's to protect my interest. Besides, with a mouth like yours I'm pretty sure you don't have men lining up at your door asking for a date."

I glared while chewing on my bottom lip nervously. Okay, I really didn't have men lining up to date me. As if I'd tell him that!? Oh, hell no. "This is bullshit. We don't even know who we are after, or if they will make an attempt for your bride anytime soon. It could be, like, weeks before anything happens!"

His eyes just stared at me, like I was the most brainless woman on the West Coast. When he didn't say anything, I continued, "This is only good until I find who is after the princess right?" I babbled as my panic started to escalate.

"It's indefinite, or until I decide otherwise. I'm Fae, we like to own"—his eyes moved to my chest and back up to meet my eyes— "things."

I swallowed down the urge to scream, because it wouldn't help me now. I squirmed in my seat, my nails sinking into the expensive leather of the booth's cushion. My stomach was pitching, my mind running wild with the knowledge of what I'd done. "How long before I can be released from this contract?"

His eyes scanned me carefully, his lips growing taut as he considered it, but said nothing, just sat there and watched my reaction.

I'd tried to save my friends, and, in the process, I'd lost my soul to him. If he wanted to fuck me, all he had to do was demand it! "I can't do this. I can't," I sputtered, needing to get outside to get air. I was up and moving in the direction of the door before I had the words out from between my lips.

His hands dug into my flesh as he stopped me. I did the only thing I could think of…I threw a punch blindly, which connected with his nose. Before I could even think, "Oops," I was pinned against the far wall of the club by two hundred pounds of solid Fae pinning me there.

"Next time you touch me, I *will* punish you!" he roared.

My lips shook as my body followed suit, violently. The need to get outside was greater than the need to live, or breathe. I clawed against him, my feet trying to find the floor unsuccessfully. I was having a glorified panic attack.

As if this day couldn't get any worse, no—I had to go have a panic attack in front of the Dark Fae. I knew the moment he sensed it, or guessed at what was happening, because his fingers went slack and he allowed me to slide down the wall. The moment my feet touched the ground, I was gone.

The bouncers at the door both moved, opening the doors so I could get outside before I threw up all over their club's shiny floors. Outside, the air couldn't fill my lungs fast enough. I'd been prone to panic attacks after the death of my parents, but it had been ten years since the last one happened.

"Syn, you okay?" Adam said with concern lighting in his green eyes as he followed closely behind me.

I shook my head forcefully. My stomach heaved as tears swam in my eyes. This wasn't fucking happening. Alden knew I was against anything pertaining to the Fae, I'd had so many assignments that I had turned down without any hesitation, because they'd included the Fae.

"Synthia, slow down. This isn't as bad as it sounds. He's trying to scare you," Larissa said, speaking low and calmly as she came into view. She must have been outside, or waiting for me.

Like she knew? She wasn't the one who'd just

signed a bloody fucking contract that gave a Dark Fae the right to use her body as food! He could turn me into what my mother had become—someone willing to kill her own child! Stars burst behind my eyelids and I had the startling realization that I was going to pass out—right before someone caught me and everything turned black.

I awoke to the sound of water dripping. Hushed voices played across the room, talking as if I wouldn't hear them.

"I don't know. She's never passed out—ever."

"Why didn't the Guild disclose her previous history with the Fae before this?" Ryder's voice was angry and to the point.

"You would have to talk to Alden about that one. I only know that it took us over a year to get her to even speak after they found her. She was a mess, angry at everything. I was the only one who could get through to her—reach her wherever she'd gone inside her mind so to say. Later on, she only let Larissa and Adrian in. She was a child, traumatized by *your* kind. The things she's seen—" Adam's voice filled with pain.

"Which neither I, nor any of my people, had anything to do with," Ryder pointed out angrily.

I heard Adam's snort, felt his ire raise as he defended the child I'd been. It was why he was one of my best friends; he was always there for me. "She was five, man. Five! Inside her mind, you're all the same; you're what she fears most. She's so fucking terrified she had some jack-off tattoo a spell on her neck. There is one lesson they teach us at the Guild, and that's to put the most valuable spell on your neck—and she wasted it, to protect herself against becoming what her mother—"

"Don't," I whispered, struggling to sit up.

I was not letting him give the Fae more weapons to use against me. Ryder stood with his back to the wall, his arms crossed against his massive chest. Those golden eyes of his took in my anger, without so much as a single flinch. Adam scratched his dark head and scuffed his feet at the floor, like a child being berated for misbehaving.

"Where am I?" I asked softly, realizing I was in a bed, a very big soft bed.

"We are in the club's sub-levels. You passed out," Ryder said, never taking those dangerous eyes from mine.

"I don't pass out," I said obtusely.

"You did," he replied with his lips jerking up into a wolfish grin.

"Whatever. Are we done here? I need a shower," I grumbled, feeling dirty for being in any bed around him.

"You need to finish reading the contract. You stay with me until this is finished. Inside my estate," Ryder growled, his eyes daring me to challenge him.

I did the only thing I could—I challenged him.

"Fuck that. I'm not staying alone with you—ever." I folded my arms over my chest, aiming for the most stubborn look I could make, while sitting in an oversized bed of black silk.

His eyes took me in, raking heat up my body as he did so. I was up and out of the bed before he could comment. Only then did I notice I wasn't in my jeans and the black flimsy panties were not enough protection from Ryder. I doubted full armor would be enough to protect me against his eyes.

"Who the hell stole my pants?" I barked, jumping back into bed, much to the amusement of the two men in the room.

Adam coughed and tilted his head in Ryder's direction. Ryder turned his head, giving Adam a look that would make most men run and then growled low in his chest. Adam turned to leave me alone with him.

"Adam, don't you dare!" I yelped, but Adam was already at the door and only threw me a sheepish grin before he was gone.

"You think that boy could protect you from me?" Ryder inquired, letting his arms drop to his side. He'd changed. His jeans rode low on his hips, and the long sleeve white shirt was open far enough to expose his well-muscled chest and a peek of the tattoos he was covered in. As he stepped closer, I realized he was also barefoot.

"Maybe," I whispered, trying to backpedal. This wasn't happening.

I watched as he stopped at the end of the opulent bed. It was big enough to fit seven bodies on. What the hell was up with him and his orgy sized beds? He didn't get on the bed. Instead, his eyes raked over me slowly, intensely, hungrily. Chills crept down my spine, my mouth dried and the scream in my throat sat paralyzed on the verge of coming out.

"Get over it. You said you are not a victim. You came highly recommended for this job. If you're not useful for it—I will find something you *are* useful for," his eyes lowered to my lips.

I stuck out my tongue and then almost bit it off

when he smiled. Guy needed to get knocked around a little, break his nose or something. He had a masculine beauty that left me boneless. Those wicked lips kept taunting me. His eyes had the eerie glow to them once more. It was a look I didn't want to see on any Fae. I swallowed and refused to lower my gaze from his.

"I'm not defined by what your people did to my parents, but I'm not stupid either," I said after what felt like hours of silence, but in reality, had only been seconds. That damn stare of his was unnerving!

"Not *my* people. Make no mistake of that. Do not damn a race for the deeds of a few bad apples."

They were words I had heard before, and they didn't help. The fear was still there, and in an enforcer it was a fatal one. I was known for putting my foot in my mouth, but I needed him to know one thing. "I'm okay with the entire contract, except one thing."

He raised a dark eye brow. "Which is?"

"I'm not sleeping with you. I don't care if you're starving and writhing on the fucking floor. I'll walk over you and out that damn the door. I'll drag someone *else* back to you—but it won't be me you feed off of, *ever*."

His lips twitched, but his eyes stayed emotionless. "Writhing on the floor?"

"Writhing," I confirmed.

"I do not writhe on the floor, *ever*."

"Good, then we are on the same page." I said smoothly.

"The contract says you will. It's a blood oath—so if I start writhing, you will spread those creamy thighs and let me in. Do you know what going back on a blood oath means?"

I swallowed, raising both my brows as I tried to think if I knew what it meant. I exhaled. I was about to learn something new. Marie would have been happy, since she was a staunch believer that you learned something new every day. "No, but I have an inkling I'm about to."

His lips twitched again, but it was subtle—if I had blinked I would have missed it.

"Let me enlighten you. If you go back on it, under any circumstances, I can kill you, or worse. You belong to me, in every way that matters. If I want you in my bed, make no mistake, that palm of yours will itch, and you will be helpless but to fulfill my needs. I say jump, you ask how high. You are bound to me, body and soul, until I say otherwise. You took part of my soul. I just took a piece of yours. Getting it now? Or do I need to show you for you to understand?"

I wanted to scream, or rip his eyes out. "I'm not a piece of fucking property! I cannot be owned!"

"Quite the opposite…you *are* mine. As of right now, you belong to me, Pet."

Chapter
TEN

I'd taken off like my ass was on fire, the moment I was released from Ryder to retrieve anything I would need for the next few weeks. I'd run into my room and thrown open my laptop, starting it up the moment we'd come inside from being dropped off by the Fae. Turns out I *couldn't* weasel my way out of the damn contract. He had to end the deal. I couldn't.

The contract was indeed a blood oath, sealed by our blood. It was legally binding in the eyes of the Fae and the Witches Guild. It went above that, though. If I broke it or refused to acknowledge it, I would become his in every sense of the word. If he wanted my soul—he just had to say the words. Unless we could find another loophole, which I would need to start looking for now.

How could I have been so stupid? I glared at the laptop. This was idiotic! I shouldn't have to move into his house, estate, or whatever he called it. He had mind-fucked me, and, in doing so, he'd backed me into a fucking corner. He'd made me see red, and then he'd baited his freaking hook with Adam dipped in chocolate to ensure I signed those damn papers.

I had cross-checked the contract, using what little

information was available on the Fae in the Guild online library. The Fae, being the weasels they were, counted trickery and coercion as legit when forcing a contract—but I'd already known that without needing to confirm it. I jumped as a soft knock sounded at the door. I stopped pacing long enough to answer it and allow both Adam and Larissa into the room.

"What's up guys?" I asked carefully.

Adam was still regretting showing up at the Fae's club. I'd chewed him out the entire way home and felt like an ass for doing so. "Syn—"

I cut him off, knowing he was settling into another long apology. "It's okay, Adam. I'm over it, and I'm sorry for biting your head off. I need a few things, though—spell-wise."

He nodded his dark head as his eyes took in my suitcase. "You thinking some soft spells, or more hardcore?"

My lips twisted into a naughty smile. A man after my own heart. "Hardcore. I don't want to be inside his house more than I have to be."

"Alden is going to flip out, Syn. Is it really so bad? You could be finished with this assignment before you know it. This guy is pretty badass, if you haven't noticed."

Adam and I had both stopped to look at her. She was always the voice of reason, but she hadn't been with us inside that room, nor had she been there when he proclaimed ownership of me! "You don't understand, Lari; he *owns* me now. He can decide to keep me! You don't see a problem with that?" I asked outraged.

She shook her head and dropped her hands to

her sides. She was of slim build. Her long dark hair had beautiful natural curls that most girls would kill for. Her eyes were the color of freshly grown spring grass. She was everything a guy would look for in a mate—unlike me, who was a normal blonde, which I considered to be a dime a dozen, since the Light Fae had joined the party, bringing with them a new view of what a perfect blonde should look like. Forget Barbie—the Fae gave new meaning to feeling inadequate.

One of my Guild instructors had been quick to point out that I was indeed not the type to ever listen or follow rules, let alone make him a sandwich. I'd agreed—oh I would have made his ass a sandwich, but he'd have worn it in his face.

"Yes, I get it. If he reneges on the deal, then I'll be first in line to fry his balls, Syn. But right now, there's more at stake than what either of you have been told." Adam snorted as Larissa left the room, only to return moments later with a file in her hand. "This is what you were really brought in for."

She tossed the file on my bed and crossed her arms while she waited for me to pick it up. Adam and I stared at her and then at the file that sat discarded on my bed. The red letters C-O-N-F-I-D-E-N-T-I-A-L were written across the manila folder, which caught and held my eye. "We couldn't tell you until you agreed to the contract, and, well, I know it isn't something we normally look into, but they need us to do this case. We think this has to do with the person or persons trying to get to the Light Heir."

I looked up at her as if she'd grown another head.

"Read it already!" Larissa scolded, picking up pacing where I had left off.

"What is it?" Adam asked, afraid, like I wasn't going to pick it up.

I blew him a raspberry before picking it up and undoing the metal hook that kept it together. Pictures of dead women slid out of the folder. Gruesome pictures that made bile rise in the back of my throat. "What the hell."

"Witches from the Seattle Guild. Some from the Guild itself, others are from some of the smaller covens across the state. Oftentimes, their mutilated bodies have been found with some of the dead Fae." She paused, nibbling on her lip as she considered telling us more. "They're somehow tied to whomever is trying to kill the Light Heir—that's all we know. None of the Guilds sent them out to work with the Fae, and, yet, they were strung up beside them and killed."

I sat down as my knees threatened to give out. Adam did the same. This wasn't happening, but Alden throwing me to the wolf made sense now. I stared at picture after picture of dead Witches and Fae. "Their spells are missing," I said, pointing out the missing skin of the Witches.

"And their tongues. The Fae are missing glands and other goodies. It's like someone is building a Frankenstein, so to say," Larissa said, finally stopping long enough to point out the mutilated Fae that were indeed missing pieces.

I considered it, moving to another picture. This one had been picked over. Most spells were written in ink and placed in the skin. They were written in Latin though, which meant whoever was doing this knew the language or was working with someone who did.

"The Fae...what are they missing, exactly?" I

asked, trying to scan their pictures without throwing up. Someone had cut them open and dissected them—and the Fae did not die, which meant someone had some sort of mythical weapon, or had figured out some way to kill them.

"Sex glands, among a few other things. Another is missing her milk glands. They seem to pick out weak ones; at least, that is what the Fae seem to think."

"If they are killing Fae and Witches, they have to be killing other creatures."

We both looked up at Adam. And waited.

He shrugged and continued, "Witches and Fae have nothing in common, so why them? Why not other creatures?"

I narrowed my eyes and scrunched up my nose. "We both have magic. But why not just hire us, if that is what they want?"

"The Fae also reported a child stolen three days ago, from a Fae compound in daylight; no one saw anything. Whoever this is has magic, but we think they want more," Larissa said oblivious to the looks I and Adam were now throwing at her.

"Just how long have you been working on this, Miss I *Hurt* My Ankle?" I barked accusingly. How could she work a case without telling me? I was her Head of Coven. She was supposed to report any missions or findings to me, and, yet I'd known nothing of this before now.

"I knew you wouldn't be too mad, Syn, because they found this at one of the scenes. And I couldn't tell you. Alden insisted it be kept quiet until we had more information." She tossed a small trinket on the bed.

It was my mother's locket. I flinched and picked it up, placing it in my hand. "How? Where did you find this?"

"At one of the first scenes. No connection can be made between them, or your parents, so far," Larissa said and smiled sadly. "We were afraid it would dredge up the past too much for you."

I snorted. "You should have told me, Larissa. Why would someone be killing immortals?" I asked myself out loud. It made no sense, but neither did the murders of innocent women. "Are we sure it's only women?" I asked, as an afterthought struck me.

"So far. Why? What are you thinking?" Larissa said, narrowing her eyes.

"And the Fae, they're actually dead? Not regenerating?"

She nodded in confirmation.

"So, whoever this is can kill an immortal Fae and is strong enough to withstand Witches' powers?" I asked, trying to think of what, if any, creature I'd ever encountered could manage a feat that great.

"Alden thinks so, but it makes no sense, since they're killing Witches and Fae for body parts. The only break we've got is they had pictures of Arianna inside one of the crime scenes. With a giant red X on her face." Larissa hesitated, her eyes turning to take in my pale complexion.

I'd had enough of the Fae, and Ryder. My eyes drifted over the charm, simple yet beautifully crafted. It was hers, and I'd watched the Fae tear it from her neck before leaving the strong beautiful woman who had raised me reduced to nothing but a mindless body. Those empty eyes haunted my dreams; *she* haunted them.

"Alden says that this might just be a serial killer, but one who is doing it on a massive scale and can kill immortals."

The phone in the kitchen rang, and Adam jumped up quickly, leaving the room to answer it, which was a habit of his since he spent more time at our place than at his own.

He came back a few seconds later and tossed a curious look at Larissa. "Alden's on the line. Says it's urgent."

We both watched as Larissa exhaled deeply and headed for the kitchen alone. Two seconds later, we followed her, too curious as to what Alden wanted to stay in the bedroom and wait. We rounded the corner in time to watch her eyes go wide, and then wince, at whatever was being said on the other end of the phone.

"That can't be good," Adam said, jumping up to sit on the bare counter and reached for a jar of peanut butter.

"Yes, I understand," Larissa was saying in a strictly professional voice. "Yes we'll go to the scene," she paused, biting her lip and nodded, as if Alden would be able to see the motion. "No, I understand, and we'll be strictly professional."

She hung up the phone and turned to Adam, who had grown bored with the conversation, and was focused on licking peanut butter off his finger, sucking on it for a moment before he noticed us both staring at him.

"What? I got hungry."

We both looked at him and shook our heads. I narrowed my eyes on Larissa. My brain knew what was coming before she said it. It wasn't good.

"They found another dead Fae. Alden's sending us, since you're now working for the Dark Prince. His men will assist us at the site."

Just freaking peachy!

"Let me guess, the prince himself will be there?" Adam said, falling in line with my thoughts.

Larissa sighed and nodded slowly. "You guys need to be professional. It's one of their own that was killed and for them—it's huge—someone is killing off immortals."

"And Witches," I piped in, making sure she hadn't missed that fact. We weren't immortal. She seemed to be forgetting that there was a trail of bodies and a killer of Witches and Fae alike on the loose. Whoever it was, needed to be stopped, and fast.

Chapter
ELEVEN

We pulled up at the dead Fae's house shortly after five o'clock. The sun was beginning to set on the horizon, bringing beautiful, contrasting colors to the sour mood of the crowd gathered around the crime scene, trying to catch a peek at the body of the deceased.

Apparently, a dead immortal brought out all the freaks. It was a nice yard. Vivid green bushes continuously flowed to the mailbox in the front yard of the small green house. From the flowers and roses planted throughout the yard, it was easy to tell that the Fae who lived here had been blessed with green thumbs—or was an actual Fairy.

The Guild had figured out that the difference between Fairies and the Fae was small, but there, the lines between the types of Fae often seemed blurred. Ryder and his merry men had more in common with the mythical Elves, minus the pointy ears, and they were not exactly gentle folk. These guys would kick your ass, mess with your head, and then probably steal your soul just to liven things up a bit. Fairies, on the other hand, were gentle creatures that preferred to live alone, unless mated. I was willing to bet that since I heard no pitter of wings, or crying from family, that this one had been alone and unmated. Fairies, like Sprites and Dryads, were connected to nature and drew from the earth and not the Human race, which made them worth keeping around in my book. Myths and legends often had a basis in fact—how many types of the Otherworld creatures were out there was uncertain and the Fae weren't sharing that kind of information anytime soon.

I opened the van door and stepped out, waiting for Adam and Larissa to pile out of the beat up van designated for official Guild business since it had the Guilds name in red down the otherwise white side. My eyes searched the Dark Fae closest to us and found a pair of narrowed golden eyes watching as we moved closer to the scene.

"Here, put these on," the closest Fae said, holding out a pair of cloth booties you would see in an operating room on a surgeon.

I kept my comment to myself as I took them and put them on over my sneakers. I'd changed into black fatigues and tank top, which was protocol for members of the Guild on a crime scene, or so Larissa said. "How many dead?" I asked quietly, taking in the broken window I could see from the front porch.

"One," Ryder replied, moving over to where we stood. "It's gruesome—sure you can stomach it?" he questioned me.

"It's a crime scene, I think we can handle it," I mumbled, ignoring his hard stare as I looked around him to the glass shards on the porch. I narrowed my eyes, considering it, and then looked at the untouched flowerbed right in front of it.

Ryder turned to stand beside me, the electrical current of his power sizzling over my flesh reminding me of everything he had done to me today already. I dismissed him from my mind, going into enforcer mode, blocking out every sound as I took in what the naked eye would miss. There was an aura trail leading around the back. It was faint, but there none the less. The aura was green and was already fading.

"The body. Who's been in to see it so far?" I asked.

"We were waiting for your Guild; wasn't aware they were sending you in to help us," Ryder didn't sound any happier about me being here than I was.

"So, no one has entered yet?" I said, stopping and turning my head around as he ran into me.

He pulled back instantly, as if I had burned his flesh. "No, we looked in through a window."

I nodded and started walking again. The trail around back was growing fainter with every second. "It's not a Witch, or Fae—I've never seen a green aura; has a slimy feel to it."

I could feel his penetrating gaze on my back as I followed the trail, ignoring the house as I walked around to the back. It was as green as the front yard was, with flower pots bursting with beautiful flowers in every hue of the rainbow.

My feet hit gravel, and I stopped. The green trail from the aura was gone. "There was a car parked here for a quick getaway if needed, but the killer wasn't in a hurry." I scanned the gravel, kneeling down to touch the rocks and measure out the tire print from where the killer had been parked, "There was at least one female in heels here," I said, coming back up. "The car is most likely a Dodge charger or a similar model." I turned, looking at the garage, which had a small fleck of red paint on the corner, which had been hit on the way out. "Red, blood red."

"Do you realize how many red Chargers there are in Spokane?" Adam whined.

"Yep, I'd say she was around one hundred and thirty pounds. Maybe more."

"You got all that from following a trail?" Dristan asked, coming up behind us.

I turned and gave him a leveled stare with a slight nod, before turning back to the garage. I chewed at my lip, before looking closely at the lock for tampering. "You guys smell that?" I asked, turning to take in the Fae's reaction to my question.

"Yeah, it's fertilizer from Faery," Ryder said, crossing his arms over his immaculate white lawn shirt. He wore loose fitting jeans with off black boots that made him seem almost Human, if he wasn't glaring with his brutal air of authority.

"Hmm, it reeks," I complained, before walking off in the other direction without waiting to see if anyone followed me. The evening air was chilling, but manageable. The sunset was now vibrant shades of orange and red, with a cloudless sky.

It was chilling how beautiful it was outside in the face of a tragedy. The world around us had not stopped because of the tragedy inside. I think that was one of the things that bothered me the most the day my parents had been brutally murdered; outside the sun had been shining, welcoming. It had pissed me off, even at five.

"Planning on killing the sun?" Ryder asked, keeping up with me easily with his long gait.

I stopped and removed the booties on the porch and held out my hands for new ones, slipping them on just as quickly before I stepped onto the porch and looked through the window. "The glass is outside," I remarked.

"Yeah, they broke the window to get in," Dristan said quietly from behind me.

"No, she let her killer inside. If they had gone through the window, the glass would be on the inside from being broken *into*."

"Smart. So the killer broke it on their way out?" Ryder asked narrowing his eyes on the glass at our feet.

I nodded carefully, keeping my eyes on the figure slumped in the small wooden chair in her kitchen. Ropes held her in place, and she was missing part of her face; there were also holes in her shoulders from either being stabbed or pinned by something. My stomach rose at the sight, but I pushed it back down, shaking my head.

"It's bad inside," Ryder said in a low voice.

"You don't investigate things like this normally?" I asked, trying to dispel the image of my father that filtered briefly through my mind. I pulled my eyes away from the body to look up into his eyes.

"No, it's not often we find our own dead," he growled from low in his chest, moving to open the door.

I followed slowly, the stench of death overwhelming as the door was thrown open wide. I scanned the room briefly. Two tea cups with green tea sat on a breakfast nook table, along with knives that I was betting had not been part of tea time. The carpets that were once white now were splattered with blood from the brutality of the murder that has occurred here.

I tilted my head, looking at the eyeless face that was facing the floor. She'd trusted whomever she had let inside her house, and she'd paid for it with her life. Blood had been used to write scribe marks across the wall in the language of the dead.

"She knew her killer enough that she made tea and sat down with her to talk," I said, narrowing my eyes on the symbols on the wall. "Can you read the message?" I asked carefully.

"It's a warning and a draining glyph. Myrsa didn't have much power, though. She was, after all, a simple earth Fairy. Good at growing, but otherwise not powerful by any means."

"No, but she was beautiful. Maybe this killer isn't just sucking out power, but beauty as well," I mumbled, tilting my head to better look at the missing skin of the poor woman's fingers. "She is missing her eyes, her fingertips, and—oh wow," I swallowed violently against the nausea rising once more.

The white pants were open, and her woman parts were completely missing, including her womb. "Was she—" I stopped, clearing my voice again as I took an involuntary step backward. "Was she breeding?"

Ryder hissed with anger, his eyes doing his glowing thing again and filling with his outrage. "No, she was in waiting. She was to be married to a Water Sprite next week. She chose this house because of the portal one block over that leads to the main garden inside Faery."

"That makes no sense. Why would someone steal

her organs? Eyes can be used for certain spells—"

I switched into second sight and took in the scene around us. I instantly felt the air crackle and the room went deathly silent. As if everyone knew what was coming, but couldn't do anything about it. The air was charged, and everything felt as if it was moving in slow motion. The Fae looked at us, as we looked at them. Horror filled the small room as I turned and looked at the body of the deceased. My hand began to itch painfully.

Adam and Larissa's hands sought my shoulders as they pushed their own powers into me. The moment the connection and circle was made, I brought my hands out wide, mimicking them in a circle before my palms slapped together—and the room exploded.

Wood from the roof splintered and hit the protection field I'd created, violently sending spasms through my body. It was a part of me. I was consuming the damage, so that the others could be protected. The Fae might have been able to live through the blast, but my friends wouldn't have.

I turned, looking over at the Fae, who still stared at us; Ryder's eyes narrowed as he took in the pinched strain on my face. Blood was pumping loudly inside my ears, making it impossible to hear what he was saying. Sweat broke out on my brow as Adam and Larissa kept their hands touching my flesh, feeding me power to keep the protective barrier up.

The room was still glowing from the bomb that had gone off. The body was no longer in the chair that once held it. This had been a trap, or a warning. We needed to get outside, but I didn't have enough power to move the bubble, even with the added powers.

"Syn!" Larissa shouted as blood erupted from my

nose. Ryder moved in, closing the distance, his eyes scanning my face.

"Why is it hurting her?" he demanded in an angry voice that scraped on my nerves.

"She took the brunt of the explosion. The spell is a reflection of herself. Her magic is the base of it, so she takes the damage portion of it."

I wanted to tell Larissa to shut it. Ryder didn't need to know my secrets, or that I was the only Witch who had ever been able to wield this certain spell.

I felt my body growing heavy. The room was still ablaze; thick, putrid smoke that could suffocate my team still lingered. I turned my head, ignoring the dizziness that assaulted my mind as I searched for the door. It had been blown closed in the explosion.

Ryder noticed where I was looking and moved into action. "Dristan, we need to get them out of here. Zahruk, clear the room."

They all ducked as Dristan and Zahruk stepped up and held hands, chanting in the language of the Fae. It was taking every ounce of energy I had to concentrate while keeping the barrier between the fire and us in place.

In the few moments it took them to get the words out, the house gave an audible shake that I felt down inside my bones and exploded outward. The moment it did, I fell and almost hit the floor, but Ryder was quick as he reached out and grabbed beneath my arms and pulled me against his tall frame, already moving away from the carnage that now looked as if a nuclear bomb had been dropped on the house instead of a small bomb.

I closed my eyes, unable to keep them open any

longer and gave in to oblivion for a moment. The warmth that surrounded me was welcomed and comforting, even if it was because I was now being cradled in the Dark Prince's arms.

"Lay her down gently. I can heal her," Larissa assured him, but I felt him tense, as if questioning her motives.

"Please," I whispered, hating that I had to ask him for anything, but I needed her to heal the pain that was threatening to become relentless. I felt the cool grass as it met my tender skin, wet with the evening dew.

I felt Larissa's hands as she placed them, one on my heart and one on my forehead as she performed the healing white magic she was known for. It was also why she wasn't included on a lot of our missions. Enforcers didn't normally need a healer for killing.

"The scene," I whispered, realizing that any chance we had to find the person responsible for the brutal murder was gone.

"Destroyed," Ryder growled, standing up to his full height.

I stretched my neck, testing out the pain in my head before I sat up. I then stood so he wasn't so tall. Not that it helped, since the guy was freakishly large, but looking at him from flat on my back on the cold, damp ground was just not an option.

When I had made it to my entire five foot six stance, I felt down my back and hips making sure I was still in one piece. This day sucked—big time. I'd felt an itching in my hand, long before I felt the air sizzle around us—a reminder that I was connected to him now. As if it wasn't bad enough that we had been standing inside a house with a woman missing her most delicate parts, the only reason I knew something was wrong was because of the blasted contract!

I needed more coffee before I could deal with this crap. I wasn't sure if there was enough coffee in the entire world to deal with the Fae, though. I turned, watching the smoke waft up into the chilly night air, thick plumes of it as a stark reminder of how close we'd come to death this night.

"You prevented us from taking damage, thank you," Zahruk said softly, surprising me more than if he'd said my ass was on fire.

"I saved my coven," I replied quietly, unsure how to accept his compliment.

His lips twisted up into a smirk. "Still, I don't fancy a night in a healing tank, so thank you."

I nodded, at a loss for what he expected. He was Fae and thanking me for saving him from being harmed. It went against everything I stood for, and, yet, with the binding of the contract, I'd been helpless to do anything less than save Ryder, which was a bitter pill to swallow. I turned back, looking at the onlookers.

No one in the crowd stood out. The green aura wasn't present among any of those standing across the yellow line of tape. I'd never seen that color of aura before, not from any of the creatures we had trained to combat or assassinate, which wasn't a good thing.

"What creature has a green aura?" I asked as Adam stepped up beside me, his eyes scanning me for bodily damage.

"Ask them," he tilted his head in the direction of the Fae. I scrunched my face with distaste.

"Hey, you guys know what leaves a green aura trail behind?" I shouted, loud enough to be heard by the Fae and not the press who had just arrived on scene.

Ryder looked past me to where the press was currently setting up their cameras and gear to start filming. If they hurried they would make the eleven o'clock news. "Time to go. Now." He growled as his men fell in line with his long angry strides.

As he walked past us, I watched his jeans hugged his firm backside. The crowd erupted, raising the noise level as more press charged the line, having seen the Dark Prince as he walked in the direction of the black Cadillac SUVs. He stopped a few feet from me and turned back, and lifting a single dark brow.

"You need to come with us. I trust you finished packing before you followed secondary orders?" he asked smoothly, his thick, rich baritone flowing through me.

Secondary orders? "I belong to the Guild, first and foremost, Ryder. I am packed, and, like a good little doggie, I will follow on your heels—in *our* car." Which I highly doubted could keep up with his. Sarcasm dripped like honey from my lips—if he heard it, he chose to ignore it.

"Do so," he replied in the same casual bored tone he had when I had signed his bloody binding contract. He smiled, showing his teeth as he turned and walked the short distance to his car.

This is keeping my coven alive. Just breathe, Synthia, just breathe. I repeated the mantra inside my head. Apparently I'd developed passing out as a way to deal with this entire freaking situation, and that was just not okay.

"Was that professional enough for Alden?" I asked, watching Larissa nod as she spoke quietly into the phone. It bugged me that she had been in the know of what was happening around us and had excluded us from it.

She'd known I was being set up for the interview. She'd known how much I hated the Fae, yet she'd kept it to herself. We were supposed to be a team, and, since most covens had ten to twelve and we only had three, we depended on honesty and the closeness we shared to stay alive. Larissa following Alden and keeping us in the dark wasn't something I could let slide. Our lives depended on it.

~~*~*~*~*~*~*~*~*

Chapter
TWELVE

We followed them out of Spokane, back down the highway I'd already been on twice today. The van was filled with silence—something unusual for our group since we normally had a lot to talk about, even if they were mundane things.

I replayed the scene over inside my head. It had been horrific and calculated. We were dealing with someone who liked to watch the victim endure the pain, who got off on the perverse sadistic need of the kill.

The victim had known her attacker; had let them in. If her house was anything to go off of, she'd been planning on the killer visiting—just without the whole killing part. It meant she'd known her killer, and had wanted to make a good impression. I still wasn't sure if there were more killers that might have joined them after the first killer arrived.

I shoved thoughts of the crime scene away, as we followed the dark SUVs in through a twelve foot high metal gate that safeguarded Ryder's personal living quarters located just a few miles from his club.

When I opened the door to get out, Adam stopped

me by placing his hand gently on my shoulder. "Syn, be careful. I know you only signed to keep us safe— but we're nothing without you."

I smiled sadly. "Adam, you're stronger than you think you are. You guys—" I paused, needing them to know they would be okay if I didn't make it back to them. "If I don't make it out of this, go back to the Guild. Damian has a great coven, and he's a fair leader. I need to know you'll be okay if I don't make it back."

They both stared at me. I could see the confusion in their eyes, but it wasn't like I was giving up on them—just the opposite. I was giving them an out. If I fucked this up, they would be used against me. I was smart enough to know that it wasn't *if*; it was *when* I did.

"No fucking way, Syn. We were a team since before boot camp. No fucking way, we belong together—we always have. We knew before we started this that it was a touchy group. We knew he'd want to use us, so let the fucker try," Adam seethed.

I exhaled slowly. "Adam, I can't do this if I'm worrying that you're okay. I need to know before I step out of this van, if I fuck up, you're protected. Give me this. Do you understand what I'm saying?"

I met his green stare as he struggled to agree with what I needed him to. Larissa was struggling, too, but it was by no means as much as Adam was. I should have questioned it, but I could feel the hard eyes of the Fae watching my back as I tried to make Adam agree.

"This is stupid. You're coming back to us."

"You're right, Adam, and seriously? I'd always come back to you."

"How cute," Ryder's voice tore away the seriousness of the moment.

I turned back in the seat and glared at him. Adam's hand still rested on my shoulder with a familiar caress from being as close as siblings. Ryder's eyes went to his hand and narrowed sharply. His face took on a harshness I was not familiar with. It sent a shockwave of shivers right down to my toenails.

"Get out of the car, Synthia. Now."

"I'm saying my goodbyes…to my *actual* friends," I growled, finding strength in my anger as the shock dropped away.

"They're coming in. Alden has agreed that since the killer is now stepping up the killings, it's best if we keep your small group here, to go out as needed with a speed we can only achieve if everyone drives out together." His eyes hadn't left mine yet.

I fisted my hand, remembering the warning that he'd been in trouble before my other senses had kicked in to warn me of my own coven's immediate danger. If he was close and in trouble when the coven was around—they'd be safe. As much as it sucked, it was ideal. Plus, I'd get to keep them close.

"Fine, but they'll need to go back to town and pack a bag or two," I mumbled, waiting for him to move away from blocking my escape from the van.

"Zahruk will accompany them into town. First, we need to get the details down while they are fresh," he challenged, his eyes probing mine as if I'd argue to go with them. I'd argue anything with him—after I had a freaking nap.

"You intend to hold the meeting here in the van?" I looked down and instantly regretted it as I took in his muscular form. I brought my eyes back up level with his. "Or are you gonna move so we can get to it?"

He stepped back, but just barely. I hopped out, feeling every muscle scream in protest as I did so. Stupid bomb. Stupid Fae. Stupid killer. And oh, what a stupid day! I swallowed the cry that threatened to push past my lips and slid the van's door open to grab my bags, gritting my teeth as I hefted them onto my shoulder.

"Syn, I'll get them," Adam said, stepping from the van and reaching for the bags. Ryder was closer and faster.

"I have them. They need to be searched for weapons, before I will allow them inside the mansion."

The property was huge. In the center of the drive in front of the mansion, a giant fountain merrily cascaded water out down the pile of round black rocks it was built from. *Runes*. The ancient lettering on the flat smooth surface were runes, written in what I assumed was Fae. It had been just light enough outside to see that the mansion was a light color and a few stories tall—but other than that, it was impossible to make out the details.

"Protection runes from Faery," Zahruk said, coming up to stand in front of the group walking to the house. Ryder handed off the bags to Zahruk, holding them for a moment as they met and locked eyes briefly. I knew something silent had passed between them.

I watched his back as he took off toward the large entryway that was well-lit, considering without the lights of the city it was darker than it would normally be at this time of night. I scanned the threshold as we approached.

To the naked eye it would look welcoming, but with my second sight still up, I could see the highlighted glowing marks of the wards the Fae had placed around the property that kept anyone wishing to harm them out. Similar to the ones inside my bedroom, but these ones were a lot stronger. These ones wouldn't just hurt you, they'd kill you.

"Drop the wards," I growled, feeling fear for my coven.

"They stay up," Ryder said, guarding his expressions closely.

I turned, looking at the faces behind me and shook my head. I was so sick of this day that I just wanted it over already. "You two okay?" I asked, quietly knowing it would be heard by everyone around me.

"It's okay, Syn. I don't plan on killing anyone today," Adam said, with a smile and an impish wink.

I yawned, waiting for Larissa to answer, and when she finally nodded, I turned and stepped through the door. I felt the slight sizzle as the spell tested my mind to check for hidden threats. I don't know who was more disappointed that it let me through, Ryder or me.

I turned, shaking my head, waiting for Adam and Larissa to follow. When both had been approved by the warding spells, I turned and took in the mass of stairways that led through the upper floors.

The entryway in which we stood was lit on a major scale that made my pockets hurt, just thinking of the electric bill this place must have every month. Funny how growing up can change your opinion of being afraid of the dark and afraid of the bills.

The place looked sterile, even though it was beautiful. Rich cream colors covered the walls, and a wide staircase was positioned about thirty or so feet in that led to the upper levels. A settee sat in the middle of the room, made of deep chocolate brown suede, with standing lights on either side of it, probably so you could sit while waiting for the prince to get off his arse and make an appearance.

As we moved closer to the stairs, I looked up, taking in the magnificent wrap around balconies that circled the third floor. The layout was open, so you could see everything from the landing. This place was huge, and I felt for the maid, whoever she was.

We walked single-file, with Adam bringing up the rear, through several more rooms and hallways before we were led to a room with the mark of Trinity above the door frame. I mentally prepared for the feeling of being drained and wondered if I'd give in to being a weak-ass girl and pass out if the room was warded against magic.

Today had been too much. Tomorrow wasn't looking any better. But I was a survivor, and I had this in the bag, as long as I didn't end up bagging the Dark Prince and tossing his body in the lake a few miles away.

I stepped through and exhaled as no pain took over my mind and no blasted past was thrown in my face. I looked up in time to catch the Fae watching me. For what? I'd passed the test at the front door, and I hadn't felt any spelling of the walls here. Had I missed something?

I turned, looking back as Larissa was thrown back and landed on the floor, her face pinched with pain as she looked up at me. "Larissa?"

"How did you get through?" Larissa whispered, her eyes wide as she stood back up.

I turned, glaring at the Fae, "Enough of these fucking tests! I saved your asses today, now let them in!"

"Fine, but first tell me how you just walked through a ward that should have knocked you on your ass?" Ryder said crossing his arms over his chest to glare at me.

"Easy, I stepped the fuck through it."

"Only Fae are able to cross it without being invited," he continued.

"Then it's broken, because I assure you I am *not* Fae!"

Chapter
THIRTEEN

"Stop looking at me like that! *Witch* here, remember? I am *not* a flipping Fairy!"

"How did you pass through the spell? It's not broken. I placed it myself," the Demon growled. I'd hoped to not encounter him again. So much for hoping.

"I told you, I stepped over it. I'm not Fae. If I was, wouldn't you guys have picked up on it already?" I challenged Ristan, crossing my arms over my chest as I pegged him with a glare.

"Indeed," he snarled.

"Enough. She cannot be of Fae blood without us being able to smell it, and I for one don't smell anything besides *Human* on her," Ryder spat, like I was something distasteful, and moved further into the room, taking a seat at the far end of a huge oval table that engulfed most of the meeting room. The others quickly followed his lead and left us standing.

Convenient. His thirteen men, who always seemed to be with him, had taken seats, as if they had been pre-assigned—or in some sort of pecking order.

The room had slate black walls that mimicked stone, and under any other circumstances, I'd have given them more attention, but my curiosity was firmly on the murders.

I still hurt like hell, and the healing process wouldn't fully work until I slept.

"How do you know she knew her killer?" Ryder asked, jumping straight to business and ignoring the fact that we had been left standing like hired help.

"She made tea," I mumbled, bringing my hand up to rub the back of my neck where the pain was starting to become unbearable.

"She made tea, and that alone tells you she knew her killer?" This from Ristan, who had his eyes zeroed in on me.

"She cleaned, she made tea. Yes, sounds lame, but seriously, there was no dust in her front room, the window was broken from inside the house, the killer or killers weren't rushed, and she opened the door for them. The car was parked out back. So, if the killer had been trying to break in to kill the victim, why the hell wouldn't she go through the back window, which was low enough for her to break and slide through easily? It seems pretty stupid to even consider the fact that she would go through a window on the front porch in daylight hours, and what she did inside—" I shivered as small bumps broke out across my skin from the image of what had been inside that tiny green house. "It wasn't done in minutes; it was precise, and the killer only took what they wanted. There were no cuts anywhere else that didn't serve a purpose."

"You got all of that from the few minutes inside the house?" Zahruk said and gave a slow whistle accompanying his sarcasm.

"Yes" I replied, trying not to show how tired I was.

"You think a woman did that?" Ryder asked carefully.

"No, I don't think. I know at least one of the killers was a woman. There was mauve colored lipstick left on the glass. The victim wore no makeup. The heel impressions in the gravel and dirt also confirm my theory."

He considered it, and then spoke softly. "Why would a woman take another's uterus and ovaries?"

I ignored it. I had no freaking idea why anyone would do something so horrendous. "What leaves a green aura trail in its wake?" I asked, after a few moments of awkward silence.

Fourteen heads shook their reply.

"They took her eyes; she wasn't a power Fae. She was an earth Fairy, for fuck's sake," Ryder snapped testily.

I dropped my arm and felt my knees sag briefly before I caught myself. Ryder noticed it, though. There wasn't much he didn't notice.

"Are we boring you?" he asked harshly.

"She took a bomb today," Adam replied before I could. "She has yet to sleep which means she hasn't healed enough and needs to do so soon."

"Stop it, Adam," I lashed out, not wanting it pointed out that I was vulnerable until I had slept.

"No, Syn. You saved their fucking asses today, and ours! No one else could have prevented it from killing all of us. You shouldn't be swaying on your feet. You should be sleeping, and you know it!" Oh hell, he was pissed.

"I'm fine," I whispered, lacking the tone I had been aiming for by a long shot.

Fourteen sets of eyes looked in my direction. I felt the weight of every pair as they took in my pale skin and the blood that was still crusted to my nose. I felt on display and it burned through me, making my spine a little straighter and my eyes a little brighter.

"Zahruk, show them to the rooms I've selected for each of them and see that Synthia is placed in the red room," Ryder said dismissing us.

"Oh. Hell. No. No red room of pain," I snapped angrily. I was big into reading, and no way in hell was I entering no red room of pain in this place.

Ryder's lips twitched, but otherwise he gave no sign that he knew of what I was talking about. Larissa, on the other hand, snorted with laughter until I turned my glare on her. I was bitchy when I was in pain, and I was doing my best to stay upright at the moment.

"I assure you there is nothing inside the red room. It's a bedroom. We call it the red room, because everything inside of it is, well, red," Zahruk said, scratching his head in confusion over my dislike of red.

I nodded, unable to care any longer. I needed to find a bed and throw myself in it before I turned into a pansy-ass and fainted again. I turned without giving the Fae around the table another thought. We walked through the halls and back toward the stairway.

I lifted my head and looked up with a grumble. Grinding my teeth, I stepped forward to start up the steps, but a hand at the small of my back stopped me cold. I turned, coming face to chest with Ryder, knowing him instantly by his unique rich scent alone.

"Change your mind and decided to make me elaborate something else?" I mumbled, feeling my eyes as they grew heavy.

"No," he replied softly, picking me up as I cried out, trying to bring my legs back down to the ground. "Hold still, or I will drop you on your head. On second thought, it might knock some sense into you."

I felt him moving up the steps and, even with the fear rising, I couldn't make my mind work. My body needed to heal, and I'd been careless, knowing what would happen all along. I settled further into his arms, resting my head on his shoulder as he curved his arm around my legs, keeping them far enough from my ass that I felt safe and not lusted after for the moment.

Or maybe it was just sleep talking. I inhaled deeply of his spicy scent, before I opened my eyes to find him watching me do so. *Great, that's all I needed right now. Smell the Dark Prince, who is carrying you up the damn stairs like Cinder-freaking-rella!*

His lips turned up in the corners as if he'd heard my snappy internal comment. I was so stupid when I was tired. Luckily, I hadn't sighed with bliss as I had wanted to.

"I could have walked," I mumbled, not knowing if it had even come out, since my mind was blanketed with the calm feeling of settling into sleep.

"My ass. You are not *fine*. You can hardly stand up. Admitting to weakness after doing what you did today is not the same as *being* weak."

I didn't answer him. Couldn't. My mind gave in and sleep overtook me until I felt myself being lowered from his arms, which caused me to automatically grab onto him and pull him with me—which was just another dumb thing I had done today. I should've started a list, but I was pretty sure the pen would have run out of ink by now.

Our faces touched slightly, cheek to cheek, before he moved his face around until our lips were way too close for comfort. Mine shivered violently, which caused him to cuss as he pulled away and brought the blankets up and over me.

"You need a healer. You're the most stubborn Human I have ever met," he growled, reaching for the phone.

"No Fae; call Larissa," I whispered through the chattering of my teeth.

"She left. Z took her to get some stuff from that shithole you call a home. Besides, she already tried to heal you," he mumbled, before setting the phone back down. "I can heal you. It won't be like she did, but the only other alternative is we wait—or I get in bed with you to warm you up and stop the incessant chattering."

"I'm fine," I said, barely audible past the chattering of my teeth.

"No. The word is stubborn as hell. Choose. Either I can undress and climb in bed with you—for which I won't be responsible for what happens—or I can heal you enough that you can sleep. Decide," he growled angrily, showing his teeth set together.

"You are not getting in this bed," I mumbled, trying to keep my eyes open.

"Fine, then close your eyes," he said, already placing his hands on my shoulder, which was bare. I felt his warmth pushing through his fingertips and into my system. It felt intimate and disturbing at the same time.

"No! No, stop."

He didn't. He continued sending those butterfly fingers over my skin, caressing my shoulder, which pushed the pain away with every wave of Fae magic he pushed into my system. The rush of heat made my eyes heavy, and I wasn't able to keep them open any longer.

I listened to his breathing as he pushed healing powers through me, calm and unlabored. Unlike Larissa when she healed me. Her powers came from spells and used energy to heal, where as his must come from dark magic, bred from his race.

I fought to keep my eyes open and watched as his face took on a dark hue, his eyes turning into twin embers as they met and held mine. "If you make me, I will induce sleep so you can heal. I don't need some half-brained female mucking shit up, because she's too weak to admit when she needs to rest."

I hissed, or more to the point I tried to. It came out sounding more like a moan than anything else. "I can't go to sleep with you in my room."

"It's not that you can't; you won't. Sleep. We need to catch a killer tomorrow. If the pattern keeps, it will be a Witch that dies next."

I stared at him for a few moments, hating how much sense he had just made. There was a killer loose, and he was right. If the pattern was spot on, then we would be finding a dead Witch within the next few days. I exhaled and closed my eyes, feeling the heat of his on me as I succumbed to sleep.

~~*~*~*~*~*~*~*~*

Chapter
FOURTEEN

I awoke to the deep, rich scent of coffee. My eyes popped open to find Larissa staring down at me with a positively magical Starbucks Venti-cup. "I love you," I mumbled before coming up to rest on my elbows.

"You better, this place had no coffee. Can you believe that? Not a single freaking bean in this entire place. Who lives like that?" She droned on as she extended her hand when I had finally made it into a sitting position and handed me the hot latté.

"The Fae don't drink coffee, Lari; they drink us."

"That's so wrong," she chirped, moving from where she had been sitting in the small chair beside the bed to finish opening the drapes, allowing more sun to blind me. She was dressed in yoga pants and a black tank top, as if we were at home gearing up for our daily workout.

"Going running?"

"No, there's an actual gym they said we could use. I wanted to keep on schedule, since afterward we need to meet up with Alden and the team from the Guild to go over the game plan for tonight," she stopped talking and looked back over her shoulder, tilting her head as if she were thinking of something before she continued, "You should get up; it's almost noon now."

I blinked at her, and then over her head to check the position of the sun for confirmation of the time. "I never sleep in," I mumbled off-handedly.

She snorted melodramatically. "Remember the time we got tanked and Adrian—"

She spun around with wide eyes. We didn't speak of him; hadn't since he'd died a few years ago on a job gone wrong. "And couldn't even remember the way home? Yeah, I remember— well, I remember the morning after," I finished for her, so she wouldn't feel like an ass for bringing up his name, even though I felt the strings of my heart tug with the memory of my first love. My heart clenched as an image of him arose in my mind.

Adrian had been our fourth, but he'd been killed on a job a couple years ago. One that should have been routine, but it had all gone wrong from the start. One thing after another, and before we knew it, before we could pull him out, he'd been killed. The pile of clothes I still kept in my closet at home was the only sign of him we could find, except for the puddle of blood, too high in volume for a Human to live through the loss.

It had been tested, and the DNA test had proven that it had belonged to Adrian. Alden had been referring to Adrian when he said I got people around me killed—the job had been routine and should have been simple to complete. Instead, I'd gotten him killed, all because I wanted to prove we were the best in the Guild.

I shook my head and exhaled, before taking a deep drink of the latté. Larissa smiled sadly, as if she'd been thinking along the same lines I had been. "He'd be pissed if he could see us now," she said as her lips turned into a small smile.

"He'd be blowing a few gaskets."

"Who wants to blow me—what?" Adam said, coming in to the conversation with a brilliant smile.

"Adrian would be," Larissa said as she moved back to sit in the small leather chair.

"Let's not go there. Not today," Adam replied, sitting on the bed, oblivious to the fact that I had a cup of coffee in my hand. His plopping caused it to spill on my shirt. I looked down as I held the coffee out to prevent any more from escaping the cup.

I was wearing a silk nightgown that I hadn't put on myself. I'd passed out in my clothes. I swallowed the urge to growl and met Larissa's stare as she took in the bright red nightgown. "Did you by chance dress me while I was comatose?"

"Nope," she said, already moving her shocked stare to Adam. It had a look of hurt that she failed to hide.

"Hey, I didn't dress her. I went with you!" He was off the bed as if it had bitten his ass, with a guilty sparkle in his green eyes.

I looked from one to the other and narrowed my eyes. "Lucy, you got some explaining to do."

They both turned bright red.

"You two!"

"It's not what you think, Syn!"

"We were planning on telling you!"

My head swung as they both said something else. I reached over and set my coffee down on the small night stand so I could rub my already pounding temples. "Shit! Shit! Shit! This is not happening. When *did* it happen?" I paused the rubbing, to peer at Larissa who was now looking like she was ready to cry.

It wasn't a smart idea to date inside a coven as small as ours. If they broke up and couldn't get along, it could mean mistakes that we couldn't afford. It could turn out badly and I loved them both. Not to mention, the Guild had its own views on dating, and I couldn't afford to have either one moved from my coven.

I moved to get out from beneath the covers, but I wasn't wearing pants. Embarrassment rose to my ears, coloring them pink. He'd seen me naked! And I'd been asleep, oblivious to the fact that he'd had me at his mercy. This day was off to a great start.

"Out, both of you."

"Syn—"

"Synthia—"

I shook my head and held up my index finger to the doorway. After they left still sputtering and trying to explain, I got up and inspected my body for signs of abuse or anything else. I was still testing my limbs when a pixie walked in humming lightly under her breath.

"You're awake! Hi, I'm Malinda. Was the nightgown a good choice?" Her voice was musical.

Not a Pixie; she was a Brownie.

Brownies were Fae that loved to clean and actually fed from doing so. They'd been almost wiped out when the Humans had caught wind of it. Enslaved by some of the seedier Humans who abused them, or sold them since they were weak and easily caught; they had to clean if they saw a mess.

"Syn," I replied after a moment of hesitation. She'd dressed me? She didn't look much older than a twelve year old and was as small as one. She had whitish, wispy blonde hair and giant blue eyes that took up more space than a Human's normally would.

Her eyes widened, so I clarified it for her. "My name is Syn," I continued as I opened the drawer to find my workout clothes folded neatly. "Thank you for folding them." It was all I could think of to say. She'd gone through my bags. That irked me, but knowing she had dressed me, instead of Ryder, was instant relief.

"You are very welcome," she smiled sweetly, before she turned and left the room just as quietly as she had shown up.

~~*~*~*~*~*~*~*~*

An hour later, after showering from the workout with Adam and Larissa, we were standing in the entranceway waiting for Ryder and his men who planned on following us out to meet up with Alden.

"So, I need to ask." I looked between Adam and Larissa seriously considering slapping them both—hard. "How serious is this between you guys?"

"Very," Adam said, with a serious look on his

absurdly beautiful face.

She smiled just as bright, and nodded at Adam shyly.

"How long?"

"How long what, Syn?" Larissa asked.

I rolled my eyes as I crossed my arms over my chest. "How long has it been going on?" *How long had they been together, and how the hell had I missed it? Some friend I was.*

"Syn—" Larissa stopped before the fourteen Fae walked in.

"Finish Larissa," I said, ignoring the intrusion.

"Six months," she growled angrily.

I had to force my jaw not to drop at the look of triumph in her eyes. How the hell could I have missed that? I felt a twinge of hurt. These were my best friends, and I had missed the fact that they were more than an item. They were an actual couple.

"Syn, after Adrian—"

"No, enough," I said quickly, needing silence. The Fae were not on a need-to-know basis with this information.

"Alden called. If you three are not too *busy* we need to head out," Ryder said, his voice dripping with sarcasm. "Plans have changed."

He was dressed in a white button down shirt and jeans today, as were the rest of his crew. I'd changed into a light blue long sleeve shirt with my favorite jeans and knee high boots with a comfortable three inch heel. Casual Friday wear.

"There's been another death," he said, already heading to the door.

"What?" I squeaked as my heart sank in my stomach.

"They found a dead Witch this morning. Need me to spell it out for you?" he continued as he opened the wide double doors.

"Who?" I asked, afraid of the answer. Only a few of the Witches lived outside of the Guild. And we knew and liked most of them.

"I didn't ask," he continued walking, making me run in the heels to try to keep up with him. "Zahruk, take the other two with you in the SUV; I'll take Syn with me."

We walked out to the yard silently as a group. I heard an engine purring to life from a garage I hadn't noticed that was connected off to the side of the house. A midnight blue SUV pulled out, and the driver opened up the door and got out.

"Follow," Ryder said as he strolled toward the garage. I followed until we were standing in front of a darker SUV. As I stepped around it, and placed my fingers on the door handle, I hesitated.

"Afraid, little itchy Witchy?" he purred from the other side, his hands resting on the hood, as if he was readying to jump over it.

"Should I be?" I retorted, raising my brow line. I should be. I could see it in his eyes.

"Very." His lips twisted up into a full on smirk.

I rolled my eyes and opened the door, pulling myself up into the seat. It still had the new car smell—the seats were leather and soft against the palm of my hand as I fastened my seatbelt and settled in.

The moment he got in, the nervous energy I felt around him came slamming home as he closed the door, sealing us inside the SUV together. "Why am I riding with you?" I asked, needing to know why he had me alone yet again.

"How did you walk through the ward last night?" He got straight to the point.

"No clue, but I'm not Fae, if that is what you're thinking," I snapped.

"There is no birth record of you being born. Nothing from before your parents brought you to the Guild. Marie pointed this out; said it was strange."

"Marie said I have no record of live birth?" I asked, making sure we were on the same page.

"Yes."

"Do I look dead to you?" I replied, in a voice that dripped sarcasm.

He turned his head in my direction as he grabbed the steering wheel. His eyes flowed over my body, making the air in the SUV crackle before he turned those golden eyes back on the driveway we were driving out of, in line with the other cars.

"Adam doesn't have one either. Larissa, on the other hand, does."

I wasn't an idiot. I'd known something was up

when I hadn't been able to get my papers from the Guild or Alden, but I'd figured it had been due to the violent deaths of my parents. "Adam was abandoned practically on the Guild's steps; my parents were killed. Ever think that it might have been an oversight on the Guild's part, due to the fact that we were orphans?"

He snorted as he pulled the vehicle onto the highway and gassed it, opening the engine as we drove back toward Spokane. "Who died?" I asked, trying to change the subject.

"There still should have been records, yet yours are sealed. Adam's were opened, but only said he was found outside the Guild—by the door to Alden's living quarters."

"Should have been. What does it matter, anyway?" I was getting angry.

"I like to know everything about those I work with. Surprises can get people killed," he replied coldly.

"So, ask me what you want to know," I snarled.

"How many lovers have you taken between your thighs?" he asked casually as if he hadn't just switched topics completely and asked me something deeply personal.

I realized it was a test, to see if I would tell him the truth. "One."

"Only one?" he asked, his eyes firmly on the road still.

"Sorry to disappoint," I mumbled, taking in the passing pine trees out the window as the countryside flew by us.

"How old are you?"

"Twenty-one," I answered.

"Twenty-one, and only one man?" He questioned.

I flinched inwardly. It wasn't from the lack of men on my roster. It was because I'd only loved one, and I didn't believe in simple sex. I'd loved Adrian with everything inside of me; everything I'd been. Until I'd gotten him killed.

"I didn't feel the need to fuck everything with a dick. So yes, only one."

"Everything with a dick? No wonder you gave in so easily to compulsion; you need to get laid."

"I don't *need* to get laid. I can do the job just as well by myself."

His eyes swung over, the heat of them drilling into my head until I gave in and turned to face him. His eyes glowed with intensity, so bright I had to blink to keep looking at him. "Indeed, but getting yourself off is not the same as allowing someone else the intense pleasure that comes with allowing a release. Nor does it scratch the itch that burns inside of you. It only scratches across the surface."

"Is there a point to this? I don't think my sex life—or lack of—is any of your business," I growled, fed up with talking about how lacking I was in the entire department.

"Did you love him?" he continued, ignoring my outburst.

I felt hot tears threaten to break loose at the touchy conversation. "Yes."

"Are you still in love with him?" he pressed.

"He's dead. Change the subject."

His eyes narrowed, but he turned back to watch the road. My mind scanned over the line of questions and then discarded them quickly. It was still painful, and saying his name made my heart ache. His beautiful face was still the first thing I saw before I closed my eyes—or had been until meeting Ryder.

"How long were you together?" he asked quietly.

"Too long. I don't like to talk about it, so ask me anything else. Just don't ask me to talk about him."

"What do you remember of your parents?"

"Not much," I swallowed a sob and closed my eyes against the pain that always came with talking about them. "Is this another test? Why can't you just leave them out of this?"

"There are no baby pictures of you, Synthia."

"Maybe I was an ugly baby?" I said, grinning.

"Or maybe you were not theirs."

I wanted to scream at him. They were my parents; they were all I remembered. I hated that he was making sense. And that I had never questioned it before. "Why would the Guild lie? It's not like I'm the most powerful Witch in the Washington Guild. It's not like they are trying to hide that I am a card carrying member either, Ryder. So, what would it matter if I was adopted?"

"I'm on a need-to-know basis, and you are the only witness to the murders of your parents."

I nodded, but knew I was about to shoot holes through his theory. "The Fairy was killed by at least one woman, and there wasn't a woman at the deaths of my parents. Nor were bombs placed inside them. It's not the same killers."

"You blame yourself for their deaths, why?"

I swallowed past the lump in my throat. "Because, I could have prevented it. I could have protected them."

"You were five. What the hell could you have done to stop Fae from killing them?" He snarled.

"I'm a shield, Ryder. I could use the ability when I was five. I was the only reason they couldn't cast; because they chose not to tap the line, because of *me*. My parents were powerful, but they needed the lines to cast and doing so could have hurt me. So, technically, they died protecting me."

I wasn't sure why I told him, or why I was indulging him with *any* information for that matter. I felt as if I wanted to, which wasn't like me at all. I didn't discuss my life with anyone, not even my friends who knew it already.

"That's what parents are supposed to do."

I glared at him. "Why the hell am I telling you this?"

"It's the binding of the contract," he said smoothly with a smile twisting his lips. "The contract makes you feel comfortable around me. Basically, I can ask you pretty much anything and you'd feel the need to talk about it." He smiled wickedly.

I felt the anger boiling up. "That's shit. How

do I get out of the contract?" I asked with a hint of anger making my voice shaky.

"You make me trust you enough that I no longer need it to control you," he said, before turning those amber eyes back on me with his smile still in place.

"So, basically, if I do everything you want, I can get out of it?" I asked, hoping it was that easy, but he was Fae and nothing would be that easy with him.

"You can openly become my property." His smile turned wolfishly handsome.

"Can you hold your breath while I think about it?" I smiled back, showing him my own pearly whites. "You don't even like me, so I'm not even sure why you would offer that."

He was about to say something else when his phone went off. He reached into his pocket and answered it, his eyes narrowing, which I noticed he did a lot around me.

I watched him swipe his finger over the screen and hold the phone up to his ear. "Z, are you sure? And you confirmed it was another Witch yourself?" He listened and then continued giving me a sideways look. "Sounds good. Stop by the warehouse and get the gear," he paused, listening again. "Yes, full armor this time. No, keep the reporters out of this. No, it's out in the middle of nowhere so it should be easy to secure." More silence ensued, before... "Yes. Okay, good. We're en route now."

He hung up his phone and turned to meet my eyes. "I hope you're ready for this—it'd not the same when it is one of your own."

Great, the bodies were piling up faster than we could stop them from happening. At this rate, we would have an entire army of dead women. "Oh shit. Necromancers?"

"Necromancers, what?" he asked, narrowing those brooding eyes again.

"What if they're building a Frankenstein? Part Fae, part Witch? Think about it. They can reanimate the dead, but what if they *built* the dead?"

"Why would they? What purpose would it serve?"

I winced. It didn't make sense. They could kill them and raise them for their powers. Something was off, though. Someone was collecting pieces of the dead. Like a puzzle that needed to be put back together. I tilted my head, considered what we knew and then exhaled slowly.

"None of this makes sense. The Guild needs to recall everyone and go on lock down until we can catch whoever is killing the weak links."

"You think it's that easy? We can't just recall the Fae. We have thousands living outside of Faery."

"You might have to," I argued. "I can't find a pattern, and neither can you. Which means Washington is a hunting ground for a serial killer who likes to cut people up and play with their insides before planting bombs that ruin the evidence. Feel free to chime in if you have a better idea, but until we can find a pattern, it means anyone left outside the walls of protection is fair game to this sick freak."

~~*~*~*~*~*~*~*~*

Chapter
FIFTEEN

Beacon Hill sat on the north side of Spokane. It was a lookout where couples came to make out. Friends would sneak up here and hang out, or do other things. Today, it was empty—minus the crime scene team Alden had beat us to.

The gray clouds loomed over us, as a grim reminder of what had happened here. Belinda hadn't been home when she'd been caught. She'd been jogging, if her workout clothes were anything to go off of. She was faceless, as if it had been peeled off, but, unlike the Fairy, she had her eyes, and no surgery had been performed.

The CSI team was looking green; one of them more than the others. His normally bronzed skin was pale, and he was holding his stomach at bay—barely. Rex was his name, and he was an earth Witch, who'd been unable to tap a leyline. He'd spent most of his time digesting science, before transferring over to the crime scene unit.

"Rex, breathe in through your mouth, out through your nose," I mumbled, trying to help him as I took in the body through the helmet Ryder had demanded I wear. "I'm taking this off. I can't see shit with it on."

"Leave it on. Just because we cannot see a bomb, doesn't mean there isn't one present, Synthia," he grumbled from beside me.

"She isn't cut like the Fairy was. I don't see anywhere a bomb could have been placed."

I looked closer. There was hair around the body in clumps. The smell around us was putrid, and, yet, something sickly sweet covered the body, as well. I closed my eyes and opened them with second sight, looking for the green aura trail that had been at the first crime scene.

"Red?" I asked aloud, to myself.

"It's not green like you said the other one was, and red is the color a newborn Vampire leaves in its wake. Is it crimson, or pinker?" Alden asked, coming up to place his hand on my shoulder gently.

"It's bright red, like the color of fresh arterial blood."

"See anything else while you have your headlights on?" he asked with a serious face on.

"My sight works as well as your own, Alden," I replied, already looking around for anything else that would help us find the bastard responsible. "No heel marks like last time; no bomb... She wasn't expecting anyone over for tea either," I said sarcastically.

"Tea?" he asked, scratching his head as his blue eyes narrowed in confusion.

"I forgot you weren't at the last one—we almost died. Bomb blew up with us standing inches away,"

I said, already growing tired of the subject.

"Syn," he replied softly.

"Yeah?"

"I'm glad you lived, and I'm glad you were there. Figured I should start with that. I'm glad you were there, but if you hadn't been, we'd have a larger body count right now."

I smiled sadly. The guy had a way with words. "Me too, Alden. Too many died before you decided to bring me in on this."

He nodded and looked around the scene, his eyes scanning everything slowly, compiling it all to memory as he'd taught me. He'd been an asshole to have as a teacher. Hard on every one of us, but it had been because he'd wanted us to be prepared.

"Alden, nothing here makes sense. This scene is off, compared to the others Larissa showed me. Everyone had something inside missing; an organ, tissue, and other severely disturbing shit. But this girl?" I tossed my hands up in the air. "She isn't missing anything outside. And other than—wait, her neck," I stepped closer, but it was too late.

I didn't have time to throw the shield, or react more than saying, "oh shit". The light that I'd seen in the body had turned from red to green, and then the scene exploded. Everything stopped—the sound, the movement. Impending doom.

Knowing that you're going to die can put everything around you in slow motion. I could hear the animals running, as if they too knew what was coming. The birds that had been flying over the scene had even stopped chirping. I had time to look for my coven, and see that they were a safe distance from the explosion. Further than I was.

Rex was over the body, his eyes scanning the body with fear as he heard the click of the bomb before he exploded with it. The heat touched my face through the suit, kissing my flesh as I was thrown back against something hard and unmoving, and then blackness took over my mind, replacing the fear.

I was on my back when my eyes flew open, warm liquid seeping from my nose and mouth. Someone was shouting over the ringing inside my ears. Someone was hovering over the top of me, a dim shadow without a face. Shouting. The helmet was removed, and everything grew louder.

"Syn!"

Others were screaming around me; some on the ground like I was. My eyes gained focus and Ryder's piercing stare was looking down at me as his mouth worked, his hands shaking me. I watched his eyes grow wide as more piercing screams were ripped from around us.

"My team," I whispered, over the dirt and grime in my mouth. The coppery taste of blood was thick as I tried swallowing past it to speak.

"Adam took a few pieces of shrapnel, but Larissa was shielded by his quick response," he replied, scanning the field for them.

I tried to nod, but the pain in my head wouldn't allow it. "Your team?"

His eyes widened as his lips turned up in the corner. "They're Fae," his eyes sparkled with amusement.

"Same team—today," I whimpered as pain erupted inside my head.

"Syn, stop talking; you're bleeding everywhere."

"Same team today," I argued, ignoring the pain.

"They are fine. *Immortal*, remember?"

"Injuries? Oh my God, Alden! He was right next to me!" I cried, knowing he hadn't been wearing a vest, or the head gear I had been sporting.

"He's on his way back to the Guild. They sifted him back to a healer."

I closed my eyes. Of course, they'd taken him back. He was acting supervisor and head of the Guild. They'd have taken him back to safety ASAP at the first sign of danger. He was too important for this shit—being in this type of danger—and, yet, he wasn't the type to stay hidden, as many of the other Guild leaders did. The fact that they risked sifting with him told me volumes. Humans did not react too well to sifting, according to our reports, so the Fae gladly avoided it with us.

"Where do you hurt, Synthia?" he mumbled when I didn't open my eyes soon enough.

"Everywhere," I chirped, feeling the stickiness of my own blood beneath the tight vest. He'd been right, and if he hadn't been so pigheaded and stubborn I'd be dead right now. Not that I would admit as much to him.

"Z, get our healer up here now. Gather our wounded and get them loaded up and back to the compound," Ryder barked out orders, his eyes never leaving mine, "Someone is sending us a message; a very loud message."

A message? "What?" I asked, still trying to speak past the blood pooling in my mouth. I needed off my back, but my limbs wouldn't move. "I need up."

"I don't think so. I can smell the blood inside the vest, Syn. I'm getting my healer here to seal the wound."

"Larissa can do it. I told you last night, I don't want Fae spelling me."

"I didn't say you had a choice, and Lari has agreed that she isn't as skilled as our healers."

Lari? He was calling Larissa by the nickname *I* had given her? I felt betrayed that she would have told him, or that he felt inclined to be able to call her that at all. I watched the clouds parting, the sun's light shining down on the scene.

My team stood off to the side, mixed with his, watching us closely. It wasn't something I liked, but if it hadn't been for Ryder and his men, we'd all be dead. I'd have let them in closer, because I'd have thought I'd be able to shield them, and it would have gotten us all dead. It was becoming a pattern.

I was in over my head on this one...the killer was just that—a sociopathic sadist who wanted to kill as many people as he could. We kept running to the scene, looking for clues, as he or she knew we would. But why? To kill the crime scene investigators, or to kill those of power who were now swarming in because of the notoriety that the killer was garnering for his kills?

"I think you're right...this was somebody sending us a message," I mumbled, more to myself than to Ryder. Rex had been the only fatality that

I could see—bits and pieces of him littered the cold ground. He alone wasn't high enough, by any standard, to warrant this much planning by the killer, though. No, it had to be either Ryder or Alden who had been meant to die here.

The question burning in my mind was who, and why? Nothing was making sense. There was only the pattern, which left the question of why the killer wasn't keeping to it. I needed to talk to Alden. We needed to put out a recall to everyone who had moved out of the Guild. If we could break the pattern, maybe we could control it.

~~*~*~*~*~*~*~*~*~*

It took less than thirty minutes before the Fae healer showed up to get me off my back. Thirty minutes of Ryder sitting beside me in the dirt. Watching me. Studying me. It had been the longest thirty minutes of my life. Not to mention, the healer had pulled up my shirt and exposed my black lace bra to Ryder, like a roast on a dinner menu.

We'd gone from the crime scene back to his mansion again, where he'd tried to force me to sleep. As if. I was wired for sound after the energy the healer had used to heal the two-inch wound in my side where the vest had left a gap large enough for the shrapnel to tear through my skin.

It had been mortifying to be exposed, and, yet, he'd been right again. Larissa couldn't help internal injuries, and I'd have needed to visit the hospital inside the Guild for treatment, which I didn't have time to do. Not with trying to catch a sadistic killer.

I watched as file after file was brought into the large oval office where both teams sat trying to comb through the evidence. This wasn't going to stop the next murder from occurring. We knew that if the killer kept to the pattern, it would be Fae. Ryder had sent out a call to his people, which might slow the killer down, but it wouldn't stop them. We were missing pieces—something that was covered up by the exploding crime scenes.

"I need to call Alden. We need to call back the Witches who moved out of the Guild," I complained for the fifth time.

"Alden already has—he called an hour ago to check and make sure you were still breathing," Adam said, coming over to where I was set up on a white sofa with a flannel blanket to keep my body temperature up.

I rubbed my temples and shook my head. "The aura today was red, which means undead—more likely a newborn Vampire, or a fledgling, five years or younger. The neck was torn and it could be a cover-up. The murders are on the front page of every tabloid and newspaper out there. This one feels wrong—like a set up."

Ryder nodded from where he stood with his back to the wall, his arms folded over his chest in a leisurely stance. "The bomb and pattern fits, though."

"Yeah, it does. But her throat was ripped out, which is common among the vamps that can't control the feeding urge. The bomb in the last victim made the headlines yesterday. So did the disfigurement of the face of the Fairy. This victim, however, had no missing parts. Just the skin on her face was missing."

"If you're right, that means the real killer has yet to make his move on a Witch to keep his pattern up," Adam said softly.

"Who is guarding Alden?" I asked.

"The Paladins," Larissa said, grinning.

The Paladins were knights that protected Guild leaders and others in the world of supernatural beings; an elite group who could wield magic and enchanted weapons. It's who you called when all hell broke loose, as it just had.

"Who called them in?" I inquired.

"Not sure, but the two Washington Guilds have called in Paladins now. Protocol, I guess. Alden said he was recalling; not who, though. It's likely they would only call back those who are without coven. It's not likely the killer would go after a full coven, since they are stronger together." Larissa finished off with a sad smile.

"It's going to take them too long to bring them all in, which means we will have a new crime scene soon," I winced as I moved my arm, causing my side to move, and the injury pinched from the movement from where it had yet to fully heal. Fae magic took time to work, as it healed from the inside out, sealing the internal organs first.

"You need to rest, Syn. We can go through these alone. You've almost been blown up twice now," Adam said as he sat down and allowed me to curl up against him. The glare Ryder gave us was worth it—his eyes narrowed as a possessive glow lit in his molten lava depths.

"I'm not sleeping while someone else dies, Adam. According to all these files, only Witches and Fae have been the targets. What if it's not just Fae and Witches, and the others are doing the same thing we do, which is keeping the problems of our own silent?"

Ryder pushed off the wall and walked toward us, pulling out a chair and flipping it around to face himself. He straddled the chair and set his hands on the back of it. "You think other groups are being victimized and not reporting it?" I asked.

"You think they could keep the newspapers from finding out better than we could?" he countered.

"Who do you report it to when dead bodies pile up?" I replied back, hiding the wince that threatened to show in my face, as I settled in more against Adam's chest.

"We don't report it, we handle our own," he said, with a deadly glare leveled right at me.

"Bingo, and no one from the Horde reports their deaths now that the Horde King decided to tuck his tail between his legs and go into hiding."

Everyone inside the room stopped and looked directly at me. Ryder's eyes glowed with anger as he narrowed them on me. "I can assure you that the Horde King is not tucking anything, or hiding. He's a busy man, and if I were you, little Witch— I'd watch that pretty pink tongue of yours while speaking of him."

I snorted. "He's been gone for years, and I'm pretty sure his caste is slinking around fucking shit up while he's gone. He's the King of the Unseelie, Ryder—one of the most powerful Fae in the universe—and, yet, not one flipping Fae knows where he went, or why for that matter. So, yes, he is missing right now. And while he's gone, his Horde is running around leaderless. So, who the hell do you think they're reporting it to while he is gone? No one. Instead, they're handling it by themselves. Hell, for all we know it could be him running around in lipstick, killing people!"

Thirteen males growled in unison. The sound alone was enough to make the hair on my neck stand up straight.

"You think the King of the Horde is out prancing around wearing lipstick, while he implants bombs inside body cavities?" Ryder asked with his sexy little smirk plastered on his full mouth.

I considered it, lifting my head off of Adam briefly before letting the air from my lungs on a soft sigh. "No, rumor says he can blow people up without bombs. He's one scary SOB. But my point is, his people are left without a leader while he's gone. They have no one to report to if they have any problems, and they're Unseelie, the Darkest Fae. They wouldn't ask for help, *ever*."

"That I can believe, but I wouldn't tell anyone else that you think the Horde King prances, or wears lipstick."

Somewhere, some place, someone was dying, and I could feel it. "We have to figure this out; comb through these and find out what is connecting these victims. A place they go, or, hell, I don't know, a dating site maybe?"

Ryder laughed, and the sound vibrated through me, making my body respond in ways it shouldn't have been able to after almost being blown up twice in two days. His face changed from hard lines to smooth, and almost playful. I wondered what he would look like if he was making love to me—

His eyes flashed with heat as the thought occurred inside my head, making me lose my train of thought, which was probably for the best. I needed to dig up more info on the details of the contract; ones that wouldn't be common knowledge via Google. I was beginning to think he could tell when my thoughts tilted toward the gutter—and I was damn good at shielding my mind from everyone—but him.

Yet, his eyes were damning, ancient ones, that if you looked too long in them you could get lost inside their dangerous depths and never find your way out again. I shivered in Adam's arms. It didn't go unnoticed by him, or Ryder, who awarded me a roguish grin.

"If you're cold, Syn, I can grab you another blanket," Adam said against my ear.

"If she's cold, I can take her to bed," Ryder injected smoothly, his smile still in place.

"I'm fine," I snapped too sharply, which caused Ryder to widen his grin to a radiant smile. I melted further against Adam, as if he could protect me from Ryder. It was futile. I don't think anything could save me from the Dark Prince now.

Chapter
SIXTEEN

We poured through the files for hours and found nothing. It was horrifying to find out that these murders had been happening for a little over a year. Alden had known about them and kept me out of the loop on purpose. Everyone was locking down, even Alden. Ryder was on the same page as the Paladins and wouldn't let us out of his house, in case we had made the hit list.

As if. I had a huge reputation for being damn good at killing those who needed it. I'd been great at puzzles—when they weren't missing most of their pieces, that is. This one had so many missing it was hard to tell which pieces fit and where they should be placed. I had grabbed several file folders and retreated to my room to look them over with as little distraction as possible—or one big distraction.

"Coming down to go swimming?" Larissa asked, with a bright smile on her strawberry red lips.

I looked up from the pile of folders and shook my head. "Too much work to do. Go have fun with your boy toy—which we still need to talk about, Larissa."

She dropped her smile as she folded her arms

across her white knitted bikini top. "You had Adrian, Syn. You loved him enough to chance hurting the coven. Why should you get to be the only person to be happy?"

I rolled my eyes. "Adrian is dead, so if you have a point to make, do it. I don't want to talk about him right now. Besides, you have no idea how much shit Adrian and I took from the Guild about our relationship."

"You got a chance to be happy with Adrian. We deserve to be happy too. Yes, this might be a huge mistake—I get that—but it's ours to make, Syn, and ours alone. If you could get over Adrian, maybe you could see that others pine over you. Hell, Rex was in love with you, and you didn't even know the poor guy existed! Get over Adrian already; we buried him in the cold ground years ago. You need to go dig up your heart, because I'm pretty fucking sure you buried it in that box with him." She spun around on her heels and left the room with quick, angry steps.

I exhaled deeply. Maybe she was right. Maybe I was the Ice Queen, frozen in time since the moment I fought to gain Adrian's soul and lost it, like I had my parents. He'd been everything. If I faltered, he'd held me up, but it was so much more than that.

Like Adam, he was one of the people I could run to when I had to get away from everything. He would hold me through the tears, even though he had been through hell too. He would sing to me, and he'd taught me to dance in the rain when I thought I couldn't even smile anymore. When we'd grown closer, and became teenagers, everything had changed.

We'd gone from friends to lovers at seventeen, and told each other how we'd get married and have beautiful babies, but I'd lost him to my pride— cockiness that seems to be part and parcel of practicing the Dark Arts, which we'd been introduced to by Alden since we'd been the top of our class. Everything had gone downhill from there.

Larissa was right. I was stuck living in the past. Carrying around the scars of things I couldn't fix. Couldn't overcome.

"She was harsh," Ryder said from the doorway that led to the connecting rooms.

I glared at him before staring back down at the piles of paper that were strewn unceremoniously over the red sheets of silk. "Ever heard of knocking?"

"Not when I own the room," he said, pushing off the frame to come further into the room. His long strides brought him easily to where I sat in gym shorts and a tank top that said "Try me" across the front of it. "They found another body."

My eyes locked with his. "Why are we talking, then? We should be looking for clues before it blows up."

"Not likely, Synthia. You have come close to death twice now in less than two days. I won't chance a third. We're going to go talk to the Vampires tomorrow night. See if they have had any unexplained murders, or if they have committed any and tried to cover it up."

"You have no sway over the Vampires, they could get seriously pissed if we go there asking questions."

"Not if we enter someone in one of the many contests they run over at *Nightshade;* it's a club that Vlad runs."

"Uh, Vlad—as in Vlad freaking Tepesh? As in freaking *Dracula* himself? Great idea; good luck with that." I wasn't an idiot. Vlad loved to bite, and I wasn't into it. I had also heard he was skilled in the art of killing anyone with a beating pulse—which I had.

"He won't kill you. Not if you leave the necklace on while you take everything else—off." His eyes slid down my body slowly, covering each inch with leisure. I could feel heat in every inch he took in as if his hands were caressing my skin instead of only his eyes.

"Stop looking at me like that!" I blurted before I could think better of it.

"Why? Does it make you uncomfortable, Synthia? Make you ache in certain places?" He smiled wickedly. "Good."

"You're looking at me like I'm a freaking Scooby Snack."

His lips twitched as he held in a laugh. I wanted to hear him laugh, and it shocked me more than it should have. Maybe a dunk in a cold pool wasn't such a bad idea after all, but then I'd be intruding in whatever the two love birds were indulging in.

"You buried your heart with your lover?" His habit of changing subjects rapidly was giving me whiplash today.

"Love is for idiots; it's just something people think they need." I griped, fed up with hearing about Adrian.

"Love is but souls meeting and connecting, *isn't* it? I wonder, Pet—did he touch your soul?"

"What the hell is that supposed to mean?" I snapped.

"It means, did he look in your blue eyes and touch you *inside*. Love is more than just feeling something, it's the connection of two souls that intertwine and cannot be without the other. It's not just saying you love someone—it's showing them with every fucking breath you take, every look. It just is, simple as that. That kind of love doesn't die. It withers the soul without the other to keep it alive. Eventually, it turns you bitter and cynical."

"You tell that to all the girls?" I snapped. His words made a lump form in my throat; I wanted that kind of love. But I'd be damned if I admitted it to him.

His teeth flashed as his smile faltered. "Destiny doesn't ask you if you want it, Syn; it just forces it into your lap, and you deal with it. In the meantime, you should find something to wear to impress Vladimir. He's into tight bodies and blondes with spunk. So naturally, you get to strip your clothes for the Undead King—unless you want me to send Larissa in?"

"You know this could go very wrong, in so many ways, Ryder."

He nodded his dark head before sitting in the chair and throwing his feet up on the bed, crossing them low at the ankles in a lazy pose as his hands covered over his lap. He was once again wearing a white long-sleeved shirt and casual jeans, which made him look almost Human if you could get past those devastating eyes.

I gave him a questioning look as he watched me. "Practice time—find something sexy and short."

"As *if*. I am *not* taking my clothes off in front of you!" I bellowed, coming up to my knees on the bed as I started to scoot backward off of it.

"So change in the bathroom—I need to approve of the outfit. You have yet to abide by any of the terms in the contract, besides sleeping where I want you. It's time to prove how willing you are to get out of this contract you hate so much."

I wanted to wipe that self-assured smirk off his lips...with my fist. Instead, I got up and stopped abruptly. "I don't own anything short, besides actual shorts, and I can only hold the full glamour for a few hours or so before it drains me too much—it's an illusion you can feel, but if I have to strip it'll be useless."

"Are you asking for money to buy clothes, Synthia?" he inquired, smiling still, amused by my outrage.

"Nope...we can leave the tags on it and return it when we're done," I smiled back. No way in hell was I owing him more than I could pay back with my measly paycheck.

He brought his laced fingers behind his head and awarded me with a wicked smirk. "You truly are the most infuriating woman on this planet."

"I'm sure I'm close. I don't need any handouts, and I will *not* leave here owing you a damn thing. I don't need to be kept, and I'm not some fucking plaything you can dress up and show off, Ryder. I'm a damn good enforcer—top of my class at the Guild. Show me someone who needs to die, and I will make it happen—I'll bury the fucker six feet deep and no one will know the why or who of it. But I am *not* arm candy!" I was shouting with my fist balled up on my hips when I finished.

"You won't owe me anything. The only way you will get inside the club will be if you impress the bouncers who know their lords taste in women. So, I will send Claire to get you a dress—size 5?" His eyes skimmed over me slowly, ravenously.

"Yes," I wondered how he knew what size I was from just looking at me, but then he'd probably dressed—and, more to the point, undressed thousands of females. And Claire who? Not that I would be asking him, since I wanted to scream right now.

"You will dance for me, so I know you can do it when it's time," he answered smoothly.

"No. Freaking. Way."

His lips twisted up, "Okay, then Larissa can do the job. She's to his taste as well, and she does not seem to argue as much as you do, Synthia."

I closed my eyes and counted to ten. I wouldn't let Larissa do this. She was too sweet to go into a nest of vipers like the vamps. She'd more than likely pass out at the first sight of Vlad. I opened my eyes to catch Ryder's sparkling with interest.

"When and where?"

"My room, now," he purred.

My body responded instantly. It disturbed me on so many different levels that I was getting mental whiplash from it. "I am not coming to your bedroom—not willingly. Ever."

"Is that so?" He moved silently as he stood up, towering over me. This man was carnal, his beauty mixed with a frightening twinge that left me boneless. "I could force you in there, or you can walk. The choice is yours. Decide now."

His eyes slid down to meet mine, challenging me,

daring me to say no. I opened my mouth to do just that, but the words I wanted to say didn't come out. Instead, I stood there with my mouth open as his eyes burned with his need to feed. "I'll dance for you, Ryder, but that doesn't mean I'm on the menu."

"You think someone like you could feed me, Synthia? I'm a Dark Prince of the Fae. I need more than some little itchy Witch with a big mouth for dinner."

Ouch! I wasn't sure why his words made my stomach hurt and plummet to my feet, but the fact that it did bothered me. "Good."

"Fifteen minutes—I want to see skin." His eyes slid to my shorts, as I bit my bottom lip waiting for him to say more. "I'll have Claire bring you something for now. If you can manage to impress me, I won't ask Larissa to go to Nightshade."

Claire came in a short time later, all leggy, beautiful, and impossibly Fae. Her long blond hair was the perfect shade of platinum, with milk chocolate eyes the perfect shade as well. She was incredibly beautiful and friendly.

She was overly excited about helping me dress, almost annoyingly so. I held my tongue and allowed her to give me any advice that would keep Larissa from having to do anything with Ryder, or Vlad Tepesh.

Chapter
SEVENTEEN

Ryder's room was in the lower level of the house, on the ground floor; larger than his room back at the Dark Fortress and more sadistic. He had chains hanging from the ceiling, and some sort of chair set up that I was pretty sure I didn't want to know what it was used for.

The bed was as big as the others I'd seen, easily fitting an all-out orgy party. Black silk sheets covered it invitingly, like a tractor beam to catch and hold you within its smooth clutches. I'm sure they were a distraction for what he did to the women who ended up in it.

I stood, barefoot and alone, inside his room. Claire had manifested a skirt that barely covered my ass, and the shirt was barely made with enough material to cover my breasts—she also suggested that it might be a good idea if I went braless in order to get more of a reaction from Ryder.

It was idiotic to do this—hell, it was suicide to make a Fae want you sexually, and, yet here I was in nothing but a hooker's outfit with no panties on! My head was telling me to get out, even as my hormones demanded I give in and make him want me—and oh so much more. I reached back for the doorknob, when I felt his eyes on my skin.

Electricity flickered over the surface, scorching my flesh. I turned, looking over my shoulder to take him in. His white button up shirt was undone completely, his smooth chest exposed to my greedy eyes. The top buttons of his jeans were undone as well, showing a thin line of dark hair that trailed low into his jeans.

"Leaving already?" he inquired, sauntering further into the room from the archway he had just entered from.

I bit my bottom lip, struggling for courage to see this through. "This is a bad idea."

His dark head tilted as he took in the slutty clothes and bare feet. I was shaking, and it had nothing to do with the cold, and everything to do with being half-naked, inside Ryder's private domain.

"Afraid you might like it, my little Witch?" His voice came out gravelly, as if he was feeling the same thing I was. Lust.

"No, I just have more of a sense of self-preservation than most women."

I blinked at how husky my voice had sounded.

"Is that so? You're shaking...cold?"

I could have lied.

I should have lied.

Should of, would of, could of.

"No," I whispered, dropping my eyes to the floor so they would unlock with his bronze stare. They locked on to his bare feet. It was intimate being in his bedroom, both of us missing our shoes. My hands trembled violently as I balled them into fists to keep them from being noticed.

"Bed or the chair, Pet. What's your poison?"

My nipples hardened at the word "bed" flowing from his lips. Bloody hell, I was lusting after my sworn enemy, and he knew it. "It doesn't matter—pick one."

"Bed it is," he flashed me a devastatingly wicked smile before his fingers snapped together; the iPod dock clicked on, and the music started playing. I followed his movement as he watched me with those animalistic eyes—not glowing yet, which was good.

I meant to start for the bed, but my feet wouldn't move. They were glued to the spot where I shook like a leaf with the reality of what I was about to do—with *him*. I could take men to their beds to murder them—yet, I couldn't walk toward one where I would pretend to be aroused enough to pull off a stupid job. This was ridiculous.

Why the hell had I let that stupid woman talk me into no panties? I wanted to turn around and run from the room—run from this place and never look back.

"I can still get Larissa to take your place, Synthia," he rumbled, forcing my eyes to swing to his.

I couldn't put Larissa and Adam through this. I'd told them what was going down when Adam had come up to see what was wrong with me. We had a strong bond; we could sense each other's distress, and when I'd explained it to him, he'd cursed, but agreed I was the better choice for what we had to do tomorrow.

I strengthened my spine and straightened my shoulders, telling myself I could do this. It was only another interview—right.   The last one had gotten someone killed! *Stop it you freaking wussy! Get it together. Now.*

"No Fae-fucking me, Ryder. Promise me that you won't."

His eyes lit up, but he shook his head.   "Not unless you piss me off, but I won't fuck you. I don't fuck unwilling Humans, Syn. I have thousands who actually want my dick.   I don't need an unwilling one." He settled on the bed with his back propped up—every inch the predator he was.

I swallowed past the thickness of my tongue. Nine Inch Nails was pounding from the stereo. The beat of *Closer* was erotic and perfect for what this was. A show.   "Good," I replied, forcing my feet to move, one after the other as I walked toward my impending doom.

When I was inches away from him, he held his hand out, and I flinched away, as if his skin would burn me.

"Relax. If you can't do this, how are you going to pretend to be my fiancé in front of Fae who will see you for the fake you are? They will see the tension and know you are not Fae instantly; we are a very sexual race, Syn. To pull this off, you are going to have to get over this aversion you have to me."

He was right, which failed to make me feel any better about what I was about to do with him. Even if it was only just another part of the show.

His hand came up and cupped my cheek softly, stroking my skin like a lover's touch.   My eyes flashed to his and locked on the amber glowing fully now within his molten depths. His free hand went to the small of my back, and he drew me closer, unhurriedly, allowing for me to escape if I needed to. My breath hitched in my lungs as thousands of different sensations ran wildly through me.

"Ryder," I sighed without meaning to.

"Stop thinking, Syn. You keep over thinking everything."

My lip trembled with the need to either kiss him or run. I settled on biting it softly while his hands held me in place. The one on the small of my back came around softly, pressing against the silk of the skirt as he rubbed his hand across my ass through the wispy material. He lifted my leg and placed it on the bed carefully.

I watched his nostrils flare as the glow became more apparent, and he allowed me to see the full fire that I'd created in him. "No panties?" he questioned through a guttural tone.

"Claire said it would guarantee you—I mean Vlad, chose me for the job," I murmured. My hand was instantly smoothing the skirt to assure myself it was still covering my core.

"Did she?" His voice was barely above a whisper, before he groaned, and released my face to rub his hand down his own.

"I can go change," I blurted, trying to remove the leg he still held in place.

"No, it's too late for that," he replied, rasping his words as he lay back on the bed, releasing my foot in the process. "Make me want you Syn."

I fought for strength as I watched his eyes search my face carefully. I exhaled a shaky breath and placed my hand on either side of his hips as I climbed onto the bed to sit on my knees above him. His hands came up and cupped my hips as he watched me straddle his hips.

I could smell him, the exquisite smell of male, rich and toxic to my hormones. His mouth turned up in the corners, his roguish smile back in place as he watched me through hooded eyes. One hand pulled away and he snapped his fingers, making the song restart.

I moved my hips slowly and sensually as his hand came back down to rest on it. This was just a job; another one. I could get through this. I brought my hands up, caressing my breasts, which got a curse from his lips, empowering my inner vixen.

He wanted a show? I'd give him one he wouldn't soon forget. I dropped down slowly, temping him with what he knew was bare beneath the skirt's flimsy material. My hands rose to my hair, removing the ponytail and letting it fall sensually down my back. I leaned over him, placing my hands on his shoulders, before bringing my face close to his.

His eyes never left mine. I heard his quick intake of breath as my lips lowered to a hairsbreadth from his own. My tongue snaked out to lick his full upper lip, slowly, eagerly. I dropped the last inch, rubbing against him, which was a mistake.

I was sex-starved, and he was sex incarnate. His hands released my hips, and one went to the back of my neck to hold me in place—as if the thought of escape had even crossed my mind since touching him—while the other cupped my ass and pushed me down on his full, hard erection.

His kiss was searching. His lips touched and found mine, gently at first and then demanding as we lost the fight, colliding together like two cars out of control in a head-on collision. One minute I was above him, and the next I was beneath him as he devoured my mouth hungrily, intensely, savagely.

Together we were explosive. I gave him back as much as he was giving me. The demand I felt in my body was complete and naked need. Intense and erotic. He ground his huge erection against my naked core until I could feel the storm building inside of me. I wanted him. I wanted him at this moment; it was unlike I had ever wanted anything else.

I called his name over and over as it built inside of me, until I thought I would break into a million pieces. His feral growl was low and harsh as he pushed me off of him and stood up, backing away. It was a reality check—his breathing was as labored as my own, the need inside of me winning over self-preservation. I fought to catch my breath, my chest heaving with both breasts exposed to him. My hands shook violently as I righted my clothes and fought to control the urge to reach down and finish the job myself.

One touch and I would explode; one touch and I'd come for him.

"If you do that to anyone, and I mean *anyone* else, Syn, I will lock you up inside this fucking room. That wasn't dancing, not by *any* fucking means." He paused, turning his full hungry Fae eyes in my direction.

I was angry—at myself, at him, at this entire situation. "You Fae-fucked me."

I was thrown back onto the bed before I knew he'd even moved. His hands caressed my body as his mouth crushed against mine, and every thought that had been inside my head was gone. I had one need, and it was to please him, to give him what he needed of me.

His cock pushed against his jeans, and I wanted it inside of me. I told him so, begged him to give it to me. Even as my mind screamed somewhere deep in the recesses, deep inside where I was still myself, to fight him off. My body refused to listen, and I instantly knew the difference.

The first time had been *me*—giving in to the hormones—but, this time—this time it was *him*. I felt the storm building again, violently and painfully. His body vibrated with his need, and the sensation was intoxicating. I cried out as I exploded, my body shaking, legs trembling, my eyes open but sightless as I watched a multitude of colors explode where his face had been.

"I could bury my cock inside of you right now, Pet. You'd allow it wouldn't you?" He growled.

"Yes," I whispered, knowing only one thing. I needed him, now.

"I could part this sweet pussy and bury myself inside of you, and you'd fucking take every inch I offered while begging for more. Wouldn't you, Pet?"

"Yes," I replied, pleading as I shook my head.

When I drifted back to earth, I cried out as my body shook from smaller orgasms still ripping through it. His eyes watched me intensely, angrily. "That's the difference between me mind-fucking you and your body needing release. I suggest you never forget the two, Syn, or I will *gladly* remind you of the difference."

I blinked at him, unable to make my lips work now that he'd released me from his spell. Angry tears exploded from my eyes, flowing down my cheeks. I turned away from him, forcing him to move his face from mine. He moved away completely, standing up and marching to the door, where he opened it and held it there with his eyes still hungrily on me.

I sat up, swallowing the sob that threatened to steal from my lips as I tried to make my legs work for a hasty retreat. I moved past him in quick, angry strides and continued down the hall until I heard his door slam closed.

My knees gave out the minute it did. On my hands and knees on the thickly carpeted floor, I sobbed. I had been so stupid. I'd just baited a fucking beast in his own domain, and then I'd lashed out at him because of my own traitorous body's reaction. I'd blamed him for my response that he brought out—the inner wanton that I'd starved since Adrian had died.

I was out of my league with Ryder, over my head in the deep end without going through swimming lessons first. I inhaled and exhaled before holding the wall to help myself up off the floor, and made my way back to my room through the maze of hallways that led to the top floor of the mansion.

Inside my room I'd cried, I'd berated myself for being stupid and then I'd go to find Ryder and apologize because *I* had been wrong. I'd blamed him, and I wasn't the type to not admit when I'd wrongly accused someone. And I had, as much as it sucked to admit it. I'd been mad at myself for reacting. I'd known the difference before he'd shown me.

When I reached my room, it was to find Larissa and Adam both waiting for me. Their eyes bugging out at the outfit I wore. "I think I got the job," I whispered, grabbing clothes from the dresser without looking either of them in the eye and headed for the oversized bathroom before either could figure out I had been crying.

Inside the bathroom, I clicked the lock into place and slid down the door only to jump as Adam pounded on the door I was leaning against.

"Syn, are you okay?" he shouted as if I couldn't hear him.

"I'm fine," I said, not bothering to raise my voice.

"Yeah? Then why is my bullshit meter going off?" he retorted angrily.

"Adam, I just need a few minutes." *And then what? Tell them what I'd just done? That I had just come all over Ryder's jeans like some FIZ slut?*

Larissa knocked next. "Syn, can I come in?"

"Seriously guys, I'm fine. I freaked out because he's Fae. We knew it was a possibility; it just happened. I just need a shower, and then can we go get some dinner?" I held my breath, hoping they'd take the not so subtle hint to get lost.

"Is it because of Adrian?" Larissa continued.

I didn't answer. I hadn't even thought about him while I'd been dry-humping Ryder. I'd loved Adrian with everything I had to give, so why had I been so easily tempted by Ryder with no thought to my first and only love when he was around?

I'd tried dating last year, but I'd compared the poor guy to Adrian in everything, which eventually made the guy break it off. No one deserved to have to listen to a person they were interested in discussing their dead ex-boyfriend. I was pathetic, which was why I'd sworn off dating and sex altogether.

I lifted my head, taking in the huge, rounded tub. It would easily fit as many people as a hot tub would. I had yet to use it, since I was more accustomed to showering since the Guild had open shower rooms; one for the boys and the other for the girls.

I pushed up off the floor, setting the clothes I'd brought in on the wooden vanity beside the sink. This bathroom was larger than my entire room in our crummy little apartment, but as crummy as my room was, it had become my home. I needed to get back to it, and back to being the self-assured person I normally was.

Here, I was at Ryder's mercy, and he knew it, which made him dangerous. It made me weak and reckless, not being in charge of my own destiny, or my coven's. The sooner I got done with this little charade he wanted me to do, the sooner I could get back to being myself.

Chapter
EIGHTEEN

Showered and redressed in my own clothes, I felt more reasonable. I headed out to find Ryder so I could apologize before I met up with Adam and Larissa for dinner. I found his Demon walking the halls, as if patrolling, and asked where I could find his master, to which he'd replied growling something about, "fucking Witches and fucking office."

Ryder's office was a mere four rooms from his bedroom, which meant I had to take the same walk of shame to apologize that I'd taken back to my own room in tears. It chapped my ass, but I needed to apologize. My coven's fate was currently in his hands, and right now, those hands were probably itching to be around my neck. I found the door that was labeled "Ryder's office" and opened the door.

And my jaw dropped to the floor. Ryder had Claire sitting on his desk as he pounded a massive erection into her. I gasped, but I couldn't look away from it, or what he was doing. I watched his body punishing hers, and found myself wanting to take her place, wanting to be the one he fucked. I couldn't look away from them.

My eyes locked to what they were doing and his

sleek masculine body as he fucked another woman. I grew wet with need and my mouth watered for his kiss. I shook my head as if it would wake me up, with no success.

She was whimpering and crying out as he drove himself inside of her over and over again. He wasn't saying anything—her noises were the only sounds inside the room. Those eyes of his glowed molten fire, which told me he was feeding from her as he hadn't done from me earlier. I bit my lip as heat flooded my core with the need to take her place. I'd left him starving when I'd left him inside his room. I'd seen it in his eyes.

"Either strip and join us or get the fuck out, little girl," he growled with his eyes now leveled on me.

I turned and ran as fast as I could away from him.

His wicked laughter taunted me, until I rounded a corner and collided with a very solid form. Zahruk's hands steadied me as he searched my horrified expression. "You left him starving, little Witch. He's Fae and he left, instead of feeding from you."

"I—I—uh."

He smiled coldly. "Do you know how many Fae could have walked away after smelling your need?" At my puzzled expression, he continued. "We have to feed. You might not like it, but it's life for us. And you smell in need of a good fucking, girl. We can all smell it on you. Too bad Ryder isn't willing to share his new pet. If you were mine, I'd share the fuck out of you and enjoy every scream you gave as we took you, filling you up until you could take no more."

I stared briefly before taking a big step back. What the hell did you say to something like that? "I'm not his pet," I swallowed and continued. "And I know what he is. I'm well aware of that. I only came to tell him I was sorry for accusing him of Fae-fucking me, when it was me who had reacted to him."

I watched his blue eyes shine with laughter, but there was more there in their depths. "You have suffered at the hands of the Fae, Synthia, and we understand that. But we were not there when your parents died. Ryder's a good man—he has thousands who he has to make hard choices for, and he's a damn fine man when it comes to making those choices. Most would have become power-hungry, but not him. I'd follow him into the depths of hell to guard him. Remember, little Witchling, if you push him, we will all push back."

I narrowed my eyes and folded my arms across my chest as I glared at him. "Is that a threat?"

"No, I don't make idle threats. I make promises that I always keep. He's trying to save an entire species from fading away to the pages of a history book. You? I think you're only interested in one thing—revenge, and that always plays out badly for everyone involved."

"I don't take unnecessary risk with my coven. *Ever.*" I felt the need to make sure he knew it.

His smile was sad as it spread over his full mouth, never touching his eyes, "If that were true, Synthia McKenna, you wouldn't be standing here right now. We *all* make bad choices occasionally."

I blanched at his words and watched as he turned and walked away in the direction where Claire's ecstatic cries were still coming from down the hall. I turned and fled, needing to get out of there. Once again I'd been enthralled by Ryder, and, this time, it had been while he fucked someone on his desk! I needed a cold reminder of what I was, and why I did what I did. And fast.

I stole keys from the entryway before peeking through the window to outside. I quietly opened the door and snuck out of the house, sneaking through the door that led into the garage, before pressing the unlock button to see which car beeped. I growled when three made the same annoying loud beep. Stealthily, I slipped into the first one.

I sat in a midnight blue Lamborghini, and smiled like a naughty child with her hand in the cookie jar. Oh. Hell. Yes! I hit the button on the keychain to open the garage as I turned it on and pulled out onto the long driveway. I winced when I saw the closed gates, but as I approached them slowly, they slid open.

I let out a slow shaky breath and passed through, waving to the guard like I was supposed to be in Ryder's quarter-million dollar car, and smiled like an idiot. I didn't relax until I hit the highway, and then I opened the car's engine and allowed it to purr to life.

My mind went back to Ryder inside his office. I'd considered his option—way too much. I'd almost taken the step that would have told him yes. I'd seen his hunger shining in his eyes, and I'd wanted to fix it. Of course, I told myself it had been because I'd been the one to enrage his appetite and leave him hanging.

I was lying to myself.

I was getting pretty damn good at making excuses for why I did stupid shit around him. I wondered if they would notice the car's absence, since it was unlikely they would notice mine at all. Ryder was partial to his cars, and it showed in the way he drove them. The way his hands caressed the leather—oh hell!

I switched on the radio and flinched as Nine Inch Nails roared to life from the speakers mounted in the doors. I clicked it back off and rolled my eyes at how pathetic I was acting. *Synthia McKenna, Fae killer extraordinaire, is giddy over the Dark Prince*. I could imagine it on the headlines of the Guild's paper already.

I pulled up to the Oak Ridge Cemetery gates and nodded at the gatekeeper, before slowly making my way to the unmarked grave in the back close to the tree lines. It was one of the oldest cemeteries in the state. It was also the only one with no names on any of the graves—just numbers.

It was a way to keep track of the dead without giving out their family names or place others on the Human's radar. Even though we're technically Human, we didn't really fit in with them or the Otherworlders. We just continued to protect them, even though they didn't accept us any more than they did the Otherworlders, who couldn't pay them enough to be accepted. Money made the Human world spin. Always had, and would continue to do so, until someone decided they weren't worth keeping around any longer.

I parked in the back and exited the car, grabbing for my purse before heading to where Adrian was buried. I'd bought his plot, since he didn't have family to do so. It was the least I could do, since it had been my ego that had gotten him put in the ground to begin with. There had been nothing to bury but a few pints of blood and some hair.

No soul lay inside this cold ground to be reborn. I had to live knowing it. Knowing that I'd failed to save him. They said the dying had it easy, that being reborn was easy and peaceful. What about the living who had to remember it? Had to carry the burden of knowing they'd failed, living with the memories of the dead? I think we have it worse off, since we don't forget.

I cleared the grave of the pine needles the wind had shed on his resting place. I pulled out the iPod from my purse and stuck in the ear buds, feeling the call of the dead tingling on my skin. None of my dead were buried here; they hadn't been that lucky.

I would release Chandra. Give her peace until she was reborn. I didn't have my coven to help as her witnesses, but I had a graveyard full of dead souls who had yet to pass onto the Ever-after, stuck here for some reason or another and unwilling to pass on.

Good thing I was one of the few who could raise souls. I'd raised this entire cemetery by accident soon after Adrian had been buried here. It had been just another botched attempt to release the souls of my parents. I wasn't even sure I could release them. After all, I'd messed up at taking them in, but I'd only been five.

Most Witches couldn't master taking a soul until their late sixties, and it was risky to do so at any age. I sat with my back to his grave marker. "I miss you."

I waited, as if he would answer me back.

I exhaled, trying to find something else to say, anything.

"I'm the world's biggest slut now—almost gave in to a Fae. Go ahead, roll over in there, A. Lord knows my parents would be right now." I smirked, finding irony in the fact that I was confiding in a concrete slab with numbers on it. "I miss you," I repeated. "Larissa and Adam are totally bumping uglies, by the way. Cue more eye-rolling—I know you would be if you were here. I told you he liked her," I smiled, imagining the wide grin he used to give me when he found out I had been right about something. "Okay, let's do this."

I stood, feeling eyes watching me. I scanned the area, finding nothing out of place in the thick greenery on the edges of the cemetery. I pulled the small blade from my purse before pulling out the ear buds to listen for a second longer.

The wind howled, but, other than the Witch posted at the gates, I felt no one close enough to be considered a threat. I whispered the words for the candles to be lit, feeling the surge that came before the flames leapt to life in the candelabras that had been scattered throughout the graveyard.

The feeling of power running through my veins was heady after being useless for two days in a row. Throwing a shield didn't give off the same kind of thrill casting did, and nothing gave the feel of raising the dead, even if it was only souls that I was actually raising here.

I took the headphones off and placed the iPod on dead shuffle, which I'd made for doing this, since the dead loved to dance. Most would consider it odd, but not me. Since they couldn't talk, it was about all they could do and not look like zombies. Okay, well some still looked like zombies.

12 Stones *Let Go* blared to life over the iPod's small speaker. I whispered the words for the releasing of the soul I held, hopeful she would leave my body without a fight when I released the blood.

No such luck. Chandra was still pissy about ending up among the dead, which I could understand.

I whispered the words for the dead to rise, watching as hundreds of spirits rose from their graves. My eyes flickered to Adrian's empty grave with sorrow.

Mrs. Gracie, who had been dead from the early 1800's, wafted over, her feet never touching the ground as she watched me. She had taken some time to get used to. She wore an old-fashioned school-teacher dress in black and white, which made her wide blue eyes seem out of character, since it was the only thing left in color on her.

"Good to see you, Mrs. Gracie. You should seriously think about crossing over, because if you don't, I'm going to have to change your name to Mrs. Gray." I watched her shake her white curls—they had been blonde three years ago—violently, before she put her nose up in the air and headed to a far off spot to sit and watch me.

Next came the kid, which I couldn't find any information for off his numbers alone, nor did Alden have any knowledge of who the small boy might be. I called him Billy Goat Gruff, which he didn't seem to mind at all. Or maybe he did, but it wasn't as if he could tell me. Whoever he was, he needed new clothes, but I wasn't about to dig him up and redress him.

"Pick your poison, Billy," I smiled and nodded at the iPod.

I said the words to enchant the iPod as he tried to push his not so corporal finger through it. The kid had taste at least, but of course there weren't many songs I had on my iPod that I didn't like. Linkin Park's song *Iridescent* echoed through the normally quiet cemetery.

I smiled and watched him thump his foot on the

grass floor of the cemetery. I watched as the spirits started doing the same, waiting for a constant beat to dance to. They wouldn't be finding one inside of this song, but Billy wouldn't let them down with the next one.

I sliced through the flesh in my hand and whispered the binding words backward to release Chandra. I felt the anger, the taste of betrayal she felt at being killed. When she did come through, it was a brilliant green flurry of lights, and then her soul exploded; sending sparks everywhere as her soul shattered into a thousand different pieces.

"What the hell?" I asked the ghosts, who all ignored me as if someone hadn't just exploded into tiny pieces of ectoplasm. I closed my eyes and shook my head before opening them as the song ended and everyone stopped and turned to Billy.

He stopped, turning his small angelic face toward the bushes. I turned, looking in the direction, but still couldn't see anything. I turned and tilted my head, waiting to see what he did next. His fingers started crossing his skin, and I realized he was telling me as best as he could to put up protection.

"Well shit on fiddle sticks, Billy," I mumbled, before cutting my hand deeper to get enough blood to draw the Celtic cross on my cheek.

When that was done, I drew the power around me, and watched my arms as the Italic written words *Never Forget* and *Always Remember* lit up on my forearms; as every other white ink tattoo I had lit up until it reached my eyes. I lifted my face and watched Billy smile wide.

I stood out like a sore thumb like this. Most Witches wore their branding under glamour. Adam,

Adrian and I had been the only ones to receive our brands in white ink that were invisible to the naked eye. If we stood under a backlight, we'd be screwed.

I watched, picking up everything around the thick bushes. Someone was there, standing just outside the cemetery watching me. Unless they were of mortal blood or could withstand the wards, they wouldn't be coming in. I turned, listening as Billy messed around with the iPod, finding his next song of choice.

I was surprised when he turned on Gun's and Roses *Don't Cry*. I winced. The dead loved to dance, and this wasn't one they could dance to. What surprised me more was when they got into couples and actually danced together, except Mrs. Gracie and Billy.

Billy floated over to me, his eyes taking in my glowing brands. Everything was off-kilter tonight. Maybe I was affecting them with my own dysfunctional issues? I felt the ice of Billy's touch as he traced my arms, and then indicated with those same icy hands for me to flip my arms around for him to continue.

His touch, like all the dead, was an icy reminder that they were no longer alive to us. His young chocolate brown eyes lifted to meet mine when he was done tracing the word Remember. He poked it a few times, before he turned his head to the outskirts again and then he disappeared without his usual flourish.

I looked over the now empty cemetery and stifled the shiver that ran down my spine. *November Rain* came on next as a figure walked over the graves, coming in my direction. I held my brands up, watching and waiting.

Ryder came into view a few feet away from me as Z came up the middle of the cemetery, keeping a safe distance from me. I watched the awe in Ryder's eyes. Not many knew we could do this—light up like a freaking white Christmas tree.

He just stood there looking them over, much as Billy and Mrs. Gracie did. I could see the darkness surrounding him in this view. It was much better than second sight. I could see though and surprisingly, besides the darkness I knew would be there, he had a pure soul.

"You glow in the dark, Synthia," he said softly, as if he was afraid he would wake the dead.

I didn't reply. He wouldn't understand me if I did, anyway, since I'd taken the powers I was using from the dead. Which meant it would come out in different languages; maybe even some Latin.

He watched me as I turned my eyes to the grave in front of me and swallowed, trying to calm the power inside of me, to dump it where I had borrowed it from. I felt his eyes taking in every spell that was visible on my arms; I'd left in a tank top and jeans with sandals since I'd dressed in a hurry.

I felt power slinking away slowly as my mind grasped onto the part where he and his men were inside sanctioned and spelled grounds. "Grounds, not for you they be." I winced as my words came out sounding as Yoda.

His lips twisted up into a wicked grin. "Be that as it may, I told the guard you were mine. You stole my car."

"Borrowed it I did, return it I will."

Oh bloody fucking hell.

"Okay, Yoda, can I have the woman whose body

you stole, back?"

"My body it is, yours I am not. Dead I speak, until drained I am," I smiled, unable to help myself. The expression on his beautiful face was priceless.

"You speak the language of the dead?"

I smiled, knowing he wouldn't be able to make sense of it. Billy chose that moment to poke his head up from the ground and wink at me. "Billy, you knew they were here?" I said to him, but Ryder wouldn't hear it as such, he'd hear some weird Yoda version.

I watched the child bob his head happily, before he went to the ground again. I raised my eyes in time to catch Ryder staring at the ground in which Billy had been in. "See the dead you do."

"You can raise the dead." Not a question… statement, it was. I shook my head and refocused. I'd started thinking in Yoda form now, too, and I wanted to laugh at myself for it.

I nodded carefully, watching his face register the news.

"But you cannot raise your parents, or your boyfriend," he continued.

I shook my head from side to side, ignoring the pain those words always brought with them. The light around us started to dim as the power diminished back to where it had come from, slowly. Ryder narrowed his eyes, as if he was considering the implications of what I had done tonight.

"What are you?" he asked carefully, his eyes sizing me up.

I narrowed my eyes at him and pointed to my

brands. He nodded his head, right before he scratched it, while his features turned questioning. The music changed before he could ask any more questions.

I watched him and Z both jump, as if they were under attack, but I knew it was only the ghosts getting in one last dance. They liked to scare anyone who came in on our time together. Not that I was anything special.

I laughed as Billy blasted House of Pain's *Jump Around,* and did just that, along with the rest of the ghosts, before my power drained. My head bobbed with him as a smile lifted across my lips. This was my favorite part of coming here.

Ryder and Zahruk both looked at me like I was nuts as I danced with the ghost, at Billy's insistence. Dancing with the dead—boy, they would think I was completely nuts now. I shouted over the music to Billy, who would tell the rest. "Next time, dance sooner! Powers fading. I should be back in a few weeks."

I turned to Ryder, who wasn't watching my face as I jumped around in place. His eyes were locked on my boobs, which were bouncing, even in the confines of the bra I wore. Billy saw it too, kid was crazy—or, well, he was dead, so it wasn't like he could be killed again. His finger was pointing at Ryder and me, while he continued to jump up and down.

Zahruk was trying to count the dead jumping around, instead of watching bouncing boobs. I knew the instant he figured out there were thousands of them. More ghosts than headstones stood inside the cemetery, and I'd brought most of them here. His eyes flew to mine and locked, even as I still jumped with Billy.

"Necromancer," he growled in warning.

I shook my head slowly, carefully. I wasn't a necro, but I could manipulate the dead like one. It was just something I could do since I'd taken on dark arts. As the song died off, I turned to look at it from their eyes. I had a cemetery of dead, dancing to some one-hit-wonder from the nineties. They all jumped in perfect unison, even though their feet never touched the ground.

"You need to explain how the hell you can raise that many spirits," Ryder growled.

I ignored him, placing my hands palm up to watch the branded words fade away. His eyes searched the words intently. As they faded away to nothing once more, I lifted my head, searching for the knife and grabbing my iPod, before watching the flowers bloom on Adrian's grave as they always did, thanks to the dead surrounding the soil.

It was the deal I had with the ghosts. I dance and bring the tunes, and they grow the flowers once a month on Adrian's grave. I flattened my palm on the headstone. "Always remember, Adrian." I looked to where the car was parked and started forward, not bothering to look and see if the Fae followed.

"You can raise the dead, how?" Ryder persisted.

"Dark Arts," I mumbled as he caught up to me.

"No mortal can do that massive scale of magic on the dead. So, how the fuck did you?" He shouted, grabbing my shoulder to spin me around.

"That's a lie, and just because you think it shouldn't be done, doesn't make it wrong," I shouted right back with my hands on my hips.

I turned back toward the car, but he stopped me again.

"Yet you haven't tried to raise any of the dead the serial killer is taking out?" he continued with his voice still raised.

"This is a cemetery, stop shouting!" I growled right back.

"Yes it is, but I just watched you bust a move with the entire blasted place. I don't think they are resting peacefully."

I smiled at his term for what he had seen. Busting a move? We'd been jumping, since it was the best the dead could do, unless you considered their botched up attempt at couples dancing. He'd seen me lit up with the brands and hadn't made any glow in the dark comments. He hadn't said anything else—which meant he'd seen it before, but how?

"Get in the car. Vlad might be leaving town soon. We need to go in by tomorrow night to ensure we see him."

I watched his eyes narrow on my face, and tossed Zahruk the keys that I held in my hand. He caught them and nodded, before heading to the sleek blue sports car.

"What?" I blurted, when he just continued to look at me with his tense amber gaze.

"In the office," he started.

"Stop! I was coming to say I was sorry. I—I shit… Okay here it is, Ryder, I don't trust the Fae. Never have; probably never will. It was my fault today, and I'll admit to that, and, yes, I should probably get laid before I have enough hormones to sell them at auction. I was wrong to blame you, and that was why I was coming back to your office."

"You wanted me," he said precisely, slowly making me tingle from the huskiness in his timbre.

"It was a mistake, and, besides, I'm a lesser being, so the point is moot. I won't put myself in that position again."

He smiled wickedly. "What—grinding on my cock, Syn? Or watching me feed?"

I swallowed past the lump forming in my throat. It was going to get stuck in there if I kept hanging around him. "Both."

"I could make you." He licked his bottom lip seductively. "Maybe then, you would loosen up some."

I held up my middle finger, and opened the passenger door, before sliding into the seat and allowing the last bit of the power to leave my body as the night's events sank in. Tomorrow night, I was going to meet Dracula in the flesh.

~~*~*~*~*~*~*~*~*

Chapter
NINETEEN

"Tell me the plan again," Ryder growled, still upset that I hadn't been able to explain how I could raise the spirits of the dead last night. But then, it wasn't as if he was on a need- to-know-everything-about-me basis.

"I go in on your arm, and we separate. I'm to make myself look unavailable since Vlad likes what he can't have. I play dumb blonde and make myself sexy." I glared as Adam barked with laughter at my words.

"No going off of the plan. When he takes you in the back room—and he will—you work the information out of him without blowing your cover, or *him*."

I shot a glare to Ryder. "I have no intention of bobbing on Vlad's knob. Or yours," I tossed in to remove the wide smirk my response had given him, and it worked.

"No surprises in there. If you get in trouble this ends. Do you understand me?"

"Yes, *master*," I grumbled, and then winced at the heat that flashed to life in his eyes.

"Mmm, I like that word on your lips."

"Whatever…let's get this done. I need sleep."

Adam and Larissa spoke into the mics they wore, testing them before I left the bus with Ryder. I fidgeted with the short black lace-up vinyl skirt that matched the lace-up top of the same tight material. I seriously looked like a hooker with matching shining black heels that were well over six inches high.

"Stop fidgeting. You look fine," Ryder whispered as he slid his hand down my naked back.

"I look like a cheap hooker," I grumbled to distract myself from the feeling of his hand on my skin. I had more make-up on tonight than I had worn in my entire life. He stopped me by moving his hand further down my back until it rested on my backside. My breath hitched with the fire his hands were igniting inside of me.

"You need to get over this reaction you have to me."

I snorted. I wish it was that easy. "Try *not touching* me."

His golden eyes slid down the thin silk shirt to where my nipples pointed up with need. I chewed my lip, but stopped when I tasted the bitterness of the lipstick. "Work on it, or I will see if I can replace you with Larissa for the Gala. I cannot have my soon-to-be-bride shying away from my touch."

"Lari can't use glamour the same way I can."

"She could, if I helped her—" He let the words hang in the air between us before continuing. "Arianna cannot die. Especially not while under my protection. It would create an unbalance that this world might not recover from. Do you get what I am saying?" he growled fiercely.

"Got it," I growled right back.

The bouncers at the wide doors separated as Ryder held up some kind of badge. Both gave him a respectful look and nod, and allowed us entrance, much to the groans of the long line of Humans that waited for a chance to get inside Nightshade.

Inside was exactly what you would think a Vampire club would look like. Red velvet seats covered a long wall, while bottles, partially filled with water dyed red, lined the walls. A throne chair sat on a stage where a band was currently playing and doing their best to avoid the chair.

"How cliché."

Ryder turned around and looked down at me sharply in warning. "Showtime, Synthia. Kiss me."

My mouth went dry. All the fluid inside my body went shooting straight to my vagina. I licked my lips nervously. "Seriously? That is like the opposite of what I just said outside."

"Prove you can do this—now." His eyes searched my face, and with the single look I melted for him. I was pathetic. A pile of fucking mush from one single look!

I reached up, running my fingers through his hair, even as they shook from what I was doing. I was doing exactly what I'd said I wouldn't do, just last night inside the cemetery. I had to do this. It was a job. I kept saying it like a mantra inside my head.

His eyes remained locked with mine until our lips met softly. His felt of the finest silk, and, yet, I'd sampled their need last night and it had literally made my toes curl. He wasn't making it easy on me. He didn't deepen the kiss, so I did, pushing my tongue past his lips in search of his.

When I found it, he growled low in his chest and held the small of my back as he caressed my tongue gently with his own, matching the tempo perfectly. The room around us faded away, and the only thing left inside of it was us and this kiss. He pressed me against his body, and I didn't fight him. Instead, I melted against his much larger frame and moaned my need into his mouth.

When he pulled away, I was left breathless, and my body hummed with unshackled need. By his playful smile, he knew the effect he had upon my hormones. I so needed to get laid—but not here. And *not* with him.

"The usual table?" A female vamp dressed in a dark sapphire blue evening gown asked.

"Yes, Eve, please," Ryder purred as his eyes slid over her ample bosom.

I felt a slight twinge of regret in my chest, but pushed it away. He was getting married for fuck's sake, and here I was getting territorial. And, like that wasn't bad enough, he was Fae! I liked having my soul intact, even if it was immersed in darkness from practicing the Dark Arts.

"Will your companion be joining you, or is she unmarked?" she continued eye-fucking Ryder right in front of me, as if I wasn't even there.

"I'm not—"

"She is not fully marked, *yet*. I'd like to see how she does on her own tonight," Ryder interjected, stopping my next words before I could tell her I wasn't his damn anything.

I smiled coldly at Ryder, who ignored me completely.

"Shall I find someone with more attributes for your meal, or do you prefer to hunt for your own?" She said, looking me over and finding me lacking.

I almost growled, but decided it was time to split before I cursed her with some magical STD for shits and giggles. "Copy," I whispered testing the frequency for my team that was still outside monitoring us. I almost groaned when I realized they'd heard me kiss Ryder.

I approached the narrow bar and looked at the red liquid inside the bottles. Freaking Vampires. Rumor had it that they were a "made" branch of the Horde. No one knew how it happened—we had heard that it started with some Fae creating these beings that started out life as Humans, so they had much of the beauty, magic, and deadliness of the Fae, but, unlike the other castes of the Fae, they fed from blood, while other Fae fed off essence and emotions. It was getting obvious to me, after the vamp-signs at the last crime scene, that the Horde needed to find their king. He was the only one who could possibly keep his people in check.

"Pick your poison, baby girl," a deep voice said from the other side of the bar.

"Gin and tonic, please," I replied back, before remembering I didn't have a wallet or my purse on me. "Crap, never mind," I said shaking my head.

"It's on the house. First time in here?" the bartender said, friendly enough.

I turned, taking in his dark features—his black hair was multicolored in the lights from the dance floor, his eyes a beautiful silver color that marked him Fae in origins. He had well-defined features, which made him both beautiful and deadly.

I smiled. "Is it that obvious?"

He smiled wide, showing off a set of wicked looking fangs. "I always remember a pretty face."

"I bet," I mumbled, turning to take in the club's clientele, "They just come in and offer you their throats."

"Some do; others come in to see what we offer. Some come in and beg to be turned."

"They have no sense of self-preservation. The fact that this is a Vampire club should get them all an *idiot of the year award*."

"And here you sit, inside the undead and unfed section."

"I didn't come here to be a snack," I replied smoothly.

His silver eyes sparkled. "No, you came in with the Dark Prince...not fully marked, but undecided if you want to be his?" He reached over the bar and grabbed the necklace I still wore, pulling me forward. "Try a Vampire." He licked his left fang and tilted his dark head to the side. "Before you commit yourself, that is. I promise you won't be sorry."

I reached up and removed his ice cold hand from the necklace Ryder insisted I keep on. It was more than his mark; it was a name tag. His. I allowed my eyes to slide down the Vampire, who wore the club's logo on a plain black T-shirt and vinyl pants that hugged his waist seductively.

He wasn't as big as Ryder, but I could see the well-defined body beneath his clothes. I watched as he turned around and started flipping bottles with a shocking speed that my eyes could barely register. I had to refrain from switching on my second sight to be able to keep up with his speed.

When the glass was full, I smiled and accepted it with a thank you and took a drink to help calm my nerves. "So, the real Dracula runs this place?" I asked, trying to pull information from him.

I felt bad using his kindness against him, but we needed to know if what had been happening to us was also happening to them. His smile faltered as he looked over my shoulder briefly.

"So, you want to sneak a peek at Dracula? What's so fascinating about him? Or are you looking for the whole tortured soul thing?"

"Tortured souls are over rated. Just curiosity, I guess."

He smiled and winked. "You know what they say about curiosity right?"

I gave him a full smile before replying. "Do I look like a pussy—cat?" I winked back at him while he laughed outright.

He placed both his palms on the counter and grinned impishly. "If you were a—cat, I'd chase your tail through any dark alley." His fangs grew as his eyes swirled. I blinked, and his face was back to normal.

"Cool trick," I whispered, before taking another drink from the glass in front of me.

"I got a few more." He wiggled his eyebrows and moved to refill another woman's glass. I spun in the chair to look at where Ryder had been, but his table was empty and the bar wench was missing as well.

"He's in a booth," the bartender said when he came back.

"Figures," I grumbled and turned back around.

"So, you never told me your name," he said.

"You never asked," I replied, enjoying the comforting burn of the alcohol as it warmed my skin.

"I'm asking," he continued, his smile still in place.

"Synthia."

"Pretty name, for a pretty girl," he said, offering up his hand for me to shake.

"And yours is?" I asked, holding up my hands to take his.

"Dracula."

I blinked slowly. "Seriously?"

"Oh, I get it…you think because I'm a legend that I should be all blah, blah I vhant to suck your blood?"

I chuckled unable to help myself. "Something like that."

"You should smile more often, Synthia. You could take anyone in this place home."

"Is that so?" I flushed from the compliment.

"I'd take you home," he said as he leaned in closer to my face.

I swallowed and gave him a small smirk as he refilled my drink again. "If I didn't know any better, I'd think you were trying to get me drunk and take advantage of me."

"You'd be right about the first part. The second one," he sighed dramatically. "I don't relish my death at Ryder's hands."

"You think a prince could take you out?" I inquired, needing the information. I knew Ryder was deadly, but I hadn't found very much on him while researching him. It was like he'd popped up on the Fae-Human radar somewhere around sixteen years ago.

It was common for Fae to disappear and then resurface years later, but he had no backdrop story. Nothing I could use to get out of the contract, or use against him.

"He's a very powerful man, and not one I plan on pissing off," he replied carefully, as if he knew why I was asking him. "Show's about to start, and your man just walked back in."

I snorted and finished the second drink, setting the glass back onto the smooth counter before replying. "He is not my man."

I stood up, wondering how to bring up the subject of the killer without making Vlad back off and become suspicious of me. When I turned around to speak, he was gone, and in his place was a buxom blonde, who also had wicked fangs showing.

I looked around the room, but didn't see any sign of Vlad. Shit! Ryder was walking toward me, scanning the area around me, so I decided to meet him halfway. The moment I stood up and started walking, the club went dark.

I stopped. Sending out feelers, knowing the minute I used my high beams to see around me, this adventure would be over, and I'd be outed, due to glowing in the dark. I held still, listening to everything around me. I could make out the Humans from the vamps by the sound of their breathing as if they anticipated being in the dark with the Vampires—freaking idiots.

The Vampires made no sounds at all. I moved my eyes to where Ryder had been walking toward me, but the moving, glowing white brands made me gasp in surprise as Adam walked toward me slowly. Why was he out of the bus? He should be there protecting Larissa from the shit load of Fae shoved inside it.

When he was inches away from where I stood, the lights came back to life, and everything inside of me froze. My heart stopped beating. The air in my lungs froze on a whimper. My bottom lip trembled as hot tears shot to my eyes with disbelief.

Turquoise eyes so strikingly bluish green watched me as his brands glowed, even with the lights of the club back up and running. My hands itched to run over his chest, but I knew this wasn't real. This was a trick. It couldn't be real. I watched his features come into view. He was so beautiful; so alive. His dark, blackish-brown hair looked longer, the smooth lines in his face more defined now. He was more beautiful than I last remembered.

He smiled, and I saw his fangs. *It's a trick... only a trick.* The Vampires knew who I was. They'd known we were coming here. I gave up on caring, and flashed on my second sight, seeking to see beyond the glamour the Vampire wore. Crimson aura floated around his body, but he wore no glamour.

I inhaled and pushed away the tears as he stepped closer and lifted his hand to cup my cheek. His touch was shockingly cold—he was undead. I placed my hand over his, as tears broke free and ran down my cheek.

"Adrian," I whispered, through a broken sob that exploded from my trembling lips.

Chapter
TWENTY

"I buried you!" I cried, pushing his hand away as everything inside of me cried out in denial. This wasn't real. It had to be someone using something.

My earpiece shook as Adam spoke loudly. "Syn, this is not the time to be thinking about him. Pull yourself together."

"Thinking? Adam, I'm fucking looking right at him!" I whispered, not caring that Adrian was listening to the exchange.

"Fancy Face," he said in a soft husky voice that vibrated through me, kick starting my heart back to life.

"This isn't real. Why are you doing this to me?" Tears made my voice sound strained as I choked out the words.

"I'm real, baby," he said, before stepping even closer and placing his lips gently over mine. He was cold, but his kiss started a spark I couldn't deny. It was a soft hello kiss, gentle and not forceful.

"Why?" I cried as I pushed him away from me.

"Why," it was all I could manage to get out as my mind raced, trying to put pieces together.

"I chose this," he said carefully, his eyes scanning my face and then lower as he took in the vinyl I wore. "New look? I like it. Who would have thought that you had a darker side, Syn?"

I watched him close the distance between us and wait for me to push him away again. His skin was still bronzed and golden. His body was still a solid wall of muscle. His touch still sent shocks to my toes as it had the very first time we'd been together.

"You left me," I cried, feeling as I had the day I'd discovered his blood covering the floor of the parking garage and the walls. "I mourned you, dammit," I growled with my chest heaving from the loss all over again.

"You buried nothing, Syn. I taught you better than that. I taught you to never take anything at face value. You buried a box, and I told you before, Baby…you never believe anything is dead, unless you killed it yourself."

"Oh my God!" Adam and Larissa said from behind me as they came to a stop, as shocked now as I had been at Adrian's resurrection.

"You knew we were here," I whispered, shocked at the knowledge that he was using the coven's bond to track us, which meant someone very powerful had made it so we couldn't feel him prying in on it. Someone was shielding him from us and had been since the day he'd died.

"I did. I needed to know if you let me go," Adrian whispered, leaning his forehead against mine.

"You abandoned us willingly?" I whispered

brokenly.

"It's hard to explain, Fancy Face. Dance with me?" He didn't give me a choice as Guns N' Roses' *Don't Cry* played through the club's speakers. His hands wrapped around me, holding me close as his lips played against my ear. It was the same song Billy had played last night at the cemetery.

"You need to tell me why, Adrian. How could you do this?" I asked as my eyes searched and found Ryder's golden eyes narrowed on us with murder in their depths.

"Not here, Syn. I'll come to you when you're alone and explain why I had to do this," his breath feathered over my skin making me shiver.

"You killed Belinda."

I didn't ask him; I knew he had. No one else around us had the same crimson colored aura as Adrian did right now; not inside the club tonight, anyway. He laughed, but it was cold, sending a shiver racing down my spine at how hollow and empty it was. His tongue was hot, unlike the rest of him as he flicked my earlobe with it, before nibbling on the tissue of my ear gently.

"I needed to get your attention, Syn. Going through the Guild wasn't an option, and, since you seem to be playing with the enemy lately, knocking on your door wasn't an option either."

"So, you killed her to get to me?" I swallowed past the bile that pushed up with a vengeance as his words rocked through me.

"She was turning us onto inside information from the Guild, Syn. Believe it or not I still love you enough to protect you. She was looking into you specifically.

I found hundreds of pictures inside her apartment. Of you. We never asked her to look into you, Syn, which means someone else had. When she wouldn't give up the information, I took her out."

"And the bomb?" I snapped, angry at everything happening around me.

"Had to make it look like the killer who keeps taking out immortals to get you to look into it, and hopefully come here."

"You killed Rex! Hell, you almost killed me, Adrian," I whispered vehemently.

He stopped moving, his eyes flashing with regret. "You don't normally go to crime scenes. How was I supposed to know you would've been there, standing over the fucking body?"

"Next time, call my fucking cell phone, or send a fucking letter, Adrian. Like normal fucking people do."

"Oh and say what, Syn? Oh, by the way, I'm not dead, and could you come with me because we found something that could or couldn't be from the serial killer? No, because I know you, baby. You wouldn't have listened to anything I said without slamming the door in my face," he shouted, making those around who hadn't been staring before, do so now.

"Well, maybe if you would have kept your fucking pulse beating you wouldn't have to hide in the fucking shadows!"

"I made a choice. I was given an ultimatum, and I took it. I couldn't chance the coven's lives, and I couldn't be with you, because you wouldn't either. This way, we can be together!" He was growling now, his words coming out hard and sharp.

"Yeah? Ever consider the fact that I don't fuck dead things!? What did you think this would do? Did you even fucking think about asking me how I felt? Did you think we'd live happily ever fucking after if you did this?"

He smiled sadly and shook his head. "No, Syn, nothing is that easy with you. I was given a choice; one that could ensure I'd be strong enough to protect you from the things that killed your parents. But, hell, maybe I was wrong, since you're currently fucking one."

I slapped him before I could think better of it. The sound was audible and harsh over the song still playing. "Fuck you, Adrian," I snarled, seeing red at his words.

"If you're not fucking him, Fancy Face, then why the fuck are you wearing his mark? Why the *fuck* are you shacked up in his fucking house? Explain why I felt you react to him more than once tonight?"

"I buried you! I fucking mourned you Adrian. You have no fucking right to be pissed about anything I do or don't do. Not anymore."

"You think I don't want to leave you alone, Syn? I've tried. Believe me, baby, I've fucking tried, and, yet, no one can replace you. Hell, they can't even come close to giving me what you have."

I felt more tears push at the back of my eyes, but I refused to allow them to fall. This was too much—I had buried him, and he'd been a few blocks from my apartment the entire time. He'd become something else entirely and he'd *chosen* to. I pulled further away from him, which was harder than it should have been.

I wanted him to hold me, to tell me this was some

sick and twisted joke and that he was still Human, but he wasn't. He *lacked* a pulse. "I came to find out if you guys had any bodies piling up, Adrian."

"I just told you I wasn't over you, and you ask about dead bodies."

I turned and took in the ashen color of Adam and Larissa. They were in shock, which meant neither of them had known he was alive either. "I can't do this right now, Adrian."

"No, you just don't think I am the same guy. Take me for a ride, Syn. I promise it will be one you will never forget."

"Seriously? You want me to just forget that you pretended to be dead, or the fact that you left me and the coven you vowed to protect, and you used us!" I was poking my finger into his solid chest with anger now. "Ride you? I want to kick your fucking ass, Adrian! What you put us through is unforgivable."

His eyes started swirling as he moved closer to me, his movements that of the undead—quick, deadly, and calculating. "You belong with me, Syn. You always will."

"No, I belonged with the Adrian I buried. The one I loved is dead. You had my heart, but you played it. You left me for them. Not because you needed it. Not because of me," I swallowed and turned to Ryder. "Did you know he was alive?"

"No," Ryder replied with honesty.

I turned to face the Undead King. "You have my attention. I'm walking out of here in about two seconds, so if you have something to say, I suggest you say it now."

Vlad searched my face intently before he spoke. "You might be a target for the serial killer. He sent us a female child. She's in the back of my club, hidden. We have had nine born Vampires turn up with missing pieces. Your face was all over the news coverage for the Fairy that was killed. Adrian said you were different than the Witches at the Guild. Was he wrong?"

I narrowed my eyes on Vlad. "Describe different."

"You are currently owned by Ryder. No coven has ever given one of their own over to the Fae, and, yet, the Guild leader didn't hesitate to hand you over, which is curious, to say in the least. I heard you signed a blood contract, which means if Ryder told you not to disclose information to the Guild, you would have to comply with his wishes." He turned and watched Ryder nod his reply.

"Your point?" I inquired carefully, wondering where he was going with this.

"She seems to know you. She said your name and Adrian showed her a picture, and she just replied with Synthia Raine McKenna. She was with the killer for an entire night, and yet she is completely whole. Someone is killing immortals and your name just keeps popping up," Vlad continued.

"That makes no sense. I just found out about this case; just started to investigate it. The murders have been happening for a while, and, as best as I can tell, it had nothing to do with me." *Unless someone was hiding the facts from me,* I thought with curiosity.

"Seems you're involved, whether you know it or not, Synthia," Vlad purred, before nodding to a man who had been standing in the doorway that led to the rooms where Ryder had been with the serving girl.

The guy stepped aside and pushed the small girl's shoulders gently, encouraging her to move forward. She opened her vivid green eyes and tilted her small cherubic face, bouncing her burgundy curls out of her face as she did so.

Everyone watched as she took small steps, until she stood directly in front of me. She was dressed in a small pink summer dress that had short sleeves and she was barefooted in a Vampire club. Her eyes took me in and found me lacking. I almost laughed; I found this outfit lacking as well.

"She looks Human," I blurted, feeling brilliant.

Vlad choked and looked horrified. "For someone hanging around Fae, you don't know dick about them." He flicked a quick, nervous glance to Ryder, who nodded almost imperceptibly. Vlad knelt down to the child's level. "They look Human until somewhere about twenty or twenty two and then they go through 'Transition'—it's a bit like puberty—but a helluva lot more violent, as they come into their full powers during this time. At this age, they could be mistaken for Witches' children—cute as all get-out—with a lotta magic." Ryder chose that moment to growl, cutting anything else Vlad might have said off.

When the child indicated for me to come down closer to her level, I winced.

Ryder had taken up a position to my right, and Adrian was on the left; Adam and Larissa were still rooted to the spot they'd taken since coming in and finding Adrian undead. I pushed the vinyl closer to my skin as I bent my knees, trying to keep some semblance of modesty, while getting low enough to be eye level in the heels.

"Synthia," she said, barely audible, even at eye

level. "I have a message for you."

I swallowed and nodded, wondering what this child had seen at the hands of the killers. I hadn't noticed Ryder's men coming inside. Every one of them made a semi-circle around us, which I was gathering was for protection more than just for looks—which they all had, since they were immortal Fae or Demon.

"Which is?" I asked the child in a firm voice, which belied the emotions running through me at being singled out by the killer.

"We know what you are. Nothing can stop what is coming. Not even you, Synthia. What we did to those who hid you, is nothing compared to what we will do to those protecting you now. You cannot hide from destiny; you are a missing piece."

I almost fell over from my perch. "Who told you that? How do you know my name?"

"You can't stop him; can't stop them from coming—they know what you are. What is coming cannot be stopped," she said softly, as if she wasn't aware of what she said at all.

"Who sent you?" Ryder interjected, pulling me up and against him as Adrian growled at his actions.

The child chose that moment to crumple into Vlad's arms as we all watched in silence. I felt the power, putrefied by evil, slither over my skin. My knees buckled as I recalled the last time I had felt an evil this powerful. It had been when my parents had been murdered.

"Breathe, Syn," Ryder growled against my ear as I took strength from his warm body pressed against mine.

"It's them. They were controlling her somehow. How the hell did they find me?" I whispered, shocked by what the child had said. Was it possible the killer knew, or was working with, the Fae who had killed my parents?

"We're leaving now," Ryder growled, but Vlad stopped him with his other hand as the child sat up and started to whimper.

I watched her small green eyes meet and hold mine. She was afraid. She'd been through hell, and I knew she'd seen horrible things just by the sheer panic I could read in her young eyes. I pushed from Ryder's hold and went to my knees again. "I'm Synthia— you're safe here."

She said nothing, but giant tears rolled down her cheeks as I held out my hand for her to take, which she did with trembling hands. She was the only link we had between the killers and their victims. Something inside of her had been worth stealing or using, and we needed to know what it was that had attracted them to her.

"Synthia," Ryder and Adrian said in unison.

"She's been through hell," I said, not moving, since she was terrified of us already.

"They entered through her to get that message to you, baby, and they could do it again," Adrian said, as Ryder growled at his term *'baby'*.

"She isn't yours anymore. She is mine for now," Ryder growled, not helping the situation we were in at all.

"You guys can compare dick sizes later. Right now, we need to get her medical help because I would think that the only way to take over another Fae is by implanting some very painful devices, or powerful magic. So, if you're done fighting over someone who, by the way, belongs to neither of you, we need to get her to a medical facility specializing in Fae."

Ryder was the first to respond. "We have a small medical facility inside the mansion, and you are mine under contract."

"Syn's not Fae; she's not obligated to consider the contract binding," Adrian growled, but Vlad stepped in, placing his hand on Adrian's shoulder as his eyes flickered to Ryder in fear.

"He's young, sire. Please excuse his rudeness."

"Sire?" I asked carefully. Why the hell would Vlad call Ryder sire? Unless the Vampires had decided to team up and become controlled by the Dark Fae. But, if the Horde King ever came out of hiding, it wouldn't bode well for either of them, since we'd heard that the Horde King was *the* alpha among the entire Fae race and the other was the reclusive Blood King.

I jumped as a small hand folded into my other hand, and then I was thrown on my ass when she crumbled into my arms. "It's okay; you're safe. I won't let them use you again, little one."

I looked up to catch Ryder giving me a weird look, as if I was a mystery, which wasn't the case. The fact that she'd been around the men who had killed my parents wasn't comforting. They had been evil to their core, and she'd made it out alive. The vamps wanted me here, thinking this had to do with the serial killer, but the child was talking about the Fae who killed my parents—how could these killers be connected?

"They're afraid of you," the child whispered as she pulled herself up to look down at me.

"What makes you say that?" I asked, narrowing my eyes.

"You are the only one who can stop them," she replied before placing her silky hair back in my face as she held on, as if I would disappear from beneath her at any moment.

"They won't get to me. I have the Dark Fae helping me find them. See that scary man standing there?" I asked her, flicking my eyes to Ryder so she knew who I was referring to. "He's the Prince of the Dark Fae, and do you know what that means?"

She sniffled and shook her head. "He's scary," she mumbled while sniffling more.

"Yes, but it means they have to get past him to get to me," I said, hoping she would understand it. I held Ryder's eyes briefly. For the first time since signing his stupid contract, I was glad I had. He was deadly, and he was under contract to protect me, as I was to serve him.

I heard Adrian cuss as he understood what I was saying. I was giving Ryder the right to protect me and my coven, while telling him that I was his verbally. I couldn't put this on the Guild; Alden was under lock and key, and unless I wanted the same fate, I had no choice but to truly give in and trust Ryder.

He was deadly, as were his men, and I had just had a pretty red bull's-eye tattooed on my rear end, by some sort of supernatural Jack The Ripper serial killer, or the Fae who killed my parents—or were they one and the same? I had my coven to consider, and the child, who was now sobbing into the vinyl lace-up top I wore. I met Adrian's eyes briefly, and then walked out of the club with the child in my arms.

~~*~*~*~*~*~*~*~*

Chapter
TWENTY-ONE

The ride back to the mansion had been wrapped in uncomfortable silence. I could see the tension and anger riding inside Ryder's golden eyes. Adam and Larissa held onto each other, as if at any moment the sky would fall. Adrian had demanded to come back with us, but Ryder had stepped in and, thankfully, stopped it from happening.

I wasn't processing it—my mind was shutting down, and exhaustion was settling over me from the day's events. I stayed long enough to ensure the child had been put under by Ryder, and whatever it was he did that made it so you could do nothing else but pass out cold.

I needed to figure out what he said, and what language it was so I could use that instead of the sleeping pills I'd been taking since I was a child to escape the nightmares. I made it all the way to my room and had enough time to change out of the skin tight vinyl outfit and into some boy-cut undies, before the door was opened, and Ryder walked in with his usual confidence firmly in place.

"We need to talk, Synthia," he said, closing the door and settling into the single chair.

"I'm tired. Can we do it in the morning?" I asked, hoping he would say yes.

"What are you?" He came straight to the point, ignoring the fact that I was in my undies and topless, with only my arms shielding him from my naked breasts.

"I'm tired and mentally fried, Ryder. And, at the moment, I'm half-naked, so either turn around, or get out of the room so I can get dressed."

His self-absorbed smile spread over his mouth. "I own you, and I don't mind at all."

I ignored him—spinning around so he couldn't see anything as I slipped into the tank top—and turned back around. "You don't actually own me Ryder, and the contract didn't include late night visits to my room. I have no idea what she was talking about, or what they think I am. As far as I know, I'm a Witch; I can't do anything that I haven't read or learned from the Guild, or a book."

And I had read a lot; I loved books.

"Indeed," he mused as I walked over to the bed, and plopped myself down in front of him folding my legs Indian style, and facing him.

"What else do you want to know?" I was giving him honest answers. He looked young and, yet, he was ageless because he was Fae. I knew he was older than our records said; they had him being only a few years older than me, but his eyes told another story, with their endless depths of knowledge. I was pretty sure he had to know more than I had learned in my entire twenty-one years.

"How old are you?" he continued.

"Twenty-one years old…Going on one hundred."

He smiled, but it was all teeth. "Funny girl."

"The child said *they* were coming for you. Any ideas on who it is, or why?" he asked, watching my face for a reaction.

"They've never tried before. I don't see why they would now."

"Fair enough. I need to examine the brand on your neck, Syn. May I?" he asked, cautiously, as if he was afraid I would say no.

"Why?" I asked just as prudently as he had.

"Because it doesn't protect you from me fully, and I am pretty sure if I had one of my men come in, it wouldn't work against them, either. You have somewhat of a natural immunity to the Fae, but I want to test it to see just how resistant you are. I can make you feel things, but you don't turn completely mindless from my touch."

"Fine, but no funny business." I swallowed. I was pretty sure I'd been both mindless and boneless in his room.

His lips quirked as he stood up, and moved closer. "I need you to lie on your stomach and hit your *on* switch."

I hesitated as he got closer, my courage breaking away. I shook my head as I scooted further onto the bed to give him some room, and lay down on my stomach slowly. "No funny business." I turned, meeting his eyes briefly.

Those eyes filled with molten heat as they lowered to meet mine. I turned my head back around and dropped it to the bed, wondering what the hell I'd just gotten myself into. I had gone from trained killer to blushing bumbler since meeting Ryder, and it was pissing me off.

I felt the bed move under his weight and hissed as his fingers swept my hair away from the brand. I stretched my neck, wondering why he would think it wasn't working. I'd never had any issue with the Fae, until him.

"When did you get this?" His voice resonated from above my head as his hot breath fanned against my neck, sending heat pooling between my thighs.

"Around thirteen."

"Any idea what it says?" His voice was hoarse, and not helping the fight that the damn butterflies were having inside my abdomen.

"No, only that it is supposed to protect against the influence of the Fae."

"I can't read it," he said, as though he was puzzled.

"But?" I'd heard the '*but*' in his tone.

"It's old, the branding is. This isn't from the Guild."

"Of course it is. I don't let just anyone write brands on my skin, Ryder. And every brand is supervised by Alden to ensure it is correct."

He didn't reply. Instead, his fingers traced over the invisible ink that he shouldn't be able to see at all, and he hadn't asked me to turn the ink on for color, which meant he could see it plainly. "You can read it as-is."

"Only this one…the others are undetectable unless

you allow them to be seen. I'm going to take a gander that it was intended to be that way deliberately."

I turned over until I was lying on my back and looking up into his eyes. He didn't push the answer out. Instead, he waited for me to decide how much I wanted to tell him about it. I inhaled his scent and let it rush through me, relaxing the tension the day had caused on my nerves. "The brands, with the exception of the one on my neck were placed on me with ink designed by Alden. It's enchanted to react with our powers. It's supposed to keep us grounded from the lure of the Dark Arts. Since we only started messing with them a few years ago, he decided to use us."

I watched his mind run through the implications, the knowledge sinking in that I hadn't been branded by normal ink, ever. He lifted his eyes and scanned my face before saying anything. "You didn't have ink before thirteen? I thought all the Witches receive ink before then—so, you had nothing but the stars?"

I flinched, remembering why I had them. They were for my parents—one for each, with traditional black ink defining the burns into the true stars on the front of my shoulders. "Correct. I didn't need any ink at first, and then we received the white ink."

"Can I try something without you freaking out, Synthia?" he asked, watching my face.

"Do I have to be naked for it?" I countered, narrowing my eyes, watching his mouth turn up into a beautiful mischievous smile.

"No, but I have to touch you. I want to see if the brands protect you from me when activated. Or if it affects me at all."

I swallowed past the uneasiness that flared to life

inside my stomach with his words. "You want me to invoke my powers while you try to use yours on me. What if we end up forgetting who we are, like we did last time?"

"I didn't forget who I was, Syn. I knew exactly who I was, and who I was with when I lost control with you."

My body responded to his words even as my breathing grew labored. "I can't be with you, Ryder; it's not allowed while I work for the Guild."

"To have sex?" he asked, narrowing his eyes again.

"No, I can have sex. Lots of sex, with lots of people. Just not of the Fae variety. I'm not sure I could ever be with any Fae. Besides, what if something happened and I got pregnant? I mean, the Guild has us on mandatory contraceptives designed for us, but something could always happen and none of the Fae accepts Changelings. Not to mention—I wouldn't wish me as a mother for any child." I was rambling, so I stopped when he noticed.

He smiled forlornly. "The Horde does," he answered, flashing his smile back to full force.

"Yeah, but their King is missing, and, unless I'm mistaken, the Vampires are changing sides already. *Your* side to be precise, which means he's either gone, or he's in play."

I watched his face shut down, going completely emotionless. "You watch too many conspiracy movies, Synthia."

"Be that as it may, Vlad called you Sire tonight, Ryder."

"I'm a Prince. Besides, I'm higher on the food chain than he is and I've earned their respect."

I tilted my head and considered it. It could have been, or it could have been that Vlad was leaderless and seeking out a new alliance, and Ryder, being Dark Fae, would be the closest to the Horde. Unlike the Light Fae, the Dark Fae got along with the Horde. "Could have been, yes."

"I have no plans of making any new alliances."

I nodded, and then shrank back as his hand came out to rub against my palm, sending a tremble through my entire body. His thumb traced over the small wound on the palm of my hand softly.

"How easily can you summon your powers?" he inquired, never taking his eyes from mine. I should be running from him instead of indulging him.

I didn't answer him. Instead, I invoked them and watched the white glow light up in his eyes. His smile faltered as he moved closer, lying down lengthwise beside me until our faces were inches apart. He was the most sexual male I had ever encountered in my life. He oozed power from his pores. I shouldn't trust him. And yet, I trusted him more than I thought I did.

"Your eyes don't match when they light up," he whispered, resting his head in his hand while his elbow sat on the bed.

"So I've been told," I whispered back, fighting to keep my voice from trembling. His close proximity was playing hell on my hormones. My hand shook where his thumb still played over the sensitive flesh, which was weakening my willpower with every slow stroke.

"You ready, Pet?" he inquired, looking a little too

eager.

"For your little science project?" I asked, making sure we were on the same page.

He grinned wolfishly before he leaned over close enough that I could smell the mint on his breath, as if he had come here planning on kissing me. "Something like that. I need to see how this thing works. I know it doesn't work against me completely, but we need to test it."

If I'd been using my brain, I might have asked why, but Mister Sex Incarnate was inches from my lips, and the only thing I could think of was what he had been doing to Claire in his office, and how I had wanted to trade places with her, *which was crazy*.

When his mouth found mine, it wasn't a crushing kiss, or hard. Instead, it was tender and firm as he tested me. When he touched me, it was electrical, like standing next to a live wire while sparks flew from it to land on you, and, yet, you were trapped in place by its beauty. That was the only way to describe his touch and kiss. It scared me. It was intense—more than I had ever felt with Adrian.

I knew the instant he pushed his Fae powers on me. Everything else faded away, and my only need was to take him. "Ryder," I said with my voice filled with need.

"Do you want me to stop?" he asked, pulling further away as he pulled the magic with him.

I swallowed, but pulled him back down. "Did you get what you needed, for the science thing?"

His eyes lit up, and he shook his head as more Fae magic pushed into my mind. It was painful at first, but gone instantly when his lips caressed mine.

I moaned and pushed against his mouth with need for him that was so hot and fierce, I was afraid I'd be left in a pile of ash if he didn't continue and give me more of his mouth. When he pulled away, I cried from the loss. "Ryder."

"What's your name?" he demanded in a husky voice, filled with hunger.

"Syn. Now shut up and kiss me, Ryder."

His lips tugged at the corner before he kissed me again, more demanding this time, his hand cradling my neck as he moved over the top of me and ground his erection against my pelvis. More power filtered in, and he kept asking my name or other questions as I answered and demanded more of him.

My body was an inferno, my center saturated with the proof of his sexual allure and power he held inside of himself. My body willing, my mind was still intact enough that I knew who I was and where I was. I shook with it. My hands found his head and pulled him back down as his knee slid between my legs and pressed against my core.

"Do you want me to stop? I need to know, because if we go too much further, Pet, I'm going to bury myself deep inside of you," he asked, pulling away from the kiss.

"I—" I didn't know. For the first time in my life, I wanted to tell a Fae *yes*, I wanted *him*. And *only* him.

"I want to feed from you so fucking badly, Syn. I need to part your legs and drive my cock inside of you. I want to see you as you come undone for me."

His words penetrated my brain, like a knife through an eye socket. "No, Ryder, I can't."

"Can't, or won't, Syn?" He growled in frustration.

I was about to answer when a soft knock sounded from the door. Ryder was up and fixing his erection against his jeans before I could say anything else. My eyes latched on to it as it stood proudly against his navel. I licked my lips, wanting to ask him to stay, but not knowing how to. I knew where he'd go after this. I could see his hunger burning in his eyes.

"You keep saying you can't, and it's a lie. You *won't*. You hide in the fucking past. You're not living, Syn; you're just going through the motions of it. You want me, I can smell it—you need it as much as I do, right now. The difference is, I can admit to what I want—you *can't*."

I gulped in air and fought for something to say while he waited, watching me struggle internally. He snorted and turned for the door. "Wait, Ryder, I—"

"Save it," he interjected, cutting me off. "I own you, Syn, so know this… While you're under my roof and my protection, the only release you will get, is from me. Not by your hand or another's. When you can grow the fuck up and admit to me what your body already knows—well, you know where to find me."

I watched him turn and walk out of the room as Larissa and Adam walked in, wide eyed.

"Oh hell, Syn, your lips are kiss-me-silly swollen," Larissa said, with wide shocked eyes.

"She's more than that, baby," Adam responded when I couldn't find the words. He was holding her hand, and I wanted to cry. I'd never have that again, the love they felt for one another. It would be forever beyond my grasp.

"So, what's up with you and Ryder anyway?"

Larissa asked, floating in to sit on the bed while she dragged Adam with her.

"Nothing," I lied, and felt a pinch of regret for doing so. "I'm immune to him, apparently—well, mostly. He can't turn me into a mindless zombie, but I do feel his powers; just not on a level I should."

"That mother fucker tried to turn you FIZ? I'll fucking kill him!" Adam was enraged, and off the bed in seconds, taking long strides to the door.

"I asked him to...well, sorta," I said quickly to stop Adam from getting his ass handed to him, which I was pretty sure Ryder would do right now if disturbed with Claire and his damn desk.

"Wait, wait a minute. You hate the Fae. What the hell is wrong with you?" Adam demanded, coming back over to sit on the bed beside Larissa.

I blew out a deep breath. "This brand on my neck...it's not for the Fae, Adam. Ryder doesn't know what it says, and I'm pretty sure he's older than dirt."

Adam narrowed his eyes and shook his head. "What do you mean it's not for the Fae? What the hell did Titus put on your neck?"

"No idea, but we need to figure it out—and soon," I replied shaking my head.

I tried to remember what Titus had said while tattooing the ink, and gave up. I licked my lips nervously and spoke low so only those inside the room could hear me. "I have no birth certificate, according to Ryder, and you don't either, Adam. There are no pictures of me inside my parent's house before I was six months old."

"I was left at the Guild, so no surprise there, but

there has to be some pictures of you as an infant—well unless you were an ugly baby."

I snorted at his response, since it pretty much matched the one I had given to Ryder. I considered my options, and then turned to look at Larissa. "If Adam cut it off, you could heal it, right?"

"Oh hell no! We can't just cut it off, Syn. Have you lost your mind?" Larissa said, turning a light color of green.

I rubbed my eyes, tired from everything I had dealt with today. "Adrian is alive," I mumbled, knowing that was what they had come here for.

"Technically, he's—Ow!" Adam whined, and rubbed his ribs where Larissa had just elbowed him. I barely contained a smile as he continued to do so.

"I know! How could he do that to us? I mean, he actually got turned into a Vampire. I can't believe it! And he was all over you. He thinks he can come back here after we buried him? Seriously, the guy is going to send my ass to counseling!" She shouted in her best outraged voice for my benefit.

"If you want, I can grab my notebook and a pen and you can lie on the couch?" I teased her.

Adam laughed and lifted his green eyes up to meet mine. He wasn't fooled by the jokes I was using to deflect the conversation at all. "He doesn't deserve you, he left us. All of us. He left the coven to become more powerful, Syn."

"Yeah, I get that. But, why? He was already powerful," I replied, thinking it over.

"No idea, but now that Larissa has fed her curiosity of why Ryder was inside your room and no voices could be heard from the door—I bid you goodnight," Adam smiled as Larissa glared at him, before he walked out and closed the door behind him.

"You can't be with Ryder, *ever,* Syn," she said hastily.

"I know that. He was trying to figure out what the brand on my neck was for. Just don't worry about it. It's my ass, not yours. Why are you so worried about me, when you have Adam?" I asked, deflecting her statement.

"I've liked him since we were little. I just need to see where this goes," she moved her hair behind her ear and smiled sadly.

"I'm doomed. I think I should become a nun," I smiled, trying to lighten the mood.

"We're both going to hell, but at least we will be there together," Larissa said, grinning.

"Not anytime soon, though," I joked halfheartedly.

If we didn't catch this killer, it might be sooner, rather than later.

Chapter
TWENTY~TWO

The next few days were difficult, but we'd managed to settle into a routine of sorts. My coven worked out in the morning together, as we always had, while Ryder and his men disappeared to wherever it was they went to during the days.

Communications were short and kept to a minimum. I trained with Ryder and Zahruk, who seemed to be his second in command. I'd even managed to hold a tea cup in the correct way. Who knew there was an actual right way to hold a flimsy little china cup? Today, I was being instructed on how to dance. By Ryder himself.

Ryder said to pick out something suitable to dance in, so I was relieved when Larissa showed up, holding an ice blue dress and shoes. It was backless and soft, not something I would normally wear, but I was limited on choices. I slipped into it and stared at my bare feet.

I slipped on the matching shoes, decided to leave my hair down, and slapped on some light make-up. Zahruk knocked, opened the door. and nodded, before offering his arm, so we could head to the room in which we'd be dancing in.

Adrian had never wanted to dance—the other night couldn't be considered since all I'd done was move my feet while he'd held me. I'd been too stunned to do much more than that. I just had to train for one more night, and then I'd been promised we'd be allowed out, even if only for a few hours. Adam and Larissa had both begged to go to the Guild's Samhain party.

I peeked around Zahruk's wide shoulders to watch as several couples twirled around the dance floor. Surprisingly, Adam and Larissa were one of those couples. I smiled as I watched them glide smoothly to the music, and wondered how I could have missed the relationship. They looked happy together; complete.

"Coming in, or do you plan on hiding behind me all day?" Zahruk said with a wide grin that lit all the way to his vivid blue eyes.

"I don't dance—not like that, anyway," I mumbled looking around at the faces, stopping when I realized I was looking for Ryder.

I stepped forward into the room, and everyone stopped as the music halted. Zahruk herded me toward a set of chairs that had been set up. I was told to take a seat and watch. Easier said than done as Claire and Ryder came in together, smiling, from where I had just entered the room myself.

Ryder was dressed in the casual clothes he normally preferred; white long sleeve shirt with low slung jeans. His hair was wet, as if he'd just come from a shower. His eyes flickered to me briefly before going back to Claire's perfect chocolate depths.

Claire gave me a haughty look, before she said something to Ryder as he allowed her to curl up against him and the music started up. I swallowed down the foreign feelings that rushed up and fought to control my mind. Why should I feel anything if Ryder had his mistress in his arms, and they were currently dancing slowly to music?

I bit my lip and looked away from the happy couple, turning my eyes to the door as more of Ryder's men walked in wearing white T-shirts and jeans. Muscles and tattoos pulsing against their bulging and bronzed perfection showed through their T-shirts. I almost bit my lip off as Adrian and Vlad walked in close behind them.

What the hell were they doing here? I sank lower in my chair, trying to become one with it. No such luck. Adrian walked over and sat beside me as Ryder detangled himself from Claire's clutches, leveling a glare at us.

"We need to talk, Fancy Face," Adrian said, without looking at me as he watched the couples still dancing.

"No, we don't."

"I need to explain why I did this, so you can make peace with it," he continued.

I watched as Ryder's men gathered in a corner, pulling out folding chairs and sitting in them. Some were straddling them, while others pulled out two and sat in one while kicking their feet up. Were they expecting a show? *Great, more people to witness my disgrace.*

I watched as Ryder came over and held out his hand, while Claire did the same to Adrian. I stood, meeting Adrian's turquoise gaze while I accepted Ryder's hand, and allowed him to pull me across the floor to stand between some of the couples that had paused for us to join in. He placed his hand on the small of my back. His other held my hand as we waited for the song start. We didn't have long to wait.

The music started. Even as the butterflies played with my insides, his eyes locked with mine as the song started up slowly. David Cook's *The Time Of My Life* came on, the music filling the room around us. I stumbled when he moved, and started to apologize until I caught the smile on his lips. "I can't dance, Ryder. You never said anything about dancing when I signed the contract."

"Take off your shoes," he countered, already releasing me and bending over to take his own footwear off. I watched him as others did the same and eventually I ignored the brilliant blush that crept up to my cheeks and followed suit, stepping out of the borrowed strappy heels.

Ryder smiled and I stared at him. He was shockingly beautiful and ethereal. Like a lion, you wanted to touch him, but knew by doing so he'd consume you, body and soul. I swallowed and held my hand up for him to take it.

"Put your feet on mine, Synthia," he said quietly, aware that everyone was watching us.

I exhaled and obeyed him, knowing his men were watching us, as well as my coven. When the song restarted, he carried us both, his hand once again on the small of my back, rubbing it softly as his fingers settled against it. My heart raced from his touch. The deep desire in his eyes made it flip-flop as he swept me around the room, until everyone else faded away, leaving us alone inside the room.

I smiled as I looked down to see our feet together. I was nervous at being so close to him and doing something I had only ever done with my father. It had been the last thing we'd ever done together. But with Ryder, it was intimate, sending heat flooding through me. I looked back up, the smile still in place, to catch him staring openly in wonder at me. "What?" I asked, growing self-conscious.

"You're very beautiful, Syn," he whispered tenderly.

I swallowed and tried to repay the compliment, but thought better of it and lowered my eyes. The butterflies had left, but in their place were a million reasons screaming that I should be running; that I was treading on dangerous ground with him. When I looked back up, he was frowning softly as he watched the emotions playing upon my face.

"Not used to getting compliments, are you?" he asked, moving us closer together until my body was completely flushed with his.

"No," I replied honestly.

"I scare you, Syn—make you feel things you're afraid of admitting to yourself."

I met his eyes and refused to answer him. He already knew I was turned on by his touch, and I wasn't going to draw it out for him. I lowered my eyes and then turned them over to where Adrian was dancing with Claire. "Why is he here?"

"Because they will be attending the Engagement Ball, and we can use all the help we can get right now to keep Arianna safe. I won't take chances with her."

"Where is she? If you guys are getting married, I'd think you'd be dying to be together already. I know I would be—well, with—" I was tripping over my tongue and his amused smile told me he was enjoying it. "If it were me, Ryder, I'd want to be with you." I watched his smile fade, and then I replayed what I had just said. "That came out wrong."

"I'd want you close as well, Synthia," he whispered close to my ear. "Maybe I should ditch her and take my chances with you."

"That wasn't how I meant it at all," I squeaked, even as he smiled wider.

"And what if I did?" he asked, still smiling.

"Well then, I would say you are crazy," I said and watched his smile fade away to the normal wicked grin.

"You think someone would have to be crazy to want you?"

"Well, you—yes. Because you don't like me, remember? I'm sarcastic and stubborn, and those are just a few of the things you don't like about me, I should start a list—to keep track," I said softly.

He did the last thing I expected him to do. He threw his head back and laughed while still moving us around the dance floor without missing a step. I had to remind myself to breathe. Smiling was one thing, but watching this man laugh took years off of his face and replaced him with a rogue who was irresistible, and his laughter was contagious.

Everyone inside the room was watching us closely. Those who had been dancing had moved from the dance floor, and the song had also changed, yet I'd been too wrapped up in Ryder to notice anything. His touch, and the sound of his laughter, had instantly made my body flood with heat, and it was unacceptable.

He growled seductively, pulling me out of the

panic before I could get too deep into worrying about it. His eyes narrowed on me, his body pressing further against me. "Come with me tomorrow night, Synthia," he said huskily.

"Where?" I asked, even though I shouldn't have. I would have been attending the Witch Guild event tomorrow if I hadn't been under contract. I'd cleared it for Larissa and Adam to go, since I had no reason to keep them from attending the only holiday the Guild celebrated.

"An event my club is throwing…just something small," he replied smoothly, but his grin had come back with blinding effects.

"Posing as Arianna?"

"No, Syn, as yourself."

I narrowed my eyes on him, carefully thinking over everything he had said. I had to be missing something. "Why would you want me to come as myself?"

He narrowed his eyes, his lips drawn back. I was walking in uncharted territory here. He'd never really been kind to me. Hell, we weren't even friends. More like enemies, with slightly twisted benefits. He could choose from any woman he wanted, and he was choosing me? Or maybe I was reading too much into this. Maybe he wanted to take me somewhere private and kill me. It was the more likely scenario.

He leaned in close again, his hot breath fanning on the hollow column of my neck, before lifting to my ear to whisper. "You're doing it again—over thinking, over analyzing everything. My club in action would better prepare you for the ball. It's a win-win situation, Syn."

I shivered as his lips pressed against my ear; he inhaled deeply before moving back to where I could read his face. "No tricks?"

He smiled, but it was all teeth. "No tricks, just us being who we truly are."

"No using your powers on me," I swallowed with the memory of how they felt.

"Not unless you ask me to, and then I won't hold back."

I blinked and made a mental note to, under no circumstances, ask him to use them. I tilted my head, thinking of what else I needed to ask, but I was coming up blank. "This is for research only."

"No, Syn, this is to get you to let go. You keep struggling to control everything around you. It's impossible. Well, unless you're me. Think you can handle that? One night of letting loose, just being yourself and not this tough shell you show off to everyone else?"

"I'm not a shell, and I don't try to control everything," I narrowed my eyes, "Okay, so maybe I do try to control things. The unknown can get people killed, Ryder. If I lose control, people die in my line of work."

His lips turned down as his eyes narrowed. "Mine too, but I still allow myself one night to—well, one night to let loose and be myself."

He'd hesitated, Ryder never hesitated. "If you tell me when you will end the contract between us…it doesn't have to be a date, but it has to be a time frame, Ryder. If you can give me that, then I will give you one night of just being myself."

He tilted his dark head and stopped dancing. I stepped off his feet, and watched him as he held out his hand to shake on it. Or so I thought, until he gripped my hand and brought it palm up, to place a gentle kiss in the soft flesh. "It's a deal."

Oh, sweet baby Jesus, what the hell had I just agreed to do? The blood in my body was draining to one place, and it was as good of an excuse to use as any. When I was around Ryder, I spoke gibberish, and my brain was located in my nether region. I had to get away from him, and fast, before I did something I would live to regret. You didn't sleep with a man like Ryder and walk away the same woman you had been before. If I gave in, things would change inside of me, forever.

I turned in time to watch Adrian storm from the room, Adam following close on his heels. Larissa stood silently, watching them leave as I did. Ryder's men closed in around us, and I wondered what I had just missed.

~~*~*~* *~*~*~*~*

Glorious mind fuck, she's addictive. It makes my mind go to places that it hasn't even fathomed before. She denies me while denying herself. She's growing weak. I can feel, as she trembles against me, her walls coming down slowly, even as she struggles to keep them up. The scent of her need makes me want to pull back the delicate petals of her flower and devour it, consume it, fuck it.

She's a drug; a virus in my system that needs to be eradicated. Nothing about her makes sense; she's a walking contradiction. She isn't what they say she is. I'm old enough to know the difference. See the difference. Yet, unable as I am to figure her out or why her blood calls to me—why? Why should it? If she is what they say she is, the only thing that should respond to her is my cock, and, yet, my mind is on her. Every. Fucking. Minute.

When she came to my room, glorious with need, I wanted to take her, make her need my cock more than she needed to breathe, and, yet, I couldn't. I want her to come to me of her own accord—strange for me, as I take what I want without guilt. Without remorse.

She isn't Human; not even fucking close. It's driving me crazy inside trying to figure out what she is. I can feel her hunger, as if something is struggling to get out from under her skin. I can smell her need— raw and unmasked with a desire so fucking hot, it makes my cock throb to be buried in her sweetness.

I smell her need, sweet and addictive. She's young, her mind works differently than my own, I need to fuck her—hard. She needs to validate why she should, stupid. Fucking just is, but I don't think fucking her would be the same as Claire, and she was simply food. Syn wouldn't be; she'd be so much more. I can feel the draw, her body calling to mine as animals do in heat. I'd fuck her like an animal; raw, hot, and fucking hard.

She made me lose control—again. She shook my hardened exterior and made me want her, an impossible feat for someone of my age and hers. It shouldn't have happened; wasn't in my plans. *She* wasn't in my fucking plans. And, yet, when I am alone, the only thing I see in my head is her; all I hear are the hungry noises she made while she dry-fucked my cock.

Those red fucking full lips that are hard to miss when she speaks. The glorious fucking things they could do—will do. I want to fill her—slow, deliberate, deep—her juices sliding me in further,

her spine aching from the fullness of my cock as she succumbs to it until she can take no more. Oh, but she will; she will take it all, filling her thirsty need to fuck. The electric blue fire that lights in her eyes…I want to watch it as it takes me, feeding my beast. I want to feel her swollen flesh pulsing around mine as she comes for me, over and over again; hear those fucking noises as she explodes on my cock.

Maybe I should drain the life from her, watch it recede from her eyes and end this before it goes further. She's an unknown, unpredictable, and yet something inside of her is struggling to grow, and I find myself wanting to cage her, just to watch her fucking struggle and overcome it. She's a puzzle box, and I want to take her apart and watch as she puts the pieces back, one by one until she is whole again. Why does she draw me in? I've been with thousands of women and wanted to keep none.

None of them drew me like she does. She's quicksand, and I am treading into it quickly. Maybe it's the brand below the worthless one on her neck. Maybe it has clues to what she is, or why she attracts. She doesn't even know it's there. Fucking puzzle box. Addicting.

I want to hold her hands above her head and feed her inch after glorious fucking inch of my cock, and watch her eyes as she takes me inside her body, hungrily, greedily. Her mouth opening to gasp as she makes those sweet intoxicating sounds that drive me insane with the need to turn from noises, to screaming as I fuck her until she trembles and gives me what I want—her unrefined lust. She'd be magnificent in hunger, wild and unimaginable. She is making me violent with lust, unfed Fae—fuck! I shouldn't be feeling anything for her. I'm here for one reason, and one reason alone. She thinks I'm less than I am. I'm so much fucking more. Deadly is an understatement.

When I reveal what I am—this world will never be the same again.

I almost had her—her eyes watching me as I fucked Claire, she wanted to be her, wanted me to use her soft, supple body instead to slake my unending hunger on. It took everything I had to keep the beast from going after her as she tore from the room, scared, her fucking scent flooding my mind. Claire didn't even satisfy. She left me cold she was just useless flesh that takes any of my men anytime. She'd been convenient before, but not anymore.

Syn is scared. She should be fucking terrified. I want her and nothing will stop me now. Not even her newly risen love. If he gets in the way, he will really go to his grave. I own him now. Another fucking pawn on my growing board. His supposed death broke her, and I intend to pick up those pieces and use them to get inside her beautiful, fucked-up mind.

She knows there is something different about me, but she's smart enough to keep it to herself. Smart, because I'd have to snuff her out before she's had a chance to live. Living—she hasn't even fucking begun to live. She's so locked in her fucking past that she doesn't even see the way everyone watches her. She's as clueless as Arianna, who will never become anything more than a fucking means to an end.

Tomorrow night. Mmm she has no fucking clue—tomorrow; she will be mine if only for the night. It won't be enough to sate the hunger I feel inside for her, but it will be enough to brand her skin and mark her as my own. Then no one can question who she belongs to. She's mine, and I will have her in every fucking way possible until she becomes a problem. I'll cross that bridge when I get to it. Until then, I plan to take her until she only knows one name—mine.

~~*~*~*~*~*~*~*~*

Chapter
TWENTY~THREE

I sat in the room, listening as Adam and Larissa droned on about the Samhain celebration the Guild would be throwing. I'd be missing it this year to go with Ryder. He'd been cryptic about what it was that we were going to, but he'd said he'd give me a time frame for when I would be released from his contract.

That alone was worth attending a Fae event for. I could have said no, but something inside me wanted to see him in his natural surroundings. There was something deeper to him, softer than I'd seen before. He'd almost seemed Human while we'd danced together.

If I was smart, I'd play sick and not go, but something darker inside me wanted to see him around his own kind. Wanted to explore these darker feelings he was pulling to the surface inside me.

Adrian had left a mark. He'd torn a huge part of my soul out when he'd died. His miraculous return only tore the wound open again, and maybe that was why I was pushing Ryder's buttons while pushing my own boundaries. But this hunger that Ryder was pulling from me was primal, an intense fire that was burning out of control and leaving ashes in its wake.

Those feelings demanded to be explored, even as my mind warned me of the consequences.

I considered the consequences, and, yes, they scared me. He was pushing my boundaries, pushing my self-control. I was tempted to allow his seduction. I was fighting it, but it had more to do with the fear of what he could do, more than what he would do. His kisses pushed me further, consuming my mind with a desire that scared me and exhilarated me at the same time. I wanted to find the passion I felt with him, and yet, I was attracted to the one thing I'd been scared of my entire life.

He consumed my thoughts. I needed to get away from him, and fast. He was quicksand, and I was sinking. I should be focused on the murders, and who would be next. It had been quiet on that aspect, and we were no closer since Vlad had sent us that message, or sick and twisted invitation, or whatever you wanted to consider it.

It meant that somewhere out there, someone was dying. Being tortured for vital organs, while we sat around and waited to find a body. I was going stir-crazy inside the house, even though I normally stuck to my bedroom, reading in our apartment. Being inside this place with Ryder, under the same roof, was driving me insane.

I almost jumped as a knock sounded from the door, disturbing my thoughts and the couple chattering on the other side of the room. Wasn't sure why they were inside my room prattling on, but I was glad they were there. I was just about to yell open, but the person had already walked in before the words left my lips. Adrian stood there with his eyes locked onto me.

I came off my back quickly, placing my bare feet down onto the carpeted floor. I swallowed the lump that swiftly filled my throat as his turquoise eyes swept the room and landed on me. I didn't know what to say. I wanted to ask him why he was there, why he had lied and hidden from us, but I knew I wouldn't accept the answer, no matter what it was. The truth was he'd left us.

"Can I talk to you, Syn?" Adrian asked, shoving his hands firmly in his pockets.

I looked around the room and nodded, still unable to talk over the growing lump. Adam and Larissa had remained silent, waiting to finally get the explanation from him as I had been. I stood nervously, already reading his expression...we'd been that close.

"Alone?" he asked the others.

I turned to ask the others to leave, but Adrian stopped me.

"Outside, Fancy Face. The walls have ears," he said smoothly as his eyes looked at the walls, as if they would object.

"Okay," I said, looking down at my still bare feet. "Let me grab something for my feet." I bent down, turning the flip flops over, and dug my feet into them.

As we moved down the hallway, Adrian commented on their relationship. "Knew they'd end up together," he said with a grin.

"Did you now?" I mumbled sarcastically, trying to stop my hands from fisting up as I figured out what to do with them. I settled on crossing them over my chest as I stood awkwardly in my pink sweat pants that said *Sassy Girl* across my butt. The shirt I was wearing wasn't much better. It was the White Zombie one I'd gotten at the concert we had gone to as a group a few years ago, that said *Living Dead Girl* across the breast area.

"They hate me," he said silently.

"What do you expect, Adrian? You ditched us, not the other way around," I said through clenched teeth.

"Ryder said we could talk by the pool, but I think I'd rather walk the grounds," he said as we made our way down the stairs. It was awkward to be walking next to someone you had spent years wishing you could have one last conversation with—one last kiss.

I couldn't think of anything I wanted to say, and it all seemed so different now. I was a different person than I'd been before meeting Ryder. If this had happened before I'd met him I would have thrown my arms around Adrian without caring what had happened, or why. Don't get me wrong, I'd still be pissed, but I missed him, and it was a relief to know I hadn't gotten him killed.

We ended up walking a trail that started from the driveway and walked through thick greenery. Neither of us said anything at first, as if we were afraid to. I definitely was. He wasn't the same guy he'd been. "What's it like?" I finally asked, letting curiosity get the better of me.

"Being dead?" he asked with a sexy smirk.

"Yeah." I quickly looked away as something crunched a few feet away from us.

"It's not as bad as I thought it would be. I don't care for the having to feed part, but mix it with sex and it's amazing," he replied, still smiling as he placed his hands back in the pockets of his jeans.

He'd been having sex, and I'd been Miss-Do-It-Myself. Great! I waited for the jealousy to come, but it was muted when it did. I rubbed my arms, feeling the cool air flow over them as my eyes scanned the area, wondering if we had been tailed.

"I didn't have a choice, Fancy Face. The Vampire who did this to me…well, he handed me a picture of you. Said he would turn you, if I didn't change. Vlad was worried we'd be sent after him, so he sent his version of a hit squad out that night. I did what I had to if it would keep you and the others safe. You didn't know it, Syn, but they were inches from you that night. Showed me where you were and then showed me the vamp standing beside you. We were so cocky back then; reckless," he smiled as I turned to look at him.

"So, you went with them? We were strong, we could have fought them!" I was pissed. "That should have been my decision to make, Adrian, and you took it without asking us. We'd have fought for you!"

"And died, Fancy Face…you would have died. That wasn't something I could have lived with— ever."

"And what if we had won? Then you would still be alive," I blanched and continued, "Or more than you are right now, anyway. Damn it, Adrian, I buried you!" I was shaking with anger, rage, and guilt.

"Baby, I couldn't take that chance." His eyes searched my face as he closed the distance between us and curled me against him in a tight embrace. "You were my life, Syn. I couldn't chance it, because I knew you would fight them, and I knew you'd die. It was a choice—me for you. I took it, and, yes, maybe I should've had more faith in you, but at the time, I was given a choice and I made it."

He was cold. His body was more muscled than it had been, but where it had once been warm, it was cold and his scent had changed. He smelled of earth and the cologne he had always worn—it made me smile. I listened to his empty chest before pulling away in time to catch him sniffing me. *Did I stink to his undead senses?*

I looked up into his face as he cupped my cheek in his cold hand. "Did you miss me?"

"Would it matter?" I asked, knowing he already knew I had missed him.

"I saw you at my grave, every day for the first few weeks after I left. Then, when work got busy at the Guild, you came on the weekends. Do you have any idea how hard it was to stay away from you until I could contain this eternal fucking hunger?"

"Is this where I say sorry? Because *I* would have fought. If we had died, then so be it. Everyone dies sometime, and I'd have died to prevent what you've become any day of the fucking week."

He frowned and nodded, letting his arm drop from my face. "I can change you, Syn. We could be together forever. Never grow old. Never be apart."

"I wouldn't abandon my coven so easily, Adrian— and who says I don't want to grow old? You made a choice. Don't assume you can make mine as well. I'm what I was born to be, what my parents died for. They died, making sure I stayed alive. I won't change that because you went and made some stupid decision. And it was, Adrian. It was stupid. We needed you, and you broke me. You left us weakened by your loss, and who knows what could have happened while you were out fucking everything with a pulse!"

"I wasn't fucking anything, Syn. I was so busy trying to figure out how to get you back that I couldn't get my dick up! I had to feed, though, and, well, it goes hand in hand. So yes, I've taken lovers, because I had to. I was just buying time, Syn. I was unstable." He threw his hand in the air with frustration. "I couldn't control it. I gave my life to protect you. Going to you while I couldn't control the bloodlust would have been stupid."

"It changes nothing, Adrian. You left us exposed. You left me in *fucking pieces*!" I shouted, uncaring if whoever was listening, heard us.

"I came back damn it; just in time to find you wearing his fucking name on your neck Syn. Are you fucking him, too? He isn't what you think he is; he is so fucking much more, and he's playing you. Did you fuck him? Call out his fucking name while he was fucking you!? Like you did with me?" He sneered.

I slapped him before I knew what I was doing. All the rage and anger I'd been holding inside since seeing him came out with a vengeance—the pain and betrayal I felt didn't help either. I turned to go, but he was on me, his fingers biting into my shoulders as he tried to turn me around to face him.

Big mistake. I don't play well when I am angry. I pulled every ounce of power from the air around us and pushed it at him, watching the shock on his beautiful face, his electric eyes as he was thrown from me, violently into the air. I could hear blood rushing through my ears, through my veins, as I allowed the power full reign inside me. I wasn't a fucking victim, and I wouldn't become one at his hands.

I watched him stand up slowly, carefully. He was linked into my power. I could feel him tapping into it, pulling from it. His death had not severed his connection to the coven. He'd known this entire time where and what we were doing. I could see his eyes registering the mistake he'd just made. I held perfectly still, waiting to see his next move.

"I didn't mean to hurt you, Syn. I am still learning how to control it," he whispered, looking down at is hands, as if they were foreign objects.

"What I do is none of your fucking business, Adrian. You chose a different path that doesn't lead to me," I allowed the power to drain slowly, watching as he did the same. "*If* I sleep with another, it's not up to you to decide if it's wrong or right. It would be my choice. *My* choice."

He shook his dark head, his hair falling into his turbulent eyes. "He isn't what you think he is. I'm trying to protect you."

"I'm a big girl, Adrian, and I don't need protecting. Not anymore."

"You do against him! Fuck, Syn, we all need to be protected against him. Are you that fucking blind? Wake the fuck up. You're smarter than that." He growled as his hands fisted at his sides, as mine had.

"Then, what the fuck is he?" I asked, narrowing my eyes. I could tell when Adrian lied, I could feel it. He was also holding back, trying to shield the connection we had through the coven.

"I can't tell you. Not because I don't want to, Syn, but because, if I do, I forfeit my life and maybe even yours."

That wasn't a lie. I watched him as my mind ran wild with what he was saying. If Ryder was something else, wouldn't I have noticed by now? "Adrian—" I said, shaking my head as nothing he was saying made sense, but the connection between us was telling me he spoke the truth.

"I can't," he said dejectedly as he dropped his shoulders and shook his head. He stepped closer, and I instinctively stepped back from him as I watched him closely. "Just don't take anything around here at face value, and don't fall for him, baby. Promise me that somehow we will be as we were before we separated. Promise me we will be together when this is over."

A sob escaped my lips before I could stop it. I couldn't promise him anything anymore. He was undead. He'd left me, and, even though it wasn't maliciously done, it was done. I stepped further away and turned back toward the house. I couldn't promise him anything, but I still loved him...just not in the way he needed me to, and it hurt to not be able to say it.

"Syn!" he called, but I was already moving, refusing to fold, because, if he caught me, I'd lose this battle. And this relationship would be the death of me—literally. I was halfway to the house, blinded by tears, when I ran into something hard and unmoving.

"Did he hurt you?" Ryder's voice was angry and sharp.

I shook my head and tried to push past him, but it was like pushing a concrete wall. I looked up with tears swimming in my eyes, trying to make my tongue work, but whatever he saw in my eyes must have showed him I needed to be alone, because he let me go and followed at a close distance behind me.

When I reached my room and moved to close the door, he held his hand up on the wood frame, stopping me from closing it. "They found a few bodies. I need you ready to go, Syn, and I need to know what he did to make you cry. In that order. You're mine to protect, and he overstepped. He said he wanted to explain why he had done it. You needed closure—you all did. But no one makes you cry; not on my watch."

"Ryder, this is none of your business. As I told him, I'm a big girl, and I can take care of myself."

He bowed his head, giving me a dark, dangerous smile. "Keep telling yourself that, Syn, and you might eventually believe it."

"I don't need you to believe it, or myself, for that matter. I have to protect, endure and live for my coven. *In that order*. I'll be ready to leave in five minutes. Let me just go grab my big girl panties," I said, leaving him at the door.

"I'll be strong for you, Syn…if you need it. You don't always have to be the strong one. I'll be your glue if you want to crumble. I'll hold you together," he said, lifting his eyes and meeting mine.

"And what if you're what's making me crumble, Ryder? What then?"

His lips lifted into his sexy smirk. "Then I'll put you back together. I will never tear you down, Syn. I will always protect you from anything and everything that would. I've yet to find anything in this world, or any other, who can take me on—keep that in mind," he said, lifting his eyes to meet mine, before he started to turn away.

I was startled by his words and what he had said earlier when we were dancing. He didn't like me, did he? "That's what I'm afraid of."

~~*~*~*~*~*~*~*~*

Chapter
TWENTY-FOUR

I quickly changed into jeans and a different shirt that covered my arms. The fact that the other bodies we'd examined had blown up had a lot to do with the long sleeve shirt—shrapnel hurt like hell. I put on leather boots, which were not pretty, but would protect my feet, and headed to the door hurriedly. I was just going into the fourth minute of the five I had told Ryder I needed to be ready.

He was in the hall when I came out. Leaning against the wall, holding the vest that had saved me last time. "The other gear is in the car. We don't know what to expect this time, but there are five bodies. I'm taking no chances with your safety, Syn. This one could go south in a hurry. I want you on the perimeter, not on scene, until the dogs have finished."

My heart sank in my chest. Hot tears stung my eyes as I felt the loss of the five people this crazy asshole had taken from the world. "We need to catch this killer, Ryder. This has to end soon." He had bomb sniffing dogs? *Why didn't he bring them to the last crime scene*? I wondered as I turned to ask him just that.

"I just got them, so before you go yapping off and

demanding to know why I didn't think of it before—finding well trained dogs that can sniff through Otherworld bullshit is harder than it should be."

Well that settled that! I narrowed my eyes, wondering how he had figured out what I'd been about to ask him.

"You speak through those pretty blue eyes. Try to work on it if you don't want the world to know what's going on inside that brain of yours."

Fuck you, Ryder. I put it in my eyes, with a smile lifting my lips, even though I really didn't feel like smiling, while we went down the never ending stairway to the front doors where his men waited with my coven. This was going to be a long day.

The crime scene was like the others—half torn up bodies lounged in chairs, while some sat in different positions up against the walls. The only difference at this scene was the sheer volume of bodies. Some looked no older than twenty. A few wore dresses, while others were in workout clothes. "They're all in shape," I mumbled more to myself, trying to figure out what we were missing.

"What would that matter?" Zahruk questioned, coming up with his face crumpled in disgust.

"Nothing, but that they're all in shape, which is the only connection, besides the fact they all come from a faction of the Otherworlders, which brings us back to Necromancers. They choose victims who they can benefit from controlling. Strong bodies to use, but if it was Necros…well, they forgot the bodies. So, we can check them off the list of suspects."

He smiled, which looked off with his forehead

crinkled from the rich scent of death. He was Fae, and they could smell everything ten times stronger than I could, and I was fighting the churning of my stomach that fought to release the coffee I'd sucked down earlier today. "Good to know, I guess; no dead fucks cutting people up," he replied.

"They went off the pattern, though. Most of these women are Fae. So the body count is higher for the Fae than it is for the Humans. Our Fairy knew her killer. She let her inside her house. These women looked surprised, as if they never saw death coming. Unlike the Fairy, they were not at their homes," I scanned their feet, most wore shoes, except the two who were currently footless. The others had on either running shoes, or dress shoes. I leaned down to examine a young female whose hands were held above her head in full rigor mortis. She had handprints on her wrist, her feet had been bound, but her eyes looked lifelessly at something in front of her. She also had those damn holes in her shoulders as if something had pinned her to the chair, but nothing inside the room was small enough to have been used.

"Two killers, or more," I said horrified. It had been bad enough to be looking for one sadistic killer, but now we had two to find.

"You sure?" Ryder asked, coming over to stand next to Zahruk by the female's body.

"Someone held her hands above her head while someone else dissected her organs. She has handprints on her wrist, with nail marks in the tissue, so we're looking for at least one female. She had to have been killed a while ago, her blood stopped flowing about seven hours ago or so. She also has the same holes in her shoulders as the Fairy and all of the other victims. It's possible that whatever the pins are, it could be what is sapping their powers."

"So, you are saying there are more killers than we originally thought we were looking for?" Ryder asked, clarifying what I had just said.

"Yep, two sadistically twisted fucks—or more. To kill on this level? They had to have had help. I don't see two people killing this many women in this little time, Ryder. We have three Fae and two Witches with an empty spot but a blood pool, so someone else was here before we were, taking their dead with them when they left."

I watched Ryder nod his dark head once before he clicked open his phone and hit redial. I waited, trying to figure if he was calling the Guild, or who it could be that he thought his people needed to be informed.

"Vlad, now," he barked at his phone, "No, this cannot wait, put him on the fucking phone. Get him on the damn phone now!" He waited briefly and then Vlad's smooth voice came through the other end loud enough for me to hear.

"What is it, Sire?"

There was that title again.

"Did you remove a body from a crime scene?" He waited and then hung up. "It wasn't a Vampire. Vlad hasn't removed any bodies."

"So, it wasn't a vamp, which leaves Light Fae. These are all Dark Fae," I said, scanning the room briefly before resting my eyes back on Ryder.

"I would smell it if they had a Light Fae inside this room."

"We're missing something. You said the dogs picked up nothing. Not even a trail, so what if the killer is using the body parts on him, or herself? It would confuse the dogs and why didn't they put the bombs in—too many bodies, maybe? But they could have gotten the same results using just one to destroy the crime scene," I mused looking around and finding a picture sticking out from beneath one of the bodies. "Arianna, again."

She was dressed in a business suit. Her blonde hair piled and pinned on her head. With a red X painted over her face. "This is the same picture we found at a different crime scene."

"So it is. I'm glad she agreed to extra security," Zahruk said as his eyes settled on the body the picture had been under. "She kind of looks like Ari, Ryder?"

Ryder was already squatted next to the body with his elbows resting on his knees as he examined the corpse. "She does, but so does that one," he pointed to the body in the chair.

"Think whoever is doing this has something against Ari?" I asked, looking at the faces of the other victims.

"Hard to tell right now. She's a gentle creature, timid at best," Ryder replied as his eyes evaluated the other bodies, "I cannot see anyone holding a grudge against her, which was why we were shocked when news of the assassin's interest in her came."

"How did it come?" I asked, wondering how they would know an assassin was trying to take out his future bride. It wasn't like we posted it on the telephone poles and said "hey, by the way, we plan to snuff out your life." No, we just got the assignment and carried it out silently, making damn sure no one was the wiser that we were coming.

"We got a tip, from one of Arianna's people,

that someone was trying to kill her; someone highly trained, and very deadly. We don't take chances with our own."

I narrowed my eyes on him. "So someone just walked up and told them, *hey, we plan to kill the Light Heir,* and you believed them?"

"No, we investigated it, but we couldn't find any leads, and since your Guild was the only one in the city, we came to you. If the Guild Master offered to help, we knew it wasn't from within your Guild. Marie sent me a letter a few years back, claiming you were different than the others inside the Guild— better, faster and smarter. I made sure to ask for you. Alden was only too willing to give you to us for a price. So tell me, Syn, if you had been told to take out my bride, what would you have done?" He asked, watching me closely.

"I would have observed her movements for around two weeks or so, until I knew a time and location where she would have been more available, and with fewer guards. Then I would have gotten the team together and taken her out before a single word of what we had been told to do could have gotten out—clean, simple, and painless. I wouldn't have told a single person who wasn't in on the hit about the target. When you take a mark, you don't want retaliation, so telling anyone else would be off limits. A breach of contract. So let me ask you this, Ryder—who would be so sloppy to get word out about taking down a target, unless your future bride placed it on herself?"

"Why would she do something like that?" he growled, obviously upset with where my mind was going.

"Because she loves attention, and being targeted by assassins has only garnered the newly found Light

Heir a truck load of it. I don't know, Ryder, the Fae are secretive and yet she seems to be loving the limelight of being on the front page of every fucking tabloid in Washington State. In fact, Larissa brought in a copy of her having tea with the Governor. So, if she was so worried about dying—why is she at the Capitol building, having tea in a place easily accessible to an assassin?"

"Enough, she wouldn't be that careless. You are forgetting that pictures are easily forged."

"That's true, Ryder. But she's incredibly excited to be the new Queen-In-Waiting of the Dark Fae and couldn't ask for more in her new husband who is generous and handsome—the exact words she fed the press last week in Spokane at the Mayor's settee where she had tea *with him*. Same exact thing she told the Governor."

His teeth ground together as the tick in his cheek flared to life. "Enough, Witch."

I smiled. I was back to being just a Witch. Back where I knew what my job here was. "I'd like to try something, if we can clear the room, and get to a safe distance."

"What do you have in mind?" he asked, his eyes still narrowed dangerously. He was touchy about his future bride. So was I. I had forgotten that he was spoken for, and yet, I'd come close to losing myself in his arms. Easily done, since he was Fae, and they didn't follow the same rules about marriage as we did.

"We clear the building and try to see if I can make it explode," I smiled impishly crunching my nose at him as several cameras from the others on scene were going off, taking in every detail of it.

"After the CSI team clears it; you think the dogs missed one?" he asked quietly as he tilted his head as if listening for something.

"If we missed them, Ryder, the dogs could have. Something we did at the last two scenes set them off, and if I'm right, it was magic. Thing is, if I'm right, that means the Vampires have more knowledge of the crime than they are letting on."

"It's possible," Ryder said as we waited for the crime scene unit to finish with their pictures.

When they finally cleared the scene, and we moved a safe distance away, I put up my shield, but nothing happened. I closed my eyes, replaying everything I had done inside the other scenes and smiled when I found what it was. Second sight, I'd used it moments before the bomb in the body cavity of the Fairy went off, and I had been using it when the one at the Vampire's sad excuse for a calling card, went off.

I pulled in just enough power to use it, and sent it seeking around the crime scene—nothing happened. I stepped a few feet closer while Ryder talked to his men, and sent it out with a force that would reach inside the house where the bodies lay mutilated.

The house exploded with enough force that I was thrown from the spot I had been standing in, and ended up landing on something hard. I coughed as smoke took to the air, making it thick and un-breathable. Noise exploded as my ears started to work again, I tried to sit up, but the once solid object gave in as my hands pushed on it, and a deep growl sounded next to my ear.

"I hate when you're right," Ryder said inches from my ear as I turned over to find his face close to my own. I'd landed on him. It was becoming an irritating pattern. I smiled brightly. I didn't mind being right, not at all.

"Thanks for breaking my fall," I whispered, not sure if he would hear it over the fire crew we'd called to be on standby as they rushed to stop the fire from spreading while we had waited for CSI to move from it.

He laughed. The sound vibrated against my chest, where our bodies were fused closely together. "Anytime you want to be on top, just let me know," he said, wiggling his eyebrows, which was entirely out of character and made him boyishly handsome.

"Pervert. A building just exploded. We should be acting professional," I mumbled, already detangling myself from his limbs.

"True, and you were right, which means I need to call a Vampire and find out what he knows."

"If nothing else, they know the person who is creating the bombs, and it could get us a lead on these sick whack-jobs."

Chapter
TWENTY~FIVE

The next afternoon, I helped Larissa prepare her outfit for the Samhain celebration at the Guild. She had picked out a corn-yellow silk dress that had an imperial waistline and would make her green eyes pop. She always looked good, no matter what color she wore. Her perfection and her smile were contagious.

"Syn, I wish you would reconsider and come with us tonight instead of going with him. Who cares about the stupid contract? I just wish he would commit to releasing you back to Alden after we figure out who's trying to kill his fiancée."

"What if he doesn't? What if this was all just an elaborate scheme that we played into? The picture at the crime scene was the same one at the others that you showed me. All of the victims in the files match her description from the tabloids."

"That's a whole lot of what ifs, Syn, without any hard evidence."

I sighed dejectedly, she was right. I needed proof, something that was substantial enough to make people understand that something about these murders had to deal directly with Arianna. It could be as simple as the killer having an infatuation with her, but what didn't make sense was the fact that the Fairy had been killed, or where a woman would fit into it, other than some creep being infatuated with the Light Heir?

Speaking of fairies, Malinda walked in with a stack of shopping bags. She smiled as Larissa and I jumped up to help her from where we had been sitting on the bed talking. "Oh thanks! Ryder sent me, told me to tell you he secured an outfit he would like you to wear tonight," Malinda said, grinning from ear to beautiful ear.

I bit my lip as Larissa's eyes swung to me questioningly. I knew what she was thinking—hell, I was thinking it, too! He'd bought me an outfit, and there were bags filled with shoes and other things, as well. "It's not a date!" I blurted, causing both women to turn around with beautiful matching smiles. "It's not," I grumbled.

Malinda tipped her head and examined me. She crinkled her nose at my sweat pants and tank top. I waited, watching her mind work—yeah—good luck making me look beautiful. Tomboy I could do, deadly assassin—in the freaking bag, but beautiful arm candy? I almost laughed at the thought.

"Ever considered cutting your hair into an actual style?" Malinda said as Larissa snorted from beside me. I tossed her a cool leveled glare.

"What's wrong with the style I have?" I asked, feeling self-conscious.

"Nothing, but I don't think it has been cut in years—and I can see from here that it is a few different lengths. I am very good at cutting," Malinda said softly.

"Yeah, so am I," I retorted, meaning something else entirely.

"Can I trim it a little? I promise not to touch your bad girl image," Malinda said with a mischievous smile.

I was about to put my foot down when Larissa caught my eye. She looked excited about this, and the fact that I was doing something really girly. "Fine," I said before I could think it over too much.

~~*~*~*~*~*~*~*~*

It took Malinda a few hours of primping, waxing and some very painful plucking before she had me stand in front of the mirror she'd brought into the room. Larissa stood, primped up perfectly herself, but I had done a full transformation.

I had straight hair that had been curled to frame my face. Malinda had put on a light blue eye shadow that made my eyes strikingly electric-blue. She'd applied a light blush to my cheeks, which gave my face definition and a touch of softness that was usually hidden by the tough exterior I hid behind. My lips had been glossed, but she'd left them alone otherwise, stating that they were already perfect.

The dress Ryder had secured, was an expensive designer work of art. It came to mid-thigh, leaving my legs and most of my thighs exposed. It had a sweetheart neckline and was sleeveless, other than the two straps that flowed over my shoulders and crisscrossed around the back to meet the only other strap that held the back of the dress together. They also kept the dropped V-line back from showing off my rear.

"Syn, you look stunning," Larissa said fanning

her eyes, to keep from messing her mascara up.

I smiled at her from where I still faced the mirror, I didn't think I came close to matching her beauty, but I was one hundred percent woman. I let my eyes drop to the stunning small heels and smiled. They laced up my ankles and had tiny ruby-like jewels that matched the necklace with the twin dragon pendant on it that he'd sent to replace the Celtic one he'd given me days ago.

"Wow, Malinda, you managed to make Syn speechless," said Larissa. "You're amazing, simply amazing."

A knock sounded at the door right before Adam walked in, and stopped dead in his tracks as his eyes filled with love for Larissa. "Wow, you look amazing." His eyes swung to me as I watched through the reflection of the mirror. "Holy shit bricks, Syn. No way in hell are you going anywhere with Ryder, looking like that."

I smiled and crinkled my nose. "It's not a date. It's simply research, so I know what to expect from the Fae at the ball."

"Yeah, keep telling yourself that and eventually you might buy it. I'm a guy, Syn, and I'm telling you straight up, we don't take women looking like that anywhere for just research."

"Well, it's not like that," I said, wondering who I was trying to convince more, myself or him. My smile faltered with the reality of what I was doing, and who I was going with, as it came rushing back. I closed my eyes briefly, knowing I was making a mistake by going with him tonight.

"Adam! Get out. You always put your foot in that

fat mouth of yours. She is going for research. Who cares if she is the hottest damn thing in the club?"

I blinked as Larissa went off on Adam. She thumped her foot as she crossed her arms and waited for him to leave. I knew better, he wouldn't walk out and leave her upset, he wasn't built like that. "It's okay, really," I said when Larissa didn't let up.

"I don't like her going out with him, not without us as backup, baby," he said, messing with the suit tie he wore.

Larissa's sternness gave way with a huff of air as she rushed forward and threw her arms around Adam's neck. "I know. Me either, but she won't change her mind. Looking like that she could have any guy inside the Guild, and we could watch her back."

I snorted, "I'll be fine. If not, I'll call you. You two enjoy tonight. We need to let loose once in a while. Just remember not to make a huge show of your newly found feelings tonight, never know who might try and use it against us. Just be safe and have fun."

Adam smiled roguishly. "Right, so I shouldn't grind my erection into her on the dance floor?"

"Ahh." I held up my hands, covering my ears and making a dramatic show of it. "My ears!"

We all laughed, including Malinda, who had been watching us. Adam released his hold on Larissa and stepped up until I had no choice but to turn around and face him. "Be careful tonight, Syn, and call us if you need us. We'll come," he said, before pulling me in for a hug carefully so he wouldn't wrinkle the silk dress. "You look beyond amazing tonight. Just remember, one call, and we're there."

I smiled. "Considering I don't even know where *there* is, you're just going to have to trust that I am able to take care of myself for once."

He swallowed and nodded. "We're well aware that you can, Syn. That's never been in doubt. It's all this shit with Adrian coming back, it has to be driving you crazy knowing he was a few blocks from us this entire time, and you're vulnerable right now."

It was my turn to swallow and nod. "You guys remember what I told you earlier about Adrian's reason? I mean it doesn't change what he did by leaving us, but you guys should know that Adrian is still tapped in to us, and our power. I need to release him; just couldn't do it yesterday."

"Shit, so he's been connected to us this whole time," Larissa said, putting her hand over her mouth in disbelief.

"Yes, but I didn't realize it until yesterday, when I knocked him on his ass. He pulled from my power I'd tapped into. He was able to draw power from me." I exhaled a shaky breath and continued. "I'll take care of it, but I needed you guys to be aware of it. He's chosen a side, and if he was ever against us, well, he'd know our moves before we would."

~~*~*~*~*~*~*~*~*~*

I walked out of the room with my friends by my side. We'd all be leaving close to the same time, and I was as ready as I would ever be. With my heart in my throat, I looked down the intricate, long stairwell, and found Ryder watching us.

He was decked out in a black suit. He was mind-blowing in his finery. I had to remember how to breathe as I took the stairs carefully in the heels. He was devastating tonight. His short hair was loose, falling over his ears as he watched me through his perfect bedroom eyes. His hands folded in front of him as that damn smirk—*Who knew a smirk could be so sexy?*—covered his beautiful mouth.

When we reached the bottom of the stairs, he came over, his eyes roving over my body hungrily. His wicked sexy grin was blinding compared to the usual cocky air he showed. Tonight, it was gone, and in its place was a sexy, intriguing male who is oozing *fuck-me* vibes that sent heat pooling to my molten center.

"Syn," he said, lifting his grin into a smile as I accepted the arm he held out for support. "You look beautiful," his eyes slowly slid down my body with naked desire in their fiery golden depths.

"You clean up pretty good as well, Ryder," I mumbled, before biting my lip as I smiled.

Adam leaned in, and whispered in my ear before he and Larissa went out the doors. "It's *so* a date."

I blushed, turning to watch his retreating back as he turned, smiling back at me and wiggling his eyebrows childishly over his shoulder. Ryder only laughed as we followed them to the waiting limos outside. I looked at it and smiled. It was black gloss in color and had tinted windows.

He opened the door and we climbed in silently. When we were fully inside, he sat across from me, his eyes dangerously sexy as they caressed over me. I crossed my legs and leaned against the seat for support, which I needed in any form I could get right now.

I managed to pull my eyes from his hungry look,

and watched as we drove away from the mansion. The loud sound of a cork being removed from a bottle made me jump and place both hands on the soft leather seats.

Ryder laughed. "Scared to be alone with me, Pet?"

I watched the bubbles flow from the bottle, none of them landing on his crisp, freshly- pressed suit. "Not at all," I lied.

"You're a horrible liar, and you should be afraid. The things I want to do with you right now—I could think of a few hundred things to do right now that don't include ending up at the club tonight."

I swallowed, and narrowed my eyes on him. "This isn't a date. You promised to give me a time frame for when you would release me from the contract."

This isn't a date. Yeah nice, Syn! He hadn't said anything about it being a date.

"So I did," he said as he reached into the window box, pulled out two champagne flutes, and held them in one hand as he filled them before offering me one, which I accepted without a second thought. I needed it to calm my nerves. Or at least, that is what I told myself.

"Are you going to?" I asked, prompting a reply from him.

"At the end of the night…is what we agreed on. Until then, you promised to relax and not try to control everything. So drink and relax, Syn. Loosen up and enjoy the night. Tomorrow we have to continue the search for the killers."

"What is it you expect from me tonight exactly, Ryder?" I asked, watching his dangerous eyes flick to my legs.

"The possibilities are endless, Synthia."

~~*~*~*~*~*~*~*~*~*

Chapter
TWENTY-SIX

We entered the sub-level of the club through an elevator, which I hadn't noticed the first time I'd been inside Sidhe Darklands. It had been a short visit, and I'd been bordering on hysterical when I'd been here signing his contract. This level was exclusive. Security was thick inside the club tonight, as if they were expecting trouble. I fisted my hands at my side as my eyes wandered and took in the assortment of creatures inside the club. It was something out of a nightmare—different branches of the Fae, many kinds I had never seen before, mingled with Humans who looked to be here willingly. Of course, I looked willing—which was really still up in the air.

"Having second thoughts?" Ryder asked, close enough to my ear that his breath fanned my neck.

I turned to look at him as the elevator behind us opened to allow more Fae into the room. One approached us, not even trying to hide what he was. He was dressed immaculately, his long hair tied at his nape with a strip of leather. His eyes were red with orange around the irises, his hair coppery red.

"Ryder," he said, stopping to bow to Ryder who tipped his head to acknowledge the newcomer.

"Altius," Ryder said, dismissing him with a nod.

The Fae moved on without another word as Ryder's men, who had come earlier, moved in around us. Tonight they looked wild, as if they were fighting against something and losing. Zahruk's eyes were wild, his mouth tightened from strain. I was about to ask if he was okay, or if we should worry, when music started up from the stage set up in the front of the small intimate club.

We were moved further in as more and more Fae showed up, each acknowledging Ryder before moving deeper into the club. "You know them all?" I asked, turning my head to watch his response.

He smiled wolfishly, his eyes turning to lock with mine. "Why wouldn't I?" he asked quietly which I barely managed to hear over the pounding music.

"Because most look like they might be from the Horde," I said just as quietly.

His smile grew bigger. "Someone has been doing her homework," Ryder replied, his eyes now challenging me to say more.

If he was moving in on the Horde in the King's absence it was none of my business; not unless it caused a war which crossed into my world. Until then, it was his problem. I smiled and let it drop for a moment, which only seemed to amuse him.

"Dark Fae consorting with the Horde," I whispered more to myself, but Ryder heard it anyway.

"Dark Fae and the Horde are allies, Synthia. This isn't a well-kept secret. It's fact. We help them when needed, and they help us."

"Funny, I thought the entire Fae race loved to

fuck each other over. And right now their king is missing. Meanwhile, your father isn't. Sure you're not trying to step into the Horde Kings shoes?" He smiled mischievously and watched me as he refused to answer. I rolled my eyes and watched as Zahruk stepped up closer to Ryder.

"Zahruk, Tara is heading this way. Tell her to give me twenty before we start, and make sure she explains to our people the rules, as well as the others," Ryder asked of his man, before offering me his arm once more.

Zahruk didn't reply more than to nod his head and run interference with the busty blonde, who was even now trying to get past him to talk to Ryder. Her vibrant green eyes locked on me as her lips twisted into disgust. She was one hundred percent Fae—of which kind I wasn't sure. She was definitely pissed-off Fae.

"Girlfriend?" I asked as he pulled me over toward the dance floor.

His sexy smirk was irritating as he dodged the question and pulled me against his chest smoothly. "Jealous?" he asked as he scanned my face.

"Hardly," I said, grinning.

"You look beautiful tonight, Syn." His eyes burned with an intensity that made me hesitate as I placed my arm around his, until he pulled me around to stand in front of him.

"You look nice," I replied, not used to giving out compliments to guys very often, unless you wanted to count telling Adam he looked good goofing off, which he did and often.

He rewarded the comment with a half-smile as his

hands settled around my waist. "*Nice* is what you tell your brother when he does something stupid."

Wow, this guy was good. I smiled, even as I tried not to, considering I had been thinking the exact thing when I'd said it. But the funniest part was his disgruntled look. It was as if I'd just insulted his person. "You look like a rogue who is intending to do very bad things, while looking very debonair, Ryder," I amended.

His smile brightened wickedly, his eyes alight with laughter. "Maybe I am—would you let me, Syn?" he asked, all traces of the laughter gone instantly.

A silent shiver crept up my spine as his fingers touched my flesh, his eyes caressing me more than his hands could ever manage. I licked my lips and considered lying. Ryder was beyond my boundaries. I'd set them for a reason, and yet, to tell him I didn't want him would be just that—a lie.

"I want you, Syn. I shouldn't, but it doesn't change the fact that I still do."

I swallowed and turned my face away the best I could manage, to keep him from seeing the brilliant blush that flowed over my cheeks. "I'm not like Claire, Ryder. I won't be used because you want sex. That's what it would be—right?"

If he said yes, then it would be so easy to just walk away. He was unpredictable. The dancing we'd done had been intimate and surprising. He'd been gentle, and so unlike himself on that dance floor. Here he was once again, a sexual male. Ryder was not the kind of man you walked away from. He was the type you crawled away from, trying to remember your own name after he was done with you.

"I want you, and I make no excuses for what I am, Syn. Claire satisfied a hunger—one *you* created. Would you rather I had taken you, even though I knew you were not ready? I'm not that person. I don't take unwilling females—*ever.* Don't have to." His hands moved up, his finger and thumb cupping my chin, so I was helpless to look away from his exotic eyes. "You want me, your body trembles with it."

"And if I don't want to be yours, Ryder?" I questioned, fighting the urge to claim his full mouth.

He smiled as Zahruk motioned to him from beside us. "I told you, tonight is all about being yourself, Syn, but it's more than that. You get to see us as our true selves; as Fae. You will be mine tonight, even if I have to hunt you down and claim you."

"And if I run?" I asked, narrowing my eyes as he stepped back from me, his hands releasing my chin and lowering back to his sides slowly.

"I enjoy a good chase."

"I'm not a dog, Ryder," I growled as an overwhelming urge to run hit me.

One minute, I wanted to kiss him, and the next, I wanted to run from him, or kick him. I wanted to run from the pleasure I could read in his eyes. He was enticing. The sexual pleasure I felt just being around him was intoxicating. My body felt the need to give in to the truth of his words, but my mind knew he was quicksand.

"No, Syn, tonight you are mine. You're the white stag everyone will be chasing." His smile turned dangerous, his eyes glowing brightly, even in the dimly lit club. A shiver crept down my spine as his words filtered in.

"Deer, dog—I'm neither."

"You want to be chased. You need the choice taken away from you. You fight your own desires, because you think you cannot handle it Syn. You punish yourself for something that happened long ago, something you couldn't have changed, because destiny decided it before you were even born. I'm just giving us both what we want."

"Fuck destiny. I decide my own destiny, Ryder. Not some fucking preordained bullshit," I snarled, tired of listening.

"Fighting destiny," he shook his head and smiled. "Every time I think you can't become more of a puzzle, Syn—you throw in a new piece. Go ahead and add more pieces, Syn, it only makes me need to put them all together, and see what the end result is."

"You're a bastard, Ryder," I hissed, trying to turn away and put distance between us. He didn't allow it; he moved with Fae speed, my hair flying from the wind he created, wafting over my cheek.

"I don't make excuses for what I am, or what I do. I play hard. I love hard, and I fuck even harder, Syn. I am what I am. So if you play games with me, keep in mind, I will be more than happy playing them with you—and I always win," he growled close to my ear before his lips gently fanned against mine. When I looked up, he was once again standing beside Zahruk with his lips twisted in a devastating smile that was a touch of seduction and amusement.

It was the first time I'd seen him move like that— no not move. He'd just sifted time and space. I had known the Fae could do it, and even though I'd known he should've been able to, it still shocked me to my very being. I'd never seen it done before, ever.

I brought my hand up against my lips, still feeling his kiss burning against them. I shook from the need to chase him, and see where that kiss would lead. I didn't. Instead, I turned away from him, searching through the crowd for an empty spot to stand in, away from what my body was feeling for Ryder.

I didn't find a place. Instead, I found Adrian standing back in a dark corner with his eyes watching me intently. I stepped forward and headed directly toward him. When I stepped closer, I could read overwhelming desire in his eyes.

"You shouldn't be here, Syn," he whispered.

"And you should be?" I retorted as I watched his face close off once more. He was hiding something, I could feel it. "Adrian—what are you hiding?" I asked him bluntly, tired of playing word games.

"I told you as much as I could, Syn. You should leave the club, *now*."

I scanned his beautiful face. His face was covered in the same strain as Zahruk's was. I took a look around the room, noting several other Fae in close proximity looked the same as if they were struggling against something. The air had also grown thicker inside the club, a loud thud echoed as metal grates were pulled across the only exit I could see.

It looked like a fog machine was sending a thickness into the room, making it eerie and dangerous. I turned, looking back at where Adrian still watched me carefully, his eyes pleading as his head bent forward. "You need to run fast and deftly when the time comes, baby. Don't stop running until you're safe." And with that, he disappeared from where he had been, vanishing from the spot completely.

"Adrian?" I called, not caring how stupid I looked

talking to thin air.

A microphone sounded as someone tapped it and welcomed the Fae.

"I see we have some fine hunters here tonight." A tall leggy brunette said as her emerald green eyes looked around the room, her smile was filled with amusement as growls sounded around the room in confirmation to her words. "The fun will start shortly. Until then, find the prey you brought with you and make sure it is marked."

Howls erupted from the men next to me, along with several others who joined in. The fine hair on the back of my neck stood up with their unworldly sounding noise. I turned around and started back in the direction which the elevators had been, but I must have had it wrong, because in their place was a wall of solid glass.

"Going somewhere?" Ryder asked from behind me.

"Home," I whispered breathlessly, as I took him in—he no longer looked Human. He was taller, his features more defined as he watched me. I truly was his prey in this moment; his eyes tracked everything I did. When my hands fisted at my sides, his eyes flicked to the subtle motion, his head tilted slightly to the right as if he had just found the most exquisite prey.

"There is no turning back now, Syn," he said thickly, his voice leveled with gravel in his tone.

"Ryder, something isn't right here," I breathed.

His wicked smile sent my pulse racing as he closed the distance and sniffed my hair, his hands resting on my exposed shoulders. "I can smell your fear, Syn, your heart beating wildly as it realizes what it truly wants." His mouth pressed against my ear, making heat flood my center. "You want this; you want me to catch you. To make you my mine in every sense of the word, don't you?"

I placed my head on his chest as his hands drifted lower, his fingers tracing softly along my naked arms. I lifted my head as he took my hands and rubbed my palms with his thumbs in small circles. "And if I don't want this, Ryder...What then?" I asked out loud.

"Tell me you don't want me, Syn, make me believe it, and I'll open the fucking doors and let you out now."

My gaze locked with his as his dangerous golden fire searched mine. He'd hear the hesitation if I lied, I sensed he'd know it in this form. His smile was beautiful, his eyes rimmed in obsidian, caressing their golden depths. I considered backing away from him and running, but I wasn't sure where to run.

"Ryder," I murmured, watching as he moved closer, his head still tilted as he closed the distance between us.

"I promise to be gentle with you." His mouth pressed against mine, his tongue pushing against my lips, demanding entrance as he invaded it. I melted against him, his kiss stealing my mind and taking my will as I took his mouth and allowed him to continue. When he broke the kiss, I held on to him. Not because I wanted to, but because my legs had stopped working along with my brain. I gasped as his hands held me pressed tightly against himself. "That's why I brought you here, Syn, because you need release and you would never give up this tightly controlled self-image you have of yourself without it being this way."

What the hell did he mean by that? I liked control. I didn't like unknown factors, and right now I was *inside* of one. I stepped backward, and watched as he followed me step for step until I was pressed up against the solid wall of glass. "I'm not that girl, Ryder. I don't want to become food for anyone, or a plaything to you."

He stopped and narrowed his eyes sharply. "Who said this was about that, Syn? This is about making *you* lose control." His hand reached up and tilted my face until I was staring up into his inhuman eyes. "I want to see you wild, see who you are inside." His finger drifted up from my navel to my heart. "Inside here. Not what you pretend to be for everyone else."

I snorted. "I don't pretend to be anything that I'm not, Ryder. This *is* me."

He smiled and licked his teeth slowly. "No, this is the battered five year old who doesn't want to be afraid. The same one who watched helplessly as her parents were murdered. She's afraid to be hurt, or getting attached to something she might care too deeply about and lose one day. This is the hurt little girl that got a little too cocky on an assignment and lost her first love. You're afraid of losing, of paying the cost again because beneath it all, you're scared. You're afraid that you might like it. But once in a while you need to let go, Syn. You need to live."

"I'm not that five year old. She was *helpless*. I will *never* be like that again," I choked out, while fighting back tears. I hated that he could read me like an open book as if he had a window into my very soul. I could feel him *inside* me, touching, opening up pages, and reading me easily.

"No, Syn, you're a beautifully skilled killer. One who shows no emotion, and yet, you wear your bleeding heart on your sleeve. Everyone else just failed to see it. But I do. *I* see *you*."

I was about to tell him off when howls erupted around us, coming from the Fae close to the stage. The female announcer was back. She was wearing some kind of cloak. The only things visible were her ringlets of brown hair and ruby red lips.

"It's time to hunt, my beautiful brethren. We honor the Horde King and give him strength tonight, in hopes of his swift return back to us." When the last word came out, the room erupted into a mass of guttural screams.

I shook as the room began spinning around me with the realization of what was happening. I knew Ryder was watching as everything fell into place inside my head. I should have known, should have been smarter, and shouldn't have let him distract me. I was in a room filled with several different castes of Fae on Samhain Eve.

"The Wild Hunt," I whispered breathlessly, afraid to be right, afraid that if he said yes, then I'd been brought here by him to be hunted and claimed as his prize in a contest filled with skilled hunters.

His head tipped slightly as his smirk tugged at the corners of his mouth. He removed his hands from me and started undoing his cuffs before removing the jacket and deftly working the buttons of his crisp white shirt, opening it to reveal his wide span of sinewy muscles with his brands pulsing on his skin.

I shook my head in disbelief, this wasn't happening to me. "He's missing, why honor him?" I offered, hoping it would stop this, but knowing it wouldn't.

"Why not, Syn?" With his shirt undone, he shook easily out of it, and handed it to Zahruk who had come up behind him, right on cue, as always. The other men from his group once again circled us, but Ryder didn't stay. "Have her ready, and make sure she knows the rules, gentlemen."

I watched him walk away as his men closed in around me. I was shaking from the mere rumors of this event. I was so stupid. How could I have missed it? A club of Fae, on Samhain! *How fucking stupid was I?*

Zahruk handed off the dress suit jacket and the shirt along with it. He nodded at Dristan, who left and returned swiftly, carrying a glass of red liquid. "Drink, Synthia; it will help steady your nerves."

"Get me drunk and then make me run?" I asked through chattering teeth.

He smiled. "Trust me, it will help you."

Dristan handed me the glass, his eyes roving over me from head to toe before he walked around and lifted my hair, his fingers grazing my skin as he removed the necklace Ryder had given me for protection. "Run fast. He isn't marking you for death, Syn. He's earning the right to claim you as our ancestors have done for many millennia. When he catches you—and he will, you will have to decide if you want him. Unlike the others, he will allow you to choose to become his for the night."

"Decide what?" I howled, shivering as Zahruk and the rest of the men smiled coldly.

"If he is worthy to have what he has caught. If not he will release you for the next hunter to claim. Just remember, not all follow the honor code Ryder does; some won't care if you scream *no*."

"There's a flag, right? If I make it to the flag I don't have to choose," I seethed as anger from what was about to happen set in.

"Not quite," Zahruk said crinkling his forehead.

"If you make it to the white flag, you get the hunter who won last year in your bower."

I raised an eyebrow in question, "And who won last year?"

Zahruk smiled impishly. The others were laughing, and snickering around us. I closed my eyes and counted to twenty, hoping I'd wake up in my bed, and this would all be a twisted nightmare. No such luck. I took the drink from Sevrin that Dristan had handed off before removing the necklace, and gulped it in one drink, much to his boisterous amusement.

"Sevrin, go get her one more," Dristan said carefully.

"I need to tell you the rules, Synthia," Zahruk continued. "They're going to open a portal into the enchanted forest, and you will get a short head start. Don't touch anything; no flowers—they're poisonous. If anything calls to you—stay the fuck away from it. Only death calls to you inside Faery. The hounds will scare you at first, but they are trained to find and protect until their rider gets to you. They have been given your scent already. They follow a hunter; only a few can tame the hounds. Nod if you understand what I am telling you."

I nodded while sipping the red liquid down slowly.

"Nothing is safe inside Faery; *nothing*. Ryder will find you, Syn, and he will protect you," he said again.

I snorted, enjoying the heat of the alcohol as it rushed through my system. The room had stopped spinning, but my heart hadn't stopped pounding yet. I swallowed yet another drink before meeting Z's level gaze. "If Adrian joins the hunt, what happens if I go with him?" I asked, letting curiosity get the better of the situation.

The men around us growled with disapproval, but not Zahruk. He was calm, his face showing no signs of anger or disappointment. "If you choose the pup, Ryder *will* kill him. Inside the hunt he won't care who he takes out, Syn, Human rules don't apply inside Faery. Don't be stupid. Don't make him do something he will regret later. With his mind consumed by the need to hunt, he won't be himself. The hunt brings out the true side of the Fae."

"So I go to him, no matter what, unless I tell him I don't want him?" I asked, and when he nodded, I continued, "Why didn't you just start with that?" Dristan smiled charmingly in reply as if he'd already told Z that. The rest seemed not to care either way.

Zahruk narrowed his eyes and shook his head before smiling. "And to think, Ryder said you would be fighting us every step of the way until we got you inside Faery."

"I know when to fight; just like I know when I'm fucked. Right now, it would be futile to argue or fight. Either way I do this ends up with me inside of Faery with Ryder hunting me down. I could kick and scream if it would make you feel better?" I smirked as he shook his head.

His lips broke into a smile. "Nah, you have balls, Syn, you might just have enough to give Ryder a run for his money."

I flinched as the woman started up again, her voice flowing over the noise of the crowd easily. "Are we ready to hunt?"

Shrieks and howls once again erupted as I bent down to undo the heels that laced around my ankles. When I stood back up, I handed them over to Zahruk. Metallica's *Of Wolf and Man* came on, as the wall across the room shimmered to reveal a portal into Faery.

~~*~*~*~*~*~*~*~*~*

TWENTY~SEVEN

The room around us vibrated with powerful magic. It took a very powerful Fae to call open a portal this big. It also meant there was a leyline directly beneath Ryder's club. It was wide open, drawing from this planet and Faery alike to open it.

Wind rushed through as the hole opened, a wide meadow with a forest bordering at the edge of it stood where the wall had once been. I looked around trying to see through the wall of men that surrounded me.

"He isn't inside the club anymore, Syn. He opened the portal," Zahruk said, noting my quickly measured scan as he held the heels awkwardly; as if he had never held a pair before.

"Here," Dristan said, handing me a white cloak. "You're the white stag," he mumbled as he met my stare. "Put it on before you go through the portal."

I accepted it slowly. The material was soft and cool against my fingers as I unfolded it and shook it out. I inhaled and let it out slowly as I hung it over my shoulders, lifting my face in time to watch Adrian push his way through the wall of men around me.

He swallowed and nodded at Zahruk, who nodded back, and the wall of men turned as one, giving us their backs to allow us privacy. "Tell me to fight him, Syn, and I will."

"He would kill you, Adrian," I murmured as my hand went up to stroke his cold face softly.

"I'd die for you, Syn. I did it once, and I'd do it again," he smiled impishly.

"I told you, Adrian, I don't need saving."

"He's going to—"

"Stop," I cut him off, not needing it drawn out on paper for me. "I know exactly what he will do, Adrian. I'll be okay," I replied barely above a whisper, knowing the wall was listening.

"It won't change, if it happens—it won't change how, or what I feel for you, Syn," Adrian growled hoarsely.

"You have to let me go, Adrian; just let me go," I rasped as women started moving in the direction of the portal, laughing. They had no sense of self-preservation inside of them. They smiled and laughed, taunting the hunters with hot looks, or sashaying their hips. "I get it now, Adrian. I get why you sacrificed yourself for us. You did it because I would have done it for you."

He smiled and nodded sadly. "I would again, in a fucking heartbeat, baby."

Zahruk spoke low, but clear over the noise inside the room, "Synthia, it's time."

I exhaled and squared my shoulders. Shook off the tremor that threatened to come and stepped forward, pressing a soft kiss to Adrian's forehead. "I got this, Adrian. I agreed to come. I can handle this."

I scanned his face as I placed it between my hands to say goodbye, but I let them drop as I felt the power ripple through the club. Electrifying and intensely powerful dark magic. My mouth went dry with whatever words I'd been about to say still inside.

I didn't need to turn around to know he was there. I could feel his power caressing my skin, his intense stare searing into my soul. I could smell his scent wafting thickly in the air, wild and untamed, sending my senses into overdrive. He'd opened the portal and had come back to openly taunt me.

"Run fast," he whispered as he stepped beside me, to look down at me with a roguish grin that promised he'd catch me—and fast.

I didn't reply. Not because I couldn't think of more than one hundred different ways to tell him to shove that smile up his ass, but because I was smart enough not to goad my soon to be chaser. Nope, I was his fucking rabbit today. He was the wolf, and if I was lucky I'd make it out of this with some shred of dignity. "You shouldn't have done this, Ryder," I whispered, meeting his piercing stare with one of my own.

"I suggest you stay away from the other females," he tilted his head, drilling his challenge in as his eyes warned of what he meant. "And the other hunters— for their own protection."

Legends of the Wild Hunt hinted that not all of the women here would make it out alive. I turned my head, looking at the women and wondering if they knew the truth, if they would panic. Run, or scream maybe. I couldn't save them, and, from the smile and defiance in some of the women's eyes, I could tell some were well aware of what was at stake.

"Do they know?" I asked in a small voice as my eyes came back to rest on his. His eyes grew somber as his smile grew tense.

He bowed his head, his voice harsh as he spoke, "Are you sure you want the answer, Syn? You should be more concerned with what I plan to do with you once I have you at my mercy."

I wasn't worried with what he would do to me. I already knew. Surprisingly, I wanted him to catch me. I wanted to feel his touch on my skin, his mouth seducing my mind. I wanted him, and it burned inside of me like a fire out of control. It was unlike anything I had ever felt before, a need so primitive and wild that it consumed me from within.

The brunette made her way through the crowd, her full ruby lips smiling as she walked to the front of the portal. "You have a head start. I would use it wisely. When the hunters are released, the portal will close," she smiled coldly, "Locking you all in. You can only return with whichever hunter you succumb to. You may pass now." She moved to the side as women took off running in every direction.

I stood, watching the others run as if their very lives depended on it, which for some it did. I watched them with a calmness I shouldn't have felt. Well I was calm until every eye in the place turned in my direction, because I had yet to exit through the portal. I smiled and turned back to Ryder. "Good hunting."

His mouth opened, and closed, as if he couldn't believe I'd just wished him luck hunting my own ass down. His smile was brilliant when it flowed onto his face. "Better run fast and hard, Pet, and I suggest you get started. I'm already impatient to catch you."

"Bring it, Fairy," I smiled, before walking off barefoot into the Realm of Faery.

It felt as if I had been wandering around for only a few minutes, but time had no bearing inside Faery. Worse than that, I had no idea how they calculated it. I'd passed the flowers Zahruk had been talking about—with women laying around them, doing things to themselves best left unsaid.

The forest was growing denser, and my feet were screaming with every step I took. I'd considered stopping and just waiting for him to find me, but he didn't deserve an easy catch. He deserved a punch in the nose, or worse.

I jumped as a ripple tore through the air, the green leaves shuddering from the force a moment before the air grew thicker, tainted with a growing disturbance. I turned and ran forward as fast as my battered feet would take me. I could hear hounds howling and snarling in the distance as I moved further into the wooded area.

Adrenaline kicked into overdrive, my mind screaming. I calmed the overwhelming urge to panic, pushing away the sound of the hounds as they howled in warning of the approaching hunter. Water beat against rocks to the west. I turned and ran toward it, hoping to cover my scent from the hounds.

I ran over grass and branches and came to a skidding halt on the edge of a cliff. I peeked over the edge and scanned for a simpler way down, I looked back over my shoulder as the beating of hooves grew closer. The hounds and a hunter were growing closer.

I swallowed and turned completely around. Waiting, watching.

I'm not sure how I knew it was Ryder that approached. Maybe it was the pulsing of power radiating from his body, incredibly stronger here, where it had been dampened inside my world. He sat atop a beautiful stallion, the horse stomping on the ground as it fought the rider for control to run freely, its sleek black body shining in the sun's burning light as its wild red eyes searched frantically for more open field to run through.

The hounds broke from the bushes and circled the horse, heads low with ears drawn back as they watched me closely. I stepped back as I lifted my eyes to Ryder, who had found me faster than I thought he would. He was incredibly beautiful atop his mount. His eyes glowing from within the cloak gave him away.

He looked like something from an age long past, or a battle scene depicted in a museum. A long, heavy cloak with a hood was drawn over his head in a heavy obsidian fabric that looked as if it could absorb light. Under this, he wore a tunic and trousers of the same fabric. Thick black straps studded with onyx jewels set in dulled silver crisscrossed his chest and held a variety of wicked looking blades as if he was expecting a fight.

I licked my dry lips, and stepped even further back and had to work to keep my balance as rocks fell from the cliffs edge. When I was back on solid ground, I flung my eyes back toward the Dark Prince. His eyes swirled with adrenaline from the hunt, his wild electrical current, wickedly abundant here, sizzled over my flesh, kissing it.

"Careful, Syn," he whispered as he lifted his hand

to remove the hood, exposing his face. He was even more beautiful in full Fae form. His face was lit up with his brands, his chest displaying them enticingly where his cloak was open enough to show them.

I said nothing, just watched him as he did the same to me. I looked down once more, judging the distance between the top of the cliff and the enchanting pool below it; a waterfall pounded into the water from the other side relentlessly. It was beautiful and serene, so unlike the emotions and adrenaline pulsing through me now.

He narrowed his eyes as he figured out what I was planning, "Don't you even fucking—"

I spun around and jumped.

A few things go through your mind when you do something stupid. Like, oh hell this was stupid, along with that moment of perfect clarity that this might be the last stupid thing you ever do. I'd just swan-dived off a cliff without any knowledge of how deep the water was, or if it held the Loch Ness Monster in its watery depths.

I didn't have long to wait before I hit the water smoothly. Luckily it was deep enough to dive into. I turned my body around and pushed off the rocks slime-covered tops and crested the water's surface effortlessly. I scanned the top of the cliffs for Ryder, but he was no longer there. I turned toward the shore and kicked my legs sending my body in the correct direction. When my feet were able to touch, I walked up and sat on a rock to catch my breath.

"That was stupid," Adrian said from behind me.

I spun around and took him in. He was wearing a cloak similar to Ryder's but Adrian's was crimson instead of onyx. I backed away from him, my feet once again in the watery pool. "Adrian," I warned as he lifted his blood red eyes to me. They matched his cloak. Looks like Ryder wasn't the only one who looked different inside of Faery.

"I won't fight him, Syn, but I'm damn sure that I'm not leaving you unprotected in this Fairy cesspool. Don't ask me to," he said, taking the place where I had been sitting on the rock.

I stood in the pool's cool embrace, letting the soreness from running wash away with the crisp, cool water. "What's it like, Adrian?" I asked, lifting my eyes to meet his.

"Don't ask me if I sparkle—so fucking tired of being asked that," he smiled, but it wasn't the same as it had been when we were together; he now had fangs that took away from it and left it cold. "It's different; I was able to keep the connection I had to you, though. I should have let it go, but I couldn't bring myself to do it, since it would have been felt by the coven. Didn't want you coming to look for me; it wasn't safe."

"You should have. It left us open, Adrian."

He was about to reply when he turned his head and disappeared just as he had last time. I stood in the water, not daring to move as Ryder walked through the clearing to the water's edge. "You jumped off a fucking cliff, Syn."

I smiled and nodded my head as he stepped closer, his hounds surrounding us silently. When he reached me and stood inches away he sniffed the air and shook his head, his eyes slowly searching my body for injury.

"I'm an enforcer and oftentimes an assassin Ryder. I free fall from buildings when needed. I jumped, but

I'm fine—besides being wet," I said icily. I wouldn't be in this situation if it wasn't for *him* anyway. I gave him my best smile before wading further away from him, back into the water.

He followed me in slowly, his boots making the water ripple as he walked up behind me and pulled my body back against his heat. "Decide, Syn," he said quietly.

"Either way I end up with you, Ryder. It's not a choice." I spun around in his arms and lifted my face to him. I wrapped my hands through the cloak's soft material and watched him as he lowered his head slowly.

"I need you to say it out loud, Syn. I won't force the answer from you," he replied before dropping his lips to fan softly across mine.

I gasped at the connection; it was sizzling. My mind went blank as his arms pulled me in as his kiss deepened until air was insubstantial; everything faded away but him and the need to have him, to allow him to dominate me. He pulled away as I gave in. "Let me have you for one night." His eyes searched mine briefly.

"Yes," I replied with more heat in my tone than I thought would be there.

His mouth claimed mine in a demanding kiss. When he pulled away, dragging me toward his massive stallion, I had to run to keep up for fear of being dragged in his haste. "Where are we going?" I asked, taking in the sizes of some of the hounds who now followed us. They were huge—and one had emerald green eyes that watched me intently.

He spun around and smiled victoriously, his hand

releasing mine as he reached into the cloak and pulled out the silver chain I'd been relieved of inside the club. His eyes locked with mine as he leaned in to place it over my head and click the clasp back into place, I moaned against him as the pleasurable emotions flooded through me once more. He held me through them, his eyes watching the reaction with pleasure. "I'm taking you some place we can be alone. Come."

Alone with Ryder. I shivered, but managed to hide it from him as he easily jumped up to straddle the horse and offer me his hand. I'd never even been on a horse before; sure I'd seen a few in the sprawling countryside, but riding them was an entirely different thing than looking at them as I passed them in a field.

He pulled me up to sit in front of him. I almost screamed when the horse decided to buck once under the weight. Ryder's boyish laughter was the only thing that kept me on the monster's back. "He can feel your unease, Syn. Lean back against me," he continued.

I leaned against him, and he took off at a slow trot, the hounds easily keeping up with us as he made his way south, down a small trail. It was hard to think of anything else besides Ryder as we made our way through the dense foliage. I closed my eyes and enjoyed the feel of his massive body beneath mine. Like this, with him, I felt safe as if I could let go and not worry about protecting everything around me.

I opened them as I felt the air grow thick around us, power radiating from the male behind me as we stepped through one scene into another. I gasped as the sensation of being in two worlds collided through me, intense and overwhelming, yet painless. "You sifted us?"

I looked around marveling at the scenery. It was beyond anything I had ever imagined. The sky was a mix of vibrant oranges, blues and reds as two moons sat on the horizon, cresting over the top of a mountain. The area around us was a grassy knoll with a thin body of illuminated water that flowed into a pond, which was fed from a waterfall.

Ryder leaned his lips against my ear when I sat up to get a better look around and whispered, "Welcome to the Fairy Pools, Syn." Wicked laughter followed his words. "And, no, I didn't sift us, so much as I opened a new portal to Scotland; a Scotland unlike any you will ever see from a tour guide as this side is in Faery. These pools cross between our worlds and feed the Fairy Pools of the Human world."

"The Fairy Pools?" I asked, turning my gaze back to where the water looked illuminated from beneath the glowing surface. I'd heard about the Fairy Pools in Scotland, had always wanted to see them. The algae glowed beneath the water and created an enchanted beauty which had earned it the name of the Fairy Pools. "It's beautiful," I said when he said nothing.

He dismounted and held his hand up for me to do the same. I did so willingly, as the horse instantly started to thrash without his master mounted on his back. Ryder released the reins he held in his other hand and slapped the horse's hindquarters, which sent the wild beast running. I watched it run to the edge of the water and lower its head to drink.

I dismissed the horse as I turned around to find Ryder staring at me, his eyes smiling with victory. His smile was captivating, if not a little bit too cocky. "So what happens now, Ryder?"

"Now, you finally give in and admit you want me," he purred huskily.

I snorted. "Okay, I want you."

He crinkled his nose and smiled. "That's not what I meant, and you know it."

I grinned. "Oh, Ryder, I can't wait to feel you over my skin; touching, tasting me, teasing my body—"

I stopped as he tossed back his head and laughed outright. Okay, I was being sarcastic, but I had planned on teasing him and then laughing at him. Not the other way around. When he was done laughing, he snapped his fingers and licked his teeth. "Get inside, there's a bath in the second room on the left, Syn."

"And where the hell—" I stopped, noticing a structure that hadn't been there just a moment before when I was talking.

"We're inside Faery. I can manipulate everything with magic here far easier. Go bathe, Syn. I will join you in a minute when I get the hounds settled," he said, turning to whistle down the sprawling countryside.

I shook my head and started toward the small, cozy-looking house that was lit from within. It looked right in place with the sprawling countryside around it, as if it belonged here. At the door, my hand hesitated. I looked up at the starless sky and twisted the knob.

Chapter
TWENTY-EIGHT

Inside was another story; it looked nothing like it had from the outside. Where the front room or entryway should have been was a sprawling bedroom, the bed, like all the others was big enough to fit a few bodies on it. Metal framed, with white silk covering the mattress. Pillows sat over the top of it, varying in shapes and sizes. The walls were covered in gold crisscross patterns while a plush carpet of the softest fabric covered the floor.

I stepped in and let my feet sink in, exhaling slowly. I looked around for the door Ryder had mentioned, since a heated bath sounded amazing after running and jumping into the lake's cold water. I gasped as I stepped into the outrageously stunning room.

Hot water welcomed me, bubbles covering the surface, and a bottle of wine sat chilling in a silver container filled with ice.

The entire room was sky blue with a huge dark blue oval soaking tub, big enough for a few people. I raised my eyebrows, wondering why everything involving Ryder was always big enough to fit an orgy inside of it.

I was still standing inside the large bathroom when he came in behind me, his close proximity causing my nerves to rise, his hands came around me and pulled the skirt of the dress up slowly. "Ryder," I said softly.

"Having second thoughts Pet?" He whispered against my ear.

"No, I just need you to promise that you won't feed from me," I answered him quietly.

"I told you I wouldn't, not unless you asked for it…most do, you know," he murmured against my ear softly.

His fingers caressed my skin as he lifted the dress up and over my head silently. My breathing grew labored as my lungs took in air and released it in quick, short gasps. My heart was racing from his touch, from knowing what we would be doing soon. It had been a long time since I'd even considered having sex.

His hand came up and pushed my hair to the side as his breath fanned the back of my neck. His lips touched it slowly, making small bumps break loose over the surface. He growled as his fingers looped through the small thong panties I'd worn. His breath fanned down my spine as he bent lower to remove them completely, kissing my skin as he did so.

I don't know what I had expected from Ryder, but this hadn't been it. Not this gentleness from him. He kissed his way back up my legs, sending small bumps and gentle waves of heat to my core until he reached my ass. I felt his teeth a second before they sank in, softly nipping at the skin. I yelped and spun around.

He was naked, his Celtic brands pulsing beneath his skin. His eyes glowed with liquid gold as they looked up at me from the floor as I stepped out of the panties. I exhaled shakily as he bared my flesh for his inspection, slowly coming back up, watching me with dangerous fire lighting in his eyes. "Are you wet for me, Syn?"

I moaned as his fingers pressed against the growing ache he was creating inside of me, his fingers rubbing against my naked sex as his mouth lowered until it found mine and kissed me softly. I captured his moan with my lips. His tongue pushed through my lips, demanding more. He pulled away, leaving me breathless as his wickedly handsome smile flowed up to shine in his bronze gaze.

"Get in the bath, Syn, before I bend you over and fuck you right here, right now."

I shook from the intensity in his voice, smooth and commanding. I turned and stepped over the edge and sank beneath the bubbles hurriedly. The water was warm and comforting even with my nerves fighting to take control. I watched Ryder from the corner of my eye as he stepped into view with his playful grin still in place.

His legs were thickly muscled, but bare of tattoos, his manhood stood up erect as it pressed against his navel. My lungs stopped working as I took it in. Nerves flared to life inside my mind as I considered high tailing it out of the tub. The guy was amazingly, sexually appealing, his body a sleek and well-defined mass of muscles.

"You keep staring at my cock, Pet, and this is going to move faster than either of us wants it to," he said, rasping his words as if he was as hot and bothered as I was. This bath was doomed to a half-life with the heat level inside the room.

I tore my eyes away from him with a nervous laugh bubbling inside of me. He stepped in and slid his magnificent body slowly into the water. "Relax, Syn. I promise to be gentle—the first time."

"The first time?" I asked hesitantly, meeting his hard penetrating stare.

His eyes challenged me, but he remained silent as he pulled one of my legs out from where I had been holding them up against my body. His eyes stayed locked with mine as his fingers rubbed the pads of my foot. "This isn't going to be over fast, Syn. It's going to take more than once to get you out of my system."

I wasn't sure I wanted to be out of his system. I should have been happy to hear it, but it sat like a rock on my chest. "You really think you can fuck me out of your system?"

"No, Syn, nothing with you could be that easy," he said, showing his teeth as he pulled my leg and made me lose my balance in the water.

I splashed on instinct, caught off guard by his heated words. His laughter now echoed through the room as he pulled me closer by my leg. I sputtered, spitting bubble bath from my mouth as I came up inches away from his lips. "You're an ass!" I tried to sound stern. Instead, it came out followed by laughter, which only grew as he watched me.

"By the Gods, you're so fucking beautiful," he whispered as the laughter died down. I swallowed and tried to think of something to say back to him. I gave in and kissed his lips instead. It was the first time *I'd* really kissed him, and I wasn't ready for the fire that ignited inside of us.

He picked me up easily, water cascading from our

bodies as he stepped out of the tub without breaking the kiss and carried me into the other room. When he did break the kiss, I growled with the need for him to continue; it made his eyes constrict with heat. I allowed him to set me slowly on the floor as his hands trailed down my body.

"I need you to know that we are leaving here within twenty-four hours, and I'm going to use every fucking minute of it, Syn."

"Ryder," I whispered, not sure how to get out of this unscathed.

"Twenty-four hours, anything I want to do to do you. Give me that much, Syn," his voice matched mine and was raspy, hoarse. He was one hundred percent Fae in this place, hunter to the core. His eyes tracked every minuscule move I made.

My core jerked awake with his words. Twenty-four hours of giving Ryder what he wanted. The image of his body fucking Claire's came floating into my mind. My throat closed as my mouth went dry. The idea was terrifying and enticing at the same time. Ryder wasn't the type of man you walked away from. You crawled on hands and knees; trying to remember who you had been before his touch corrupted you.

"Decide, now."

"One condition," I whispered, knowing I'd already lost the fight.

He cocked a dark eyebrow and tilted his head, listening.

~~*~*~* Ryder *~*~*~*~*

She thinks she can bargain with me. I can smell her pussy already. Begging to be fucked *by me.* She's succumbing to the alcohol in her system. She's not on edge here, not yet. Her eyes are constricting with need; her pussy clenching with the need to be punished and used by me.

My hands itch to touch her, to grab her hair and make those pretty fucking lips wrap around my cock. I want to watch her fuck me with her mouth until I come inside of it. I watch her pupils dilate and constrict, her lips flaring.

She's all woman, tempting me when she shouldn't be. She's less than I am and yet I can think of no one else, nothing else besides how she is going to feel and look when I fuck her raw. She fights me, fights her needs, and, yet, I can still smell it on her. Every. Fucking. Time.

She smells erotic, her wetness drenching her pink folds. I need to watch heat ignite in her vivid blue eyes as she accepts me inside her body. I want to watch as the heat from lust fills inside her endless depths as her pussy grows moist with her need while I'm driving my cock deep inside of her.

"Say it. Agree to it, Synthia," I growl; my cock is hard, hard as fucking steel with the need to be fucked by those juicy red lips, to dominate her completely.

She doesn't answer me, and it pisses me off. "Syn—" I warn her, letting the need I feel in my cock enter my voice.

"Don't make me forget it, please," her voice is filled with her resolve. Her answer shocks me. I would have thought she'd ask for the memory of tonight to be erased. I hate that I can't fucking predict what she does, what she says. In my world, it's deadly.

"I'm going to fuck you, hard." She needs to know

I won't be myself. I'll be driven by the need to fuck her until she submits to me in every way possible.

She lowers her eyes briefly. She's hiding the fear my words flare inside of her. When she lifts them again, I see more resolve and lust. Her body tightens with need. She wants this—wanted me to remove the option of saying no for her. I had seen it in her eyes as she watched me fuck Claire in my office. She wanted to take her place. She wanted me to bend her over and spread her apart and feed from her, instead of Claire. And fuck if I wouldn't have done so in a fucking heartbeat if I hadn't thought she'd run afterward. The hunger she created was wild and undeniable.

I watch as her nipples harden with my words. The musky scent of her wetness drifts in the air. My hounds growl fiercely and howl wildly into the night, feeling my excitement from where they are outside the door, guarding us from intrusion. The hunt makes them wild, lets them become the beast for a while.

"Say it," I growl, struggling against the urge to fuck her, here and now. If it was anyone else, I would. But this is Syn, and she needs to be shown the difference between a boy and man.

"I'm yours for twenty-four hours," she whispers, her eyes narrowing with self-loathing. She hates it as much as I do, this fucked-up electrical pulse that ignites the air around us when we are near one another.

"That's not what I need to hear from you. Now say it."

Her tongue snakes out, trailing over perfect fuckable lips as she watches me through narrowed eyes. My cock jumps with excitement with what those red lips will be doing to it soon.

"Anything you want, for twenty-four hours," she corrects her earlier statement.

I barely contain the growl that rushes to my lungs. Excitement makes my pulse increase as she moves to step closer to where I still stand. Her hips flare, and she moves closer to me slowly. I hold my ground, letting her come to *me*. Those tight hard buds stand up proudly as her tight breasts jut forward begging to be pinched and kissed.

I'm going to use every fucking minute of my time with her. When she walks tomorrow—if she can—it will be with soreness between those thighs, reminding her that I fucked her. And she's going to be sore—*everywhere*.

Chapter
TWENTY-NINE

I wanted to cry, and yet I couldn't. It was a weakness I couldn't afford with this man. I shouldn't be excited and yet I was and it floored me, because I shouldn't be. I was wet—for him! It was unimaginable. My body was traitorous; already moisture pooled between my thighs for him. My nipples begged to be touched.

The images of him bending Claire over the desk, his rock hard cock making her scream—it had been haunting me ever since I watched them. I was giving him control, giving myself over to him for an entire day or more if I was right and his agreement was based on Fae standards.

Why did I feel so much excitement when I was supposed to hate his kind? His hand came up as he wrapped it around my back and brought us together, placing his lips on my neck. I blushed as I realized he could feel the hard pebbles my nipples had become.

"Is your pussy wet for me, Syn? If you lie to me about this, I will punish you," he growled thick with lust.

I brought my eyes up as my hands went flush with the sinewy muscles of his naked chest and washboard abs; his touch warmed my body instantly. I bit my lip and considered what I should say. If I lied, he would abuse me, and I *might* like it. If I told him the truth, he would know I was already weak with need for him. "Yes," I whispered as I felt his lips as they curved into a wicked smile on my neck from where he was standing against me.

I could feel the evidence that told me he was affected by me as well. My fingers curled with the need to grab and stroke the silken shaft that was poking against me.

"I could fuck you right now, right here, and you would let me. Wouldn't you?"

"Ryder," I growled, needing him to do as he said right now.

"You want it now, want me to take you. You want me to spread you apart and shove my cock deep inside of this sweet wet pussy. Don't you, Pet?" His voice was hoarse, rough with need.

I would have let him do anything to me at this point. He didn't need me to answer his question. I couldn't if I tried. His fingers were stroking and touching my skin, along with his tongue caressing my neck, and it was too much. I could feel the storm building, close to the surface with his touch; the fire kindling, igniting and burning out of control—*for him*.

"Get on the bed and face me, Pet. I want to see you."

I stepped closer to the bed and hesitated as my stomach swirled with nerves. This was it; no going back. If I did this, I'd never be me again. If I did this, there would be me before Ryder and after. No middle. He was the fucking Dark Prince! And right now, he wanted me. And even if it made me less, I wanted him. I sat down, deciding right then that it would be worth it in the end.

"I need to taste you…to part your sweet pussy and fuck you with my tongue until you fill my mouth with your sweet honey," he growled before pulling away, his eyes wicked as he watched my body spasm from just his words.

My knees grew weak as my body leaned closer to him. He watched me as his hand explored my sex leisurely. His words left my head spinning. My mouth watered with the image he had set. I hated myself for it because I wanted him.

He raised his head and the dangerous intensity in his eyes, the raw need he had for me almost dropped me to my knees. "I choose when you come tonight, Syn. I can smell your pussy. You're close to coming, and I haven't even begun to start with you," Ryder growled huskily where his mouth hovered next to my ear.

"I need to come, Ryder," I replied with a layer of gravel in my voice.

I closed my eyes briefly, fighting to regain my mind. It was a red haze of need; need for the Fae whose words were taunting me.

Those dangerous amber eyes met and held mine captive. I was so fucked. I would never be the same girl I was before I chose to walk into the party with him. I turned away, afraid of the desire I read in those eyes. Afraid of what I felt for him.

The feeling of being watched made me bold as heat ignited in my nether region with the thought of what was to come. I laid my head on the softest pillow and turned in time to watch Ryder.

He stalked me from the edge of the bed, knowing I was already his. His eyes feasted on my naked flesh.

"Spread your pussy for me," he whispered thickly.

My hands lowered to my flesh, and I hesitated briefly, shaking with the urgency to please him, which shouldn't be there. I'd never allowed another to watch me touch myself. The act was sensual and private, intimate. In the end, the urgency won, and I allowed myself to do as he asked and part my flesh for his greedy eyes.

I watched as his nostrils flared. I'd long suspected he could smell my need, but I'd refused to believe it. His eyes started to glow with lust, plain and simple. My eyes lowered to his cock, and I groaned. He's hugely endowed, and fear of it licks inside my sex-starved mind, making it work against me.

He is bigger than anything I have known or tried before. His lips turned up creating a wickedly sinful grin. "Touch yourself for me, Synthia," he growled as his hand slid down to cup his sex.

"I want to hear your noises; make yourself wet." The heat in his timbre excited and ignited the flame inside my inner vixen. She raised her head and smiled wickedly.

The harsh intake of breath that erupted from him as I smoothed my hands over my breasts excited me and I watched him as he moved closer and watched. When I raised my eyes to meet his I was amazed at the raw need I saw in them, my skin grew taut under his greedy gaze.

I caressed my naked flesh and watched as flames leapt inside his eyes. He watched me for several more minutes while he did the same to his cock.

"Get on your knees on the bed and face me," he growled hungrily.

I did it, bending over seductively, allowing the seductress inside of me to splay my hips and ass for him as he had ordered me to. When I faced him again, he stepped closer, his hand stroking his shaft. His eyes landed on my lips.

I didn't need a guide to know what he wanted from me, I'd done this before, and most of it was instinct and the need to please your lover. My smaller hand replaced his as I looked up to see if it was what he had intended for me to do. His eyes searched mine intently. I lowered my mouth and opened it, using my tongue as I flicked the tip of his cock with my tongue. I wouldn't be able to take him completely—but I was damn well willing to try.

The hiss that broke from his lips was all the encouragement I needed. I kissed him and licked around his flesh, curving my tongue around his silken length. He was too big, though my tongue still molded to the sensitive side of his hugely thick cock, enjoying the feeling of his heart beating inside my mouth.

My hand tightened around him, jerking him off slowly as I fed my mouth more of him until I felt it pushing against the back of my throat.

"Your mouth is so fucking hot, Syn. Fuck, you drive me crazy. Look at me. I want to see your eyes as you fuck me with your mouth," he growled, fisting his hand in my damp hair. He pushed himself further in and began to move inside my eager mouth. He fucked my mouth with his cock as his eyes seared into mine.

My teeth scraped against his soft sensitive skin,

gently but firmly enough that he growled. His legs strained to keep himself upright. I smiled around his cock seeing the muscles tense as he pushed in again and again, the saltiness of his pre-cum igniting the fire inside of me.

He pulled out, leaving only the head entombed inside of my mouth. His eyes locked with mine in a silent battle of wills before he pulled out completely and used my hair to push me back onto the bed effortlessly, forcefully, in a show of dominance. He was showing me that he was in control.

"My turn," he said, dropping to his knees and gripping my hips as he pulled me to the edge of the bed where he had kneeled. I moved my body, sitting up until I was perched on my elbows in an upright position so I could watch him.

His eyes still locked with mine as he reached up and gripped my hips. He lowered his eyes to what lay bared to him and grinned devilishly. His hands moved slowly as he spread my legs even further, until he had full access to my soaking slit. I was wet—for him.

There was no hiding the evidence of my desire from him with my sleek wet heat bared to his greedy eyes. I watched him lower his mouth closer without touching it, without giving me what I needed. "Ryder—"

I almost screamed as his tongue came out and licked the sensitive bud softly, yet firmly enough to make my body shake from it. I dropped my head as he caressed it sensually. He hissed, as if he was angry. But his voice, when it broke through the haze, wasn't angry—it was seductive.

"Look at me. Open your eyes and watch me fuck you with my mouth, Syn."

Shivers erupted over my skin as I forced my head to stop swaying and come back up to meet his hungry eyes. The moment I did, he parted me and licked the soft slit slowly, methodically. Watching him as his tongue stroked my most sensitive parts was highly erotic. I moaned as he continued, his eyes taking in every emotion I experienced from his touch.

My head felt as if it weighed a thousand pounds and eventually it rolled back once more and he growled as we lost eye contact again. He stood, making me cry out at the loss of the heat his mouth had created on my flesh. I watched as he stood and leaned over me, his cock warning me with what was to come as he stretched up and grabbed the pillows easily with his tall frame.

His brands pulsed and moved with a life of their own. I moaned as I imagined how it would be to finally give in to the urge to trace them with my tongue, to see how he tasted. He pulled on my hips, adjusting them until I was perched with my ass on the pillow and exposed to him.

"Break eye contact and I stop; everything stops. I want to see you as I fuck you, Syn," he warned heatedly.

"I need release. I need you to make me come, Ryder—now," I begged.

"Not until I tell you to come, Syn. In this place, I *am* your master, and you come when I fucking allow it. Your pussy gets rewarded when you please me. Do you understand, or do I need to teach you how to serve me?"

I moaned, but I managed a nod of agreement.

Twenty-four hours of this? I'd die; but what a

glorious freaking way to go.

He sank between my thighs once more, and I willingly opened for him, exposing myself to him as he demanded. My legs trembled from the need for him to continue his ministrations to my core. I watched as he placed soft kisses to my thighs as his mouth got closer to where I urgently needed him to be. My hands came up and gripped his hair, but his own hand came down stopping mine and removed them easily as he held them down on my own stomach.

I felt his fingers as he trailed his free hand down my stomach to my sleek core, touching, feeling and exploring every inch with a leisure I wasn't feeling. "Ryder," I growled, and shivered as his husky laughter sounded from between my thighs.

"What's wrong, little, Pet? You want to come don't you? You want me, a *Fae,* to fuck you hard and fast, don't you? And I will, Synthia, I plan to fuck you until you're sore from it; until your pussy is swollen and tender, and then I will fuck you again. By the time I am done with you, you will be ruined for every other fucking man in this world and the next. Tomorrow, when you walk, if you *can* walk, it will remind you that I was I inside of you; that I fucked you until you couldn't remember your own fucking name. And that you allowed a Fae inside your body and *lived*."

My womb constricted, my pussy tightened and juices flowed that shouldn't have come from his wicked words. He'd just slapped me with what and who he was and I couldn't have cared less, just so long as he made good on his words. I cried out as his mouth hovered, his tongue lapped at the juices his heated words had created. Fear flickered in my eyes as I considered his words.

He was killing me slowly. My body was so hot,

on fire, so ready to explode, and he knew it. He was taking his time, driving me past the brink of rationality. I cried out as his finger slowly entered me, his eyes low and filled with intensity as he fed me them.

"You're so fucking tight, Syn. You want more don't you? You want to ride my fingers until your pussy comes all over them." His voice was strained.

I cried out as yet another finger entered me, filling me. He pulled them out to the tips and rammed them back in several times before his mouth descended on my clitoris, sucking it in and releasing it in perfect rhythm with his fingers. I was so fucking close, my body was straining, flushed with moisture from the need to find release.

I felt my body cresting the glorious peak, but just when I thought I would detonate from it, he stilled all motion of his hand and mouth, thwarting me from coming. My muscles tightened around them, milking them for more, but he refused to allow me to come.

"Ryder, please," I pleaded, needing to go over, needing to crest that magnificent precipice and ride its waves.

"Not yet. Don't even think about it. I'll tell when you can come, Pet."

His mouth lowered, his hot breath fanning my core before his tongue flicked against the soft, sensitive nub. He put another finger inside of me this time and the fullness was overwhelming, painful and pleasurable as he slowly, meticulously pushed them in the tightness. Preparing me for his massive size— without this he'd tear me apart and we both knew it, but knowing didn't make my body agree with it; this was fucking torture.

"You're too tight. I want to put my cock in you so fucking bad, Syn. I want to drive it in until you scream my name. Do you want it, Witch? Do you want this Fae cock fucking your tight pussy until it comes for me?" He growled as I nodded eagerly, uncaring if he was Fae. "Say it. Tell me you want me to fuck you, say my fucking name." His eyes captured mine.

"Ryder, I need you—" I moaned it, unable to make my mouth work correctly as he drove his long fingers inside of me and his mouth sat inches from the sensitive spot that would make my release instantaneous if he allowed it.

"Tell me to fuck you, Syn, tell me to fuck this pussy until you come."

"I want you to fuck me, Ryder; fuck my tight pussy. Make me come," I screamed as my body quivered with the need to release. My muscles sucked greedily at his fingers, pulling them even further into my core.

"Such a contrast to your normally cool façade. Your body wants me, Synthia. Even as you struggle against what your mind is telling you. You want my fucking cock; you want it buried inside of your tight body and right now you'd do anything I asked you to do, just to be fucked by this hard cock. Wouldn't you?" He growled, and my body responded violently clenching against the pain and pleasure his fingers were creating deep inside of me.

"Yes!" I screamed, needing his touch more than I needed my fucking pride.

He lowered his mouth, hovering even closer than he had been, his eyes locked with mine as he pulled and pushed his thick fingers inside more as he prepared me for his splendid cock. "Not yet, Synthia," he warned, his voice filled with gravel.

I pushed against his fingers, raising my hips to take even more of him and give him more access, more depth inside of my tight confines. He opened his mouth, watching as my eyes grew lowered with desire. He was going to allow me to finally find release from the need that he'd created, and nothing else mattered.

His hand that had been holding mine to my stomach was removed, allowing me to grab his hair the second he released them. His lips hovered, rubbing over my clit softly—I didn't want soft. I needed fast and hurried. I needed to come; needed my release. Now. "Ryder, now please; I need it now," I cried, feeling it as it started to build. My hips rocked, trying to force his mouth down to where I needed it.

"Good girl," he whispered, "Come for me," he smiled and dropped his head to my soaking core.

He drove his fingers deep inside at the perfect tempo with his mouth, sending me instantly over the cliff he'd been holding me on. My body trembled violently as sweat broke out on the back of my neck, small goose bumps flooding over my skin as my nipples hardened even more, if it was possible.

This was why women flocked to the Fae; for *this*.

I was still coming back down to earth when I felt him pushing against my entrance with something hard and silken. I cried out as he entered me roughly, swiftly, his magnificent cock tearing me apart as he entered using my own release to slide himself inside of me easily. Or it should have been.

He was too big. Pain tore through me instantly. My body tightened against him, trying to expel him from my body. I scratched his sides as I tried to fight against my own pain until I saw his stamped on his beautiful face. He was staring down at me while holding perfectly still as if it was hurting him as much as it was currently scaring and hurting me.

"It hurts," I cried, feeling a single tear slide down my face and land on my breast where I was still propped up.

"Try not to move, Syn. The pain should lessen in a moment. I didn't expect you to be this tight. I knew it would be a tight fit, but you fit me like a fucking glove and it's been too long since you have allowed someone else inside of you."

That was easier said than done, since I felt an overwhelming need to move with him inside of me. His hand came down, holding my stomach still as he ground his teeth in pain. "You're so fucking bloody tight, Pet. Your pussy is stretching for me, adapting to the size. Your pussy is growing wet to give me more access. Can you feel my cock pulsing inside of you, wanting to move, to fuck your tight, wet pussy?"

My muscles released slightly, and it was only then that I realized he wasn't even half way inside of me yet. "You won't fit," I whispered softly, and then winced at his hoarse laugh.

"You want me inside of you, Syn, and I want to be inside of you. You're strong enough to take me. I'm past the point of no return. I couldn't stop if I wanted to now. I need to be inside of you, Synthia; right now. Relax, wrap your legs around my hips and tilt that pretty soft flesh up and let me show the difference between a boy and man fucking your sleek heat."

I considered saying no. But as he kissed away the tear, catching and trailing soft kisses back to its source, I gave in. It was such a gentle contradiction from the Dark Prince I knew. I rocked my hips, enjoying his grunt of pleasure as I did so. I wrapped my legs around his back with a little help from him and tilted my core giving him a better angle to feed me his cock.

And he did, he pushed further inside with his soft words of encouragement driving all the pain away as he put inch after glorious inch deeper into my core until I could feel him pushing against my womb with his cock.

"Bloody hell, woman, you were made for my cock," he growled as he brought his lips down softly to press against mine, his kiss was hard and driven by his need. I met his pace, giving him back everything I had. He started to move his hips slowly, and I cried out from the fullness he was creating inside of me, his mouth catching and smothering it.

He pulled away, his eyes locking with mine as he pulled himself out and rammed it in—hard. My body shook with the need to come, to explode and shatter against his silken shaft. My legs trembled from the sensations; nothing in the world could have prepared me for this.

Nothing could prepare anyone for something as beautiful as this dark sensual creature that was between my legs and buried inside my body. His amber eyes watched as I just felt him moving, his fullness and his touch as he rode me. I forgot to think when he was inside me. The only thing that mattered was this storm he was creating.

~~*~*~*  *~*~*~*~*

Her body consumes me, unlike anything I have ever had before. I'm losing fucking control, like a fucking youth in Transition experiencing his first feeding. She's so fucking tight and sweet. I need to move harder, faster. She's as glorious as I thought she'd be as the need to fuck is overriding her mind. She's moaning and begging me for more.

God her *pussy*—so tight, so fucking gloriously tight and hot in her need. Slick from her release and another one growing inside her already. Her pupils dilate, the storm of her body tightening, building. She's a fucking Goddess, and *she's mine*. The beautiful chaos in her eyes drives me insane.

I need more. I need everything she can give me. I need to push her from my system. Twenty-four hours is not enough time, I'm not sure a lifetime of fucking her will be enough to sate the beast inside of me. Teeth grinding, her small little sighs and moans drive me insane as her pussy milks me, sucking, pulling me further inside her sleek heat—I growl as the beast demands to move deeper, demanding to punish her body for making us wait for *this*, for *her*.

She won't deny me after this. She can no longer pretend that this electrical fucking attraction doesn't exist, not after this. Not when she's moaning for more, and her pussy is soaking wet—*for me*.

Her body tightens, nipples puckering up and demanding my touch. My mouth. My cock. Tight fit, yet she took it gloriously, wantonly. She's so fucking beautiful, so wild in her lust. Her hips spread and her nails demand more of it. It is so fucking hot to watch her eyes grow hazy with lust, her teeth worrying at her lip as I shove my rock hard cock further, allowing the beast to add his inches for her greedy pussy.

Her eyes widen as I grow larger inside of her, pushing against her womb, demanding she take all of it. I pull out a few inches and watch as she demands them back. She's lost in the throes of need, beautiful fucking chaos. Her body trembles for the release that

I'm holding at bay, teasing her body with. She isn't ready for this one; the last was only a sample. The next is going to send her over the edge, and I plan to watch her as she falls.

"You're so fucking tight. I need to fuck you hard, Syn. I need to fuck your pussy hard. Are you ready?" I growl it. She's greedy, and her body is taking my cock and accepting it. She cries out, her sultry fucking voice makes my balls tighten with the need to release. She's fucking exotic, a diamond in that fucking pile of rocks.

I shove myself in until my nuts scrape across her tight ass, hitting it hard as she takes me inside of herself willingly. Her legs quiver with the need for more. I pull out. She cries out from the loss of my cock. It's good to be me right now. Never has a pussy looked so welcoming, so pretty from the abuse of my cock. I reach down, flipping her over swiftly until her glorious ass is in the air, bared to my eyes.

I bring my mouth down, awarding her with the heat of my breath against the tight ass, before I smack it just hard enough to hear her cry out with pleasure. She clenches tight. She thinks I'm going for her ass— and I might, but not tonight. Tonight, I just want to be buried inside of her tight pussy.

I spread her legs, lifting one and holding it until her pretty pink pussy is fully exposed to me, for my cock. It's growing more for her. Even now, her hips push for more, juices flow as her lips part to welcome me. Red and angry from the abuse I'm doling out and she's taking. I'm not even close to being done yet; I plan to use every fucking minute of the time I was given, driving my cock into her welcoming sheath.

I nudge myself at her opening and she cries out, feeling the tip as I push inside of her slowly. She wants it fast, and she will get it, but she's more exposed this way. More open and vulnerable. She has no bloody fucking clue what is pushing into her, what she is allowing to fuck her pretty pink flesh. If she did, she'd run. My brands pulse with the need to feed. I smile as I grip her ass and sink further inside of her.

She's so fucking sweet. Her muscles tighten around it, sucking my cock, milking the tip as if it's in her mouth. I add an inch, and she cries out, her head tossing with need as she pushes against me, wanting it all. She's so fucking hot in her need, her wetness increases and drenches my cap. I reward her with another inch.

"Ryder, now," she cries with gravel deep in her voice. Sexy as fuck.

"You want this dick don't you, Pet? You want me to give you all of it. I feel you growing wetter with need. I can feel your pussy drenching my cock as it makes room for more. You're so fucking tight, so fucking wet, Synthia. I want to come inside of you. Do you want me to?"

She nods emphatically, stupid. She has no bloody fucking idea what it is like to be claimed by something like me. She's so innocent and so sweet in her lust, in her need to come for me alone. I give her a few more inches and watch as her hips slide even further apart, taking what I give her without complaint. Not many have fed the beast and lived, yet she laughs for him and just spreads her hips and takes more.

She's so fucking mine now.

~~*~*~* *Synthia* *~*~*~*~*

I cried out with need as he refrained from pushing himself in all the way. I needed him to fuck me hard.

Now. He was immensely huge, and my body was greedy for him, it needed the rest. I tempted him by pushing myself further, impaling myself on him.

Encouraged by his grunts and groans as I took more, every fucking inch he gave me was glorious. "Ryder, fuck me harder!" I cried out and was rewarded with more of him buried inside of me. I rocked my hips, adjusting to take him.

His laughter was husky, heated. "Greedy little, Pet. You want more?" he purred before pushing more inside of me.

I moaned and buried my head to stop the cry that threatened to come out. He grabbed my hair, yanking my head backward and crushed his mouth against mine. I felt him pushing further inside me, and I celebrated in it. My muscles contorted, clenched and milked his cock with a vengeance. His growl deepened as he kissed me harder.

I was behaving like a slut, and I didn't care. Here and now, it was me and him. There was no room for regret, no room for fear of tomorrow. I bucked against him and enjoyed the feel of his teeth as they scraped against mine. He gave a husky growl of approval as he pulled away and released my hair. I grabbed the sheets to hold on and knew he was about to release his control.

I was right. He pulled out and slammed himself hard inside of me. I released a scream and pushed against him, pulling him back inside of me. "Harder," I cried, needing him to let go.

"I could hurt you," he whispered, straining as he fought for control.

Ryder wasn't one to ever give up control and the

idea of my body making him lose it was seductive. "Fuck me, Ryder—hard. I'm asking you to just give it to me, everything. Stop holding it back."

I gasped as he pulled out yet again, but I could feel it. The air sizzled around us, the sweat beading my neck was now dripping. The storm was brewing. Even the air was growing thick with it as he gave in to me and finally gave me what I asked for.

Thunder shattered the air around the cabin as he released himself and drove into me with a renewed vengeance. I was helpless to do more than hold on. The battering of his body against mine was harsh and oh so gloriously blissful. My muscles clenched and released, unable to keep up with the relentless pounding of his cock driving in painfully, deliciously.

"Fuck you're tight, so fucking tight. Come for me, Syn. I want to feel your pussy around me as you come."

"Yes! Oh God, yes, Ryder," I screamed as I felt his hands tighten on my hips, the speed picking up and his groans got louder and then he cried out, his cock still relentlessly battering against my sleek heat as his own heat added to it.

My body responded, and, for the first time tonight, I knew I was in real trouble. Everything went blank around me, my legs trembled as my womb clenched, and stars burst behind my eyes, even though they were still open. Heat surged through me violently, as if someone had detonated a bomb inside of me. I screamed as my body clenched brutally, over and over, my womb sucking him in.

I shivered as my body exploded more until it shattered completely, still impaled on his shaft. I felt his hands as he pulled me up and kissed me passionately, but my mind was threatening to fragment; it was perched on the verge of emptiness, threatening to go over. I bit his lip and tasted the crimson tanginess of his blood and listened as his breathing went ragged again.

Messing around with a Fae was one thing; resisting his allure yet another. Accepting his foreign seed into my body was risky since most Fae could claim you with less. I was tempting fate now and fuck if I didn't want more of him. I wanted him to continue or else my mind would come back with too many reasons I shouldn't be here with him, that I shouldn't be fucking him.

"Synthia," he whispered as my eyes focused on him. I leaned over and claimed his mouth and enjoyed the throaty sigh that mine caught from his. His hands slid behind my back as he pulled my body closer and laid us down on the cool sheets.

"Again," I growled, fueled by the need not to think. Already the consequences of what I had allowed him to do were sinking in.

"You need a few minutes," he replied, searching my face with a brilliant smirk.

"I said again, Ryder…unless you're not up to it?" I taunted him, feeling the motors inside my brain turn with the implications of my actions. His smile faltered, his eyes glowing with intensity as I felt his cock stir against my stomach, awakening again.

"Do you know what you are asking for, Syn? I won't be as gentle as I was last time," he warned with steel in his tone, already pulling my leg up as he sat up. He settled between my legs, with his cock poised at the entrance.

I clenched with the knowledge of what I had just done, but I needed this. It was the only time I would allow myself to have him. After the twenty four hours were up, we would go back to the way things were before. "Less talk, Fairy, just fucking—" I groaned as he entered me hard and ruthlessly.

He drove himself in roughly, punishing me. I gloried in it, the feeling of his still growing cock as it turned to hard silk inside of me. He was driving himself inside of me hard, but he was holding back still. I could see the strain in his eyes as they locked with mine, he was testing me. This time I'd goaded him into it, and he wanted to teach me a lesson.

"I know what you're doing, Syn. You think if I hurt, or punish you that it will make it easier to hate me. I won't give you that satisfaction. I'll fuck you. I'll even give angry fucking sex. Who am I to say no to what a woman wants, when her pussy is open and bared to me." His eyes searched my face closely. "I'll even make you scream and beg my Fae cock for mercy, if it's your desire, Syn."

He was too big, bigger than he'd been before. His hands clamped against my skin biting into the soft tissue of my thighs as he fucked my body harder, exactly as I had asked him to. My legs quivered from where he held them up and apart, to use for support as he buried himself deeper. He didn't stop, and, when he did, it was only to toss another pillow beneath my ass and tilt me up so he could punish me more.

This position gave him more depth, and he took advantage of it until I could fit no more of him inside of my body. I cried out, struggling against the pain and pleasure of the fullness he was creating inside of me. He laughed coldly, his eyes filling with heat as he continued to ride my body relentlessly. I didn't want him to stop, *I* wanted this. Still, I could feel the storm building, readying the bliss that would render me oblivious once more.

"Don't you fucking come yet, I'm not ready for you to." He growled fiercely with anger tainting his tone. He was pissed that I'd challenged him in the bedroom after he'd told me he was master here.

"Fuck you, Ryder. I'll come when I want," I ground out between moans of pleasure.

"You think you're in fucking control? No, Syn, you're not. *I'm* fucking you. *I'm* in full control of my body. Are you?" He murmured before he lowered his teeth, scraping them over my nipple, his mouth clamping down to suck hard before he did the same to the other. He released his hold on my leg, and his fingers stroked my clit, knowingly, seductively. The storm cresting, only to stop when he once again stopped moving, showing me exactly how much control he had.

"I said not yet," he growled seductively with a wicked smile back on his full mouth.

I rocked my hips, needing him to move, the fullness was too much when he stopped the friction. My lips quivered from the pain until he realized the problem and started moving with renewed force.

"Take it, take all of it," he ordered, grating his teeth as he pushed and pulled and drove it inside me until I whimpered and shuddered with pleasure. I could feel him pulling it back, reducing the size, and it pissed me off.

"Good girl, that's it. Take it all for me, Pet. You're so fucking wet," he ground out, his eyes never leaving mine. As if he could see inside my soul.

I bucked against him, even though it took more

strength than I had, his eyes lit up as he realized what I was doing. I moaned as he gave in and rode my body with vigor. His mouth was covering mine, but I wouldn't let him in. Instead, I bit softly against his lip, tasting the blood from before still on his lips.

My animalistic hunger fed his. Together we fed off each other's anger, which was quickly transforming to white hot passion. It was hard, angry, sex; soul-altering and life-shattering sex. In this moment, we agreed on this one thing together, fucking like savage animals without a coherent thought of what would happen afterward.

I pushed away from his cock, fighting his hold and was surprised when he stopped and pulled away from me. The dangerous hint in his eyes telling me he'd recite everything that I had agreed to if I stopped this now. He wouldn't need to, not by a long shot.

"Get on your back," I growled, enjoying the fierce growl that resonated from his throat.

Defiance lit deep in his amber eyes making them feral as if he was considering defying the order. He didn't want to give me control. He was a true dominant male inside the bedroom and outside of it. I pushed against his chest as we both stood on our knees, facing each other. "I said, on your back. I want you in my mouth," I growled, feeling bold with the sexual allure my body was giving me.

He finally obeyed and laid his lengthy frame out for my greedy eyes. His cock jutted up thick and proud, making me wonder if I was as bold as I thought I was, probably not. But I was a bitch in heat, and he was the cure. The biggest need inside of me right now was to make him lose control and scream for *me*.

I gripped his cock hard, enjoying the gasp that

escaped from between his lips as I bent over and took the glistening head between my lips. His hand tried for my hair, but I backed up removing it carefully, enjoying the startled look that stopping had caused him.

"Hands off, Fairy, or I stop," I growled huskily.

When he complied, throwing his hands up in surrender, I took him back inside of my hot mouth, flicking my tongue over the engorged head, brazenly meeting his eyes as he had done with me. I took more, rewarding him for doing as I had told him to.

He tried to touch me again, so I pulled back, running my nails gently over his thighs. I crawled up his body slowly, knowing this was hell on him. He was so used to being in control. So used to being the one calling shots with everything in his perfect little world. When I was sitting on his waist, I smiled wickedly into his beautiful eyes.

"This has to suck, wanting a lesser creature. You want me, don't you Ryder? *Your* cock wants *me*; wants to be buried inside of my heat. Doesn't it?" I chimed, smiling impishly before I reached behind my ass to stroke him. "He wants to feed from me, doesn't he Ryder? He wants my pussy. Doesn't that piss you off?"

"Don't tempt me, Pet," he growled, struggling to get the words out past the feeling of my fist as I pumped it around his erection.

I stopped and lowered my face. I was in control of this and he needed to know it. "You want me, and it pisses you off. I'm not in your plans. I don't fit into your perfect little world and your cock here doesn't get it, and it wants me, regardless of who or what I am. It wants to be buried inside of me."

I positioned his cock at my soaking entrance rubbing it over slowly. Somehow instead of being fully in control as I had planned my body was in control; it grew wetter with the knowledge that he would be invading it again. I wasn't prepared for what he did; his hands gripped my shoulders, and he shoved me down on his cock—hard.

I cried out as he pushed, and I pulled until my nipples hardened with the impending orgasm, but he stopped before it exploded. "Must suck, my little Pet, how much your pretty pink pussy craves me just as much as I crave you."

My head swam with his words. Not his cock, not his body. *He* wanted me. He realized his mistake at the same time, a violent cuss leaving his lips. I pushed him down forcefully as he tried to sit up with his cock still sheathed inside of me. I rocked my hips, watching as the anger drained from him.

He'd never admit to saying it, not tomorrow. But tonight we wanted each other, in every sense of the word. This wasn't driven by primal needs. We were just a man and a woman fucking like there was no tomorrow because for us, there wasn't.

I allowed him to flip me over so I was beneath him again when he'd had enough of my teasing him with the slow gentle ride. His lips claimed mine in a crushing, devastating kiss that curled my toes. When he pulled away, his eyes searched mine for something. "Tell me you want me, Syn. Tell me you want me right now, here, in this place; that you want this from me."

"Here and now, Ryder, I want to be yours. Completely yours," I whispered, knowing it wasn't what he had asked for, it was more. It was a treaty of sorts until his time was over, at which point we would probably become enemies once more.

His kiss was soft when he claimed my lips again; his thrust inside of me was gentle. Driven not by anger or need, but by an urgency to make every second of the time together count. And he did, driving himself inside of me until we exploded yet again.

He was gentle and hard and insatiable with his needs. When I thought I couldn't handle anymore, he healed the pain with his magic, and we started all over again. He was gluttonous, his stamina off the charts as he continued battering my body pleasurably. He was beautiful and wild with his need, his brands pulsing as he exploded with release.

Ryder had explained the time difference to me between bouts of making love. We'd been inside Faery for two days, according to Faery time, while in the Human world; only a few hours had passed.

We didn't leave because Ryder had been done with me, or that the twenty-four hours in the Human world that we agreed to were up. We left because everything changed horribly. The hounds had gone off howling and whining until Ryder had gone outside to check on them, only to come back in with anger pulsing from him in hostile waves.

"Get ready to leave. I had Malinda pack you an overnight bag." He nodded toward a corner and was out the door before I could ask him what was wrong.

When I was dressed in a t-shirt and jeans, I walked out, still barefoot, onto the porch, where the thirteen stood glaring at me. "What's wrong?"

Ryder growled low in his chest, hatred in his eyes, "What's *wrong*? Your fucking Guild attacked my club while *you* kept me distracted, *Witch*," he snarled.

Shock swept through me. "No way. They wouldn't.

That would be a suicide mission, for the entire fucking Guild. Alden wouldn't give that order, Ryder, ever!"

"They did, and those who openly attacked have been slain," Zahruk growled.

I swallowed, a feeling of hopelessness settled on my shoulders. This wasn't happening. Alden would never have given those orders, not unless he was trying to wipe out the entire Guild, which would be the end result. "When is my contract up?" I asked, not meeting Ryder's angry stare.

"When I fucking say it is." He smiled coldly returning to the old Ryder effortlessly.

~~*~*~*~*~*~*~*

Chapter
THIRTY

He sifted me back, barely slowing to throw open a portal and uncaring of any damage I might take. He was in as much of a hurry to get to his people as I was. Only he wouldn't let me go to mine. I'd fallen on my ass as we had sifted in, the world spinning as I fought the urge to throw up everywhere.

Gone was the demanding, sensual man that had laughed and made love to me while we were in Faery. I struggled to my feet with my hand on my head as he watched his men, who had sifted in shortly after us. I had no idea what had happened, or why he was acting like this, other than Ryder had said *we* had attacked them.

"Where's my coven?" I asked, through the lump in my throat.

"Go to the room you were staying in and don't come out unless you're invited, Synthia," Ryder growled.

"Fuck you! Where are they?" I demanded and was instantly shoved up against the wall with his hands around my throat. I didn't cry out. I didn't flinch. "Where the fuck are my friends?" I snarled, not caring if he tightened or loosened his hold as long as he told me where they were.

"They're in the fucking basement, chained to the walls because they were in my club when it was attacked. I'd watch your mouth, unless you want to join them. I should have known it was a fucking act, should have seen through it," he seethed.

I smiled coldly. "Is that what you think? That I fucked you just so they could do it? I don't play games, and I had nothing to do with what happened— if you're really stupid enough to believe that I would do that, then *please* put me with them, Ryder."

His eyes narrowed, and his teeth ground together as he tightened his hold around my neck.

"Go ahead, finish it, Fairy," I whispered, feeling the blood as it rushed to my head. I met his eyes and held them with a challenge.

"If you think I wouldn't, just because we *fucked*— think again," he growled.

I struggled to keep focus. "Fuck you! Fucking means nothing to the Fae—I'm smarter than to think just because I fucked you it would change a damn thing between us. Either finish it, or let me go, Ryder—*decide*."

His smile faltered, or maybe it was the stars rushing up around me that made it appear so. I felt his hands release my neck. I felt my body go limp as my legs gave out, unable to hold myself up any longer. He caught me before I fell. I saw the flash of remorse briefly before he covered it up with anger.

"Pussy," I said, or I think I did.

"Say again?" Ryder tilted his head.

"Pussy," I ground out through the pain in my throat, tears rushing to my eyes.

"You, Synthia, have a fucking death wish," he snarled.

"So do you," I challenged him, I knew it was suicide, but if I couldn't get to my coven through my own stubborn pig headedness, they'd absorb my powers through my death, and Adam would channel the power; he'd feel the bond sever.

"I'd behave, if I were you, or you might find yourself chained to my bed," he replied huskily.

"Right now, I'd choose death over your bed."

His men snickered. I was upset, scared, and fighting for my life and the lives of my coven. If we had attacked, nothing short of a miracle would keep the Fae from wanting our blood. What the fuck could Alden have been thinking to attack the freaking Fae?

"Take her to my room," he growled.

"I *said*, I'd rather fucking die," I said, with enough force to mean it.

"No, you choose death because you think it will save your fucking coven, but *it won't*. I won't kill you, Syn, but I could think of many uses for you—"

I dropped and kicked his legs out from beneath him and jumped back up—Dristan was there defending Ryder the moment he hit the floor. I kicked his legs out, and as he came down, I lifted my leg and smashed his face against my knee with the use of his hair. Once more, I went crashing against the wall, my bones jarring while my teeth clattered from the impact.

"Fucking move, and I'll feed from you, Syn. I'll

keep you as my fucking *pet*," Ryder warned, his tone harsh as his eyes swirled with anger.

I lifted my head, defeated. "Let them go," I cried. I would beg if he just let *them* go. They couldn't pay this price; they were everything to me. Everything worth fighting for.

I felt him pushing against my mind before he released me. "Put her in my room and chain her."

"Ryder, if you do anything to them—a*nything*— I'll fucking hunt you down and cut your fucking heart out," my words came out crisp and clear, and I meant every fucking word of it.

"I know you would, Syn. That's why they're locked up, instead of dead like the rest who walked into my club and *killed* my people," he said softly, no longer meeting my eyes.

"*No*, Fae *can't* be killed. Not by any weapons we own," I argued.

"You could have, Syn; you tied my fucking soul to yours," he retorted.

I smiled. "Yes, I *can*. Not them. Me. Ryder, I was with you—unless you have forgotten already."

"You're saying they couldn't have done what you did?"

"No one else knows how to tether souls," I swallowed, realizing I'd just given him ammo to use against me.

His lips twisted coldly. "Good to know. Chain her in my room and gather the others."

~~*~*~*~*~*~*~*~*~*

I was dragged down the hallway and taken to Ryder's room by a Fae I hadn't met before. He was silent, yet I could feel the sliminess of his aura pressing against my skin. This was all wrong, it made no sense. Alden wouldn't have done this.

I was pushed into the bedroom door frame as he threw the door open, my face taking the brunt of the damage. My nose exploded, blood bursting from it, to run down my chin and onto my shirt. I should have fought and run. I wouldn't leave this place without my coven though, and Ryder knew it.

"Fucking whore, move it," the Fae barked as he pushed me further inside the room. He pushed me again, even though I'd stopped in front of the bed. I knew where the chains were, I'd seen them on my one trip here. "Take your clothes off…let's see what is driving Ryder to fuck something so beneath him," he said crudely as his hands grabbed my breast.

"Wrong fucking girl," I growled as I spun, using my hands as weapons; one grabbed his ear, and the other connected with his chin and twisted, a sick crunch echoing through the room as Zahruk walked in.

"You broke his neck," he replied calmly.

I wiped the blood that was dribbling down my face without any sign of stopping soon on the back of my arm and replied coldly. "He deserved it."

"He did this?" His hand indicated my face. "You are deadlier than we had thought."

I gave him a nod. "And?"

"And, you could have easily done so to Dristan, yet you chose to only damage his legs and his pride," he mused as he closed the distance between us silently.

He was trying to surprise me so he could take me down easily. He, like Ryder, had a raw electrical current that was palpable when in close proximity. I considered my options as I stood watching him. If he chained me, I would be able to undo them easily. I wouldn't be able to get away if I took any more injury. I sat on the bed with a calmness I wasn't feeling. I watched as Z removed the subdued Fae from the room, before coming back to place the chains on me.

"You need your nose looked at," he said, moving my hair to secure a white metal collar around my neck.

"You gonna let Larissa do it?" I asked, but his eyes narrowed as he shook his head. "Pass then."

"She's okay, a little shaken up but otherwise she and Adam are fine," he replied.

I scanned his face. He looked as if he was telling the truth, but I'd already trusted Ryder, which had been a huge mistake I wouldn't be repeating anytime soon. When the collar was on and secured with a chain that attached to the metal bed frame, he grabbed a remote and turned on the oversized television that was mounted to the wall and tuned in to the local news channel. I sat numbly watching it—we'd attacked. We'd killed. How the fuck? We didn't have any Fae killing weapons. No one except the killer had them—

Zahruk left the room for a few minutes, leaving me to absorb the news that played on the TV. This wasn't fucking happening. Not now. I'd given in to Ryder, just to have him do exactly what I'd been afraid of. I knew better, I was better than this. I shut down my mind and listened to the reporter.

Anger pulsated inside of me. It was a fucking set up. Smart. Calculated. They were pitting us against each other. And what was worse, it was fucking working! I lifted my head as Zahruk came back, his eyes lowering to my nose as he tossed a clean set of clothes on the bed.

"That needs to be healed. It hasn't stopped bleeding, Synthia."

"It will. Took a door frame to my face, I'm pretty sure he meant it to hurt," I said, through the thickness in my mouth.

"You know you're stubborn as fuck, right?" Zahruk said with a soft smile on his face, he was making it impossible to hate him.

"Go away," I replied, turning away from him to watch the news.

We'd attacked the Fae, or so it had been made to look. The reporter said the Guild had been locked down and unavailable for a comment on why they had invaded the club which had resulted in the deaths of seventeen Fae.

I scratched at the collar and eyed the clothing that lay folded on the bed. My shirt was covered in blood. My entire body shook with anger and pain. I exhaled as I moved off the bed and flicked my eyes to the door, which stood open a sliver. I unbuttoned my pants and shimmied out of them, using the top I had worn to wipe away some of the blood on my face.

Dressed in a form fitting tank top and some short spandex shorts, I curled up on the bed, not caring that blood was oozing out on the pillow. I should have let them heal me, but right now I didn't trust them—they wanted revenge. Revenge for something we hadn't done and we were close at hand to take the brunt of their anger.

I closed my eyes and tried to focus on a plan, any

plan that would get us all out. I couldn't focus. I could feel my power draining as I lay there. The blood wouldn't stop and had only increased in flow since Zahruk had put the stupid collar on. I pushed away the feeling of needing to close my eyes and struggled to sit up, but couldn't. I cried out, fighting the dread that was consuming my mind.

I had expected Z to come back, but instead, Ryder stood over the top of me looking down. "What the fuck? Syn, what the hell did you do?" He asked, looking around the room as if it held the answers he needed.

I gasped. I couldn't get air, my body shook as I gasped and tried to bring air in through my throat, but it wouldn't work—the harder I tried, the less air I got. I was dying. My hands clasped around the collar, my eyes growing slack as I struggled to fight against the oblivion drawing me in.

"What the fuck? Zahruk!" He was yelling, his hands working against the collar deftly as he pulled it off from my neck.

"What's wrong?" Z asked, walking back into the room from where he'd been outside, guarding the room. I was gasping for air, unable to draw it into my lungs. "Bloody hell!" He sifted, or maybe I was starting to see things.

"Don't you fucking die, Syn. Don't—god damn it! Where's the fucking healer?" Ryder was commanding me not to die. He had some serious God complex going on.

~~*~*~*~*~*~*~*

Chapter
THIRTY~ONE

I awoke to pressure on my face. It felt broken. My entire head felt broken. I didn't bother trying to open my eyes. There was no point. They felt like they were glued shut. I lay still as voices sounded from across the room.

"She's waking up, some," Zahruk said as the bed shifted, but his voice had been across the room, someone else had been on the bed. I tried to remember everything that had happened.

"Dristan?" Ryder asked, his voice low.

"The one below the useless one is a protection spell—powerful, but fading as if it's losing its juice. But Ryder, it's been there a long time. It's definitely Fae, and old."

"You're saying my little Witch is marked by the Fae? By *us*?" Ryder said in surprise.

"No, not per se, Ryder. Think older," Dristan replied coldly.

"Elaborate," Ryder snapped.

"It almost looks as if it was branded with blood

ink and some very old magic, but that's impossible, considering she appears Human and has been living as such since she was a child. Someone went to pretty extreme lengths to hide her. If she is Fae, they didn't want her being found."

"Is it possible she was stolen, or is she something else?" Ryder mumbled from across the room. "I pushed magic into her, and she resisted. It took everything I had to turn her mind to my will."

"You're saying you could not turn her FIZ?" Zahruk said and whistled low.

"I hate to butt in, but those were Fae in her house who killed her parents. Chances are they were looking for her, and the collar she reacted to was iron, Ryder," Zahruk said carefully.

"True, but why would they? The Fae don't hide their young with Humans, it would be suicide for her *and* the Humans if she hit Transition without help. And the reaction to the collar doesn't make sense if she hasn't hit Transition. She could be starting the Transition. At twenty-one she's the right age for it to start, if not a little past it."

"It's only suicide, Ryder, if you cannot control them—she is being shielded, she has no Fae abilities, she doesn't feed, she ages normally. Someone made damn sure she appeared to be one hundred percent Human," Dristan said before fingers smoothed down my neck and the hair was pushed out of the way. "It's a Triquesta. The words, well—I can't read them and this particular usage of the Triquesta looks to be a protection and concealment brand." Dristan released my hair and stepped back, his shoes making a soft thud as he walked to the other side of the room.

"If she is Fae, then why the fuck isn't she waking

up?" Ryder growled low in his throat.

"No clue, but you sifted with her. I'm going to take a guess here and say it has to do with why the tattoo is fading. You said her tattoo was darker a few days ago, and she did not know it was even there, right? You also said that you could see it before she entered Faery?" Dristan continued to be the loudest voice inside the room.

"Correct."

"You taking her into Faery weakened it then; she's changing. Question is, what the hell kind of Fae is she?"

"She could be Light Fae; with her coloring, it's possible. She has enough of their attributes as well," Zahruk replied.

What the fuck were they *thinking*? I was Human, and I was pissed—sore, but pissed. I wasn't Fae. Had the whole fucking world gone crazy this week? I blinked and moaned, wincing as I realized everyone had been whispering, even though they had sounded louder. Dristan was the first to say something.

"It lives," he said, making me cover my ears and cry out. It was like razors pounding through my head.

"Stop screaming," I whined.

I turned over carefully, just in time to catch Dristan nodding to Ryder, who stood across the room. I glared, this was his fault.

"Look at her eyes," Ryder said smiling.

I closed them. It was too bright. Sound was too loud. I exhaled and tried it again. A scream ripped from my throat as everything around me grew brighter, more vivid—painfully so. Something wasn't right. I'd been dying when I'd last seen Ryder. I groaned. "So help me, if you turned me into a fucking Vampire, I'll bite your dick off!"

Dristan exploded in a fit of laughter. Ryder didn't find it so funny, on the other hand. His eyes narrowed and ran over my body slowly as if was trying to figure something out but couldn't. "The tattoo on the back of your neck, Synthia…who put it there?" he asked, ignoring my outburst.

I shook my head and pulled my hands away from my ears fighting the nausea rolling in my stomach. I tried opening my eyes again and was relieved to find the room as it should be. My eyes swung to him accusingly. "Fuck off, Fairy," I growled.

His lips jerked at the corners before he sat beside me, making me scoot over to keep distance between us. "*I'm* a fucking Fairy? Tell me, how is it that you had no idea *you* were a fucking Fairy, Synthia," he whispered, cold and tonelessly.

"Seriously, did the entire fucking world go crazy when were busy—" Shit!

"When we were busy fucking?" he finished crudely.

I felt a blush steal over my cheeks, I hated that I had given in and allowed him more ammo to use against me. Why didn't my brain work right around him? I met his piercing stare with one of my own. "Thanks for that, by the way, not bad for a *fucking Fairy*—" I laughed—"get it? Fucking Fairy?" I snorted and closed my eyes.

"I get it," he growled, his hand moving the hair from my face, making me flinch and back away from him. He allowed it, but only because one of my legs was held to the bed with a new metal cuff and a length of chain. I shot him a pissy look before laying my head back down. He'd accused me of fucking him as a distraction—something I had never done in my life.

"Tattoo guy, who is he?"

I smiled, or tried to. "Fuck off."

"Keep telling me to fuck off, Syn, and I'll see it as an invitation," his voice had turned husky.

"Keep dreaming," I growled, wishing I looked tougher, and maybe less crusted in blood—my own at that.

"Keep saying *fuck,* Syn," he argued.

"Let me go," I pressed, I needed to see my coven, make sure they were okay.

"I cannot do that, Syn. The Guild killed seventeen Fae, and that is not something they will live to regret. Tell me why your coven was inside the club when it happened, and I will consider changing my mind about them. The others were already killed."

"And if they didn't do this? If it *was* a set up?" I asked, watching his reaction closely.

"They did it, and they will pay for it. An eye for an eye, Syn. I want the name of the artist who did the red ink tattoo on your neck."

I blinked. "I don't have a tattoo with red ink; its white ink. It's *not* red."

"Stop fucking around, Syn. Someone went through a lot of effort to hide you, and I'd like to know who it was and why they did it."

My hand went to the back of my neck on instinct, my fingers touching as they skimmed over the slightly raised skin. "I'm Synthia Raine McKenna. I was born Human, and I will die Human, Ryder. I won't make it to old age. I'll die fighting—*you,* most likely, if you don't release my coven. We didn't attack you. That much I know. I would have *felt* it. *Inside*. Larissa and Adam didn't raise one magically delicious finger. If you try to tell me they did, you better have that shit on tape."

Ryder and his men left the room soon after we had agreed to disagree. They were heading to the club to assess the damages. I wasn't sticking around for when they got back. I pulled the chain and sat on the side of the bed, opening his nightstand drawer. I found nothing useful.

I shook my head and looked around the room, my eyes landing on his dresser mirror. I sent my mind out to connect to my coven, the feel of them pushing their magic into me was heady, exhilarating. They were alive and inside this house.

I wrapped my hands around the metal anklet I had awoken with and sent magic pulsing into it. Nothing happened. What the hell was this thing made out of? Platinum? I eyed the chain—screw it. I grabbed it as close as I could to the cuff and pushed again smiling as the metal melted.

I crept from the bed and cussed as the knob twisted. Jumping back up onto the bed I pulled the blankets over the metal chain and the evidence of what I had been up to as Ristan walked in. His eyes searched the room and then settled on me and then at my ankle.

"Going out?" he asked, lifting a dark eyebrow.

I narrowed my eyes. "Guess not."

"Oh, don't stop on my account. I came to let you out, anyway. Unless of course you don't want to break your little friends out?"

I considered answering him and then hesitated. "I dooooo, unless of course I say that I do, and then you go Demon on my soul. In which case, I'd politely answer with nooooo, I like it here?"

He smiled and shook his head, his eyes turning briefly from their silver and black pattern to red as he plopped on the bed and folded his arms behind his head. "You will need to hurry. Adrian will meet you at the exit road," his eyes met and held mine, "You are going to be timed, of course. Ryder will be back shortly, so you have exactly fifteen minutes to be out of here. This information comes with a price, Synthia," he smiled coldly.

"Great, you want my soul?" I glared at him unamused.

"Nah, that thing is battered and bruised. You now have fourteen minutes. I need a promise that you will stop this before it happens. If Ryder openly attacks the Guild, it will mean a full out war. While it would be a feast, I cannot allow it." He waved his hand, and I felt a cold breeze pressing gently across my face as the thick oily presence of his magic surged through me.

"So tell Ryder," I said harshly. "What did you just do to my face?" I asked, afraid of what he had done, but it felt clean and less painful now.

"I cleaned you up a bit. And you've met him, Flower. He's about as fluffy as a porcupine. He will not listen to me, or to you, unless there is powerful evidence to change his mind. There is something else…you need to get close to Arianna, and you need to look closely at her, Syn. She's off; something isn't right about her. I can't "*see*" her, and that can mean a multitude of things—most of them bad. Got me?"

"You want me to take her out?" I asked carefully.

"No, I want you to *look* at her. Ryder would kill you before you could take her out; don't be stupid. You'd start a fucking war of the worlds if you do that shit. Thirteen minutes," he replied smiling.

"Fine," I started to stand up, and groaned from the pain inside my head.

"C'mere girl," Ristan said smoothly. Before I could protest, I was pressed against his mouth with my eyes bugging out as he kissed me. When he was done, I pulled away, wiping off my mouth with the back of my hand. Power pulsed through me; raw, dirty power. Demon magic—I smiled, and started to walk out of the room, but he caught my hand and pulled me back, staring. "Fucking hell, you taste good."

"Thanks—I'm leaving now." I looked down, noticing he'd just done more than juice me. He'd given me black sneakers, black sweat pants, and a black long sleeved shirt for escaping in, rather than the bloody mess I'd been wearing before.

"Good luck. Go stop this before it's too late," he whispered before he flicked his hand and the collar appeared on his neck, his face taking on an instant black eye as if I'd hit him myself. I turned and left the room shaking my head. I wondered if Ryder would really believe that I overpowered Ristan.

~~*~*~*~*~*~*

The basement was on the next floor down. I'd

barely managed to miss being seen by two guards as I'd not so stealthily walked right down the middle of the hallway. I could sense the Demon magic he gave me with that lovely kiss was dangerous. I felt no pain, my emotions were gone. I felt like darkness would overtake my soul if I let it.

I took the stairs more carefully, my eyes scanning for body heat as second sight took over. I had to actually concentrate using it as I walked. As if I wasn't myself, and maybe that had to do with the head pounding I'd encountered with the door. When I reached the bottom of the stairs, there was only one door and it was ajar.

I pressed against the wall and peeked inside; Larissa and Adam both sat on chairs with their hands tied in front of them. I slipped inside, expecting to fight. I looked around the barren rooms. Pulsing cells enhanced by Fae magic were constructed along the walls. An enhancing spell covered the wall in black ink, and I had a feeling Ryder was creating those cells for Witches alone.

I slipped over behind Adam, who had been sleeping, and started untying his ropes. They got ropes, while I got platinum. I felt special—sorta. "Adam, untie Lari. I'll guard the door. We've got ten minutes to be out of here."

He lifted his dark head and leveled his emerald gaze on me. "Syn, he's going to attack the Guild; we have to stop him."

"Untie Larissa, Adam; he won't attack them tonight," I said feebly. I had no idea if he would, but I couldn't go into panic mode right now—not juiced up on Demon.

I turned back to watch him carefully untie Larissa

while patting her cheek to wake her up. He was gentle, his hands sure as he undid her bindings. "Baby, we gotta go."

Larissa opened her eyes and turned a brilliant smile on Adam. "Told you she'd be here to save us."

"Guys, we gotta go," I said, trying to hurry them so we would be a safe distance away before Ryder returned.

We went out through the door at the top of the stairs. I'd made a note to peek and make sure it led outside since it was a lower level, and surprisingly it looked like it was accessible without setting off any alarms. The cool night air washed over me, calming my nerves as we emerged from the back of the house.

"Two guards inside watching through the upper windows, Syn; one on the ground level, but he is looking at a magazine," Adam said, going right into combat mode.

"Get closer. I'll throw up the shield. Lari throw up a spell to shield our presence; Adam, watch our asses."

"My pleasure," Adam said with a wicked smile.

After we had everything up, we walked out onto the green grass and into the shrubbery, only stopping to fortify Larissa's spell before we headed for the gate. As we got closer, the metal bars slid open to allow several dark colored SUV's through.

"Get in the bushes!" I shouted, remembering Ryder had been able to see through my glamour a few days ago. We held our breath as the cars drove past. With the last one going through, we scrambled and made it through the gate before it had fully closed.

"Let's go. Adrian's waiting," I said. When we had made it the mile and half on foot to the car Adrian was waiting in, I froze with my hand on the car door handle. Hounds howled furiously. *His* hounds.

I turned to look back the way we'd come, sparing one last look at the dim lights in the distance before I opened the door and jumped in. I had to stop Ryder before he put us into a war we would never recover from.

THIRTY~TWO

We sat in an abandoned warehouse—it wasn't ideal, but it was an indication that we were officially at the top of the Fae's *"persona non grata"* list. I paced, burning a hole into the concrete floor. Adrian sat watching me, he'd explained how the Demon had called and told him to be waiting for us.

"So let me get this straight, the Guild *did* attack the Fae?" I stopped pacing long enough to level Adam with a glare.

"It was someone from the Guild, Syn, but they were off. We left the Guild an hour or so after the party got started. Figured the Darklands would be more alive, and, well, we were worried about you," he said, shaking his dark head as he sat beside Larissa on an old ratty couch that had been left here.

"Explain *off*—and thanks for worrying. Next time, stay where I send you," I said, tapping my foot nervously. If we had, in fact, attacked the Fae, I couldn't fix this.

"I couldn't tap their powers to stop them, but they didn't notice us either. Witches would have. Lisa was there, and she was one of them. I couldn't sense anything inside of them as if they were dead."

"Dead?" I asked to confirm, and grinned. "That's actually good. Well, not that she's dead, but it means the Guild didn't do shit. We don't come back to life—" I spared a look at Adrian who was now sitting up on the hood of the broken down car that was stored in the warehouse. "Unless someone brings us back," I amended.

"That still doesn't explain why they would be at the club attacking the Fae," Adam continued.

"Actually, it does," I said, moving over to lean against the rusted car, hoping I wouldn't need a tetanus shot after I did so. "If they thought we'd be able to figure out more about the murders and who was doing it, who would you take out first?"

"The Guild, and then the Fae investigating it," Adrian said, making us all turn in his direction. "What? It's who the Vampires would take out."

"Not helping, Adrian," I said, holding his gaze before dropping it. "So they killed Witches, somehow turned them into something cold and lifeless, and had them attack the Fae because there is no faster way to start a fucking war then to openly attack someone on their own turf. Whoever is doing this is starting a war and they know it. Smart, which makes this dangerous. The Guild should be on lockdown if they are following protocol."

"Syn, you should get cleaned up a little more. You're still bleeding a little. Are you sure you're okay?" Adrian said huskily, his eyes turning hard at the sight of blood.

"I got in a fight with a door. I've done worse," I said sharply. My head hurt. Hell, my entire body hurt right now as I came down from the Demon-Blood-Kiss high. My nose was still bleeding a bit, but I'd recover without any more magical help.

"You know, considering our line of work, you get hurt a lot, Syn," Adam joked.

"We need a plan. Ristan said I needed to get close to Arianna and look at her—whatever the hell that means," I said absently.

"The Light Heir?" Adrian said before whistling, "Good luck, she's bouncing all over the place. First, she was hiding, and now she can't get enough attention."

"Do you know where she'll be tomorrow?" I asked hopefully.

"She'll be downtown; not sure where, though. Ryder has the Fae on high alert. No one without clearance can get close to her without him knowing."

"Perfect; we have to figure out how to get around him then," I tapped my finger on my chin and shook my head, discarding idea, after idea. "Okay, listen up. We need a plan and fast. We need to figure out where she will be tomorrow, and we need to know like yesterday. We need a distraction team, something they wouldn't see coming."

"And if something is off about her? What then, Syn?" Adrian asked, narrowing his eyes, "If you take out the Light Heir, you'll start a war."

I let the air from my lungs out slowly as my head bobbed in agreement. "Yes, Adrian, but what if she is part of this? Ristan said to get close to her and take a look—what if she's not the Light Heir; what if she's something else?"

Adam sat up and swore. "That would be stupid crazy, and how would Ryder not be able to see it?"

"Not sure without being able to bounce this off the Guild, but I think there are spells that could fool the Fae—*if* she had a powerful enough Mage working with her, or a Witch. It's not easily done, but it isn't impossible either."

"If they're able to conceal it from Ryder, how the hell will you be able to see through it?" Adrian asked, swinging his legs over to sit beside me.

"Because I have something he doesn't. I have a coven who can push enough magic inside of me to see the truth, but to do that—I'm going to have to light up, which means we're going to need a huge distraction," I mumbled.

I'd barely managed to sleep, I kept dreaming of Ryder finding us and throwing us in those cells he had in his basement. I could feel his eyes on me as if he was standing right in front of me inside the crappy warehouse. As if he'd seeped inside and was watching me from within a dream. *My dream.*

I'd managed a sponge bath with water Adam, and Larissa had brought back with them, along with some extra clothes for today. Adrian had gone back to Vlad since his absence would be noticed. We had rounded up enough people to create a small flash mob, but I wasn't positive they'd be enough to draw the Fae away from Arianna. I only needed a few seconds to see whatever it was Ristan wanted me to.

There was also this restlessness inside of me as if something was fighting to get out. I'd stared in the mirror for an entire hour trying to figure out what the hell was in my eyes that Ryder had been talking about—they didn't change once. And, yet, something inside was changing, I could feel it twisting and turning as it fought to come to the surface.

Ryder said I was Fae, but that was impossible—wasn't it? Wouldn't I have known if I was? Could I have been what the Fae were looking for when they killed my parents? I had too many questions and no answers. I closed my eyes and groaned. The sun wasn't even up yet and I already had a million problems to solve.

I must have fallen back to sleep because when I opened my eyes this time, I was back in the small house inside Faery and Ryder was lying beside me playing with a lock of my hair between his fingers.

"You shouldn't have left me, Syn. I have to punish you now," he whispered.

"You say that an awful lot, Ryder. I have to stop this, before more innocent lives are lost," I replied back to dream Ryder.

He smirked and dropped my hair from between his fingers and placed his hand on my face softly. "And if your people attacked mine, Synthia? What then?"

"Then we become enemies, and I fight against you," I whispered breathlessly.

He laughed, but it was a cold and emotionless sound. "You would lose," he moved over me as he said it, pinning my hands softly in one of his, above my head. "I miss being buried in your warmth, Syn. I need to fuck you."

I smiled and shook my head. "Not unless you release me from the contract," I uttered breathlessly as his mouth moved dangerously close to mine.

"I don't think so. You still wear my mark around your neck, Syn, and I like how it looks on you." His eyes sparkled with amusement.

"Go away, Ryder," I growled, but he closed the distance and silenced my mouth with his. His kiss was soft but carried an urgency I matched as the kiss deepened. Moaning against him probably wasn't the best response since I wasn't supposed to want his kiss, but it was all I had— until the bed shook violently.

I watched him pull away and smile coldly. "I'll find you, and when I do, Syn, I won't be gentle. And I'm going to find you. I *always* find my prey, Pet." And then he was gone and Adam was above me, shaking me.

I sat up looking at him in bewilderment. I swallowed and shook off the dream I'd been indulging in. "What happened?"

"You were having a nightmare," he said, by way of explanation. Of course, he would think it was a nightmare—I had them a lot growing up. He'd always make me wake up, even when Larissa hadn't been able to.

"I'm okay. What time is it?" I asked, looking up through the broken window that sat high up on the wall of the warehouse.

"It's 6 a.m. Time to shine. This was on the door when I went for coffee," Adam said, handing me a quickly scrawled note.

"Arianna will be outside the courthouse—what the hell would she be doing at the courthouse?" I asked more to myself, but Adam answered anyway.

"Picking up her marriage license more than likely, or meeting with the Mayor?"

"Call Terrance. Tell him to meet us at nine at the courthouse and to make sure he calls everyone else," I said, taking the coffee he picked up from the floor and handed to me, I smiled and sipped it slowly letting it filter through me. Terrance was a kid who did odd jobs for us when we needed help. He was a good kid, who had been given a bad hand in life. We used him, but we paid him well.

"If this goes south, Adam, you need to get Larissa out of Spokane. The Seattle Guild is the best choice to hide from the Fae."

"Fuck that, Syn," Adam said, standing up to place his hands angrily on his hips, "If this goes bad, I'm not leaving you. You're my only family, Syn; you and Larissa are all I have."

"It wasn't a question, Adam. You will take Larissa and get her someplace safe. Ryder won't kill me. He might say he will, but he won't. Not while I'm under his contract—he owns me, Adam. I need to know you can do this. I need to know you two are safe. You're the only ones that can be used against me. Ryder knows it, and he'll use it," I said, grabbing his hand and pulling him down beside me and somehow managing to not spill a drop of coffee in the process.

"Of course," he replied, holding my hand and looking at me with love in his emerald eyes. "Syn, we can be used against you—but the same is true for us. We'd be willing to move the moon for you. We need you, so don't do anything stupid. I also need you to know that we don't just stay because no one else will join—we stay because we're family. We have each other, and that's more than most people have in this world."

I pulled his hand up to my lips and kissed it before standing up to stretch. "We need to get this show on the road. Go call Terrance. Tell him we need that flash mob today."

I wasn't good with emotions, showing them, feeling them, *or* expressing them. I wasn't the type to wear them on my sleeves. He knew how I felt without me having to tell him. This idea had to work. The Demon released me to do this, and right now it was the only lead we had.

Chapter
THIRTY-THREE

Downtown Spokane Washington was packed—someone had leaked that the Light Heir would be making an appearance. We waited at the back of the crowd in hoodies that were pulled up to hide us. The rest of the flash mob who would be causing the distraction were dressed the same to stand out from the crowd when the right time came.

We waited, the magic pulsing inside of me ready to explode. We'd spent over an hour doing nothing but collecting and depositing magic inside of me. Adam had laughed, telling me I'd be lit up enough to power the city. I was hoping it wouldn't be the case since the plan was to use and dump the magic quickly enough not to pull attention to us.

The entire crowd was hushed as if this was a monumental event in time—which it wasn't. I'd never understood the draw of the Fae until I'd melted against Ryder. His blistering heat had drawn me in like a moth to a flame. He owned my mind without having to turn me FIZ. My thoughts constantly flowed to him and our time in Faery.

"Showtime," Adam said as a sleek black limo pulled up to the steps of the courthouse. It was something they would never allow for anyone else.

I turned my head and gave him a reassuring smile and we pushed through the crowd as the flash mob started up. It was the perfect disguise for what we had planned, or would have been until Ryder stepped from the limo and his men stepped from the crowd to create a guard around the princess.

It was now or never. The mob was dancing to Kesha's *Your Love is My Drug*—as if they couldn't have picked a more annoying song? I stepped from the group with Larissa and Adam pushing power into me. Ryder's eyes landed on us fleetingly. "Shit, dance!" I said, starting to move with the group, if not horribly off kilter.

His eyes moved through the crowd and off of us. I almost exploded into laughter at how goofy and bad we danced, but the situation was dire and laughter was something we could do later when we'd finished it. As the group of men parted to allow Arianna to wave at the mob, I stopped moving with the crowd and sent my second sight searching her—nothing happened. I pumped up the magical juice, and almost threw up.

"Oh my God," I uttered. I shook my head and stepped back, as if I could not put enough distance between me and the horror I was seeing.

"Shit, Syn, go dark!" Adam shouted, but it was too late, Ryder had seen me.

"Fuck! Split up, blend in!" I shouted, already retreating into the mass of dancers. I couldn't shake the power pulsing through me. I growled, scaring a few of the Humans who had joined the tweet about the flash mob Terrance had sent out.

I could feel Ryder bearing down on me, hunting

me. But when I looked over my shoulder it wasn't me he had gone after—he'd gone after Adam. He held him by the back of his hood. Adam shook his head. He was telling me to go. "Let him go, Ryder," I shouted, wishing the music would stop.

"I told you, Syn, that when I found you I would punish you. You only feel when something is taken away from you, Pet," he turned, smiling coldly at Adam, who was now struggling in earnest to get away from him.

"Ryder, take me. Let him go," I whispered, knowing he would hear it over the crowd that had now sensed danger.

He didn't listen. Instead, he turned and propelled Adam to Dristan who grinned and touched Adam. I felt the connection I shared with Adam waver briefly—he was trying to keep me from feeling what was going on. I watched his eyes as they settled on me and locked. I shook my head in denial. Ryder wouldn't allow this.

The noise went silent around me as if I'd stepped out of reality. The only sound I heard was my own blood flowing inside my ears and my own breathing as everything went still around me—frozen in time. Dristan was trying to turn Adam FIZ. It was too much, and everything inside of me snapped as the world stopped around me. Like a vacuum. One minute I was standing silently, the next I was screaming my pain with everything inside of me, everything I had. I would die before I let the Fae hurt my family again.

Glass exploded from the limo and the surrounding buildings, crashing to the pavement below. Humans screamed in pain as they hit the ground. I couldn't stop. Something inside of me had broken open and was demanding to come out. I barely registered the shock on Ryder and Dristan's faces as they watched me.

I couldn't stop it; whatever had opened just kept coming, I couldn't focus on anything, and, yet, I saw everything. As if I was standing above, watching as my body reaped havoc on anyone foolish enough to not run away. I could see fear, *smell* it. It was intoxicating. My hair whipped with electrical current as the ozone grew thick around me.

I tried pulling back. I was in trouble. Whatever was happening—I couldn't control it. I met Ryder's gaze and locked onto it. His nose was bleeding, but otherwise he seemed to be handling my power overload better than anyone else. He spoke low, clearly, and right to me, even though he addressed Dristan. "Dristan, let Adam go," he growled, never letting my gaze move from his.

Adam hit the pavement and stumbled over to me. Larissa crawled up from where she'd been taken to the ground with everyone else. The only sound was my labored breathing. I couldn't take my eyes from Ryder. He looked worried, and that wasn't something you see him show—ever.

"Back up, now," he said as he and his men started backing up slowly.

"Syn, you have to stop now!" Adam shouted, but when I turned to meet his eyes he flinched. "Oh my God, Syn," he whispered horrified.

My chest was heaving, my face tilted to look up at him. Humans sobbed, and I tried to look at them, but Adrian sifted in and stopped me.

"Syn, look at me," Adrian said. I met his eyes and watched him flinch at the sight of me.

My coven was here, unharmed, and all trying to calm whatever was going on inside of me. They should be running away. All of them. Adrian cupped my face while Adam and Larissa tried draining the power from me. Ryder approached silently, his eyes meeting mine as I heard his shoes crunch against the pebbles in the road.

"She needs to come with me," he whispered to Adrian. "She has to release the power. If she doesn't, it will consume her mind. She doesn't have—" he stopped, narrowing his eyes as Adam touched my face and pushed Adrian aside, "—a familiar."

He frowned, his eyes lighting up emerald and lime green, *glowing*. He looked as shocked as I felt, but his touch was calming. I felt my heart start up from where it had stopped as if Adam's touch alone had jumped started something inside of me. He frowned as he met my eyes. "Your eyes are fucking purple and blue, Syn."

I didn't answer him. I wasn't sure about anything just now. I just watched him, confused as to why his eyes also glowed. His were lined in a vivid colored lime and had never been that way before now. Was it because he was taking whatever it was that had broken inside of me out, and into his own body?

"I'm—monster," I panted as tears started down my cheeks. Adam's eyes swirled with a mix of lime and emerald as he held onto me.

"I thought it was a dream, only a fucking dream. All those years, Syn. I thought it couldn't be real. It didn't make sense then—but now, now I remember. I followed you here. I felt you here—from Faery, you pulled me here, Syn, when you needed me," Adam whispered as his arm dropped back to his side.

My body shook from the drain, my teeth chattered as I backed away from him. My head shook as Ryder, Adrian, and Adam all tried to move in closer to me. "Stop, just stop, Adam. This isn't happening. We have to go. Now."

"Let's move," I whispered, turning to walk away. I felt like I was going to pass out and we needed to be somewhere safe before I could do so. I didn't miss hearing Ryder tell Zahruk to pull his men off the warehouse. He had known where we'd had been hiding this entire time.

When we were a safe distance away Larissa spun on us. "Okay, what the fuck!? What the hell just happened, and why are your eyes glowing?"

I wiped my eyes and shook my head. "I don't know. I don't know what's happening to me," I mumbled, I couldn't explain it to her any more than I could to myself. Adam looked as upset as I did. He kept looking at his hands like they belonged to someone else.

"We need to go to the Guild, now," Larissa said, keeping a safe distance from us as if we suddenly had become strangers. "Did you get what we came for?" she continued.

"Arianna, well she's made of at least a few of the victims. She's been sewn together magically, for lack of a better description—with pieces. But something or someone is controlling her. She has no blood, no heat. She's just dead. Like a puppet, taking her down would be easy, but it wouldn't stop whoever is controlling her."

"So, she's a zombie, one who is made up of other people's parts?" Larissa asked as she sheepishly looked from me to Adam and back again.

"How bad do we look, Lari?" I asked, reading the fear in her eyes.

She smiled, but it didn't touch her eyes. "You both look Fae right now. We have to get you back to the Guild; Alden will know how to stop it."

"Stop what? Larissa, you don't just choose to become Fae. If we look Fae, then we were born Fae." She was in denial; hell, *I* was in denial. I turned and looked at Adam. He looked exactly as he had before, but his eyes glowed in two different colors now. "The Guild can't help us, Larissa; they don't allow Fae inside. We need to go home and figure out how we can find the killer, before he kills more innocent people."

She nodded, but didn't move from where she stood at a safe distance. "I need to know something first." She hesitated as if she was picking each word carefully. "Did either of you know what you were? I need you to be honest, because if you did—we need to be prepared for when the Guild comes after us."

"Larissa, I don't even know how this is possible. I hate the Fae; they killed my parents. Look, we lived inside the Guild with you. How could we have known?" The panic showed in my voice as it shook with tears.

"I'm so sorry guys. I mean I know you couldn't have known. I just had to ask. This doesn't change who you are, and you're my family. Fae or not, we only have each other," she whispered, before stepping closer.

We walked home silently. The mission had been successful, and, yet, it felt like a loss. I'd felt myself changing. I'd watched the horror on the innocent faces around me that I'd hurt. I had hurt them. Not Ryder, not the dead puppet—me. Everything was happening too fast. How could I be Fae? It made no sense, and I wasn't ready to accept it.

I stood, looking at the mirror in my room, just staring at myself as I listened to Larissa comfort Adam in her bedroom. My eyes now had two layers of iris surrounding the pupil. The first layer closest to the pupil was the same turbulent azure blue it had always been and around it was a ring in a light color of purple, surrounded by a very thin black ring.

The muffled sounds, told me that Larissa was doing a little more than just comforting Adam, so I grabbed a jacket and headed out. I had no idea where I was going until I stood in front of my parents' house.

The Victorian style house I had spent a small part of my childhood in was still standing. It was canary yellow. I could still remember my father painting it. Mom had said he should've just hired someone to do the job, but he'd laughed and said it was his home, and it was a labor of love.

Had they been hiding me as Ryder and his men had been discussing when they'd thought I couldn't hear them? Why would Guild Witches take in a Fae child? I let out a deep breath, realizing it didn't matter now, no one could answer those questions since they had died protecting me.

"Synthia," Alden's voice penetrated my mind as he slipped his bigger hand inside mine. "I'm sorry."

"Sorry for what, Alden?" I whispered, turning my eyes to him.

"I always knew you were different; knew something was off about you. You have to understand something, Synthia. My sister—your mother—she loved you. Made me promise to raise you up with other Witches if anything happened to her; she never did say why, but after watching the news today—well, I can only assume she knew what you were."

"I got them killed, Alden," I murmured, wiping at the angry tears that tried to fight free and won.

"Nah, they chose to help you. They couldn't have kids; you filled a void, Synthia. You became the center of their universe. They died protecting you, from what—well I have no idea, but you need to let them go; it's time. You can't keep doing this, blaming yourself. I can't keep blaming you either. We both need to let them go."

"The Guild will hunt us now—for breach of contract."

"No, I filed a report that said we knew the entire time. Marie had me run those tests on you and that boy, she saved us—even then she was protecting us. That woman stopped me from blaming you when I found you covered in blood," he stopped, clearing his throat from where tears had grown thick inside of it. "I thought it was you and then I realized what you were doing, trying to put her back together." He stopped, rubbing his eyes. "You were so young, Synthia. You couldn't have saved them. You would have just died with them," he finished.

"I did die with them, Alden," I sobbed, no longer caring that I looked weak. "I never left that house that day," I finished, and wiped my eyes again before letting a shaky exhale out slowly.

"I know. I'm the one who carried you out, Syn. I took you to my home and then Adam showed up. He was young and left on the steps, abandoned and alone, like you. He held you for hours and eventually you both slept. When you woke up the next morning you were no longer a child," he smiled and narrowed his eyes on me. "You wanted to know how to fight, how to be stronger. Here was this little five year old girl who wouldn't talk, but was working harder than most of the graduating class that year. You did everything, right down to tapping a Leyline and pulling it to the Guild, which was the first indication that you were different, Syn."

"They said I was allergic to the lines," I said incredulous.

"You weren't. Oh, I know they said so," he held up his hands to stop me, "but you are Fae, Synthia. If they were hiding you, then they would have had to keep you from connecting to a line. Every time one is tapped by a caste of the Fae, it sends out a trail that would have made it possible for someone to follow it back to you."

"What if I tapped one, when I was young, and it sent whoever I was hiding from a signal?" I was thinking out loud.

"It's possible, Syn, but we could play *what ifs* all day long. My sister is dead. She wouldn't want you to be suffering still. I admit that I blamed you for a long time, but I let it go, you need to now as well. She wouldn't want you to live like this, Syn, and if she died protecting you—she had a damn good reason for doing so."

"Aren't you supposed to be in lock down, Alden?" I said, coming out of my stupor and noticing the twelve Paladins standing around us. Their white metal armor and wicked silver weapons challenged any threat to Alden openly.

He laughed. "I knew I would find you here, and I

knew you'd have questions. I don't have the answers, Synthia. Hell, I've probably as many questions as you do now. But I knew you'd need family, and you're all I have. Also, Ryder has threatened the Guild with payback for the killings at his club. I issued no orders for an attack; it didn't come from us, and you have his ear girl, use it."

I snorted. "Have you met Ryder? That man makes my stubbornness look like nothing. Besides that, I don't have his ear. I may be under contract with him, but I'm his enemy right now—right along with the rest of the Guild." We were talking. We'd never spoken about his sister before. Hell, we didn't actually talk to each other unless he was training me, or giving me an assignment. It was awkward, but I needed it more than I could admit.

"He's planning something, so we're evacuating the Guild. Only the Keepers of the Guild will remain. The books and records have to be protected. Syn—" he hesitated running his hand through his messed up hair, he looked as if he'd been doing it for a few hours. "I don't know all the ins and outs of it with the Fae, but now I know you're gonna need to feed eventually. Marie thought Ryder could help you. Before, it made no sense, but now it's starting to. She left us instructions in case anything ever happened to her. She told me you would need to seek him out. I figured when they requested our help that it was the perfect time to carry out her wishes and see what came of it." He shrugged his wide shoulders, "Figured if nothing happened, or if Ryder wasn't able to see anything different inside of you that maybe everyone had just been worried for nothing."

"So, you think I should feed from Ryder?" I asked, narrowing my eyes.

"No," he turned bright red as he responded. "No,

of course not, Syn." He rubbed the back of his neck and laughed uncomfortably. "I just think that the first time you do—you should be with someone you couldn't hurt."

"Or kill," I said what he hadn't.

He nodded, his face sagging with relief that I'd said it instead of him. He looked as if he'd aged since I'd seen him last—and maybe we all had. "Synthia, I'm looking into the records to see if anyone has ever succeeded in stopping a Fae from turning. I can't promise results, but maybe we can find something to slow it down until I can. I can't bring back my sister, but I can protect what she loved the most—you."

"I get it, Alden," I snapped. I hadn't thought about feeding yet, hell I couldn't even grasp the reality of what was happening. "We got bigger problems than me feeding. Arianna isn't what she appears to be. She's got pieces from our victims magically sewn on to her like a fucking quilt." I was dodging emotions again, and from the grin he flashed he was thankful I had.

Alden swore violently. "Necromancer?"

"Not quite, more like a puppet. Her eyes take in everything as if someone is controlling her and seeing through her. I need to get to her, to get to the one controlling her. Get the master's attention, maybe it will stop the killings. Problem is, I'd need to kill his puppet to draw him out, Alden."

"And doing so could start a war if you get caught before you can kill her and break whatever spell is covering up the fact that she's nothing more than a fucking puppet," he said, rubbing the bridge of his nose. "Good grief, if she is what you say she is—the implications between the Dark and the Light Fae—"

"I can't do it without a team, Alden. And I won't do it without knowing the Guild is being cleared out and made safe from any repercussions that might come back on us."

"I can't give you the okay to kill the Light Heir, Synthia, even if she isn't who she says she is," I felt my stomach drop as he shook his head. "But I can give you a team and assure you that the Guild will be safe."

I smiled slowly. "So, unofficially I have your permission, but if anyone asked—"

He smirked. "If anyone asks, this conversation never happened," he stepped closer, placing his arms on my shoulders. "I don't show emotion, kid, and I think it rubbed off on you a little bit more than I thought. I'd like to think you know that—well, that I consider you family, and have, ever since my sister brought you home in diapers. Be careful, Syn. I can't claim responsibility, which means no one will come to help if you get caught. You'd be at the Dark Prince's mercy."

I nodded and exhaled slowly. "You have."

"Have what?" He asked narrowing his eyes.

"I'm strong, because you showed me how to be. I'm faster, because you made sure I knew what could happen if I wasn't fast enough. I'm me, because you raised me, Alden. You raised us all, and maybe you rubbing off on us wasn't a bad thing. Hard lessons aren't easy to teach children. We're stronger, because you made us into what we needed to be."

~~*~*~*~*~*~*

Chapter
THIRTY~FOUR

I watched Ryder and his men moving into the room below. There were hundreds of Fae gathered inside the ballroom of the Dark Fortress, along with Human dignitaries and members of the press. Security was next to impossible to bypass, so just getting to the rooftop where we were crouched, had been a death-defying feat without the team being detected.

"Last chance to back out guys; if this goes wrong we're dead. No one will be able to save our asses. I need to know you can do this job. If you're thinking this is too much, then it probably is. I know most of you are here because the Guild is on the line. I get it; you're pissed. So am I. But the Fae are not the bad people here tonight—no attacking them unless you have no other option."

I searched each face of the team I'd trained with. I knew their weaknesses. I knew their strengths. These were my people. They were why I fought, and would continue to, no matter what DNA I had been born with. They were good people, trustworthy, but this mission was suicide. I was asking for their lives, but if we couldn't stop Ryder from blaming the Guild— they'd have to hide like rats in the sewers, and they deserved better.

Twelve sets of sober eyes looked up to me with no doubt, or reserve, about giving their lives to ensure the Guild stayed up and running. I exhaled a shaky breath and looked to Adam and Larissa, who, like me, had dressed in black leather. The others had on black fatigues.

"Adam, blow it," I said, clasping the rope into my harness.

We waited, watching the Fae beneath us as they laughed and danced, unaware that we were about to crash the party. As the glass shattered, I jumped, making sure I was first on the surface to throw up the shield to protect the others as they came down. Eyes closed, arms out from my sides, I sailed through the air with a smirk on my lips as screams erupted.

When I was a few feet from the floor, I flipped so that I landed facing Ryder. I landed hard, but tossed up the shield, throwing Fae around the room and cutting one half of the crowd off from the other as it went up smoothly. When it was fully erected, I looked up and undid the hook as I watched the rest of the strike team come down.

Ryder and his men surrounded Arianna, and that would be a problem, but it was one we'd expected. I wasn't sure Larissa's magic would be strong enough to bring them in and consume their minds. Adam signaled as he hit the floor, and the music swiftly changed to Crazy Town's *Butterfly*.

"Go time. You're on, Larissa," I said, turning to meet her smiling eyes.

I met the death shining in Ryder's eyes. He'd kill me without thinking twice now. I was technically only fulfilling my contract. It just wasn't playing out in a way he had expected. His nostrils flared as the tick in his jaw started up. I blew him a kiss and sent my residual magic into Larissa.

The team took over and kept the shield up, protecting Adam and Lari as she started moving, sending her power out to flow through the room. She'd caught enough Fae with her seduction spell to ensure only Ryder and the thirteen would be the only obstacle in my way. Only a few of the Fae had begun to follow Larissa's dance steps. The rest were glaring murderous looks at us.

Ryder strode toward us in long angry strides that made him look dark and seductive while showing just how deadly he was. His body sizzled with electrical current.

I faltered briefly. Images of his mouth pleasuring me flooded my mind. The feel of his naked skin touching mine, sweat covering our bodies while we'd fucked like animals. I pushed those memories away, locking them into a box inside my mind, to view when I was alone.

I smiled at him, flashing him my best *come and get me* smile while I watched his hands from the corner of my eye. Larissa had gotten a better hold on the crowd, and some were now following her moves. It was a slight they wouldn't let go unpunished. While the Fae were big on fucking over each other, they united when fucked with as a whole. This plan had to work; it was the only one we had. If we failed, the entire Guild would suffer Ryder's wrath. I couldn't allow him to hurt them.

"Stupid, Synthia, you shouldn't have come here," Ryder snarled as his hands rested on his hips.

"I didn't come here for you, Ryder," I replied, meeting his angry glare head on.

"If you leave now, I'll only punish *you*," he said quietly, for my ears alone.

"Promises? Save them. I'm finishing our deal; when I am done, *we're* done.   Understand?" I challenged him.

"I'm going to tie you to my fucking bed and feed from you until there is no fight left inside of you. Then I'll keep you there, and use you as I see fit. I might even bring you back just to watch those pretty eyes as they explode for me."

I blinked, my mind shifted from focus for barely a moment with his words. His face changed briefly, shadows moving just beneath the surface of his flesh. His eyes changed, a glimmer of sparks lighting up inside their fiery depths. His teeth sharpened a fracture, something I had never heard of any Fae doing. He wasn't the Dark Prince—he was so much more than he was pretending to be.

"Looks like I'm not the only one keeping secrets, Ryder," I whispered as I felt the power shift. Larissa had control of everyone, except Ryder's men and the puppet now watching me intensely.

I sent a silent prayer up as I crouched down low. Ryder did the same, matching me move for move. He crouched low, knowing the moment I broke through the shield that he'd have me. I knew it as much as he did. But I would get away from him as planned.

I'd prepared for it, practicing with Adam. I smiled and lifted slowly, watching his body ripple with power and muscles against his suit. I moved to another spot and watched him follow me, his eyes piercing and beautiful in his anger.

"I'm going to fuck you until you only know the

need to please me, Syn. Until you worship my dick. You'll beg me to fuck you, and your mind will belong to me *alone*," he growled as we mirrored each other's movements again, like some sort of crazy football scrimmage line. He knew my moves before I made them as if he'd studied me in detail.

"What if I already do worship your dick, Ryder?" I said, lowering my voice until it sounded seductive.

His eyes narrowed as his mouth shifted into his sexy little smirk. "Pet, if I owned your mind—you'd let me in right now, you'd let me take you right here in front of everyone and not care who watched us. *You* care. I'll be sure to change that," he whispered icily.

I swallowed and exhaled before I launched myself at him. I was in his arms and on the floor in seconds, his hands biting into my flesh. "You're mine now, Synthia," he growled as he rolled me beneath himself which hadn't been in my plans.

I counted inside my head as his eyes stared into mine—ten, nine, eight. I sent my senses out into the room, stopping everything, and once again everything slowed except *Ryder*. "Let me go, Ryder. I have to prove that you're wrong before you do something stupid."

"I can't let you do that, Syn. I have proof that it was the Guild. We have identified most of the people involved," he growled as his thumb trailed down my cheek slowly.

"Then I'm sorry," I said as I slammed my head into his and rolled, using his shock as a distraction. I was up and moving toward the angry men protecting Arianna instantly. Adam's wicked flash-bang grenade spell went off, and Ryder's men hit the floor as planned, but they wouldn't stay there for long. As I pulled one of my blades from its sheath strapped to my leg and met the puppets gaze, I took quick aim and whispered the targeting spell, launching the blade forcefully through her chest with a killing blow.

Her body dropped as I was thrown back by something slamming against me hard enough to crush the air from my lungs. I cried out as soon as air came back, and met Ryder's angry stare. "Why the fuck did you do that!? *Shit,* Syn," he snarled low enough that only I could hear him as he held me against the wall.

I looked down to see a blade protruding from my chest. Zahruk stood a few feet away from us—on his feet and unaffected by Adam's spell. His eyes filled with sorrow as he brought his hand down from where he'd thrown his knife—into my chest.

Ryder's eyes dropped to my chest, and then over his shoulder to where Zahruk stood, horrified by what he'd done. "Fuck!" He shouted as my body sagged. He scooped me up into his arms. Air escaped from my lungs in a sick sound that made Ryder only cuss more.

I could feel the life draining with the blood that was escaping from the damaged tissue around the wicked blade protruding from my chest. I coughed, trying to speak, but blood splattered from my mouth to cover Ryder's crisp white shirt beneath his formal wear.

"She's—" I couldn't get the words out. I struggled to get air into my lungs as I was drowning on my own blood.

Ryder's eyes showed fear and regret. "Fuck, Syn—" his words trailed off as I smiled and tried another ragged breath.

"Ryder," Ristan yelled.

"Not now!" he shouted to his Demon.

"You need to see this," Ristan persisted.

Ryder spun around with me still in his arms as he faced the Demon and then looked down at where Arianna lay, gasping like a fish out of water. "What the fuck?" he snarled, looking down at her and then at me.

Arianna had lost whatever spell had been covering up her stench. Even now, I could smell the decaying flesh and decomposed organs. Ryder released me, and I slid to the floor, meeting Adam and Larissa's horrified looks. They were under orders to leave me if I couldn't get back to them. I turned my head at an awkward angle and watched her fingers move. She wasn't dead.

I used everything inside of me to pull the blade Zahruk had stuck in my chest, out, to use on her. I pushed up and used the confusion of the crowd as they realized Arianna was pieced together with dead bodies. "I'm going to find you," I growled to the person watching from the dead, lifeless eyes. I whispered the targeting spell again, and Zahruk's blade flew from my fingers and slammed into her chest next to my blade. I watched as the reflection of the puppet master faded from her eyes.

I stood on shaky legs and looked at Ryder, who looked down at the corpse, Zahruk's and my blades now protruding from its chest. "Told you," I whispered, turning to make it back to Larissa and Adam. I got about two steps before Ryder turned me back toward himself, which made me fall to my knees at his feet.

"What the fuck was that?" he asked sharply.

I tried to speak, but I was seconds from passing out. His eyes lowered to where Zahruk stabbed me, and I watched as the full realization of what his man had done in protection of Arianna set in. "Let—go," I croaked.

"You need a healer," he growled, trying to pick me up. I tried fighting against his hold, which caused more blood to flow from the open wound in my chest. He saw it and stopped trying to pull me up. "Why didn't you just fucking tell me?"

I glared at him. Shook my head and ended up coughing more blood. I moved toward Adam and Larissa who broke the shield's protection and ran to me. "She needs a hospital," Larissa cried.

"She won't make it," Adam said, barely above a whisper, sheer terror filling his eyes.

We didn't have time to argue as Ryder reached down and picked me up, sifting out. We sifted into some kind of medical ward, more than likely the one Ryder had mentioned at Vlad's bar.

"I need a fucking healer now!" Ryder snarled to the surprised onlookers who watched us silently. "Stab wound to her chest—where the fuck is Eliran?" He continued to snarl at the Fae around us.

"I'm here. You have to set her down, Ryder," said a tall blonde Fae with wispy hair.

"Fix her or you die," he seethed.

"You have to set her down, Sire, or I won't have a chance to do so," the blonde Fae said clearly.

I watched Ryder step back after he had set me on a bed, his eyes searching my face with a rawness I'd never seen before in their molten depths. "Eliran, you have to fix her."

"What is she?" he asked, already pulling apart my clothes to get a look at the wound.

"She's unknown Fae."

"She looks Human…Are you sure she isn't?" he replied as he put an oxygen mask over my mouth and nose.

"I don't fucking know!" Ryder growled, "She's more Human than Fae right now, she has not Transitioned."

"But, Sire—"

"Just fix her, Eliran, your life depends on it," Ryder said, so softly that I thought I had imagined it.

~~*~*~*~*~*~*~*

THIRTY~FIVE

I awoke to the whispers of people speaking in hushed tones. I winced as fire spread through my ribs, but at least I was able to breathe again. Either that, or we had all died, and I'd hallucinated the healer. I blinked and tried to cover my eyes, but the IV and Kflex bandage made it a feeble attempt. The scent of bleach and sterile equipment filled the room.

"If I'm not dead, turn the freaking light off," I groaned.

"There's my girl," Alden's voice sounded from beside me.

"If you guys died too, I'm going to haunt that fucking Fairy until hell freezes over," I mumbled through my cracked lips.

Everyone inside the room laughed.

"I'm serious," I said, narrowing my eyes as I tried to move. Adam held his head over mine as I realized I couldn't move.

He laughed and shook his head. "Nope, afraid not. You're alive, Syn. Ryder saved you."

"Saved me—my ass. His guy is the reason I got stabbed!" I complained, remembering the look in his eyes. He'd regretted what had happened. Good.

"Yeah well, it's over and we won. You got her, Syn," Larissa said, smiling from behind Adam's head as she leaned over him.

"Where am I?" I asked, wishing I could sit up.

"Guild hospital. There's been a lot of wrangling while you were out. Ryder is claiming you and I are Fae and no longer fall under Guild jurisdiction—he tried to keep you and demanded the Guild turn me over, as well. Alden filed a formal complaint and injunction against Ryder and brought you back to the Guild until this could be sorted out—and, speaking of, he failed to protect you from danger, so the contract is void. You attended the Engagement Ball, which was in the contract, and by Fae law you were there by invitation—the only problem is, he said if we didn't want to send everyone else to face a boatload of charges that you had to come back willingly and renew the contract."

I blinked at the overload of information from Adam "So let me get this right…if I don't go back to Ryder—the strike team does?"

Adam sighed and shook his head. "They said they would, Syn, but that's up to you. You can choose to walk away this time."

"No," I snorted. "That wasn't an option. They were my team last night—"

"Last week," Adam said sheepishly, as he scratched his head and crinkled his nose.

"Last week?" I winced as I tried to sit up. "Why didn't anyone wake me up?" I shook my head…as much as it would allow me to.

"You were treated by the Fae. Ryder said it might take your body a while to heal since you haven't um—Transitioned yet," Adam winced and stood up fully again.

"Transitioned my ass…and, no, I'll go, Adam. Tell the team they did well, to stand down. I'll go see Ryder," I met his emerald eyes that now had that ring of lime.

"You don't have to, Synthia. I'll find a way to deal with him," Alden argued.

"Alden, listen to me. I did this. It was my idea, my team, my coven, my responsibility. He has answers, and I need them. Adam needs them too and sooner or later—without help—we will end up hurting someone, and then the Guild will have to hunt us. I can't live with that. Can you, Adam?" I asked meeting and holding his eyes before looking behind him to where Larissa held his hand.

"No," he said as his teeth ground together.

"I can do this. You made me strong enough and smart enough, Alden. Sooner or later, we have to learn to be what we are, and you haven't found a way out of being Fae yet. I can't feel my magic right now, and without it I'm a sitting duck."

"I don't like it, Synthia," Alden continued.

"You don't have to like it, we just have to deal with it," I whispered, closing my eyes briefly before opening them back up. "What happened with Arianna?"

Adam snorted, "Well she was one of us, but she'd been dead for a couple years, Syn. Her body is being wrapped and readied to be taken back by the Seattle Guild in a few days. They are going back through the missing persons files now. Seeing how many of them might have been the first victims. The press is going absolutely ape-shit crazy over this and hounding Ryder—they're camping on his doorstep. We got you out before they could connect us to anything. You got lucky, Syn—this time."

I'd killed his puppet, or her puppet—which meant, soon, we'd know who had been pulling her strings and why. I closed my eyes and tried shaking off the sick feeling that came with knowing she'd been a victim before a tool.

I stood outside Ryder's estate after fighting through the press, who even now were flashing pictures of me standing in his driveway. I was dressed in low hip hugging jeans and a baggy shirt that hid the fact that my ribs were wrapped from where Zahruk had stabbed me. I stood my ground, watching as fourteen males piled from the house shirtless. Someone needed to put a freaking warning label on these guys. *May cause hormonal overload.*

Ryder stood in the middle, his eyes sliding down my body slowly. Probably looking for damages. We said nothing. I could feel the Fae pulsing with their wild magic, waiting for me to strike, or do something stupid. I shook my head wondering if we'd get into a pissing contest next. Maybe I had interrupted their workout session, which could account for the lack of dress and pissy looks I was getting from them.

"You ordered me here," I said, finally breaking the silence.

"I did," Ryder replied with his lopsided grin that

looked more dangerous than friendly.

"I'm here," I mumbled.

"You are."

"Okay, we gonna measure dicks all day, Ryder, or are we gonna sign a contract?" I snapped.

"You don't have a dick, Syn. I would have noticed," Ryder's smile lifted roguishly.

I rolled my eyes and then rubbed them in frustration. "Your man stabbed me Ryder because he thought I was a danger to your fiancée. I broke in, because *you* were in danger. I tried to talk to you when this first went down, and you didn't listen to me then, so I'm pretty sure you wouldn't have listened to me about this. You're too fucking stubborn. We were hunting a killer, you were getting ready to marry his or her puppet, and *I* saved you. I did what you wanted me to—only there was no assassin, unless you consider the one pulling the strings on your—well, whatever she would be now."

"You broke into an engagement party with almost every house of *royal Fae* in attendance—an engagement that I set up. There was never going to be any wedding, Synthia, *ever*. I was trying to draw out the Light Fae, among other things, and you *ruined* it."

I blinked at him. *No wedding? He hadn't planned on going through with it? And why was he trying to draw out the Light Fae?* Ryder had more secrets, and I was starting to wonder if he wasn't trying to start an all-out war with the other castes of Fae. "Why would you need to draw out the Light Fae?" I asked trying to pull more information from him.

"That's none of your fucking business," Ryder growled. "You broke Fae laws, Synthia, without a good fucking reason."

"You were about to start a fucking war, Ryder, on *my* Guild. I saved lives. I don't regret it, not even if it leaves me your fucking slave for eternity. I was born to save people, and I'm good at it. I take out bad people. I do what no one else wants to do, Ryder. I get the job done." I winced and grabbed my ribs, before realizing what I had done and righted myself again.

"You're not healed," he growled.

"Nope, still Human," I said, hiding the pain in my voice.

"You're in pain."

"I'm *fine*."

"*Who* is stubborn?" he asked, moving closer to me.

"I am. Never said I wasn't."

"You should be healed by now," he whispered as his eyes met and held mine.

"Nope, not yet. I need to finish this and get home. I need to find the puppet master. He needs to die. Like yesterday."

"You won't be going home this time. You will be staying with me. *Indefinitely*."

"No, I won't. I was stupid last time to sign before reading every detail. I came here because you forced me back. You knew I'd come," I watched his eyes sparkle in answer. "Well I'm here. You didn't protect me, *you* got me stabbed. You broke our contract. Alden thought it was a temporary clause, but it wasn't. If you failed to protect me from harm, you forfeit your claim on me. That's why I'm here, because you don't like to lose."

He smiled and tipped his head. "It won't happen again, and I didn't lose, Syn. You're here, and I told you, I *always* win."

"Ahh, but remember Ryder, you're as stubborn as I. We're both hot-headed. Where there's a flame, someone's bound to get burned, and this time it won't be me."

"You burn pretty hot, Syn. I haven't forgotten," he whispered smiling softly.

"Not gonna happen. I'll be making my own contract. It goes both ways. Watch what you wish for, you just might get it."

"You're going to need to feed sooner or later, Syn," he warned as his eyes turned hard.

"Then I guess we better get to negotiating, Ryder," I challenged him back.

"Is your body changing?"

"Nope, I'm still me."

He smiled. "Your eyes are Fae, Syn; unique, as well. I have never seen a mix of blue and purple before. I'm curious as to how Adam became your familiar."

"He's not my familiar, he's my family."

"No, he calmed you down. He grounded your power with his own. Most Fae spend eternity looking for a familiar who can ground their powers. Yet you, a newborn, walked in with one in your pocket. Explain."

"Explain?" I laughed, "Okay, last week? I was a *Witch*. I knew where the hell I belonged, Ryder. This week? This week I'm a fucking Fairy, Ryder. A *fucking Fairy*—my entire life, has been a huge fucking lie. I got people who loved me *killed,* because I can't think of another reason for those Fae to be inside my house that day. No one can, but now that I know I'm Fae—or turning Fae, I know they were there for me. So explain? I have no fucking idea, Ryder—I don't even know who my actual parents are, or why they hid me. Adam is only getting pieces of what he thinks we are—hell! He doesn't even know why he is drawn to me, but he is. When I get pissed or upset—he *feels* it! Nothing in my life makes any sense now. The only thing I do know is that I don't want any of this."

"I need to know what the mark on the back of your neck is," he growled.

I threw up my hands and stood there, waiting for Ryder to invite me in so we could get this over with. When he didn't say anything I tapped my foot, impatiently waiting. I looked around us at the smiles and smirks from his men. Ristan was there, a guarded look in his eyes, a sad expression on his face. Maybe he felt bad for everything that had ensued after he'd asked me to investigate the Light Heir.

"Come, we will go inside," he said crisply.

I started forward, but it hurt. I'd done too much today already and I had yet to fully heal. I flinched as I stepped forward and felt my knees try to give away under the weight. Ryder was instantly there, catching me by the waist to steady me on my feet. "Let go of me, I can manage on my own," I growled at him.

"I think '*thank you*' are the words you're looking for, Syn. If you're not healing, we need to figure out why," he said, letting me go and heading back inside, awarding me with a view of his firm ass in his low hung jeans.

"Did you go broke and couldn't afford shirts in the budget this month?" I grumbled, having to look at his exposed skin.

"You liked my brands inside Faery. You interrupted a training regimen, Syn," he said smiling over his shoulder. "If I remember correctly, inside Faery you tried to taste every one of my brands—"

"With my tongue," I snapped back as his men fought the urge to smile.

"Don't tempt me, Syn. I've decided only to keep one source of food in my house."

"Claire?" I asked glaring at him.

"*You.*"

I tripped over my feet and ran into his back, it made the wound scream in pain, and before I knew it I was falling. Once again he was faster than gravity was. He caught me with a worried look in golden depths. "You need to rest. You're not healing fast enough."

"Sucks to be me, then. Contract."

He smiled coldly. "You drive me crazy, and I think you do it on purpose. I had to watch you almost die, Syn. Do you have idea how fucking hard that was for me? I had to watch them cut you open to stop the bleeding, and I watched you bleed out *three* fucking times before Eliran could stop it. And then I had to watch as your fucking coven came in and took you away from me, while citing breach of contract bullshit and I couldn't fucking kill them because if by some fucking miracle, you woke up and I had, you would never forgive me. *I* saved *you,* Syn, not them. You'd be dead if I hadn't been Fae. You'd have died in the arms of your coven."

I swallowed slowly and reached up against my will to caress his face gently. "Thank you for saving me. Next time—try not letting me get stabbed *first*."

He smiled and searched my face before setting me back on my feet. His hands steadied me before he released me. "I meant what I said, Syn, I plan on punishing you. Soon."

"Yeah, you like to say that, but you're going to have to get in line. I'm waiting for a visit from the puppet master at the moment, so we need to hurry this along."

Chapter
THIRTY~SIX

It took three hours to finish signing the contract. Once again, I was his property. At least for a while, but I'd stood my ground and refused to back down on some things. I was back in the Guild car and heading to my shared apartment when Larissa called to check up.

"Local morgue, you stab them, we slab them," I said, smiling impishly, knowing she'd hear it in my voice.

"Syn, how'd it go?" Larissa replied with nervousness in her tone.

"It went okay," I said, turning onto the highway and frowning. "Everything okay?" I asked, noting she lacked her normal pizzazz tonight.

"It's fine, are you on your way home?" I didn't miss the hopeful note in her voice as she asked.

"Yup, need something from the store?" I asked, wondering if that was the hope I'd heard since I was already out.

"No, I was just checking," she replied.

"You and Adam need me to stay gone for a while?" I crinkled my forehead and made a mental note to set them a schedule, or have them go to his place from here on out.

"Just come home, please, Syn. I *need* you here," she said and hung up on me.

I held the phone out, looking at it before shoving it back into the purse between the seats. What the hell had that been about? She'd sounded upset, and I really hoped it had nothing to do with Adam. No way in hell was I playing a go-between with their relationship. I shook my head and headed home.

I hit the button for the second time glaring at the doors of the elevator. I'd tried to call her again, but she'd either hit ignore call or had turned off her phone completely which had made me ignore most of the speed limit signs from the highway all the way home.

The elevator doors beeped as they slid open. I rolled my eyes and stepped in, pressing the third floor and waiting. When the doors opened on our floor, I felt a twinge of fear, but it wasn't my own fear that I felt. I groaned, hoping it had nothing to do with Larissa's fear that Adam was now Fae.

It wasn't as if we had chosen it. We couldn't change it either, the best we could do was ignore it until it became more dominant and then Ryder would help us as had been agreed upon earlier tonight. I exhaled and shook my head as I twisted the knob and found it locked.

I lifted my knee and groaned as the pain came back as I dug through my purse for the keys. I almost found them when the door opened, and a man who wasn't Adam stood in front of me. "You must be Synthia."

I blinked and narrowed my eyes, "And you would be?"

"Oh, how rude of me. I'm Joseph," he held out his hand, which I didn't take as I looked over his shoulder to see inside my own apartment. "Do come in, Syn. Larissa and I have been waiting for you."

He looked harmless enough. Maybe we had a new neighbor? He knew my name so obviously Larissa trusted him enough to allow him inside our apartment; why she'd allowed him to answer the door was beyond me though. I could see no brands exposed from the white shirt and faded jeans he wore that would mark him Fae, or from the Guild. It wasn't until I met his eyes that I found something off about him.

"Where is she?" I asked as my stomach dropped.

"She's inside," he said with a smile that didn't fit right on his pinched features. His hair was a dull brown and looked as if he had been running his hands through it all day. He had eyes that held a keen interest in a shade of gray that was creepy.

I pushed past him and screamed as I felt the sudden white-hot pain in my back. It was too late. Something was pushed into one of my shoulder blades, and I fell to the floor, unable to move a single muscle. Tears burst into my eyes as I realized I couldn't move. I could see Larissa, though.

She was tied to a chair, and blood was pouring from her face in several places. He'd come while I'd been out signing the contract. The puppet master had gotten to Larissa, and I'd failed to feel anything from her from our connection. Worse, she must have been tortured this entire time by a killer *I* had provoked. I fought to pull any magic around or to me while his malicious laughter pulled my eyes to him. He stood over me, looking down with a twisted smile.

"It won't help. Those rods were created to hold the Gods; the more you struggle, the more they lock down and drain you and your powers," he snickered, enjoying the pain that was now palpable inside the room.

"I challenged you. Let her go," I said, trying to get Larissa away from danger.

"No, she's too beautiful. She has great skin and her eyes—magical."

I felt bile push at the back of my throat; everything inside of me screamed that this wasn't happening. Not again; I couldn't watch this, I couldn't breathe. "Mine are better, I'm Fae."

"You, I plan on keeping, because you killed my masterpiece. You will get to keep your friend. Well," he crouched down and moved a few stray pieces of hair from my face, "you will get to keep *pieces* of her."

"No, please," I whispered, meeting Larissa's terrified eyes as she tried to speak through the gag tied over her mouth.

"Let's get you up. You need a better seat for the show!" He chirped as he easily picked me up and held me pressed against the wall. He had more small, thin rods in his hands. He used one hand to press my head against the wall as the rest of my body obeyed him. His free hand slid the pins in one by one as his eyes lit up. I fought the urge to scream as fire ignited and muscle gave way, tearing as each one was pressed through.

He was enjoying it, with a calmness that was unsettling. I fought nausea as I helplessly allowed it.

He was going to kill us both, and I couldn't do a single thing but watch. I was going to have to relive my past again. There had to be a way to stop this. I tried to pull up a shield that would protect us, but nothing happened except a tightening inside my chest.

Tears of hopelessness ran down my face as he snickered and backed up with his head tipped low as madness lit inside his eyes. "You took him away from me. I could have brought down the entire Fae race. You ruined it!" He lost his composure and screamed showing just how unhinged he was. "No, you will suffer and you will take her place."

He turned and picked up a knife, his other hand trailing over Larissa's bare leg where he'd cut her pants open. I screamed, shaking everything inside the room until he was forced to turn back to me. He walked back slowly, his eyes lighting up around the edges to reveal the fact that he was half Fae; *Changeling*. "That's it, baby, scream," he screamed with me, his piercing the room until he started laughing. "No one can hear you. No one will save you."

I stopped and shook inside, my palm itching with a slight tingle, and then a burn as if it was trying to work blood magic again. I swallowed and begged him to cut me, to use me. But he refused, and when he walked back over to Larissa all I could do was watch as my voice, hoarse and tired, refused to work.

He removed the gag from Larissa's bloody mouth, and my heart dropped, everything inside of me screamed in denial. "No, oh God nooooo! Lari—oh God." He'd cut her beautiful face up in several places. He snickered as he sank his blade in and watched her come back, aware of what was happening. She sobbed and shook her head, trying to move it away from his merciless abuse.

I met her eyes and sobbed along with her as I fought the hold of the pins. He was cutting her open and once again I couldn't help, I wasn't strong enough to do anything with the pins holding me securely to the wall. I screamed and fought the horror of what he was doing. He whistled while he cut my best friend open. He was fucking insane!

His body moved, blocking my view for a few seconds and then silence reigned as he cut whatever it was from Larissa's insides, the noise sickening. When he turned around, I closed my eyes. I didn't want to see, didn't want to know what he had done.

"Beautiful," he whispered, and then I felt his blood-coated hands on my shirt as he cut it up the middle.

I opened my eyes and met his. "I'm going to get loose, and when I do, I am going to cut the flesh from your bones and rip every organ out slowly, starting with the ones you can live without!"

He snickered again and groped my chest. I couldn't see Larissa. I felt the rage pulsing inside of me and yet no magic came from it, the connection we shared was now completely gone. Severed.

"You will scream for me, I promise you. When I am done with you, you will do anything I want you to. I will control your body and mind. Are you ready to scream?" He smiled coldly as his blade came up to touch my skin.

I felt the knife cut through my chest, and he was right. I screamed. I'd thought I couldn't anymore—I was wrong. The blade sliced through my skin like freshly melted butter. I looked down to watch his blade, covered with my own blood now.

He snickered, enjoying the sound of my screams as he pulled the blade out and licked it. He opened his mouth to say something, and before he could, he was gone from where he had stood in front of me. I turned my head and watched as a hooded figure in an onyx colored cloak attacked him, cutting and slicing him with a wicked looking silver blade.

Blood spurted up with every angry slice the hooded figure made. I moved my eyes to Larissa, but before I could finish making them move to her mutilated body, Ristan was there blocking the way. "Move," I cried, but he ignored me as he placed his hand on my chest and dropped his magic to seal the wound.

His skin turned bright red, his eyes matching crimson as he spoke strange words that caused his hand to glow as he pressed it against my chest, and he applied more pressure. "Ryder, she needs more help than I can give her here."

"Not—me, heal—heal *her*. Please, I need her, fix her. You can do it, please. I'll do *anything*, Ryder, *anything*. She's my family!" I sobbed uncontrollably.

His eyes met and held mine with sorrow in their ancient depths. "She's already gone Syn."

"No! You're wrong! Fix her—oh God—no, no just fix her. I need you to just fix her. Please, oh God, you have to!" I sobbed, sagging as Ristan started pulling each pin out of my skin and then Ryder was there.

"Syn, look at me." Ryder took the pins still protruding from my skin and pulled them free before he caught me and pulled me close against his body. "She can't be fixed, Pet, and you don't want to see her, not like this, Syn." I sobbed, my body shaking with each one as what they were telling me sank in. I couldn't do this, I wasn't strong enough. I buried my face against Ryder as I screamed with everything I had—my body shook hard enough that Ryder had to hold me with both hands to keep upright.

"Ristan, stay with the body and clean it up. Bring her back to the mansion when you finish. I need to take Syn back to Eliran," Ryder whispered as I pushed away from him.

"Where's Adam? He was here with her earlier. He was with her! Oh God." I fought nausea and lost. I bent over and threw up until nothing else would come out. I felt comforting hands pulling my hair away from my face, and as I looked up, I saw Larissa's lifeless eyes staring at me. Her chest had been torn open, and her heart was gone.

Everything inside of me closed down. Something broke inside of me and just stopped, and I stopped with it. Sightless, I sat down at Ryder's feet as his eyes filled with grief. "Make me not feel it. I don't want to feel it. Make it stop."

He reached down and picked me up, until I was cradled in his arms. "Find the boy and make sure you remove the body first, Ristan. No one else needs to see her like this. She deserves better."

Ryder sifted us into the medical ward, *again*. He said nothing as he placed me down on the sterile bed. "Eliran, she needs you."

"Again?" Eliran said as his eyes scanned the damage. "Ristan did well, Sire." His eyes met mine, and grew round in surprise to find them glowing.

I felt my life draining away. Everything inside of me just wanted it to stop. The pain. The death. I'd given too much, I just needed to sleep.

~~*~*~*~*~*~*~*

Chapter
THIRTY-SEVEN

~~*~* Ryder *~*~*~*

She sleeps, free from the pain that took her into this catatonic state, broke her mind, and ripped a hole in her already battered soul. She had seen too much. Her mind broke, snapping, as the past clashed together with the horror of watching yet another person she loved be tortured to death.

"I want to know why the fuck I couldn't feel her, Ristan, only her fucking pain. How'd that sick fuck block me from her?" I snap. I feel useless, something I have never felt before. Never want to again.

"No clue. I didn't see this play out, Ryder. Her future is unclear to me still, blocked. She's powerful and has a big part to play in saving Faery; beyond that I can't see anything."

"Fuck, Ristan, I don't care about the fucking future. I want to know why she won't wake up right now!" I explode. I hate the vacancy I see in her eyes. She's empty. There's no more fight inside her eyes, and I hate it.

"She's catatonic, she has to heal from within,"

Eliran says as he walks into the room we sit watching her from. Adrian and Adam had both shown up, along with their Guild elder.

The two men had wasted no time with questions. Adam shook with denial and then climbed in the large bed we'd laid Syn in. He'd cuddled her against his chest as tears ran from his eyes. He'd lost his mate—I didn't fucking blame him for needing to hold her, but I didn't like it either. They comfort her, even when she cannot feel them.

"I want a full research team on the metal pins. I want to know where they came from, how he got them, and what effect they have on her. And I want the information yesterday. Eliran, use the Mage if you need to. I want him in pain and screaming to tell us everything he knows, and why he went after, Syn."

"When do you plan on telling them that Larissa's killer is still alive?" Ristan asks, his eyes narrowing as he turns to look at me.

"I don't. Adam would want him dead. I need him alive to tell us who else he is working with. He wasn't alone. He said the others would come—I want them all dead. I'll tell *her* when she's strong enough, Ristan. Right now I just need her to wake up."

~~*~*~*~* Synthia *~*~*~*~*~*

I hear them, their hearts beating, hands touching, connecting with me—I can sense it all. But nothing makes sense. Nothing brings my mind back from where it has gone. I'm awake, but nothing computes, nothing is real. Here, there is no pain, Larissa is alive, and if I open my mind—if I wake it up, I'd have to feel it, have to admit it.

Sleep claims me again, and I allow it.

I wake; Adrian is talking to me, trying to pull me from the peace inside my mind. I close him out. I don't want to feel anything anymore. He leaves, and Adam takes his place, but he says nothing. He holds me and cries—it threatens to bring me out, and I go back to the darkness.

Someone cradles me, his scent calls to me. It's Ryder, his lips caressing mine gently as he demands I wake up, that I come back to him. His hands comfort me as he holds me against his chest and I sleep, held in his arms. I feel safe with him, and, yet, I shouldn't.

I pace inside my mind, knowing I have to come out sooner or later. It would be so easy to just never wake up, to give in to the blackness that takes the pain and holds it at bay. I felt the fracture, the crack inside my mind that I slipped into. It was seductive, the emptiness was comforting.

They take turns, holding my useless form, comforting it. I wish they'd leave it alone. Every time I need it, it refuses to save the people I love; every time. The magic didn't come. The Fae inside of me failed to help me, as well. I hate them both. Everything inside of me is useless. What is the point of having powers, if they don't come when you need them the most?

Adam lays down his hand, stroking my face and staring into eyes that see, but don't register anything. He smiles through his tears, choking on them. "Syn, you gotta wake up. I need you. I can't live without you too. She's gone, Baby. You're stronger than this. You're the strongest person I know. I need you. Damn it, Syn, I need you."

I close him out.

"Syn, you need to come back. You need to wake

up and eat. You're wasting away. It's been days now. We have to bury her soon, and you have to be there to let her go," Adrian whispered as he holds my hand tightly.

I close my eyes and sink back inside.

Hands touch my face. I open my eyes as Ryder and Eliran stick plastic devices to my forehead and click on a machine. "She is in there. See these waves here?" Eliran speaks to Ryder. I go back inside. "What the hell?"

"What?" Ryder demands.

"It's like she just completely shut off. I've never seen anything like it. There are no brain waves. She's gone."

"Gone how?" Ryder explodes.

"Like she's dead, but she still has a pulse," Eliran says as his hands grab my face and searches it. I open my mind, his machine beeps and then I close them—it goes silent. I like the silence of my mind. I go there, hiding.

I wake up. Ryder's holding me in his lap, his nose buried in my hair. He's whispering encouraging words and then nonsense, words that bring me to the surface but wouldn't allow me to breech it. I'm safer inside, not ready to break through. "I need you to wake up. Your friends have been mucking up my home. They refuse to leave, or bury Larissa. You're strong enough for this, Pet. I need you to wake up. I need you to stop shutting down, or I'm coming in there to get you."

I close him out.

Alden comes. He whispers and rubs my hands together. Comments to Adam about body heat. I'm not controlling it. I'm losing more than retaining now. I shut him out. I failed him too.

"Syn," Ryder's voice shakes me.

I turn around to see him standing in the darkness with me. He's dressed in his cloak, blending in with my darkness. He steps from the shadows and examines me closely. I don't speak; I don't need words here. I slide down the wall of my mind to sit again.

He strides forward and does the same, sitting beside me, his hands finding mine and holding them. Comforting, and, yet, not forceful. "Adam needs you, Syn. He's grieving. They need to bury Larissa soon. They're scared and need you right now."

I turn and take him in; his eyes look tired. And his hair is a mess, as if he's been running his hands through it for days without brushing it. Dark circles surround his eyes as they flow over me carefully, studying me. "I need you, Syn, need you to help me break the fucker who did this. He's alive. I need you to come back to me. Can you do it, Syn?"

I can't breathe.

My heart kicks into overdrive, pounding relentlessly in my chest.

I watched him die. I watched Ryder *kill* him.

I blink and cry out as everything comes back. The pain. The agony. Larissa is dead—because I *failed*. Tears burn my eyes, and I try to hold on to Ryder's hand, but he's gone, and once again I am alone in the darkness. But now, I can see light.

Someone is crying, screaming with pain so deep, raw, and utterly bare that it consumes and takes a hold of me. Hands pull me close as more tortured screaming erupts from within the room that sounds like a wounded animal. My ears bleed from it. The pain is too much, the shaking is too much.

"What's wrong with her?" Alden demands.

"She's waking up," Ryder replies from where he's holding my tortured body as it emerges from the depths of despair it had been locked inside. His arms tighten around me, his scent calming but nothing takes away the pain of knowing I failed Larissa, and she died because of it.

I blink as feelings of pain wash through me. I claw at my mind demanding it let me go, let me out. The screaming in the room is me, it's my own. I sob, my entire body shaking against Ryder as he holds me against him. Adam is trying to hold my pain away with the bond, but he cannot, he releases it with a shudder the instant he felt it.

"Put her to sleep! Fuck, it's too much—too much pain!" Adam snarls, his body shivering from the pain he's tasting from inside of me.

I push away from Ryder and look around the room as the scream subsides. I fight my breathing and my mind as it tries to fracture again. I meet Adam's horrified eyes. He knows what I felt, and I hate it. They didn't tell him what happened in that room— he knows now, he saw it when he tried to pull my pain away. It's playing on repeat inside my head. He shouldn't have tried.

The room is full of my friends and Ryder's men. They pity me for what I will have to endure, what I have to live with. "Where is she?" I demand to know.

"Syn—" Alden says softly, as if calming a child.

"Fuck. That. Where is she?"

"She's dead," Ryder says.

"I—" my voice cracks, and I shake it off. I fight the tears and the nausea that threatens to come out. "I know. Where is her soul?" I meet no one's eyes. I don't want pity right now. I want to know where her soul is.

"We don't know. We couldn't find it," Adrian says watching me.

I meet Adam's eyes. He shakes his head sadly, I exhale and nod. It's okay. I didn't want her to be released to the Fade. I wanted her to be born without this life, I wanted her to be able to live and grow old, without having to fight next time.

"Syn," Alden is getting ready to say sorry. *Why do people do that? Why do they say it?*

"*No*. No, don't you fucking say sorry. Sorry isn't going to bring her back, sorry isn't going to make me feel any better, and it damn sure won't fix the guilt." I was crying, sobbing as I struggled to get my point across. "She's dead, because *I* challenged him, because *I* took his puppet away. She died because of *me*, and I couldn't save her. I have to live with that. What I don't have to live with is any fucking pity, or anyone saying they're fucking sorry."

The room grew silent as they listened to my sobs. I wiped the tears away angrily and shook my head. "I bought the plot next to Adrian for me; use it for Larissa. She'd want a dress—something yellow. Her funeral packet is at the Guild, Alden—get it. We bury her as soon as we can get the arrangements together. Now, everyone except Adam get out."

When the room had fully cleared, I met Adam's green eyes and held my arms open for him. He fell into them, and I held him as we both cried together, neither one speaking until the last tear had dried. We'd all done the same when we had thought Adrian dead—this time there was no chance of afterlife.

"I failed her," I whispered against his ear.

"No, Syn, you didn't. Those pins he used took your strength and all magic, that's how he was killing immortals. There was no weapon, only those pins. Ristan said you couldn't have done anything—not even *he's* immune to them, Syn. You can't shoulder the blame here. We all knew he would come. We both failed her. I was asleep for fuck's sake, three doors down, and I couldn't feel anything from either of you. I need you too, Syn. I need you to stay awake now. I can't lose you, too."

When Adam left the room, Ryder took his place on the bed, his features empty as he watched me. We didn't talk. We didn't need words. We just lay there together, staring at each other. I wanted to say something, but I wasn't sure how to thank him.

"How did you get inside my head, Ryder?" I asked after the silence became too much.

"I wasn't inside your head. I projected an image. I had to try several times. You wouldn't let me inside until you were ready. I'm sorry about Larissa. He blocked me from you; he knew you were mine. That it won't happen again—I assure you of it, Syn."

"Why do people say that? Sorry—it's not like they killed her. I never thought he'd come to the house. She was my responsibility, and I failed her. I—"

"You couldn't have saved her, Syn. If you blame yourself, then Joseph wins. He's downstairs, gloating because he knows you're in pain. You are letting him win, just like you did so long ago with your parents. You were a child. If you had tried to take on Fae at that age, you'd be dead. You can't keep blaming yourself for things you cannot change. Trust me when I tell you this. Some things just cannot be changed, no matter how much you want them to be."

I laid my head back down on the pillow and watched as he removed his shirt and crawled back in, lifting my head and placing it on his chest as his fingers caressed my cheek. I felt secure and safe with him. I closed my eyes and placed my hand above his heart, feeling each beat of it until sleep started to sink in. "Sleep, Syn. I'll keep the nightmares at bay for now," he whispered and kissed the top of my head softly.

Chapter
THIRTY-EIGHT

We buried Larissa on a sunny day beneath the old oak tree in the Guild's cemetery to the musical lyrics of the Lumineers *Ho Hey*. We followed her wishes with the exception of the roses, she had wanted yellow ones. She got thousands of red roses. The Seattle Guild showed up en masse to honor one of our fallen and to celebrate the end of the killer's reign, now that he was locked up.

No one thought it weird that the Fae were still tight-lipped on how the Mage had created a puppet and used her to infiltrate their ranks as an Heir. Ryder and his group were careful of what they spoke of when we were around now, as if hiding something from us. I was more worried about if, or when they would retaliate against the Light Fae for the slight against them.

Arianna hadn't been Fae. She'd been a Witch from the Seattle Guild. I'd given her peace after five years of her soul being torn to nothing more than a wisp of an aura that had once belonged to a beautiful Witch. She'd been kidnapped a few years ago, which told us this was much bigger than we had thought it was. It was good news and bad news. We'd stopped one, but he hadn't been working alone. They rejoiced while we grieved.

There was no winning in this one; only sorrow as the news cameras and press sat outside the gates, waiting for the Guild and Fae to finally make a press release about how she'd fooled us all. She'd been put together to do just that, the missing pieces had been used to ensure she could do so. We'd gotten a few answers, but once again, it had left us with many more questions that needed answering.

It was bittersweet and a grand event. Larissa would have loved to see the cemetery full of Vampires, Fae, and Witches. I don't think any had ever been in the same location of their own free will without there being a threat of war involved before.

I hadn't been able to use magic yet, so Alden had done her funeral rites for me. He'd blessed her with enough magic to pass through this life into the next, even though we weren't sure she'd go there since right now her soul was in limbo.

We stood there until everyone was gone, myself and Adam with the fourteen Fae who stood at our backs as an unbending wall of muscle. Everyone filed out slowly; Adrian and Vlad waited behind with the Fae until Adrian stepped through and laid a single yellow rose on the casket. He shook his head and turned around to face Adam and myself. "I'm sorry I put you through this, both of you."

I met his beautiful eyes but said nothing. I was barely holding the sobs at bay as it was. I nodded and slipped my arm through Adam's and leaned against him for support. I had borrowed a dress from the few things Larissa had left at Ryder's house. The idea of going home had me ill.

After the funeral was over, we were heading to my

parents' house. We'd decided to move in, *if* I could do so. I couldn't go back to the apartment, and we were officially no longer welcome inside the Guild, even though we'd found the killer and, as far as they knew, Ryder had taken him out. The fact was, we were Fae and no matter how much we wanted it to change, it wouldn't.

We were having a hard time adjusting, but Adam had found a friend in Zahruk, who was teaching him what he would need to know about feeding when the time came. I had Ryder, who hadn't been pushing me yet, but the time would eventually come.

He'd been torturing Joseph for days now, and we'd learned he was only one of many seeking to destroy Faery and any caste who stood in their way. This was why they had gone after Ryder, or so we believed. We still had to figure out who the Mage worked for and why he'd targeted Fae in the Human world instead of their own.

We ended up heading back to Ryder's place first so we could drop off the entourage and take a smaller group with us to the house. Ryder was being protective, and it was chafing, but at the same time it was nice to have someone else protecting me and Adam for once.

"Syn, I need to see you in my room before we take you to the house," Ryder said, running his hand through his hair.

I nodded and followed him. I hadn't said much since waking up. I'd been a shell of who I had been before, and while I was healing, it wasn't an instant process. It still felt as if I was watching a movie of someone *else's* life play out before my eyes.

When we reached his bedroom he quietly held the

door open for me and closed it as soon as I passed inside. He leaned against the door, blocking my retreat if I wanted to run "I can't do this anymore, Syn. Your silence is fucking killing me. I miss the fucking Fairy jokes; the light shining in your eyes when you smile. I can't believe I am actually saying this—but I miss your sassy fucking mouth, Pet."

I blinked at him and shook my head. "I just lost one of my best friends, and you miss my sassy fucking *mouth*?"

His lips turned up until he was smiling, he stepped closer and pulled me against him. His eyes watched me intensely as he did so. "I need to feed, and I want it to be from you. Since I need to teach you, Syn, I could do both at once. You have yet to hit Transition, but it would show you how to when the time is right. If you don't want to—well, I won't force it. You are under contract, out of everything in it—you didn't argue my feeding from you. Just so there is no misunderstanding between us, I sent Claire back to Faery when you agreed."

I didn't answer him. Hearing that he had sent her away had created a warm fuzzy feeling inside of me though. I smiled as much as I could manage and started clumsily unbuttoning his shirt as I met his eyes giving him all the answer he needed. I wanted him, and right now he was the perfect distraction. I knew he wasn't the Dark Prince. He was more than that— so much more than that, but I didn't care right now.

He was ancient and deadly and yet he'd been gentle and comforting when I needed him most. I'd signed the contract with the agreement that he would teach me what I needed to know to live. While I didn't embrace the idea of being Fae, I had no plans on dying because I was too stubborn to feed. His hands glided down my back until he found the zipper on the back of the dress and undid it slowly.

When it was undone, I let the dress slide down my body to pool at my feet. Ryder hissed, and before I knew what he was doing, he pinned me up against the wall, his knee between my legs as his hand held mine high above my head. "I hate that I want you, Syn, and I hate that I can't stay away from you or that no matter how fucking hard I try to get you out of my head—you stay."

His mouth crushed against mine gently as I opened and allowed his kiss to consume me. His other hand reached down and pushed past my panties, rubbing over the nub that lit up my insides instantly. He groaned as I moaned against his mouth, his words penetrating my mind. He hated that he wanted me as much as I hated that I wanted him.

He removed his hand and picked me up as he pressed me against the wall. I ripped the buttons from his shirt, unable to wait to touch his flesh any longer. He grinned as his mouth claimed mine again, with a deep urgency I felt in my soul.

We moved from the wall to the bed, where he dropped me roughly and continued working the buttons on his jeans until his sex jutted out, ready, with pre-cum glistening on the tip of his cock. He bent down low as I lifted my hips, pulled the panties down and off me and then held my feet up. He held my legs apart and growled deeply from inside his chest as his eyes feasted on what lay between them.

"I've thought of little else besides fucking you since we left Faery. Gentle or hard, decide because I can't do both. I need to know what you want."

"Ryder," I whispered, not knowing which I preferred. I wanted both, I wanted him. I ran my hands down my stomach watching his greedy eyes follow them until I got too close to touching myself, he growled and shook his head in warning. "Just make the pain stop, make me not think. Make me feel dirty."

He smiles wickedly. "I'm going to fuck you, Pet. I promise not to stop until your legs tremble and the only words you can say are *more* and *now*. Syn, I'm the kinda dirty that doesn't wash off; remember *you* asked for it," he went down to his knees, still holding my feet and used them to pull me forward.

His hot breath teased, as it fanned against my cold flesh, his tongue darting out to draw small circles on my flesh as he got closer to where I needed him. He stopped, looking up to meet my hungry eyes. "It might shock you at first; if it's too much, tell me to stop, and we can try again when you are ready."

Stop? I was about to ask him what he meant, when his mouth touched my core, tongue flicking long hard strokes over my clit. I was trembling from the sensation when it started. I felt it. The throbbing need was removed with a desire so hot and wild that my body hummed with it. My eyes closed as my head thrashed from side to side as orgasm after orgasm shook my entire body.

I was so wrong before; this was why they let them feed, this was why women sought them out. Everything inside me liquefied, my thighs trembled as his mouth continued, his eyes lighting to liquid gold as he fed from me. *Me. Not Claire.* Not another woman, he was feeding from me, and I was enduring it. When he stopped feeding, I held his head in place and demanded more.

He growled, and I felt him smile against me *there*. He reached his hands beneath my legs and pulled me closer, forcing my legs over his shoulders as he gave in and sucked hard and soft at the same time. His fingers entered me and joined in the assault. I exploded again, and while I shook from the sheer force of it, when I opened my eyes he was leaning over me with masculine pride shining in his eyes.

"You're fucking amazing. You are unlike anything I have ever tasted before," he whispered, waiting as I rode the ever-growing wave that was rushing through my body. I was floating and falling at the same time. It was like a deadly drug pulsing through me and yet it was beautiful at the same time. I was lost in his golden glow, his eyes swirled as if an entire constellation of stars sat lost inside their fiery depths. "I want my cock buried so far inside of this tight pussy. Can I fuck you, Pet, can I?" He smirked.

I tried to speak; my tongue wasn't working, and it took several attempts before I could finally speak. I just laughed and laughed until Ryder was staring at me like I had lost my marbles. I laughed until I cried, and when he scowled at me, I laughed even more.

"Syn—" He wasn't sure what was happening and maybe I was having a mental breakdown, but I knew he would pick up the pieces.

When I couldn't laugh anymore, I rose up and pushed him over onto his back. I straddled his hips and lowered my mouth to his and nibbled his bottom lip, before kissing it gently as he growled his approval. I kissed his neck while my nether region rubbed the moisture he had created over his glorious hard cock.

I knew he wouldn't allow me to tease him for very long, his cock throbbed with need already. He growled low in his chest as I kissed down his jawline and then lower as I worked my way down his body, nipping and then kissing him until I rested above his cock. I flicked my tongue playfully, enjoying as his hips came off the bed for more attention as my own had just done for him moments before.

I took him into my mouth, caressing him with my tongue as he growled and rocked his hips. His hand grabbed my hair and forced himself further inside my mouth until I pushed back up and took more, and then I felt it, a tingle inside of me that demanded to be let loose on him. It wasn't dark or cold, it was intense and animalistic and yet it wouldn't fully allow me to take from him and feed. I met his encouraging stare and continued to take him in my mouth, watching as his head dropped from where he had gone up on his elbows for support so he could watch me as I took him in. He growled and then cried his release as he came inside my mouth.

I didn't stop until he was on his back moaning. It was empowering to know I'd satisfied a glorious beast such as him. *I'd* made his legs tremble until *he* exploded. I climbed up his body as he had done to me and watched his as his eyes met mine, sated and yet still glowing. I smiled as I felt him grow hard again.

He rolled me over beneath him and entered me slowly, his eyes watching me as I accepted him. It was intimate, as if our souls had connected in that moment of time, and nothing else outside this room mattered. "You are mine, Synthia. If any other feeds from you he *will* die. Do you understand what I am telling you?" He drove himself to the hilt inside of me, ripping a gasp of pleasure from deep in my chest.

"I belong to no one," I said, wrapping my legs around him as he prepared to pound inside of me, punishing me for disobeying him days before.

"Wrong. I'm claiming you, Syn. Right now, right here, *you* are *mine*."

He pulled out, his eyes glowing fire as his brands pulsed beneath his skin and his hair rustled as if a wind had just swept through the room. He pushed himself in and out until everything inside of me once again started to build toward another climax. I met his thrust, kindling the fire until it exploded, and left me shaking while I held on to his shoulders as he pounded into me until the only sound in the room was his flesh meeting mine and our mutual screams of pleasure.

The obsidian ring surrounding the gold in his eyes bled over and expanded until his eyes were black pools. He spoke in a strange language which sent a ripple of power pulsing through the room and through me, as well. He threw his head back as he found his own release and sagged until his forehead rested on mine as we gained control of our breathing.

We lay there for minutes, neither of us wanting to break the silence, the serenity that came with releases. I reached up with my mouth and kissed him, knowing I wouldn't get many more chances to. I was going to turn a new chapter, and I wasn't sure where it would lead me. I intended to help him with the details he'd mentioned in the contract renewal I'd signed, but that wasn't for a few weeks.

When I redressed and waited for him at the door, I peeked at him from beneath my lashes. He was so beautiful, masculinity mixed with a sexual allure most magazines would pay millions to photograph. And he'd been mine, even if it was only for a little while. I swallowed the urge to wrap my arms around him.

He shoved his arms into the sleeves of his new shirt since I'd ripped the buttons off of the one he'd been wearing when we'd arrived in the room. He lifted his head and met my eyes. Something showed from within—something dangerous. I blinked and it was gone as if it hadn't been there. But I'd seen it—

he wasn't Dark Fae; he wasn't any kind of Fae I'd ever heard of before. He was an unknown—that I'd just allowed to feed from me.

"Something—wrong, pet?" he asked as he closed the distance between us slowly as if he was stalking prey.

"Thank you, Ryder, for teaching me to feed," I said, ignoring the fact that I'd caught a glint of something pacing inside of his golden depths as if it was caged inside of him, or worse, a part of him.

~~*~*~*  *~*~*~*~*

She blows my fucking mind. I expected a succulent sample and got a glorious feast instead. She fed my inner *beast*. He gorged on her glory until I had to fight him for control. He wanted her, fuck did he want her!

She amazes me. She consumes my mind when she shouldn't. I've fucked thousands of women, none of them come close to how she tastes, or the bloody fucking gasps she makes when I enter her sweet pussy. Those sexy fucking noises drive me insane with need. Drive him insane with it.

Glorious mind fuck…It took me going in to bring her out. She came out stronger, not broken and shattered, as so many who fold into their minds do. She went through hell, she watched someone she loved die, and she *learned* from it, grew stronger because of it.

She showed no fear as I fed. She didn't succumb as the others normally do; no one has ever asked for more from me. No woman has fully satisfied my hunger before, *ever,* and yet she just fucking did. She gave until I was full and then demanded I take more.

Never before since my Transition has that happened.

Her eyes colored, glowing enough to show their true beauty. And that she's full Fae; full fucking Fae. Hidden from us, and kept secret. She's royal to her sexy fucking core, her eyes the most beautiful ones I have seen in my lifetime. Beautiful in her need to feed. And she tried beautifully, like a fucking Goddess. She's going to be wild in her Transition, and I plan to enjoy her when it happens. She will be mine, brought over by me alone, my cock inside of her, fucking her, tasting her.

Impossibly clueless and yet so fucking smart and beautiful. So fucking *mine*. I branded her, couldn't stop myself and couldn't stop the beast. She saw him, at a glance she saw him push to the surface as he demanded to be let loose, to show her his beauty.

Her body begs for my touch, my mouth, my fucking cock. She takes everything I give, demands more and gives everything back. She's pure, her touch excites me, makes me feel like an untried youth about to explode in his fucking pants.

Her mind is my temple, one I want to examine at leisure. See how she thinks, what she wants. How she gets knocked down and gets right back fucking up without thinking twice. She comes up swinging, harder, smarter and changed.

If the rest of the fucking Fae had half her heart, we wouldn't be in this fucking mess, our world would be safe. Our children would be thriving instead of dying before they can Transition. Her children would be fierce, loyal, and a fucking force to reckon with. *My children.*

I smile at her and watch her eyes narrow. So fucking smart, she knows I'm plotting, planning.

She's waiting for me to fuck up, to see what I am. More so now that she's seen him pacing inside my head, rattling his fucking cage to get to her. Soon, soon she will be ready for him.

Soon, she will help me track down those who are trying to kill my world, while I hunt down the one I seek, the one who can heal my world. She may hate me when it is over—I'll face that when we get there. Until then, I plan to make her mine in body and soul.

Chapter
THIRTY~NINE

My parents' house was the same as it had been when I had left as a child. Pictures of the three of us covered the shelves my father built while symbols from the Witches rituals were etched in the thick wood walls. We'd eventually have to redo it and add new wards. Not that any of the other wards had been helpful since Ryder and Joseph had both walked right though them.

I stared at the front room. The furniture had been removed, and new stuff now sat in its place. The only thing that was the same were the walls and the symbols that adorned it. We'd no sooner told Ryder that we planned to move out of the apartments and back into my parents' house that I owned, than he'd sent his men transferring mine and Adam's belongings to the yard while Alden had some of the Warlocks from the Guild moving it inside.

"You cleaned," I said, noting that the floors had been redone, and yet there was no smell of polish inside the room. "Tsk-tsk, you used magic to clean, Alden. I'm impressed."

He smiled and crinkled his nose as his eyes sparkled at his mischief. "I didn't want you to have to do it, Syn. You've been through enough."

I grinned. "You heard I was moving in here," I said, not knowing who would have told him we were moving into this old house.

I didn't have long to wait as Adam came in from the same direction Alden just had. He smiled, but it no longer reached his eyes anymore. "I called Alden, asked for a little help getting rid of the old stuff," he said.

"You two could stay at the Guild until this place is ready, Synthia. You're still family, no matter what anyone says," Alden interjected.

"Alden, I'll be okay here. I know now that I was a just a kid. I couldn't save them anymore then I could have saved—" I swallowed as tears rushed to my eyes. "No more than I could have saved Larissa. I can't live in the past anymore. I can't keep blaming myself for everything. I've been told it's unhealthy by a very smart man." I winked at Alden who stood next to Adam, both of them with their mouths slightly open at the statement.

"Synthia, I may not say it a lot—hell, I may not ever say it. But I'm proud of you, girl. To be honest, I thought you'd never stop blaming yourself," he smiled, his eyes sparkling with unshed tears. Larissa's death had hit us all hard and left no one untouched by the loss of her gentle soul. "Listen, I talked to the elders at the Guild. We can't keep you on as an official Guild member, but we can always use a freelance team if you're interested."

I nodded, but it wasn't a confirmation. I wasn't sure what the future held. I wasn't sure if I wanted to be part of the Guild without a coven. Without Larissa. I couldn't even think about it right now, let alone agree to it. "I think we're okay for right now, Alden; time off might be the best thing right now. Adam?" I asked since I couldn't speak for him.

"I signed on with Ryder," he whispered, meeting my shocked reaction with a sheepish grin. "Syn, we need them now."

"I signed so you wouldn't have to, Adam. Why the hell would you do that!?" I screamed loud enough for the Fae outside to hear. Zahruk popped his head in from the threshold, eyes scanning the room for an axe murderer.

"Everything okay?" he asked, ignoring me and looking at Adam.

"No!" I stomped my foot grabbing his attention. "You tell the fucking Fairy he better get his ass in here this instant and rip up Adam's contract, or he's gonna wish he never met me!"

His eyes swung to Adam with pity as he backed up and went to go get Ryder. Ryder came in seconds later, but Adam stood firm not letting either of us get a word in edgewise.

"Syn, this isn't your call. Not anymore. We're no longer a coven—fuck we're not even Human! You don't get to decide my life. I need this, Syn. I'm not built like you. I don't just take it in and put it inside a fucking box until my mind can handle it. I'm not fucking built like that, and this fucking need to feed on top of everything else is already screwing with my head, and we haven't even Transitioned yet! I need this, so *no*. You don't get to decide my life any fucking more," he was yelling, but I could hear the tears shaking in his tone.

"Okay," I said swallowing slowly.

"Don't fucking say—wait," Adam paused, shaking his head as he rested his hands on his hips. "Did you just agree?"

"If it's what you want, Adam, fine, I get it. We're changing. We lost—you lost Larissa, and you need something to keep your mind off it. I understand that. If you need time, I understand. Those are choices you have to make now. I'll be okay," I paused, fighting to keep the tears in my voice from showing as he had done; we were good at hiding emotions. "I understand. I'll be fine, Adam. If you need to go—do so. I'll be right here waiting for you when you need me."

"That's not what I meant, Syn," he whispered, and walked out of the room with Alden close on his heels.

"He needs time. He was planning on asking her to marry him," Ryder said, from where he stood beside the door.

I couldn't stop the sob that escaped past my lips. Or the burning tears as they slid down my cheeks. They hadn't just been dating. They'd been in love. I'd been so fucking blind, I'd been more worried about how their relationship could affect our coven and he'd been *in* love.

I nodded and turned, looking at the walls as I felt the slight tingle of magic. It wasn't until Ryder walked further into the room that it exploded. Ryder gasped and fell to his knees. I rushed over to him, but his angry look stopped me in my tracks as the room turned a violent crimson color as the walls pushed power out and into the room. Ryder's face filled with strain and anger as he ground his teeth together against the pain.

"Alden!" I screamed in fear; something was setting off the wards. A sinking feeling started in my stomach at the direction of my thoughts as my eyes settled on Ryder again.

"What?" Alden asked, coming inside and cussing when he saw Ryder on the floor and red angry walls. "We have to get him out of here. Now."

We struggled with Ryder's weight. As if on cue, Ristan came tearing into the house and picked him up, sifting outside.

"What the hell just happened, Alden?" I gasped breathlessly.

"If I had to make a guess? I'd say your parents were worried with the Dark Fae coming in and taking you away," he said as his eyes went bright with second sight as he examined the wards on the wall. "Wait, this says the *Darkest* Fae—or worse," he examined another symbol and shook his head. "This one might say Unseelie, but I can't be sure."

"As in the Darkest Faery, from the ancient times?" I asked. I was really beginning to get scared now.

He shook his head. "I can't be sure, Syn. Your parents put these up before they brought you home. I don't know where they even got these symbols from. I've never seen them before. They were protecting you from something, Synthia. It had to be something bad enough that they put up wards."

"Alden that makes no sense. Ryder doesn't even know which caste of Fae I am. I don't get it, why all this fucking mystery over me?"

"Syn, be careful. They killed to get to you before and whoever it was walked through these wards," his eyes swept to the door, and mine followed.

"Ryder? You think they were hiding me from

him?" I whispered fervently.

He shrugged his shoulders, but I could see the fear creeping into his eyes. He shook his head. "Let's hope not, Syn; not when he currently has a contract on you and now Adam. I need to take some pictures of these wards and view them back at the Guild."

I nodded and while he took out a camera and started taking pictures, I peeked out the window to where Ristan and Ryder were arguing silently across the yard with their hands moving and eyes angry. I'd have liked to have been able to hear them, but I still couldn't tap into any magic, and I wasn't about to try to tap the leyline and see if whoever killed my parents came running to answer the call.

Adam had been in and out of the house for the last few days, coming and going without a single word. He was adjusting to life without the woman he loved. I was adjusting, or more to the point, I was trying to get Ryder out of my head and move myself back into a normal routine. It had been a little over a week since we moved in and things still made no sense. Adrian had been checking in on us frequently, and nothing kept my mind off Ryder.

I was in the shower when Adam came in and hollered that he was back from where ever he had gone. I smiled sadly, but at least he'd said something. I was beginning to think he was going mute on me. He'd probably gone to the cemetery again. It was where I had gone when I needed to feel close to Adrian when I had thought he'd died. I grabbed the bar of soap and started to lather my body when I felt a slight twinge and then a burning sensation on the right side of my lower stomach near my hip.

I looked down and screamed, angry red flesh that felt as if it was on fire, met my eyes and then turned black and crimson. Adam came in, throwing the shower curtains open even as I grabbed it to hide my nudity from him. "What are you doing!?" I screamed as he stood staring at me.

"Fuck, you smell good. So fucking sweet, Syn," he growled.

I met his eyes and flinched from the heat in them, emerald and lime green sparkled back at me, glowing. He was hungry. As in Fae fucking hungry. "Adam, back up, now."

"I can't. Fuck, I'm so hard, Syn. Just need to taste you. Just a little taste, baby, please. I'm so fucking hungry!" he snarled, just before he lunged at me.

I kicked him in the balls and ran to my bedroom, throwing the door closed and locking it. He was pounding on it within seconds. "Shit, shit, shit! Go away, Adam!" I shouted, running for my phone and dialing Ryder's cell.

He was the only one who could help him, but he couldn't even come inside the house. Zahruk answered the phone. "Syn, bad timing."

"Fuck the timing! Adam's chasing me around like I'm a fucking chicken," I shouted as more pounding erupted from the door.

"What do you mean he's *chasing* you?" Zahruk's voice grew tense.

"He said he needed to *taste* me. I don't want to hurt him, Z. I need help. *Now,* and you owe me."

"Can you get out of the house?" he replied calmly.

"I'm standing in my bedroom wearing a freaking shower curtain."

"I'm sending Ristan now," Zahruk said before the line went dead.

The door splintered, and Adam's arm came through it. He tried to find the handle from the gaping hole he'd just created. I hung up, looking around the room I'd used as a child. I'd left my overnight bag in the bathroom, and everything else was still in boxes downstairs.

"I need you, Syn. Just a taste," he growled as he gave up on finding the knob, and started kicking at the door in. Pieces of wood went flying as he pulverized it and gained entry.

"Adam stop; it's me. You don't want to do this," I cried, shaking my head.

"The fuck I don't," he said, already struggling to get his shirt off.

"Seriously, if I see you naked, Adam, we can't undo that—*ever*. I really don't think you understand what you're doing." I stopped long enough to jump over my bed as he followed me with his head low as if stalking prey. He worked the button his of his jeans, removing them quickly and efficiently. "This isn't you. Pull it back. *Now*. Oh—and you're naked," I covered my eyes and ran around the bed again, only looking through a small crack in my fingers.

"Stop running, baby, I'm so hungry. So fucking hard and hungry," he snapped as he grabbed the mattress frame of the bed and flipped it against the wall, splintering the headboard into pieces.

"Adam, stop. Please."

I didn't have a chance to beg him. He lunged and took me to the floor hard enough that my teeth shook from the impact. I struggled to keep his mouth from me as he fought to subdue me. His hands struggled to part my legs. He was no longer my Adam right now. He was hungry and he was one hundred percent Fae. "Part your legs now. I need in. I hurt. I need to be inside of you. I can make you feel so good; so fucking good."

He parted my legs by force and smiled coldly. I fought the scream as my nails dug into the flesh on his shoulders. This wasn't fucking happening! I screamed as Ristan appeared from thin air, and Adam went sailing across the room to hit the wall, and slide down limply.

"Fucking hell, Synthia," Ristan growled. "What the fuck are you wearing?"

"Why did Adam do this? And my shower curtain!" I ground out as I righted the curtain as if it was a dress, and struggled to get on my feet with shaking legs.

"He's hit Transition. He's becoming immortal. And from the smell of it, my little blossoming Flower, you're getting close to blooming, as well. Damn! You didn't smell like this last week. Ryder will want you close to him now. Imagine an animal going into heat. Every fucking alley cat is gonna come sniffing for a taste of you. He wants you with him when it happens."

"That's not his fucking choice," I snapped. I spared a quick look at Adam who was just waking up; he'd almost raped me. Knowing that would kill him. "Ristan, I need him to not know what happened here. He would never forgive himself; he's been through enough."

"You care too much, Syn. I'll take him home,

where he can feed. You did right last week by letting go of him, but consider this. Females in heat bring any Fae male with a nose right to their doorsteps, and Adam was weak. He isn't immortal yet, Synthia, if you're alone when you go into Transition," he shook his head as his silver and black eyes met mine, "God have mercy on the poor fucker who tries to get to you, because Ryder won't."

"Synthia," Vlad smiled as he sifted in, eyeing the shower curtain I held like a lifeline. "Smashing get up, who knew a shower curtain could be so sexy?"

I shook my head and left the room before Adam could see me. I listened as Ristan and Vlad, who had sifted in behind Ristan, were now helping Adam up. I had yet to stop shaking from how close I'd come to being raped by my best friend. My *only* friend.

I looked down at my lower stomach. The brand had grown while I'd been running from Adam. It was about the size of a silver dollar, the background looked like a silver disc inlaid with a design similar to a Celtic cross and had three red marks the color of rubies running down the center. Resting on the top of the disc were two red dragons facing one another with their wings spread and almost looked as if they were about to fight or worse—mate.

Ryder hadn't just claimed me, he'd fucking branded me. On top of everything, this was the last straw. He'd allowed Adam to sign a contract, after having me sign one in order to keep the others safe, once again leaving me no choice. He'd been overbearing, pigheaded and stubborn since day one.

It was too much, just when I was finally getting my life back to normal. I had been slipping back into a routine, and, even though I'd been in mourning, I was dealing with it and moving on. And now this.

Branding me, like cattle!

But branding me was unforgivable. My life was not perfect right now, but it was *my* life. I'd been offered an income if I decided to take the Guild's jobs, and Ryder was also paying me to work for him. I had a roof over my head, and I had Adam.

I didn't need some egotistical maniac ruling what was left of my coven—even if it wasn't considered that anymore. I didn't want Ryder deciding any more of my life than he already did. He had enough of that in the last month. I didn't want to be immortal, and I sure as hell didn't want to go into heat like some freaking animal. But then life wasn't asking me what I wanted.

I dressed in jeans and a shirt, flinching as I pulled it over my stomach that felt raw around the site of the mark. I pulled my hair into a loose ponytail, threw on a pair of flip flops and grabbed the keys to Adam's car off the kitchen table to head out and confront Ryder.

I got no further than his front gate before I noticed something was wrong. The metal gate hung open as if it was expecting someone, so I drove through and parked in the back. Everything on the grounds was eerily silent—no movement, and there was always activity of some kind around Ryder's mansion.

I walked across the grass, and decided to sneak a peek through the window since curiosity got the better of me. What I saw was not what I had expected, or anything I could have mentally prepared for. Ryder's men were inside the room, along with Humans and Fae set in a line on their knees. Some of them looked battered, if not a little bruised. As I watched, a figure with a hood and cloak stepped up to a male who was already screaming for mercy.

I felt chills run down my backbone, and my heart

accelerated. A golden haze came from the hooded figure's hands, and the man on his knees began screaming louder the instant it did, a blood curdling howl that had me covering my ears with my hands.

It had no effect on the one using magic. He had no qualms about using his magic on the poor guy. I scanned the room, watching as Dristan came into view. He kicked the screaming man onto the floor and moved to the next male in line. I moved my eyes to the next male, and my blood turned to ice; it was a member of the Guild. There were several other men on their knees, all lined up with Ryder's crew standing close behind them. I exhaled a long shaky breath and scanned the room more.

Dristan smiled wickedly, enjoying the cries from the Warlock—the fucking *Warlock*. What the hell were they doing to them, and why did they have members from the Guild inside the mansion? I watched as he too screamed with pain as the gold haze curled around him. I couldn't tell if they were killing them, or if it was some sick and twisted type of torture.

Mathew moved into view as Savlian shoved him from the line; I knew him from around the Guild, but had no idea why Mathew would be here, or why Ryder would allow this to happen. I pushed back bile as he began to scream as the others had, begging for forgiveness and finding none. I watched his eyes roll back in his head and blood poured from his nose as the gold haze from the magic wielder's hand touched him. I covered my mouth to stifle the cry that tried to rip from my throat. This wasn't fucking happening. I stepped back, and my foot crunched over the brush littered on the ground. I looked up and watched as the head of the hooded male came up.

"Oh shit," I whispered, covering my mouth with my hand. The hooded male turned his head as if he'd heard me, and looked right at me—with beautiful, glowing, golden eyes.

~~*~*~*~THE END~*~*~*~*~*

~FOR NOW~

Coming Up

~ * ~ The Fae Chronicles ~ * ~

Fighting Destiny

Taunting Destiny

Escaping Destiny

~ * ~ An Alexandria MacReeve Novel ~ * ~

Seduced by Darkness

Keep checking back as these two sagas continue!

The Fae Chronicles